D0390960

NOTHING FORGOTTEN

NOTHING FORGOTTEN

A NOVEL

JESSICA LEVINE

SHE WRITES PRESS

Copyright © 2018 by Jessica Levine

All rights reserved. No part of this publication may be reproduced, distributed, or transmitted in any form or by any means, including photocopying, recording, digital scanning, or other electronic or mechanical methods, without the prior written permission of the publisher, except in the case of brief quotations embodied in critical reviews and certain other noncommercial uses permitted by copyright law. For permission requests, please address She Writes Press.

Published 2018
Printed in the United States of America
Print ISBN: 978-1-63152-324-3
E-ISBN: 978-1-63152-325-0
Library of Congress Control Number: 2017956584

For information, address:
She Writes Press
1563 Solano Ave #546
Berkeley, CA 94707

Interior design by Tabitha Lahr

She Writes Press is a division of SparkPoint Studio, LLC.

This is a work of fiction. Names, characters, places, and incidents either are the product of the author's imagination or are used fictitiously. Any resemblance to actual persons, living or dead, is entirely coincidental.

In memory of

Rose, Carolyn, Florence, and Lucille

PART I

1. I Hope This Is You

It was the Tuesday morning after Memorial Day, and I woke up remembering the argument I'd had with my husband the night before. We'd fought about the apartment my aunt Doris left me in Rome. I was leaning toward keeping the place as a rental property, but Michael wanted me to sell it. The fight escalated until I took a sleeping bag and went to spend the night on a mat in my backyard studio. It took me forever to fall asleep, so I woke up later than usual, disoriented in time, but knowing I had to drive Esther to school got me up and going.

Inside the house, I found my daughter having breakfast. At twelve, she was at the tipping point of adolescence. Some mornings she had the freshness of a young child. On this particular morning, her skin was broken out and she looked tired.

"I heard you and Daddy fighting last night." She looked angry.

"Don't worry about it."

"Are you going to split up?"

"No one ever said anything about splitting up."

"Half of my friends live in two places. Everybody gets divorced sooner or later." She stirred her corn flakes aggressively.

"Couples argue sometimes. It's normal."

She put her bowl in the sink, and we went out to the car. As I drove her to school, she was quiet, so I repeated, "Don't worry about it."

"I'm not worried. I'm sleepy."

"I'm sorry, really sorry, if we kept you up last night."

After I dropped her off, I drove back to the house to get breakfast. Michael was sleeping in, as he lived on a musician's schedule, often working late into the night. I returned to my studio and sat down at my computer. Right outside, a dogwood tree was blooming for a third time, having partly bloomed in January then March. Spring in Northern California is so magically long that the plants get confused and flower in stages. In the distance, the rust line of the Golden Gate Bridge seemed to swell slightly upward in an arc echoing the curve of water on the horizon. Was it an optical illusion or a glimpse of the Earth's roundness? My eye landed on a patch of sparkles scattered by the sun on the blue-gray water.

I checked my email and was jolted by a message coming from someone I'd known a long, long time ago.

From: Sergio Buria
To: Anna Stark
Hello Anna,
I found your email address on the website of an art gallery in San Francisco. I think you must be the Anna Stark I knew in Rome in 1977. A few days ago, I read in the newspaper an obituary for your aunt Doris that mentioned you as her surviving relative. I'm so sorry for your loss. I never met your aunt, but I remember your stories about her. She always sounded like a colorful character, full of life and curiosity. Please know that I'd be happy to help if you have any business here in Italy as a consequence of her passing away.

I remember fondly your little apartment near the Tiber, where we used to meet.
Kisses,
Sergio
PS I hope this is you.

The email felt surreal, as though delivered by some winged creature that had flown in from the past. I remembered Sergio vividly, as one does the formative relationships of youth—a slim, wiry man in his early thirties, with dark hair and a dark moustache, who could most often be found sitting behind a big desk in the main office at Multi Lingua, the school where I taught English. Sergio had a beauty mark on his right cheek, a gold fleck in the brown iris of his left eye, and an expression that could change in a flash from serious to exuberant, from withdrawn to loving. The soft deep texture of his voice always bewitched me like thunder rumbling at a safe distance.

I imagined him sitting across from me, offering condolences. Not that I really needed them. When grief about my aunt came up, I honestly didn't know whether I was mourning her or the young woman I'd been when I'd known her. One thing was true, though: since the news of Doris's death a few days before, I'd been flooded by memories of Rome.

To: Sergio Buria
From: Anna Stark
Sergio,
What a surprise to hear from you! Yes, it's me. Thank you for the condolences and also for the offer of help, which I might in fact need. My aunt left me her apartment in Rome. I'm not sure what I'll do with it. The legacy came as a surprise, as the last time I saw her was 25 years ago, right before I left Rome.

Yes, 25 years: if you do the math, you'll realize that the year we knew each other was 1979, not 1977. And the place where we used to meet wasn't my apartment but a hotel— the Odeon Hotel. How could you forget that?

Write me back and tell me how you are. Did you ever move down to Sperlonga as you planned?

After everything I'd been through, how could I explain the crazy joy that seized me as I read and answered his message? I looked out the window again at the shimmering Bay and thought of Sperlonga, Sergio's hometown an hour south of Rome, that sat on a promontory overlooking a smooth arc of sand and the Mediterranean. The sight of the sea always brings something up for me, I don't know what exactly—a feeling of expectation, of hope and anguish mixed together. How does one sign a letter to an ex-lover? Best wishes, yours, regards, bye? *Ciao, salve, baci?* After a moment's hesitation, I signed off as he had: *Kisses, Anna.*

I hit SEND. Music came up the hill: My husband was playing the piano in our little house across the yard. I wouldn't tell him that Sergio had contacted me. Why give him yet another reason to get annoyed? I didn't want to complicate things by bringing Sergio into the picture. Sergio! The intensity of my feelings surprised me. For years I'd longed, grieved, been angry, resentful. Now there was only elation. For a moment, I forgot the terrible end of our story and remembered only its wonderful beginning—our first night together at the Odeon Hotel, a place that, in my imagination, had achieved mythic proportions.

Located in the Ghetto, the old Jewish quarter south of Campo dei Fiori, the Odeon was nothing more than a series of rooms off a long L-shaped corridor on the third floor of an apartment building. Climbing the stairs to reach it, we got a whiff of pasta sauce and curry, strangely combined. A recording of exotic music, with sitars and high, thready chanting, drifted down to meet us. Sergio held my hand as we went up to the reception desk, where the Indian hotelkeeper handed us a key.

The room, with its old, flowered wallpaper and metal-frame bed, its worn tile floor and wooden shutters, received us solemnly as we stepped inside. I fell into Sergio's arms, as though giving into gravity. Our clothes disappeared. We were extended on the bed by the hands of time and fate joined together.

"Finally," I whispered. This was joy. This was the moment I wanted to last forever.

"Have you been wanting this for a long time?" he asked, stroking my face.

"For months."

"Me, too."

He smelled of thyme and lemon blossoms, and his skin had, even as we went into the heat of lovemaking, the cool feel of petals in summertime. I might have thought about the next day, might have put a guardrail around my heart, but what would have been the point? It was our first time in bed together, and I was willing to pay for the ecstasy with any form of trouble.

I didn't want to think about the emotional or moral consequences of what we were doing. I didn't want to think about *her*—the other woman whose happiness we threatened.

We made love twice that first night and talked, in between and afterward, until two in the morning.

The music outside cascaded up the hill like waves surging up a shore during a storm. When Michael and I were first living together, I was, like everyone who knew him, so transfixed by his ability to write, perform, *live* music that everything he wrote seemed gorgeous. But then, right around the time his music became more experimental, the novelty of living with a musician started wearing off, and I found myself judging his work, getting irritated by the way he'd start a melody, then interrupt and distort it. There was no tune to grab hold of, only a huge, tonally brash collage of sound, loud and unceasing, that made it impossible for me to prepare a class, paint, or meditate.

Sergio's email resurrected the Roman chapter of my life so vividly that I wanted to go back there immediately to see Doris's apartment, the neighborhood where I used to live—and him.

Even if I hadn't been married, the moment wouldn't have been right. My semester of teaching hadn't yet concluded, Michael traveled a lot, and I needed to be home for Esther. And I wouldn't be able to go at the end of school, either, because Esther and I were making a trip east to visit my elderly mother. She couldn't drive anymore, and I needed to take steps toward moving her from Long Island to a retirement facility in California. Italy would have to wait until later in the summer or the early fall.

A sense of entrapment came over me and, with it, the tightness in my chest that sometimes preceded an asthma attack. I put a hand on my belly and took several slow breaths.

Then I checked my email again.

From: Sergio Buria
To: Anna Stark
Hi Anna,
I'm so glad I found you! I've often asked myself where did Anna go, is she okay? You disappeared so suddenly that I was concerned. Anyway, yes, I moved down to Sperlonga, to the apartment in my father's building, which you must remember—especially a certain night . . . The town hasn't changed very much, just a few more hotels along the coast and a bit of development in the hills. What about you? Are you in New York or San Francisco? As for your aunt's apartment, I'd be happy to go look at it for you—Rome is, if you recall, just a hop from Sperlonga.

Forgive me for messing up the details of where we used to meet. My memory isn't so good anymore for dates and places . . . But now I am remembering the Odeon and some other things very well, like your stories about your crazy life, which made me quite envious, as there I was, a little older than you, trying to settle down and be respectable, while you were being so "Bohemian." What a wild girl you were.

Kisses,
Sergio

Wild girl. I loved that Sergio still thought of me that way. My memories of Sergio existed within me like a forgotten underground source, and, with each email, I lowered the bucket and quenched my thirst. But that wild girl was long gone, done in by the responsibilities of adulthood. And Sergio was no longer a young man. In 1979, I was twenty-two, he was thirty-one—nine years older than me. I was forty-eight now, so he had to be fifty-seven. Had he changed much, I wondered. Who was I actually corresponding with? Did it matter? His message reminded me of the young woman I once was—of her vitality, curiosity, wanderlust. Suddenly I wanted to resurrect her. I *needed* to.

Agitated, I stood up, exited my studio, crossed the yard with its edging of Mexican sage full of soft purple blooms, and entered the kitchen through the back door. When Michael stopped playing, he would hear me moving about; he could decide whether or not to take a coffee break and talk to me. From where I was standing, by the counter, I saw him in the living room, sitting on the piano bench, his hands moving up and down the keyboard with their own intelligence. A tall man in middle age with a bit of a belly—a big man, in short—wearing his eccentric uniform of two poplin shirts one over the other, a blue one on top of a white one that day, with the collars stacked and the sleeves rolled up above the elbow. Once upon a time, I'd reveled in his height and breadth, which made me feel small and feminine, and I'd blissfully nestle my face in the crook of his neck. Now his size felt oppressive, as though he occupied too much space. My in-breath met the tightness in my chest as I watched him stop playing and lean forward to scribble on composition paper.

He heard me, stood up, came into the kitchen, and sat down at the picnic table in the breakfast nook.

I went and sat across from him. As we looked at each other in silence, I caught a slight smell of weed. I'd asked him many times not to smoke inside because of Esther and because it irritated my lungs. Maybe he'd smoked on the front steps, and the odor had followed him inside. He'd once told me that pot helped him "tap into the Muse," but I thought it made him scattered and irritable. Still, I wanted to keep the peace.

"I don't know how we got into that argument last night," I said, "when I haven't even made a decision yet."

"You don't think you have enough on your hands dealing with your mother? And I'm swamped right now, you know that."

"I'm not going to let my mother get in the way of an opportunity. And you're always swamped."

"What am I supposed to do about my gigs if you take off for Italy? Who's going to take care of Esther?" He used the word "gig," even though it was no longer a matter of his playing with some two-bit band in a club, but of his symphonic compositions being performed at Julliard and Oberlin. "I can't help wondering how much you could get for the apartment and how great it would be to put that money in Esther's college fund."

"You mean, if I sell it?" I could picture Doris's apartment as clearly as if I'd been there the previous day—the guest bedroom where I sometimes slept, the tomatoes in hanging baskets in the kitchen facing the shaded courtyard, the living room with its black-and-white checkered marble floor. On a hot day, when opening the tall windows on both the street and courtyard sides of the building created a refreshing cross-current, I'd step out onto the balcony and take in the mesmerizing view of ocher buildings spotted with the light green of rooftop gardens in the foreground and the deeper green of Roman pines in the distance. Why wouldn't I want to *own* all that? Make it *mine*? For a while, it had been a refuge for me. Might it be one again?

"I just want you to think about what you might be getting yourself into, if you keep the apartment," Michael said.

"I *am* thinking about it. It could be a steady source of revenue—"

"If everything goes okay. If there aren't huge repairs, if you get a steady stream of holiday rentals, if Italian taxes aren't—"

"I don't understand how you can be questioning the idea when I haven't explored it yet."

"We don't have capital to draw on if anything goes wrong—"

I was exasperated that we were repeating the argument of the previous night. His being home that morning was anomalous, but it was typical that, when alone together, we would find something to fight about. Recently, I'd started taking retreats at a meditation center two hours north of Berkeley in order to escape him.

I stood up. "I've decided to go to Rome, maybe in August or September, and take a look at it. I can take Esther with me if necessary."

"She wants to be a CIT this summer and I thought we'd agreed it would be a good experience for her. Besides, for all you know, the apartment's a complete mess. Someone over there should look at it in the meantime."

"The lawyer will." I wouldn't mention Sergio's offer of help.

"All right then."

I was turning toward the back door, when he detained me. "You could talk to Julia about it when you go east—see what she thinks about it as an investment."

A financial advisor, my cousin had written a book that had turned into a big success. *Women, Be Rich* it was called, as though a mere commandment could effectuate wealth. Boy, what I would have given to be rich—and to have a little more independence!

"Sure, I'll ask Julia." There was impatience in my voice.

"I can't think of anyone better to consult."

"I said I'd talk to her."

He shot me a dark look, got up, and went back to the piano. I headed toward the back door. Michael's mention of Julia annoyed me, and not only because I envied her wealth. I'd always suspected that, once upon a time, maybe in college, the two of them had been romantically involved, though he denied it whenever I asked him. He'd slept with my other cousin Robin when we were all at Yale, so why wouldn't he have slept with Julia, too? And I had secrets I kept from him, so why wouldn't he be keeping something from me? *Oh, shut up. Breathe in, breathe out, consider the facts.* It was Julia who'd brought us together a decade later, when we were all living in New York. She ran into him in the supermarket, or was it a bookstore, and renewed their friendship; then she suggested I bring him to her Christmas party, as he and I were both living on the Upper West Side. I called him, and he came to pick me up, and I *knew* as soon as I saw him that something would happen between us. I was so attracted to him in college, something had to. And it did.

My suspicions about Julia were unreasonable, fostered by a jealous streak and an overactive imagination.

I headed out the back door toward my study then decided to take the path along the side of the house toward the street for a walk. Michael's hostility wasn't just about my inheritance or our endless power struggles; it went way, way back to his relationship with his dad, a brilliant, loving man who sometimes lost his mind and took his belt out and gave him a good whipping. Michael had a small scar on his shoulder from the worst incident. Our marriage was probably so stormy because our initial attraction to each other had to do with wounding by a parent of the same sex. We were a foursome, really—his crazy father and my alcoholic mother always in the room. Michael and I were trying to win now, with each other, battles we'd lost long ago—all of which made us a very imperfect match. Or maybe a very perfect one. If we could resolve this, we'd be in a much higher place.

The pathos of human relationships struck me, and my anger softened. I walked along our street in the hills, catching enticing glimpses of the Bay in between one house and the next. A stretch of bushes and bramble spotted with tiny white blooms made me forget for a moment that I was in an urban area. A hummingbird flitting through the branches stopped, wings whirring, to hang in space and sip from a flower. This study in joy seemed to be following me, so I stopped to look at it. As the bright red of the plumes around its throat filled me with elation, the tiny, fragile creature, which must keep moving in search of nectar to survive, landed on a twig long enough for its dot of an eye to look straight into me. For a split second, I wasn't alone. I had an ally. And I needed an ally.

When I came back from my walk, Michael was in the driveway, getting into his car. He was going to teach. I approached him.

"I hate it when we fight," I said.

"Me, too," he said, swinging his messenger bag onto the passenger seat. "I don't want you and Esther leaving for your mother's with us in a muddle like this."

"Why do we always fight?"

"I don't know," he said.

Many times, we'd ended a fight with a promise to talk things through or a hug, but, as he turned toward me, his body language—arms crossed over his chest and shoulders pulling away from me—signaled too great a divide.

"I don't know, either," I said.

And he got in the car and drove off.

For a long time, I'd believed that if I continued to work on myself, if I learned to contain my anger and be more generous, our relationship would turn back in the right direction. Now it was beginning to feel irreparable. Sigh. Esther and I were leaving in a couple of days, and there was a lot to do to get ready for the trip.

I was intending to go into the bedroom and start packing, but found myself back in my studio, answering Sergio's email.

From: Anna Stark
To: Sergio Buria
Hi again Sergio,
No, I don't live in New York anymore, though some of my family still does. A couple of years after Michael and I got married, we moved to San Francisco, and then a little later

to Berkeley, which is more affordable. I work on both sides of the Bay, teaching English as a second language—just as I did when I worked for you.

As for that "wild girl" you wrote of, I'm not sure where she went . . .

Since you offered, well yes, if I could put you in touch with the lawyer and you could—at your convenience, no rush of course—go look at my aunt's apartment and give me a report, I'd really appreciate it. The condition it's in will influence my decision. I'll email the lawyer to tell her you're acting as my agent. Her name is Marcella Solazzo. She's the daughter of an old friend of my aunt's.

In the meantime, please tell me more about your life. Did you and Olivia have children? You must have found another job when you moved to Sperlonga.

*Michael and I have a daughter named Esther. She's twelve now.
Anna*

For a split second I had a weird feeling in my head because I'd stopped breathing. I took a deep breath and hit SEND.

All day, I wondered about Sergio's children, about Olivia. I wondered how the passage of the years had treated her. I still looked good. Did she? I wanted to ask Sergio for a photograph of the two of them. He might send one of himself, but he probably wouldn't send one of Olivia. He would know what I was up to.

At dinner, I had difficulty paying attention to what Michael and Esther were talking about.

"So we're meeting at eleven on Saturday," Esther said.

"Who's meeting?" I asked, focusing in as I sensed an

upcoming demand. I'd been sitting at the table with my family and not listening to the conversation.

"Me, Cynthia and Theresa and Sonya."

In the new manipulative stage Esther had entered, she would present me with a date she'd made with her girlfriend group as a fait accompli, without consulting me first. Said dates were invariably at locations that involved my driving her a ways from home, then having to hang out nearby until she was ready to be picked up.

"Are you free to drive her or pick her up?" I asked Michael.

"No, I have a band practice set up."

"You need to consult with me first before making your plans," I said to Esther.

"But you can drive me, right?"

"We're leaving for New York on Sunday and I have a million things to do."

"So you can do your stuff in between dropping me off and picking me up, right?"

They say that the best way to parent adolescents is to choose your battles. I could have made a point about being considerate of other people's schedules, but the will power for discussion escaped me. I looked toward Michael for support just as he was standing up to grab another bottle of wine.

"I'll drop you off and pick you up," I said. "But I won't pack for you. Keep that in mind, okay?"

The following morning I was at the well again, drawing up the bucket.

From: Sergio Buria
To: Anna Stark
Hi Anna,
I'd be happy to look at the apartment for you. I've already exchanged emails with Marcella Solazzo, and will visit the apartment day after tomorrow.

Yes, I have children, two daughters who are in their twenties now. I'm happy to hear you, too, have a family.

Being manager of a language school wasn't challenging enough for me—though you teachers could certainly be a handful! Shortly after you left, I got a job in the port of Gaeta, a little down the coast from Sperlonga. I work for a shipping company that buys and transports marble and stone for construction around the Mediterranean. My office has big windows overlooking the port and the water. It's very bright, and I can see our boats at the docks. It would please your artistic sensibility—the activity and colorfulness of the shipyard with the brilliant azure sea behind it. I have to visit quarries to inspect materials, so I've been everywhere— Spain, Egypt, Turkey. And I help buyers choose materials for important projects. In short, I did realize my dream—not only to work for a bigger company, but also to have a life that takes me out of my little country and its provincial way of thinking.

On a personal level, some things have not gone so well, but with regard to work, money—what you used to call the "practicalia" of life—I haven't done badly.

Are you planning to come see your aunt's apartment soon? I would love to see you again.
Kisses,
Sergio

I was touched that Sergio remembered my use of the word "practicalia," a term I'd picked up from my father, who used it with an ironic inflection in connection with his lab experiments. "The practicalia did not go well today," he would say when he came home from work, smelling vaguely of the chemicals and animals he worked with. I reread Sergio's message. *On a personal level, some things have not gone so well*—did that include Olivia? Or maybe his relationship with his daughters?

It was easy to picture him working in a shipyard, in charge of the transportation of tons of rock. Dominant in his personality had been personal ambition and a need to do real work in the real world—something very opposite my own dreamy nature.

From: Anna Stark
To: Sergio Buria
Dear Sergio,
So you've been successful. Congratulations, and I'm not surprised. I'm not sure when I'll get over there to see the apartment. I wish I could hop on a plane and see it—and you—immediately, but I'm scheduled to visit my mother. The fact is, it's a trip I'm not looking forward to. I don't know if you remember my stories about her and the damage she did. She's old now and I have to figure out what to do about her care. My sister, Evelyn, recently moved to London and isn't interested in helping me make decisions. I should probably bring my mother out to California, if I can get her to agree to it.

I hope you don't mind my telling you all this.

Why was I sharing my worries with him, as though we were back in his office chatting at the end of the day, the way we used to? And should I not have said that I wanted to see him? But I did. I'd only written the truth. Still, it felt like a small betrayal of Michael. To compensate for my transgression, I hesitated to write "kisses" and instead signed off, *Best, A*

Thursday there was no message from him. Friday I again checked my email first thing. I was looking forward to his messages more and more.

From: Sergio Buria
To: Anna Stark
Dear Anna,
Of course I don't mind your writing me about your problems. You can write me anything you want. I remember you had a

difficult adolescence because I intuited it before you told me anything about your mother.

I met Marcella at your aunt's apartment yesterday. As lawyers go, she seems honest enough. What a wonderful living area with those black and white marble tiles and what a splendid view from the big balcony! The three bedrooms with their little balconies on the courtyard side are a plus, of course, and the kitchen is serviceable and a comfortable size. I don't think one could have a nicer place in Rome. Unfortunately, your aunt let it go in her last years. There's dry rot around the bathtubs from leaks that were never fixed, the electricity needs to be upgraded for the computer age, and the pavers in the kitchen floor have become loose and dangerously uneven.

Anna, if I were you I wouldn't sell it "as is" because you won't be paid the true value of this potentially splendid piece of property. Many Americans now own such apartments, which, as vacation rentals, create a healthy stream of income. I could make you a list of things that need to be done, and I know of people who could do them for you reasonably.

I'd be happy to oversee the work for you, Anna. It would make me happy to do so. Do I dare say—I've missed you. Many kisses,
S

I've missed you, too, I thought, but didn't write it. I wouldn't go there. I wanted to stay practical, to stick to the matters at hand.

I puzzled over the quirkiness of memory. Sergio couldn't remember what year it was that we'd known each other, but he remembered my stories about my mother . . . I tried to recall what he'd told me about his own childhood, but drew a blank. There was some awful story about his mother, which now escaped me. I wouldn't ask him about it yet.

From: Anna Stark
To: Sergio Buria
Dear Sergio,
Thank you so much for offering to oversee the repairs. I would appreciate your doing it. I remember how you redid your apartment in Sperlonga—I liked your taste, and I trust your judgment. However, to be honest, I feel I ought to compensate you for your time.
—A

His response, an hour later, knocked me over:

From: Sergio Buria
To: Anna Stark
My darling Anna,
I would absolutely refuse any form of payment. You remember how fixing up the apartment in Sperlonga was a passionate hobby for me? I love this sort of thing—you know how we Italians are about architecture and design. Besides, I feel— how can I put it— that I didn't treat you as well as you deserved, and I'd like to use this opportunity to "atone" because, Anna, you were a great love of mine and, if things could have been different, I would have been a happier man. But when I met you, I was already in so deep with Olivia, it was as though I were on a speeding train and couldn't find the emergency hand brake to get off—which led to so much regret for so many years . . . So let me do this one favor for you, okay? Having written all that, I must also tell you the truth of my situation. Olivia and I divorced during a period when she'd lost her faith. She moved up to Florence a couple of years ago and works there now. But I sometimes go up there on the weekend to help with things around the house and visit with my daughters, one of whom still lives with her mother. So—"divorce Italian-style."

Why am I telling all this? You're happily married, you have a daughter, a life in California. I don't want to meddle with anything. But please let me do you the favor of taking care of the apartment. Okay?
Many kisses,
Sergio

I brought my face closer to the computer, as though to check that the message was real. I'd never known exactly what or how much Sergio felt for me. *You were a great love of mine.* I wanted the words hand-written on paper. In email, the sentences floating against an illuminated screen can seem nebulous, slippery. Still, this was that marvelous, old-fashioned thing—a declaration of love. Here I was, a woman in mid-life, who'd had many lovers, yet I'd never received anything quite like this. But my joy was complicated by the sentence, *Olivia and I divorced.* I'd known it would never work out. She was too imbued with Catholic prudery. *Se va bene di notte, va bene di giorno,* went the Italian saying: If things go well at night, they'll go well during the day. Well, the night would have failed them, sooner or later. Olivia's heart-shaped face, with its expression of love and hopefulness about her future with Sergio—what did it look like now, what had disappointment done to her smile, her eyes? And was I, in any way, implicated in the failure of their relationship? Everything we do has consequences. For a split second, I felt awful. Then I went back to a crazy medley of feelings. *If things could have been different . . .* Reading this avowal that was twenty-five years late brought tears to my eyes. But there was resentment, too.

From: Anna Stark
To: Sergio Buria
Dear Sergio,
I had no idea you really loved me. If only I'd known . . .
Well, what happened, happened. You moved on. I moved on.

Okay, about the apartment. I'll let you make up for the past by taking care of it. Send me your recommendations about what needs to be done and how much you think it'll cost. I'm leaving for New York on Sunday. I'll write you from my mother's.

Thank you for your email. I wanted you to choose me. Part of me is still angry, though of course I was equally responsible for everything that happened.
Love,
Anna

PS This is all rather confusing. Would you send me a photo of you? So many memories are coming back and with such force . . . Our correspondence feels bizarre. I'm writing a man of—what are you now? Fifty-seven?—yet seeing you in my mind as you used to be, a man of thirty. I need to know what you look like now.

Why tell him I was angry when I hadn't yet told him why I'd left Rome and what happened afterwards? Why not tell him now?

I didn't because I couldn't, because I was still ashamed.

From: Sergio Buria
To: Anna Stark
My dearest,
You want a photo? I don't look so good in pictures anymore, though in person I'm not a bad-looking middle-aged man. Perhaps you think I'm being vain? It's not that, but rather a sense of being buried inside myself, of being now something that isn't me. Age is a kind of mask. Your memory of me is truer than any photograph I can give you.

It pains me that you feel anger toward me. You're a married woman now, I don't want to make trouble between you and

your husband but—can I call you? Let's speak on the phone;
it'll make everything better. Please. As for the photo—yes, at
some point—but let's speak first.
Kisses,
Sergio

What would happen if we talked on the phone? Would I
spill everything? Did it matter at this point? I longed to hear
his voice. I'd been longing to hear it for years.

From: Anna Stark
To: Sergio Buria
Okay, call me. You could call me tomorrow morning my
time. Esther will be sleeping and Michael in Chicago. I'd
love to hear your voice.
Kisses,
Anna

Friday morning, I went to my studio to wait for Sergio's call. I
couldn't run from my agitation, nor could I appease it. I could
only cross my legs on my cushion and breathe. So I sat in the
meditation space I'd set up for myself when my chemical sen-
sitivities had forced me stop working with paint and I'd put my
old canvases behind a shoji screen in order not to be frustrated
by the sight of them. My dear, wild canvases, with their spinning animal forms, their volcanoes and tsunamis—the places
where I used to put the wind, rain, and sleet of my soul as well
as its crazy blooms. Instead of a large easel and paints, I now
had a small drafting table, some watercolors, and old canisters
filled with pens and pencils. Thus had life forced me to contain and restrain my creativity and passion.

My cell rang.

"Hello, is that you, Anna?"

"Hi, Sergio. It's me."

"Is this a good time to talk?"

"Yes, it's fine. I'm alone."

"Your husband travels a lot?"

"Yes. He went to Chicago for the début performance of one of his compositions. He's been very successful."

"Well, it makes sense, I suppose, that as an artist you would marry another kind of artist."

"Maybe. But it's not paradise."

"Marriage is never paradise. We don't have the greatest connection, but you sound exactly the same, Anna. Exactly the same."

"I've changed a lot. What about you?"

"Inside, I'm the same," he said. "More or less. Outside, I'm afraid I'm rather different."

"We all get older."

"Hearing your voice makes me feel so . . . "

"Me too, Sergio."

"Are you crying, my dear?"

"I'm sorry, I can't help it—"

"I looked for you, really I did. I thought your family would still be on Long Island, so I found their address, I sent a letter to you there.

"I never got it. My mother can't be bothered to forward my mail."

"She had a little problem with wine, if I recall."

"Scotch whiskey."

"I'm sorry you had to deal with that."

"Sergio, talking to you—this is unbelievable!"

"Your email distressed me, Anna. Please don't be angry with me, honey. Sweet honey."

"Hearing your voice—no, I'm not angry anymore." I wouldn't tell him everything just yet, after all. I needed to revel in the sweetness.

"You can call me anytime, Anna. I hope you will. We need to catch up and say all the things we should have said years ago. Call me from your mother's."

"If I can get a moment alone, yes I will."

After we hung up, my heart was racing, my breathing constricted. I went back to my cushion and sat facing a drawing I'd made of the Buddha in the Tibetan tangka tradition, which prescribes proportions with great precision. Working in this rule-driven manner, so opposite to the wild way I'd painted before, enabled me to pour my creativity into time-tested grooves that fostered inner equilibrium. It was the terrible fallout from my affair with Sergio that had led to my attraction to Buddhism when I lived in Asia in my twenties. Then I took up meditation more seriously years later in order to calm my asthma. At first the asthma itself was an obstacle, as meditating made me more conscious of tightness in my lungs. But as I learned to focus on the feeling of the air in my nostrils, I became able to soften my chest and belly. Finding a spot of calm inside, however small, gave me the hope that I might eventually find peace of mind.

The path of meditation is full of twists and turns. Part of what happens when you go deeper into practice is that you confront feelings that have been pushed aside—what my meditation teacher called the dragons waiting just outside the cave. He used to say that, the fiercer the dragon, the more crucial it is to "invite him in for tea." That's a Buddhist metaphor for befriending one's dark emotions. Processing Sergio's phone call, I faced a dragon of shame, grief, and longing. And there was nothing to do except sit and face it. Eyes closed, I saw myself, in a daydream, sitting cross-legged like a Taoist monk in a mountainside cave in which a tea pot hung over a fire pit. I poured a little tea into a porcelain cup and handed it to the fiery dragon that stood threateningly at the entrance. With its long thin body and fiery breath, with its curled and patterned scales and claws, the creature looked like it had stepped right out of a Chinese scroll. I faced this beast with resolute stoicism.

Usually, if I meditated long enough, the difficult emotions would begin to soften and the dragon might shrink, even turn into a friendly creature. But this time, I only wanted escape, distraction, stimulation. I wanted to hear the sound of Sergio's voice again and see him in the flesh and throw my arms around him. I wanted not to appease the dragon, but to give it wings and climb on its back and fly across the American continent and the Atlantic Ocean and back in time, through dimensions of mist and light, to be with Sergio again.

But I had to go see my mother instead.

2. Motherhood and Variations

A few days later, Esther and I were flying east, playing double solitaire with a miniature travel deck. Half of the aces were on her fold-down tray, the other half on mine, so we had to reach across each other to build. Every time she leaned my way, she poked me with her little elbow to break my concentration. She kept winning because her reflexes were faster than mine, and every time she won, her laughter erupted over the thundering engine of the plane. Finally, she had enough. "What did you bring to eat?" she asked, and I unpacked our specials snacks—slices of dried mango and chocolate cookies and the drinks we'd bought after going through airport security.

I wished I were flying to Rome instead of going to visit my mother, but I was happy to have time alone with my daughter. After we ate, she took out her iPod, put in her earphones, and soon fell asleep. Outside the window, an even blanket of clouds spread into the distance, up-lit by the sun that was sinking beneath it, casting a rose light through the glass and onto my child's face. She had Michael's black hair and my bone structure. Her skin, which had been broken out a couple of days before, was at the moment without a blemish, for it could recover in a flash, with a single good night's rest. The pale down on her upper lip over her slightly open mouth shone in the light slanting into the cabin. Her head, tilted back, leaning against the glass of the plane window and set against the background of clouds, offered an exquisite portrait. Like a hummingbird sipping from a flower, I drank in her beauty.

Then I remembered my secrets. Some day—when? how?—I would tell my daughter everything that happened to me, I would try to explain why I did what I did. At what age would she have the compassion to understand? Maybe that time wouldn't come until after I was long gone.

Sergio . . . I remembered how he called me *sweet honey* on the phone and, in the calm of the moment, puzzled over the expression. Maybe an Italianism of some sort. The way they doubled and intensified everything—all the stereotypes about the passionate Latin temperament were true. And I was a sucker for it.

I would email or call him from my mother's.

My mother still lived in the house on Long Island that my parents bought in 1970, when I was fifteen and my father got a research job at the nearby university medical center. It was a traditional two-story structure, in the New England style, with horizontal siding of real wood painted white. There were three bedrooms upstairs. Esther was sleeping in the one that used to be mine; I was in the one that used to be my sister's. At night, I could hear my mother snoring in her room across the landing. Cousin Julia, who had come out for a couple of days, was sleeping in the downstairs office.

After my mother had hit another car in a drunk driving accident, she lost her license, and they'd put her on a medication that makes people violently ill if they have a drop of alcohol. A home aide from Haiti named Chantal came by every day to make sure she took her pill and to cook a little dinner. If it hadn't been for Chantal, my mother would have survived on crackers, stewed prunes, and coffee.

The morning after we arrived, my mother was working

in clay in her backyard studio when I told her about Doris's apartment. I neither needed nor wanted her opinion, but it was a way of making conversation before we got down to the matter of moving her out to California.

"So I'm not sure whether I'll sell or keep it," I concluded. "At some point, I'll go to Rome and look at it."

"I can't believe Doris was able to buy a place. What a crazy woman. Did I ever tell you about how she used to step out to get the morning paper wrapped in nothing but a bath towel?" My mother cackled. "That was her morning routine—a shower, a towel, and out to get the paper in front of the neighbors. There she'd be, her tush hanging out, parading for all of Flatbush. Once she locked herself out and had to go walking down the street half-naked, knocking at neighbors' doors—"

"Linda! You've already told me that story—" I called my mother by her first name to put more distance between us.

"You were the only one who could ever get along with her. Did I ever tell you how she once rubbed herself with a raw fish before going on a date? Brooklyn, 1952. No, 1953. Right before she left for Italy."

"Oh come on—"

"She said wanted to make herself smell like female pudenda, and she stood there in the kitchen, holding a flounder in her hand and applying it to the back of her ears and neck—"

"Stop already—"

"She was always throwing herself at men. A woman driven by her appetites, with no taste or culture, always trying to get something out of you. And the way she dressed! Always in clinging knits, to reveal her boobs and every roll of fat. The whole family found her intolerable. No wonder she exiled herself to Italy. But so smart of you to put up with her! Now you've got that nice apartment of hers, you can spend summers in Rome, if you want, and take it all in again." She wasn't one to hide her envy. "Or you could sell it and buy an apartment in Paris." She let out a big sigh.

"Sure, Doris was difficult sometimes, but it's hard to believe the stories you tell about her."

"They're all true." My mother stuck a pinkie in the mouth of the clay face she was working on then pressed it in, angrily, to make it deeper. "There. Big mouth. Or maybe a little more." She made another quick jab. "'Screaming head' is my title for this one. *Pace* Munch." She looked sideways at me. "Did I ever tell you about the time Sarah and I found a dildo in her room?" Sarah was my mother's other sister, my aunt who now lived in San Francisco.

"Come on, that I really don't believe. How, in 1940-something Brooklyn, would Doris have gotten her hands on a dildo?"

My mother snorted. "In some ways, little sister was way ahead of all of us."

"I can't believe you aren't at all sad about her death."

"I'm eighty-three and half of everybody I know is dead. What am I supposed to do, cry like a Greek chorus each time? It's too exhausting. And the truth is, about Doris, I washed my hands of her years ago." She looked back at her figure and jabbed her pinkie yet again in its mouth. "Why is it that it's the people who break all the rules who get the desserts in life?"

When my mother was forced to stop drinking, I expected she'd change, but she was the same—narcissistic, angry, bitter—a parody of a demented Jewish mother. If it was true, as it said on my birth certificate, that I'd come out this woman's body, it wasn't thanks to the so-called "miracle" of childbirth, but through an act of sorcery.

"Let's talk about moving you out to California," I said.

"I'm not going to California. You're going to put me in some 'facility' where I wouldn't have a place to sculpt? You want to drive me stark, raving mad? And why go through all the work of moving me when I don't have much time left anyway?"

"You talk as though you were actually dying of something. We could find you an artist's studio or a little house with a garage where you could work."

"No."

"How are you going to continue living here if you can't drive? And the day may come when you can't climb the stairs—"

"Then I'll sleep in the office downstairs."

On the one hand, it felt like she was an alien from outer space. On the other, she was a darker version of me. Sometimes I was tempted to throw in the towel and say, yes, goddammit, I'm exactly like my mother: I, too, have a difficult marriage and an outdoor artist's studio. And now that my asthma has forced me to give up paints, I too know what creative frustration feels like. As I stared at the charcoal crescent moons under her fingernails and the gobs of clay in her long gray hair, the similarities between us grabbed my viscera and gave them a little twist. If it hadn't been for the fact that I was on a spiritual quest—"How Californian of you," she would have said contemptuously, if I'd ever shared that information with her—I'd have felt like her twin and done myself in. But thankfully, while she'd been making figures of fat women with horrified expressions on their faces, I'd found my way to drawing Buddhas and lotus flowers. At the very least, I *aspired* toward forgiveness, even if I didn't actually feel it.

These moments alone with her were torture. Thankfully, my cousin Julia was inside the house going over the books to make sure my sister Evelyn hadn't mismanaged or—who knows? Embezzled!—my mother's money before going abroad.

"I'm going to get a bottle of Scotch and pour it right in here." Pinkie digging inside the clay mouth. "Jesus, I hate that drug they're making me take."

"You're destroying your liver, so you have to stop drinking—"

"They're prudes and killjoys, all of them," she hissed.

"I'm going inside for a moment."

The house sat on a promontory jutting into Long Island Sound, so the spring breeze was damp and salty from the sea, making me shiver as I stepped outside and crossed the lawn back to the house. I looked up toward my old room—the room where my mother had locked me in the closet and left me for the night one time she was drunk and my father and sister were away. She'd been strong in middle age, even more so when inebriated. I'd banged on the door and cried myself into a state of hysteria until I could barely breathe and threw up on myself and my shoes, while she passed out on her bed. The next morning, she let me out, pretending I'd "accidentally" locked myself in. Later that day, when my father came home, I had my first asthma attack and he took me to the emergency room. It was as though my subconscious had deferred that reaction so that I wouldn't suffocate in the closet. The things my mother had done, not just that night but others, too, now seemed like they'd happened to someone else, and not me— until I'd remember something very specific, like cleaning the vomit out of my black patent leather shoes, at which point I'd shudder, reminded that those events had indeed been episodes in my own life.

Opening the back door and going into the house, I heard the sound of some movie Esther was watching on TV in the living room. Julia was in the kitchen making coffee in my mother's ancient percolator.

"Want some?" she asked.

Julia was thin and elegant in middle age, with her tailored black pants and straight hair in a neat ponytail, a graphite shawl wound around her neck.

"Yeah, sure. In a minute."

In California, I could sometimes ward off an asthma attack by isolating myself and calming down, but that was impossible at my mother's. I went upstairs to get my inhaler, took a couple of puffs then went back down.

"How's it going out there?" Julia gave me a look of sympathy.

"She's unbearable. How's it going with the accounts?"

"The books look okay. Nothing's amiss."

"Good."

"I wish you and Evelyn would mend your fences."

"Why? We have a perfect arrangement. We keep the peace by avoiding each other." My sister, like my father, had never defended me against my mother when I was a child, and I couldn't forgive her. "Listen, I want to talk to you about something."

"Me, too. You first. Let me serve this up, then we'll sit down."

Julia went out the back door to deliver a cup of coffee to my mom. I was grateful for her company and help. Soon the door slammed again and she was back. She poured coffee for the two of us and we sat at the kitchen table.

I told her how I was thinking of keeping Doris's apartment but was concerned about the economics.

"So the apartment is just sitting there now?" Julia asked.

"Someone's taking care of the renovations," I said. "The lawyer who's the executor of her estate." The lie slipped out easily. Julia knew a little about my time in Italy, but not the whole story. "I'd like your opinion about whether or not to keep it— not that I expect you to know anything about Italian inheritance law or taxation."

"No, I don't. But I also don't think I need to, and you don't need to either. Does it matter how much, if any, money you'd make renting it? If you want to keep the apartment, you could probably break even, at the very least. Why don't you do whatever makes you happy? It seems like a rare opportunity."

"That's surprisingly impractical coming from you." I noticed she was wearing diamond ear studs. They were probably real.

"I don't know. I think at our age we have to be more aggressive about getting happy." She cocked her head at me. "What I wanted to tell you was—Ben and I are talking about adopting."

I was startled. I thought of Julia as conventional and successful, but never as particularly maternal. For a brief period she'd tried to get pregnant, and when she'd had problems conceiving, she did some fertility treatments. But when that didn't work, she hadn't been devastated. She and her husband Ben had been together since college and seemed to relish their freedom as a childfree couple. They went to the theater, entertained, and traveled a lot.

"Really? That's wonderful! Are you going to do it domestically or internationally?"

"Domestic adoptions are complicated. There's always a worry about the birth mother changing her mind. Besides, it makes more sense to us to adopt a child who's already been abandoned. We're thinking of going to Guatemala or Peru or maybe China. So we'll be able to provide Esther with a cousin." She smiled.

Those two words—"abandoned" and "adoption"—always grabbed me in the chest like a vise around my esophagus.

"So, uh, how does it all work?"

Julia started talking about it, but I wasn't listening. Suddenly I was perspiring, part of me back in that awful night in a Paris hospital twenty-five years before—waves of agony that rolled over me for hours, then morphine, evisceration, the sound of crying, more night, day again, and then months of days like nights, and the irrevocable done, no going back, no fixing or possibility of fixing, only grief, shame, and self-loathing. For the longest time I'd felt about *it* the way I felt about my childhood—that it hadn't happened to the real me, but to a parallel me, a kind of doppelganger who soldiered on with the suffering, leaving me to cobble together an after-*that* life—as though I were a disaster survivor.

"So we're going to start all the paper work for the adoption soon. It'll be an older child because we're older." Julia leaned forward, touched my arm. "Tell me it'll be okay."

The request for support, so rare from her, jolted me out of my trance.

"Of course it'll be okay. You and Ben will be great parents. You'll get a great kid—"

"Sometimes the older kids have problems, that's what scares me."

"You'll work it out, you'll get help, the child will adjust. In the end, it'll be fine."

"I hope so."

"Yeah, sure. Listen, I need some exercise," I said. "I'm going out for a walk." I didn't want to hear more about her adoption plans.

"Oh, before I forget—I was going through your mother's mail and saw something addressed to you."

Julia got up and I followed her into my mother's home office. There were piles of envelopes and bills on the table, and a couple of paper bags stuffed with junk mail.

"Thanks so much for helping with this," I said.

"Look, here's this letter for you. Seems to be from France."

Why would anybody write me from France? I looked at the return address. It was from the agency that had placed my baby.

"Goddammit, she could forward my mail to me."

I stuck it in my pocket and walked over to the foyer closet where I grabbed a light jacket. Stepping outside, I took a right and strode down the country road that went to the tip of the promontory, past white houses set on ample stretches of lawn surrounded by wind-bent trees. The lighthouse loomed up on the right, its beige stones a set of neutral blotches against the pale sky and dark sea behind it. When I reached the very end of the road, I stuck my fingers through the metal gate that kept people and traffic from careening off the cliff and into the water. A nervous shiver went through my body in waves, like a pulsing vibration. What was it that I'd done, exactly? I hadn't *abandoned*, had I? I'd *relinquished*, right? Never had the choice of a word been more critical. I opened the envelope and skimmed the letter. *Nous avons eu une demande de la part de votre enfant naturel (We've had a request from your birth child).* My son—he'd be a grown man now—had approached the agency and asked for my identity and whereabouts. I looked at the postmark on the envelope—it had been mailed six months earlier to my mother's house, as that was the address I'd left with them twenty-four years before.

A small, beat-up Mazda pulled up and a young couple got out to take some pictures. They seemed in love. Maybe they were married and would have a baby and a normal family life. I turned my face away from them and looked out at the Sound. In childhood, the sight of the water filled me with rapture. But now I wondered about what was underneath—the varieties of sea life all consuming each other, the human garbage and chemical deposits. The wind, unusually strong for early June, brushed up the surface of the water, dotting it with white caps. I was so ashamed of everything I'd done that the idea of reconnecting with my son threw me. How had things gone for him, being adopted? Had he grieved for me, as I had for him, or had I been an abstraction for him? They say we carry our early traumas at a cellular level in the body, and in some way or another my giving him away would have dealt a blow. Better not to think about it; better to stay with the feeling that what I remembered had happened in some other woman's life.

Without thinking, I grabbed my cell phone and dialed Sergio.

"Hello, Anna? You're at your mother's?"

"Yes, we got here a couple of days ago."

"A little closer to Italy, then," he said.

"I had the same thought—I'm half-way between California and Italy, so a little closer to you."

"You're in your mother's house?"

"I'm out for a walk."

"What's wrong? I can tell something's wrong."

"I—I hate coming home."

"You sound frightened," he said.

"I want to see you so much, Sergio."

"I want to see you, too, Anna. I wish I could get away and come to you, but I can't. Right now I'm getting ready to go with a shipment of marble to Turkey."

"That sounds exciting." Listening to his voice calmed me down. "I'd love to go to Turkey."

"If I could, I'd get on a plane tomorrow and meet you in Manhattan."

I sniffed back the tears. "You could hijack the ship and redirect it to Manhattan. Wouldn't that be romantic? You'd make quite a pirate." I laughed as I pictured Sergio with a black bandana and a sword.

"I'd make a rotten pirate." He laughed, too. "But you'll come to Rome soon and see the apartment, and we'll have time together. When do you think you'll come?"

"I don't know."

"Make it soon."

"Sergio, the way you called me 'sweet honey' in your email—"

"That's how I think of you."

Our connection was scratchy, as though the choppy waters were interfering.

"Maybe not as sweet as you think," I said, feeling the letter in my pocket. No, I couldn't tell him the details now, not with this static on the line.

"Yes, absolutely sweet. You want to know something, Anna?"

"What, Sergio?"

"After you left, I wasn't the only one who missed you. Olivia did, too. And when our first child was born, we named her Anna."

"You named her Anna? Whose idea was that?"

"It was Olivia's idea. She felt alone, she missed her American girlfriend, she said, 'Why don't we call the baby Anna?' and I said, 'Yes, of course, let's.'"

"So you have a daughter with my name?"

"Yes," he said. "I do. Now, what was it you wanted to tell me?"

"I can't now," I said. "I'll explain later. Tomorrow or the day after. I'll call you back and explain."

PART II

3. Wild Girl

A one-night stand is easy enough. It's the second time that things get dangerous. After my first tryst with Sergio, in the Odeon Hotel that February of 1979, I didn't know if there'd be another, but I hoped there would be. Friday evening after my last class, I was putting my books away in the dark book-case where the Multi Lingua course manuals were kept, like precious objects, behind glass doors, and Sergio was sitting as usual behind his wooden desk, his thin frame dwarfed by the oversized casement windows that rose, in the European fash-ion, to the ceiling behind him. His childhood friend Mauro, plump and relaxed-looking, sat across from him smoking a pipe. Mauro had started the school then invited Sergio to run it. Both of them always wore three-piece suits over white shirts.

"Sergio is telling me wonderful things about you," Mauro said. "It seems all the students love you."

"That's nice to hear," I said, looking at Sergio.

Our eyes met, and his whole face lit up as he broke into a smile and made a diagonal nod coming from the neck, an unconscious gesture that signaled excitement.

"If you keep on like this, you'll force us to give you a raise," Sergio said, grinning.

"Well, I must be off," Mauro said. He tapped his pipe on the ashtray and stood up. "Are you locking up now?" he asked Sergio.

"In a few minutes. I have to talk to Anna about something."

"All right then. *Ciao.*"

Sergio and I looked at each other without speaking as we listened to the door close and to Mauro's steps on the staircase.

"Is everyone gone?" I asked.

"Melitta is substituting in room five," he said, referring to the Greek secretary who spoke five languages.

"Oh." I smiled.

"I might be free later tonight. What about you?" he asked, dropping his voice. Room five was in a suite with a separate entrance, so Melitta and her students couldn't hear us, but she might surprise us by coming in for course materials.

"When will you know?"

"In a little while. After dinner."

That meant around 11:00 p.m. In Italy, my nights often extended into the next morning.

"And then will you—will you tell me—"

"Everything."

It was rumored among the English teachers that Sergio had a girlfriend, maybe a woman named Olivia, who occasionally substituted for Melitta in the office. No one was sure. Once while rushing to class, I'd seen her, but from the back, so I didn't even know what she looked like. Sergio's discretion was not unusual in the Italian context, and his secrets remained guarded by the unspoken, European prohibition against asking personal questions of people who aren't intimate friends.

"I'll be back at the apartment. You can call me there."

I went out into the night and caught the 16 bus that stopped on Via XX Settembre, not far from the school. It was a short ride past the train station and the white marble steps of the Santa Maria Maggiore church, then down Via Merulana to my neighborhood. Dimly realizing the vulnerability of my position, I reminded myself of my original goals in coming to Europe: to travel, improve my languages, have lovers, and get as far away from my abusive mother and ex-boyfriend as possible. To that end, I had recently applied for a fellowship to study and teach for a year in Asia. Sergio was a momentary blip in all this and, whatever his "situation," my affair with him would ultimately have little effect on the greater journey of my life.

I reached the apartment I shared with a guy I'd met at the Multi Lingua teacher training the previous fall. Our two-bedroom unit was tucked at the back of a courtyard and down a few steps, in a converted semi-subterranean space. Hearing music and a loud chorus of voices, I sighed, for I was tired and not in the mood for a wild party. Nathan excelled at rounding up large numbers of guests and lubricating them with drink and various entertainments. Walking in, I saw that he had requested that everyone come in costume, and the crowd included cowboys and geishas, Roman emperors and Renaissance courtesans. He and one of his buddies, Will, who was always the good sport, were dressed as master and slave, with Nathan in a makeshift toga that revealed the fawn-colored hair on his chest and Will in rags with a bicycle chain around his foot and his sweet, pageboy face smudged black with eyeliner. Sitting on the couch with his guitar on his lap, Nathan mangled Bob Dylan tunes, his British accent warping the singer's twang to comic effect. Projecting his voice over the shouting Brits, Canadians, and Italians in our living room, he sang with the reckless abandon of someone sentenced to execution in the morning, while Will, crouched on a low stool, alternated between banging on a drum and rattling his chain. Completing the picture, a college student with a bunch of grapes perched on his hat in honor of Bacchus sat at their feet, playing the harmonica.

"We're going to have trouble upstairs," I said to Nathan as he paused between one song and the next.

"To hell with the neighbors," he said good-naturedly. The width of his chest, broad and muscular from being on the swim team at university, matched the body of the guitar, which he held with amorous tenderness. "To bloody hell with them. May their bollocks drop off and rot." He had the foul mouth that Brits educated at the best institutions use to cope with the burden of their intrinsic superiority. "Hey, Foxy, bring me some more wine."

"Sure."

At twenty-two, with my big frame and short hair, I wasn't particularly foxy. The nickname came from the fur trim on the overcoat I'd worn all winter and, as a term of endearment, I didn't mind it. I took Nathan's glass and went into the kitchen to refill it.

I was bent over the sink guzzling water when some-one upstairs yelled, *"Tempo dormir! Vaffanculo!"* ("Time to go to sleep! Go fuck yourself!"), and some cans whizzed by and crashed outside on our cement patio the size of a grave. I felt mortified: We were violating Rome's quiet-after-ten-o'clock rule. Well, if my tryst with Sergio didn't happen, I could go to my aunt's. Doris would be sleeping, but I had the key and permission to use her guest room whenever I wanted.

I set the wine next to Nathan, and he thanked me with his winning smile, revealing childish teeth square as Scrabble tiles. He was still my best friend, though the day-to-day hassles of living with him—his never doing the dishes, hosting serial parties, and entertaining a steady stream of women—were beginning to wear on my good will.

He was trying to tune his guitar, an impossible task with the noise in the background, and I was back in the kitchen making myself a sandwich when the phone rang. Nathan picked it up before I could. Damn.

"Pronto." He glanced at me. "For you. Someone named 'Amedeo'." He smirked.

I put my hand out to take the receiver from him, but he held it back for a second, teasingly. "Someone," he continued, "with a suspiciously familiar-sounding voice."

"Just hand it over." I placed it to my ear and turned my back to Nathan.

"Ciao, Anna? It's me, Sergio. I'm free now. Do you want to meet at the Odeon? In a half-hour?"

"Sure."

"See you soon."

I hung up and glanced at Nathan, who was strumming again.

"I'm going out. Maybe not coming back tonight," I shouted.

"Going for another merge with Serge?" he shouted back.

"No. What are you talking about?"

"You were out the other night, my little fox. And I can guess who you were with."

"I sleep at my aunt's sometimes, you know that. Anyway, it's none of your business."

Nathan reached for my arm. "Be careful, Foxy, don't do anything stupid."

That stopped me in my tracks. No matter how I looked at it, what I'd done wasn't smart. I was living and working in Italy without papers and had slept with the man responsible for getting them for me. In a country where that could take months, if not years, it behooved me to avoid getting into trouble with my superiors.

"As though you lead an exemplary life?"

"Yeah, but I'm used to it. You're more—delicate." He gave me a look of tender concern.

"Hey, I'm not *that* delicate."

Going into my bedroom to gather my things for a night at the Odeon, I found a scantily clad, leggy model lying on my bed in a provocative position, while our friend Peep stood over her taking pictures and asking questions. Peep was an eccentric character Nathan and I had collected in the bohemian neighborhood of Trastevere. He had brought a photographer's light and stand and was hard at work, with little beads of sweat on his forehead from the heat of the lamp and too much wine. "Peep" stood for Philip and for photographer, pornographer, and paparazzo. A big-bellied man, prematurely gray in his forties, with a grizzled Amish-style beard, Peep always wore, over a white T-shirt, the same black suit, the darkness of which worked to reveal rather than conceal its filth. Dried white spots testified to his habit of guzzling quarts of milk after drinking too much wine. When eating out, he would line his right suit pocket with a stolen napkin in order to improvise a makeshift doggie bag, and on this particular night, a couple of shrimp tails could be seen sticking out.

"And so, Maria," he was saying, "missionary doesn't work for you? Stimulation-wise? What about getting your hand in there? Not possible?"

"You embarrass me," the beauty said. "Pictures okay, but no interview."

Peep looked at me and shrugged. "I don't get the modesty of these people."

"I see you're making yourself at home in my bedroom."

"You don't mind, do you? It's so white in here, it amplifies the light."

My room was indeed very white. The building owner had turned the basement into a cheap apartment with a roll of white linoleum on the floors and a coat of whitewash on the walls and ceiling. The bedspread, the melamine desk, and ceramic lamp in the corner were all white as well. The only dark piece was the antique cherry armoire, where I kept my money from teaching under the innersoles of my Frye boots.

"I guess it's all right."

"You don't want to lie down next to Maria?" Peep asked. "Maybe with your arm around her? I'd love to get some shots of the two of you together."

"No, thanks—"

"I'm after something soft and suggestive—nothing explicit, I promise—a little kiss maybe—"

"Actually, I'm going out." I put on my gray fedora, grabbed my brown Greek bag with the white key pattern and tassels, and started stuffing it with a clean shirt and panties, my toothbrush, a book, and a sketchpad.

"Where you going?"

"None of your business."

"Gimme the neighborhood, at least."

"The Ghetto."

"Why don't we grab a taxi together and stop by the Falcon for a dance and a drink?" he suggested, referring to a favorite hangout of Anglophone expats. Sure I'd agree, he turned off his lamp and patted his model on the butt. "That's it, Maria," he said and began packing up, as the model rolled off the bed, looking at me through half-closed, heavily shadowed eyes.

"Okay. I go get myself a drink." She languidly slunk away into the living room.

"I can't go to the Falcon—" I began.

"It's on the way. And this way I can chaperone you."

"I don't need a chaperone," I said, though Peep was right to be concerned. The nightlife of Rome in the late '70s was dampened by the terrorist activities of the Red Brigades, which had included the brutal kidnapping and murder of the prime minister the year before.

"Yeah, but I do," he said. "After midnight, I'm a total coward."

I laughed. "So what's the idea? We can get blown up together?"

"Yeah, holding hands. Come on, at least ride with me."

"Okay. Let's go," I said. He amused me.

With our respective bags, we fought our way out through the crowd jabbering in crescendo in the living room. Nathan was still strumming the guitar, with *Desire* now playing in the background on a portable record player. It was our only album, and I'd heard it—and him playing along with it—a thousand times. I loved and hated *Desire*, the way I loved and hated living with Nathan. As I waved good-bye to him, he looked at Peep, then at me, and raised his bushy eyebrows. I shook my head in the negative and followed my strange companion out the door.

Peep and I stood on the corner of Via Merulana, hoping for a bus or a taxi. The sidewalks were abandoned, and there was little traffic. He rested his photography equipment on the ground, pulled a shrimp out of his doggie bag pocket, and extended it in my direction.

"Want one?"

"No thanks."

Munching his treat, he turned and looked at me in the soft glow of the streetlights.

"Hey," he said, "I've been taking you in again tonight, and you got good bones and lots of flesh. I'd like to photograph you sometime."

I laughed. "'Lots of flesh'? That's supposed to be a compliment?" I'd gained thirty pounds since my arrival in the Eternal City.

"In Rome it is." He leaned over and squeezed my upper arm. "Jesus, I love that flab. In the right lingerie, you'd be terrific."

"Enough already."

"Don't get me wrong. I'm not trying to come on to you. On the contrary, I can't."

"You can't?" I laughed again. "Wounded in the war, perhaps?"

"Yeah, in the war of life. Too many hang-ups. Really. That's why I do what I do, I mean with photography. Gotta get my satisfaction somehow."

"You really are pathetic."

"*I'm* pathetic?" He chuckled. "Be careful, Anna. I know more about you than you think. Nathan told me about your encounter with him."

"You're kidding me," I said. My one sexual experience with Nathan, about five months before, had been so humiliating that all I wanted was for it to be digested and eliminated through the bowels of Time.

A taxi appeared and we climbed in. Peep's photographer's lamp extended over both our laps. I was hoping for a change in topic, but Peep continued where he'd left off.

"He said you s—"

"We're in a taxi, damn it!" I placed my hands over my ears, flushing with anger and embarrassment.

"He doesn't speak English," Peep said, glancing sideways at the driver.

"I can't believe he—and whatever he told you, I'm sure he embroidered on it."

"'Embroidered'—I like that." Peep chuckled. "Well, you know how Nathan likes to tell stories."

"And you believe them? You cross-questioned him the way you cross-question everyone, and who knows what he came up with."

"Well, I can tell you. He said you—"

"Shut up!" I screamed.

"Okay, okay."

As the taxi sped by Santa Maria Maggiore and its white stone steps, gleaming in night spotlights, I stared out the window, pouting.

It was true that Nathan liked to tell stories about his sex life, and they usually made me laugh. I just never expected to end up in one of them.

When we'd met during our teacher training months the previous September, we'd hit it off immediately. Tall and good-looking, with thick dirty blonde hair and a bristling moustache that suggested a playful snuffing and whiffing of life, like a boar after truffles, Nathan had an aliveness of expression that caught my attention.

"Sorry I'm late," he said with a British accent as he swung into the classroom. "Impediments and all that."

With outsized energy he strode in and, taking a seat next to me, gave me a good look and a big grin.

Soon we were hanging out together and, when my aunt kicked me out of her apartment one day because she wanted the guest room for a visitor, I moved into the Odeon Hotel, where Nathan was shacking up with his friend Will. At first, I had a single room across the hall from them. Then, one week when Will went back to England, Nathan talked me into rooming with him to save us both a little money. At first we had separate beds and turned our backs modestly to each other when we changed. Then came a couple of cold October nights before the heat was turned on, when we slept together, doing spoons. So it was almost, but not exactly, a brother-and-sister thing.

Most evenings Nathan and I spent walking around the Ghetto neighborhood or sometimes wandering over to the ancient synagogue by the Tiber. The river, low and muddy in early autumn, had a seductive, earthy breath at night; its dankness floated up the embankment and pulled you back down with it. When we returned to our room, we'd sit cross-legged on one of the beds, drink brandy, and talk about our college years and travels. Eventually we started telling sex stories. I had only a couple of good stories from my previous year in Paris—one about a woman I'd met at a lesbian nightclub and the other about a Franco-Slavic artist who drew broken dolls resembling his lovers. In contrast, Nathan, who'd been seducing women since the age of fourteen, had a multitude. He once told me he enjoyed talking and journaling about sex as much as having it, and that wasn't hard to believe, given how entertaining his stories could be. And unforgettable, too, because they invariably culminated in a metaphor or phrase that would stick in my head like a catchy short story title. There was, for example, the woman who liked a lick job first thing every morning, which she called "having breakfast;" then there was a woman who did a dancing strip-tease before bed, whom he named "my shining Scheherazade." He'd dubbed another lover "my Venus flytrap" because she had a multitude of freckles on her upper lip and chin.

After a good gab, we'd both pull out our diaries and start writing. He was reading *Tropic of Cancer* at the time and clearly trying to equal Henry Miller in word and deed, while

I, imagining myself a tad more refined, played Anaïs Nin in the opposite corner.

Sergio hired both of us, though he later told me that he had his doubts about Nathan and never liked him. Nathan was equally suspicious of Sergio but happy to be employed at Multi Lingua, where he promptly fell madly in love with the Greek secretary. Day and night I listened to his praises of Melitta, how great she looked in tight skirts and high heels, how seductively her brilliant green eyes shone between her thick eyelashes.

Melitta finally consented to go out with him. Because Nathan was a fast operator, I assumed he would spend the night at her place or rent a room for the two of them. So I was surprised when, drifting off to sleep, I heard the door swing open and Nathan come in singing loudly, "Melitta, Melitta, me' lita o' wine. Melitta, Melitta, me' lita o' wine."

He turned the light on and sat down on the bed next to me. "Anna, Anna, my little banana. Melitta, Melitta—"

"Oh, shut up," I said. "Get off my bed and go to sleep."

"I can't. I've got a real boner."

"Then go take care of it in the bathroom or something." I propped myself up on the pillow. "So what happened?"

"She refused me," he said. "Absolutely and completely. "

He actually had tears in his eyes. Nathan was half-British and half-Italian, and the two halves of his personality waged war with unpredictable results. One minute he was weeping over Wordsworth, the next he was Mozart's Don Giovanni adding yet another name—with color of hair and eyes and a performance rating on a scale of one to ten—to the list of conquests he kept in the back pages of his diary.

"But it was only your first date. Be reasonable."

"I can't. It's hopeless. She said I was too young for her. If I can't change her mind, I'll die. I think I might actually be in love for the first time in my life."

"I doubt it. But I'm sorry." I grinned, pleased to see his seducer's confidence shaken.

"It's not funny. My heart's broken."

"Nathan—" I began, wanting him to see his own ridiculousness. "Oh, forget it." I rolled away from him and pulled the covers up over my shoulder.

He turned off the light, took off his pants and got under the covers, pressing his erection against my ass. The warmth of his body curled around mine felt good. "It's cold tonight," he said. "Come on, roll toward me."

I faced him, and he took his briefs off and put his hand on my shoulder and pushed me down, and I did him a favor, maybe because I needed connection and he was my best and only friend in Rome. But as he moaned Melitta's name, I felt like I was whoring, to get what I don't know. Friendship? Company?

Seconds after he finished, he said, "I'm sorry. Jesus Christ, I'm such a bastard."

"Forget it," I said.

"I'm sorry," he repeated. "You're the first woman I've ever been able to really be friends with. I don't want to ruin it. This must never, ever happen again."

"Don't worry," I said. "It *won't* happen again." Pause. "And don't you dare put me on that goddamn list of yours."

"Of course not, Foxy. I wouldn't ever."

I turned my back to him, and he cuddled up to me and we fell asleep. The episode wasn't anything to be proud of, but I comforted myself with the thought that, once upon a time, Anaïs had done much more for old Henry.

The taxi approached the Falcon. I was furious with Nathan, furious with Peep.

"I can't believe Nathan told you about it—and he acted so sorry about it at the time! Jesus, what a creep."

"Don't you want to know what he told me *exactly?*"

"No, I don't. Because I'm sure it's not true, and you'll put an even less true version out there."

In Rome, people traded stories to defray the boredom of

endless social engagements, and Nathan's story would circulate, becoming more salacious with each retelling.

"Worried about your 'reputation'?" Peep chuckled. "Listen, I'd like to put the two of you together in a movie."

"Your kind of movie? Forget it."

"I'd make serious movies if I could, but there's no money in it. Erotica is how I make a living."

"I'm guessing porn is the better word."

Peep leaned toward me, grabbed my arm. "You want to be some kind of artist, right? You stay in Rome long enough and you'll go to the dogs, too. You'll see. You'll start taking photographs to 'support' yourself as a painter, and then one day you'll take a picture of a friend half-naked, and before you know it you'll have a little business doing 'artistic' photos for wealthy expatriates or perverted Italian politicians—"

"I actually have a job teaching, so I don't need to do that."

"Even with your job, you'll find yourself doing things you never thought you'd do."

That stopped me. I'd already done things I wouldn't have done back home.

"So what do you recommend, pray tell?"

"Get your experience or culture or whatever it is that you're after, then leave. Whatever you do, don't stay on and on, the way I've done. Make your escape plan now, before the city chews you up and spits you out."

"You don't think it's possible for an expatriate to live a normal life here? My aunt does."

"She's an exception. But you won't be. You're already leading a double life. You've got your apartment and your little job *alla Romana*—I bet you even have a two-hour lunch break for siesta, right?—but you're also out carousing till dawn, à la Hemingway."

"Wrong city."

"You get the idea."

Peep was right. On the one hand, I'd constructed something like a normal life, with an apartment and a nine-to-eight job with—he was correct here, too—a two-hour lunch break. On the other hand, there were too many dinners with too many people, followed by wandering through city nightscapes as drunk on color as I was on alcohol. For I was a double addict, dependent not only on how light and dark played on the city's earthy colors, but also on how wine intensified my pleasure.

"You know what? I'm having a great time and I'm not about to leave."

"And you want to be an artist, right? Where are you going to find a studio in this town? Or are you going to paint *plein air*" —he gave the phrase a sarcastic bite—"doing scenes of crumbling ruins for tourists?"

"You're a real downer, you know that?"

"Someone's gotta keep it real," Peep said.

The taxi wound its way up to Piazza Barberini and down a narrow street to the Falcon's door.

"You sure you don't want to come in for a quick drink?"

"Uh—" I hesitated. The Falcon was fun. You could walk in and talk to anybody, male or female, young or old, and hear a good yarn. There were stories of the "why I'm here" variety—the abusive father, the dead marriage, the Novocain numbness of a Canadian childhood—and tales of drugs and enlightenment from pilgrims to India. Most entertaining were the stories about expatriate life in Rome—plots to secure apartments, Boccaccian bedroom farces, and disguises assumed to escape the *Questura*'s pursuit of illegal immigrants. I myself liked to tell about the time I'd hidden in my bedroom armoire from the police, who'd come to check for papers I didn't have.

"Come on," he urged.

"No, I don't think so," I finally said.

"Sure?" he opened the door, extended a leg.

"Bye, Peep."

"Thanks for paying for the taxi. Remind me to buy you a drink next time."

Peep climbed out, slamming the door behind him. As he stepped down the stairs to the entrance of the club, I had a momentary impulse to hop out and follow him. But, as much as I loved the Falcon, I had a date with Sergio.

"*Avanti,*" I said to the taxi driver, who stepped on the gas while I, leaning back in my seat, gave myself over to anticipation.

4. The Nature of Impulse

I reached the Odeon Hotel before Sergio. The Indian hotel-keeper gave me a key and I walked into a room, placing my bag on top of the beat-up dresser. It was the same room we'd had two nights before. I glanced out the window at the cob-blestoned street, let down the wooden rolling blind, closed the drapes, and sat down on the edge of the bed. Forty-eight hours earlier, Sergio's first kiss had taken me by surprise: I'd waited so many months for him to make a move that I'd assumed it would never come. But now, this second night, waiting for him had the swirling deliciousness of pleasure foretasted. Lying down on the bed I opened a volume of Alberto Mora-via's *Roman Stories* that I'd brought in case Sergio was late. Moravia's Italian was simple enough for me to read without a dictionary, and the world he described, antithetical to every cliché about Italy the beautiful, presented lessons that deluded me into feeling forewarned. The *Conti romani* read like a series of neo-realist film scripts about soured relationships, poverty, and, of course, the occasional prostitute.

I finished a story then began to draw. In the many hours I'd spent sitting in Sergio's office, during the lunch siesta when I chose to be with him rather than go home and in the early evening when I kept him company as he tidied up, I had mem-orized his every feature. Sergio, his wiry frame inside a three-piece suit, leaning sideways in his chair, his weight on one elbow, while he held a pen and gently tapped it on the desk, then turned it and tapped the other end. Tap, tap, turn, and tap, tap again meant he was in a reflective mood, and I liked to listen to him talk about his life. He told me that during the week he lived in a small apartment in the periphery of Rome, but on weekends he returned to Sperlonga, the seaside town where he'd grown up and owned a building with three apartments. He rented out the ground floor, his father lived on the second, and he had the apartment on the third. His cousins and aunt and uncle lived across the street, in a house behind a gas station they operated.

He'd told me that Mauro, the founder and owner of the Multi Lingua chain, had grown up in the house next door. "With the exception of Mauro and me," Sergio used to say, "the people in my town are *contadini*—country people, peasants." He used the term with equal parts condescension and affection. He wanted to leave Rome eventually and move back home to make his relatives' lives a little easier. "Someday I'll work at a big company and make a lot of money," he once said. "Then we can get all of Robertina's teeth fixed," he added, referring to his aged aunt. He'd look out the window, dreaming about it.

Our conversations at school were usually in English, which he spoke well, but when he talked about his home town and family, he'd switch to his native language and, forgetting my Italian was intermediate, speak rather fast, leaving me a little confused about the details. The gist of the Robertina story seemed to be that poor nutrition during her wartime pregnancy had caused her teeth to decay. If only the Allies had landed a year earlier, then baby wouldn't have cost mommy her teeth. Nobody's fault, that's just the way things were. As for her son, poor Flavio, his teeth weren't too good either. So Sergio's story went, or something like that. The stories of hardship, his tenderness for his family, and his compassion for his elders all moved me deeply.

After so many months of us talking like that and of my

desiring him, he felt uncannily present as I sketched him, although he hadn't yet arrived. It was as though the ghost of his living body were before me. When I closed my eyes, there he still was. A slight pressure in my forehead and rawness of the throat reminded me that I'd taught many hours and was short on sleep. I imagined Nathan relating our infamous encounter to Peep and got upset all over again. Then, remembering the expression of concern on Nathan's face when I'd left the house, I smiled. I put my sketchbook down and was almost dozing off when a knock woke me. A tremor came into my body.

"It's me," Sergio said softly from other side of the old, heavy door.

Heart thumping, I placed my hand on the smooth brass handle and, stepping back, opened the door. "*Ciao*," I said.

He swung into the room.

"*Ciao*." He stepped in, striding past me with a few long steps to the center of the room. His olive skin was darkened further by end-of-the-day stubble, his moustache, in need of a trim, curled down a bit over a serious upper lip. As he looked around the room for a moment, his profile expressed an intensity of feeling that I hadn't seen before. He turned to look at me, his brown eyes filled with gravity.

I went to him, he put his arms around me. Our clothes disappeared, and we came together, one warm wave of skin melting against another in the oceanic current of feeling that landed us in bed. There was an aggression in his tenderness that hadn't been there two nights before, a quickness and grace to his movements. Notice, touch, feel.

"*Bella.* You're so beautiful."

"Sergio, Sergio." I repeated his name again and again, like an incantation.

"*Amore*," he whispered.

He touched me, opened me, entered me. It was simple, effortless. He made me feel treasured in a way I'd never experienced before. It was so confounding that all I could do was repeat his name over and over as he moved inside me—

Sergio, Sergio—and each time I said his name, he whispered, *Amore*, back to me, and I fell deeper into a loveliness I hoped to remember forever because I intuited that one day we would each be gone to the other.

Between the lines of faded roses on wallpaper and the heavy roll-down blind, between two cool white sheets, my lover held me, caressing my face.

"I thought that this might be a one-night story." Speaking in Italian, Sergio used the word *storia*, which in Italian means "history" as well as "story." When referring to a love affair, *storia* implies not only the facts of a liaison, but the romance, delights, and wounds that come out of it—in other words, the sense that an affair has a beginning, a middle, and, inevitably, an end. "But here we are again."

"Here we are again," I repeated.

Then, out of the blue, "I took someone to live with me about two years ago," he said.

"You 'took'?" The verb suggested a kidnapping in antiquity, like the rape of the Sabines. I imagined him riding into some woman's front yard wearing a leather cuirass and sweeping her up onto his horse, while she, imitating the woman in Rubens's painting, extended one arm to the skies, screaming.

"Her family is traditional Catholic. She's half-American, so I expected a more modern attitude. But they were as shocked as any small-minded Italian family. Two people together under one roof, unmarried! What would the Pope think! You know, I participated in the student protests in 1968, I was on the barricades in Rome, so I thought the world had changed. But nothing has changed. In the little towns, in the little minds of little Italians, nothing has changed at all!" His voice became staccato when he was agitated. "To make matters worse—it's a complicated story—the money her family promised us to set up a life, well, they have not yet provided.

It probably sounds old-fashioned to you, this expectation of a dowry, but it's customary here."

He seemed unaware of the contradiction between his desire for the freedoms promised by the Sixties and his old-fashioned expectation that a sizable gift would be delivered with his wife. Astonished, I said nothing.

"Consequently I'm wrangling with her family on two accounts," he continued. "One—our violation of Catholic law. Two—the money they owe us."

"What's her name?"

"Olivia."

So it was Olivia. I remembered the time I'd glimpsed her back and wondered whether she were beautiful. Whether yes or no wouldn't diminish my shock. I had somehow imagined that Sergio's other relationship was casual, disposable. Now I would have to redefine what I was doing in bed with him. I was—let's see—his last fling before marriage. Yes, that was it. How humiliating. Well then, I would think of him as my Italian trophy, one of many conquests in my career as a lusty globetrotter. And that was okay, since I wasn't planning on getting married and having kids—both of which would get in the way of my artistic path, not to mention my travel plans. It was good to be clear from the outset about the parameters of our involvement.

"So if you're living together, what did you tell her about where you are tonight?" I propped myself up on one elbow.

"I told her I had a business dinner, and tonight I can stay over with you because she went down to Sperlonga ahead of me, and she thinks I'm spending the night in our Rome apartment. We go to Sperlonga almost every weekend. I'll drive down tomorrow." He pulled me toward him, drawing me off my elbow, and squeezed me tight. "You need to meet Olivia and become friends with her. Come down to Sperlonga tomorrow. Then we can spend more time together."

"That's a crazy idea." It was also perverse and dangerous, but I liked that he wanted more time with me when we already spent the weekdays together at school.

"You'd like her. And you could use a woman friend. You're always hanging around with this guy or that one. It's not good for you."

"No, you mean, it's not good for *you*. You're jealous."

"I don't have the right to be jealous, obviously." He looked miserable.

"I think it's better if I don't meet her."

"Why?"

"You're going to marry her!"

"If it was up to me, I would never marry. Never."

"So why did you 'take' her to live with you?" I asked.

"Doesn't everyone want a companion for the road of life and, eventually, some children?"

"Not necessarily." Here was a difference between us. At twenty-two, I wanted a variety of lovers, places, adventures, whereas Sergio, almost ten years older than me, needed to settle down. "I'm tired," I said, overwhelmed by the new information. I pressed my nose into his warm shoulder, and he gave me another squeeze.

Why hadn't Sergio told me how deep he was in with Olivia before sleeping with me the first time? I puzzled over his secrecy. Was it the result of a European code of discretion or an intentional manipulation to get me into bed? The artist I'd had an affair with in Paris described himself as a libertine: he made it clear he had simultaneous partners of both sexes, yet remained silent about the details. Maybe all European men were that discreet.

There came from the street a sound of motorcycles revving up and guys barking loudly in crude Roman dialect. Something kept me from asking Sergio questions. Whatever the reason for his secrecy had been, I forgave him because I desired him. In any case, I had filled out that application for a teaching fellowship in Asia the following year and, even if I didn't get it, I would move on in that direction, with the hope of improving the Mandarin I'd started studying in college. Now that I was a reasonably good English teacher, I could go anywhere. Sergio's prior involvement was a blessing in a way, since it guaranteed me my freedom. Even as I held him tight, I held on just as tight to the vision of me crossing the Hong Kong Harbor on a junk, or riding up the hills behind the exotic city on the funicular, or having my first affair with an Asian. I loved the feeling of the open road before me, and I wasn't about to give it up.

Morning came and Sergio was still beside me. I didn't yet know how rare waking up together would be. Not wanting to think forward in time, I only gazed at his face, slack with sleep, adorned by the dark brown moustache that curled slightly over his upper lip. A moustache without a beard always struck me as a kind of misplaced object, like a nailbrush turning up in a living room. Sergio's suggested a certain shyness, perhaps even a tendency, unusual among Italians, to be socially withdrawn. I took in the faded red of his lips, the beauty mark on his right cheek. He opened his eyes and the pale speck in the brown iris of his left eye shone like silk velvet reflecting a ray of sun.

"*Cara*," he said. His morning voice delivered the Italian word for "dear," so similar to "caress," with a soft bristle.

"Good morning."

He reached for his watch on the night table, glanced at it, and looked at me. "I have to go home then drive down to Sperlonga." He rolled back toward me, stroked my face. "Take the train down today and visit us."

"I can't, you know that."

"Listen to me: I'll tell Olivia that your living situation is driving you crazy—which is true—and that you need a weekend away to get some rest—which is also true. Look at you—you're exhausted from Nathan's parties! There's a train at eleven o'clock to Formia, which is the station closest to us. I'll come get you, you can meet my family, and we can be together."

"I don't know, Sergio."

"I don't know either. It's probably a terrible idea. But it's what I'd like."

I reflected. "Does Olivia have a sewing machine?"

"I invite you to my home for the weekend and you ask if Olivia has a sewing machine? Now you're thinking like an Italian! What can I get out of this situation—how can I use it to my advantage—that's exactly the way we operate here. You're catching on. *Brava!*"

"I have this dress from my aunt that I have to alter for a gala she's organizing."

"Yes, Olivia has a sewing machine. In fact, she's working on some curtains."

"Okay, then."

"It's arranged. Let's go have breakfast."

"There's a café I like on the piazza."

He sat up, picked up my copy of Moravia's *Conti romani* from the night table. "This is so harsh," he said. "Beautiful and real, but not the right thing to read while waiting for your lover. You should be reading Leopardi, Montale . . . " He sighed. "Olivia's intelligent in her own way, but she doesn't read, with the consequence that—" He stopped himself and looked away. "But who am I to say anything about that? The son of a peasant. Lucky enough to get an education, but still— the son of a peasant."

We dressed, took turns using the one toilet at the end of the hall. Then we went to the main office where the skinny Ceylonese innkeeper was watching TV and having biryani rice for breakfast, while his wife stood over a stove in a tiny kitchen stirring a pot that smelled of coriander and ginger. Seeing us, the man rose and approached us with an odd waddle, as though his legs were too stiff to bend at the knees.

"*Buon* morning," he said. "How you *dormire?*" Perhaps he mixed his languages mid-sentence to suit us as a half-Italian, half-American couple.

I stepped back as Sergio took lira notes out of his wallet to pay him, then we set off down the wide stone staircase.

"I like him," he said, "even if he does walk like a duck."

Giving me a comical look, he took the last stairs with straight legs, swaying back and forth like a roly-poly toy and making me laugh. I liked hearing his laughter first thing in the morning, and even more I liked his taking my hand as we stepped outside. We paused in the cool mauve shadow of the *palazzo* and looked at the rectangle of morning light landing on the west side of the piazza. Then I gave him a tug in the opposite direction, nodding toward a café on the eastern, shaded side.

"They have good *sfogliatelle* there," I said. "My favorite thing for breakfast." The crusty pastries, shaped like scallop shells, were filled with ricotta.

"Are you sure? Are you sure you wouldn't prefer a little curried rice?" He stopped in his tracks. "Let's go back and ask to share." He did another little waddle.

"You're silly sometimes."

"We have a plan, that's the important thing. You'll go home, get your things, and then catch a train. Meanwhile I'll be driving down."

We crossed the small piazza and stepped into the café. Like most of the cafés in the little neighborhoods, it had sparse decoration. There were a couple of little tables to sit at against the wall and no stools at the bar. We stood at the long steel counter and ordered cappuccinos and pastries. The coffee was hot and bracing; the *sfogliatelle* had a satisfying, layered crispness on the outside and the ricotta inside was laced with orange. I smiled as I watched the powdered sugar make its way into Sergio's moustache.

"What's so funny?" he asked.

"You—you're sprinkled with sweetness," I said, dusting his moustache with a finger.

"And you—you have stuck your nose in the cappuccino." He picked up a napkin and, leaning in toward me, dabbed my nose tenderly. "That's better."

"Everything's better now."

"Yes, now that I know you're coming down to Sperlonga, everything's better."

Neither one of us considered the insanity of what we were doing. Sergio had suspended all judgment, and I took guidance only from my emotions, which were pure in their intensity. My delight in Sergio was like my delight in Rome itself: the smile in his eyes flashed like sparkles in a fountain on a sunny day; the color and texture of his skin pleased me as much as the ocher hues of the ancient buildings. When he talked to me and touched me, my whole Italian experience got condensed like fruit ripened in the sun and boiled down to a sweet jam. It didn't occur to me that what we were doing was wrong—and uncommonly twisted.

I got back to my apartment to find it reeking of stale wine and human sweat. Someone had set our record *Desire* over the top of the lamp next to the couch, and it had melted, so that half of it draped down like black lava against the white lampshade, offering a Dali-like still life. Still in costume, a couple of Nathan's students were asleep on the makeshift bed they'd made out of cushions from our two wicker armchairs placed on the floor. In Nathan's room, which I glimpsed through the open door, two more guests huddled under a blanket. As I turned toward the closed door of my own bedroom, it opened, and Peep's voluptuous model, dressed in a man's shirt and not much else, came out.

"*Eh, buon giorno,* I go to the toilet—" She slid past me and disappeared into the bathroom.

I went into my bedroom and found Nathan in my bed.

"Anna! Thank God you're back," Nathan groaned. "Save me."

Angry, I approached him. "How could you—how could you tell Peep—"

"Oh, come on Foxy. Lighten up." He extended an arm

and taking my hand, coaxed me to sit down on the bed next to him. "I mean, why must you take everything so seriously? Why?"

Nathan, like me, had gained weight since arriving in Italy, and puffed up and unshaven, with bloodshot eyes, he was the picture of Roman decadence.

"What are you doing in my bed, anyway?"

"A bloke was too drunk to go home, so I offered him mine."

"There are two people in your bed, actually—"

"Really? Who?" His eyes grew big with curiosity.

"It really bugs me when you use my bed for your—activities. What's her name, anyway?"

"Maria—or was it Sabrina? Shit. Something with three syllables."

"You're a real jerk sometimes."

"It's true. And one day, Foxy, when I've gotten all this carousing out of my system, we'll settle down somewhere and have a proper life, just like we had in that former lifetime when we were married and raised chickens. Was it in Morocco, maybe?" He took my hand and placed it on his cheek. "Don't you remember us raising chickens in Marrakech, many lifetimes ago?" He cooed at me affectionately.

I laughed. "Sure, why not." It was hard to stay angry at him.

"So, kiss and make up?"

Sitting up to hug me, he glimpsed the sadly melted album in the living room through the open bedroom door and gasped. Without any inhibition about being stark naked, he leapt out of bed with his morning erection at half-mast and stumbled into the living room. Grabbing the bent record in his hands, he cried out, "Oh, *maestro!* What have they done to you?"

I got up, followed him. "Your friends really trashed the place last night."

"Next time we'll have *your* friends instead. That should make for a fun party." He made a stiff, serious face, and we both laughed. It was a running joke between us that Sergio gave me the older, boring students, men from IBM and other large corporations—the lucrative accounts, in short—whereas Nathan got the young, hip students ready to party all night with their teachers.

At that moment, Maria or Sabrina or whoever she was came out of the bathroom.

"*Mamma mia!*" she said, looking at Nathan's nudity on display. She grabbed a stray sweater hanging over the back of a chair and tied it around his waist.

"Ha!" he guffawed.

I went back into my bedroom to pack for my weekend in Sperlonga. It seemed vaguely unfair that Nathan found sex partners so easily while my attempts to get Italian men into bed usually ended with disappearance acts. My date, Houdini-like, would escape his forward American seductress citing a curfew, another commitment, or an attack of guilt brought on by the sudden recollection that he already had—*o Dio!*—a *fidanzata*—a word that literally means fiancée but also works as a euphemism for girlfriend. The few times I'd scored, the sense of the Pope about to knock at the door had made the sex quick and furtive, belying the Italian word for intercourse, *amplesso*, which suggests an amplitude of experience. I'd have called it a *minimo* instead—the result of a culture of sexual shame, in which men, at least of that generation, were often initiated by prostitutes. I'd been getting desperate when, thank God, Sergio had taken me to bed.

I replenished my Greek bag for the weekend with clean underwear. Toothbrush and hairbrush, a book and a small sketchpad were already in there. I'd forego pajamas and sleep in my underwear. In a separate bag, I had the dress my aunt had given me, which I hoped to alter with Olivia's sewing machine.

"Hey, Anna," Nathan called out, "I forgot to tell you there are a couple of letters for you."

I saw the envelopes on the dining table and picked them up. One was from my father, the other from my sort-of-ex boyfriend, Doug. Two men who both enjoyed telling me what to do.

"You see them?" Nathan asked. He and his girl were in the kitchen making espresso.

"Yeah."

"Hey, I'm going motorcycle shopping today. You want to come along?"

"Sorry I can't—though it sounds like fun—"

"What are you up to, then?"

"I'm—uh—going to spend the weekend with some friends."

He came out of the kitchen with the sweater still wrapped ridiculously around his waist. "You don't want to tell me who and where?"

"No, I don't."

"Okay. Be careful, won't you?"

Avoiding his eyes, I stuffed the letters into my Greek bag to read on the train. "Yeah, sure," I said and left for the station.

5. A Crazy Idea

Was I really going to meet Sergio's fiancée? Anxiety came up in a wave then subsided into a ripple as I looked out the train window. The urban periphery of Rome, with its strange combination of crumbling ruins and fascist apartment blocks, relaxed me back into the feeling I'd often had since going abroad that I was play-acting, that I was having one big adventure in parentheses and nothing I did could have consequences.

Remembering the letters in my Greek bag, I pulled out my father's first.

Dear Anna,

Do you realize that you forgot your mother's birthday? She was terribly hurt, as she'd hoped for at least a card, if not a phone call. At our age we don't expect a celebratory feeling, but the day turned into an occasion for real sadness, and as a week has passed since without a word from you, she has sunk deeper into depression, and you know what that means for your mother—and what that means for me. It's a lot to bear on my own, though of course you have a right to your own life. I only hope that after almost a year in Italy you're getting some sense of direction. I doubt your aunt Doris is of much use in that department. As far as I can tell, you're navigating like a rudderless ship, so let me suggest that it's time for you come home—

For God's sake, I was only twenty-two. Did I have to have a master plan for my life firmed up already? In any case, I knew what this was really about: since I was no longer available, my father was now the object of my mother's wrath, and he couldn't take it. But he deserved it. After all, he'd spent my childhood cloistered in the university lab doing experiments late into the night while my mother abused me. Too angry to read the rest of the letter, I stuffed it back into my bag and took out the other one, from Doug.

> *Dear Anna,*
>
> *I don't understand why you haven't answered my last few letters when you know I want to visit you at spring break. You're still there, right? You haven't decamped to some other European city, have you? Even though we've taken a kind of "intermission," I still believe in us and our future together. Things are happening for me now. I'll be taking my master's exams in late May, and I already have some job prospects here in Boston. Why don't you come back to live with me in the fall? We've never really lived together. I think we ought to give it a try.*
>
> > *Your silence makes me anxious. I need to see you and I want to buy a plane ticket to Rome. Will you be there when I land? I tried calling you the other night but you weren't home—*

I put the letter down. I'd last seen Doug almost a year before when I was getting ready to leave Paris to visit my aunt in Rome. When we parted, I told him I needed my freedom and couldn't make any promises, but Doug was very in love with me and kept on writing. I sent him about one letter for every four he sent me—just enough to keep him dangling. I couldn't go on being so cruel. I had to write him and tell him not to come.

I looked out the window again. We'd pulled into flat countryside divided into small farms. This trip, my first south of Rome, felt daring. I'd heard terrifying stories about the southern half of Italy. In Naples, kids running by with a knife would slash the strap of a woman's handbag and make off with it in an instant; a gold earring might be grabbed with such force that its removal split the owner's ear lobe; drivers got their tires stolen from underneath them while their cars idled at red lights. My aunt Doris had a more amusing story about how, driving down the coast to Sicily with my grandmother Iris in the 1950s, they'd been stopped by *carabinieri*, who accused them of drug smuggling. The police humiliated them by rifling through their luggage, lingering over their lingerie and toiletries, going so far as to remove the wrapper from a tampon and examine it as though they had never seen one before. "Which," Doris said, "given the world of the Italian male, was entirely possible." All of which is to say that, in my imagination, Rome was where civilization ended and the wild west of Italy began.

The reality I found myself in was, of course, a lot tamer. Lazio, the province that contains Rome, has a modesty all around it, with the exception of its capital. The valleys, cultivated with utilitarian crops, are less picturesque than those of Tuscany, the hill towns are lower than those of Umbria, and the shore, lacking the drama of Liguria and Campania, runs more flat than not as it sweeps from one modest craggy point to the next. Still, I was curious to discover yet another corner of this region that had become home, and so, ready for adventure, I stepped onto the platform with my Greek bag and a sack containing the dress from Doris that I needed to alter. Sergio, in blue jeans and a white T-shirt, waved to me. It was the first time I'd ever seen him in casual clothes instead of a three-piece business suit.

"Anna," Sergio said, gesturing to the man next to him, "this is my cousin Flavio, who lives across the street from me. Flavio, this is Anna."

Flavio shook my hand. He was shorter than Sergio, clean-shaven, a little rotund in the face and belly.

"Welcome. Welcome to our family."

They led me to a light blue Mercedes parked behind the small station.

"What's this?" I asked Sergio, surprised. If he'd had money for such a car, surely he would have spent it on Robertina's teeth instead.

"The family Mercedes, of course." He grinned.

"It belongs to all of us," Flavio said as he opened a door to the front passenger seat for me then seated himself in the back. I got in next to Sergio, nervously stroking the tassels of my Greek bag.

"Flavio," Sergio said, "this you should know: Anna is Multi Lingua's *best teacher*. Best teacher *ever*."

"Okay, enough with the *best teacher* thing," I said, laughing. "I'm beginning to think you're being sarcastic."

"Do I sound sarcastic to you, Flavio?"

"Not at all," Flavio said, chuckling. "My cousin doesn't have a sarcastic bone in his whole body. If he says you're the best teacher *ever*, then it's true."

I was used to this particular form of Italian humor, in which praise became so hyperbolic that it resembled sarcasm.

"Flavio and his wife and baby live across the street from us. He owns a gas station. Today's his day off, that's why he's not covered with grease from head to toe."

"Today my brother Nazzaro gets to be covered with grease," Flavio said.

"Poor Nazzaro, who is consumed by a desire to go to South America," Sergio said.

"He says he's saving up to leave," Flavio added.

"Why would anyone want to leave our region, so full of economic possibility?" Sergio said, gesturing around him.

Now he was being truly sarcastic. The back road between Formia and Sperlonga took us through barren hills where scant vegetation beaten by sea winds revealed areas of denuded soil and white rock. The sparsely inhabited land bore the marks of the kind of cheap construction that thrives in a culture of poverty. The houses had only distant echoes of Italian charm in their roofs of fake terracotta tile and metal balconies with industrial-looking vertical iron bars. The plastered exteriors painted in chipping white and peach tones fell straight to the ground like stiff starched sheets, and on more than one property the frame of a structure with no workers or materials nearby suggested a project abandoned midway for lack of funds. But my eyes, seeking pleasure, went to the vegetable plots and old stone walls, and the sparkles of light on the blue Mediterranean in the distance triggered some crazy excitement inside me.

"Ah Nazzaro, how he dreams of the tango," Flavio said.

"The tango with an Argentinian beauty," Sergio added.

"In a Parisian-style Buenos Aires café with three guitarists—" Flavio continued.

"Three *mad* guitarists—three mad *singing* guitarists—*oh, oh, mi señorita*—" Sergio howled in a minor key.

"And candles on the tables all around—"

"And at the door, the watchman with a knife between his teeth. Oh, *Dio*, what an exciting dream!" Sergio exclaimed.

We were still laughing when we reached the outskirts of Sperlonga, where newer, little apartment buildings alternated with ancient houses and vegetable gardens. Sergio's building, with its fresh paint and clean windows, suggested a proprietor who cared about appearances. We parked.

"See you in a while," Flavio said, and he headed across the street, where a garage with a single gas pump stood in front of a little house.

Sergio led me to the front door of his dwelling and opened the door.

"Did you notice this is the only three-story building along this road?" he asked proudly. "My father built it, then I made some changes." Inside the small entryway three mailboxes hung on the wall. "Good neighbors here," he said, gesturing to the front door of the first-floor apartment. "Papa on the second floor," he added as we passed it and continued up the staircase. "And Olivia and I are on the third." He stopped on the last landing, looked at me uncertainly. I was about to meet his fiancée—was he going to issue a warning of some kind? No. What he said was, "I hope you like it."

"I'm sure I will," I said.

"With your aesthetic sense—" he began. "You're fussy. I don't know."

His desire for my approval, although odd under the circumstances, touched me. Wasn't he nervous about my meeting Olivia? I felt hot and cold from climbing the stairs. He opened the door.

Stepping in and making a left, we found ourselves in a large, impeccably equipped kitchen. A fridge and stove bracketed a long counter with a double sink against the back wall, and off-white stone tiles on the splashboard contrasted with dark wooden cabinets. On the entrance side of the room, a rectangular dining table was set for lunch for six. The popular magazine, *Oggi*, probably Olivia's, sat on top of a copy of Sergio's left-leaning newspaper, *La Reppublica*. Two women stood by the stove, one of them cooking, the other with a toddler on her hip.

"Anna, this is my *fidanzata* Olivia, and this is my sister-in-law, Teresa—Flavio's wife."

"And this is Bobo," Teresa said. "Say *ciao*, Bobo. *Ciao, Anna.*"

"Ow, A-a," said the child, waving his little arms.

"I've heard so much about you," Olivia said. She had a Brooklyn accent. "Sergio says you're the school's best teacher."

"I never know whether he really means it," I answered.

Olivia extended a hand to shake mine, then impulsively stepped toward me and planted a kiss on my cheek. She was a tall woman, a little stout, with a heart-shaped face and a sweet smile.

"How was the train ride?" she asked.

"Fine. A lot of stops. Seems like the equivalent of the Long Island Railroad."

"So where are we, then? Probably not Garden City, but

Huntington, right?" She chuckled, mentioning stops on the North Shore line. I hadn't expected to meet someone I might like. At a loss for conversation, I looked out the window at the sea, visible in the distance to the left of the old town, as my stomach did a little flip.

"Oh no," Teresa interrupted in Italian. "No English. The American girls do *not* get to gossip in English."

Teresa was much shorter than both of us, but her massive bust and darkly shadowed eyes gave her an air of authority, as did the child on her hip. The conversation quickly shifted into a dialect difficult to follow, as it not only dropped word endings, Roman-style, but was also inflected with the local lexicon.

Sergio, who had disappeared into another part of the apartment, returned and reined Teresa in. "Standard Italian, please, for our guest," he said, gesturing deferentially toward me, at which point Teresa went over to the TV hanging above the dining table and turned on a loud and glitzy game show.

"Aren't Flavio and Nazzaro eating with us?" Olivia asked.

"No, they went to get a part for Donato's hot water heater," Sergio answered. "We're going to help him fix it after lunch."

I would never be introduced to Donato. Like most Italian men, Sergio had a large tribe of male friends whom he'd known since childhood, and I would never master all their names and identities.

We sat down to eat, and Olivia served us minestrone then some grotesque-looking but delicious innards from who knows what creature. Out of the corner of my eye, I took in the reality of her existence. She had been, until this moment, an abstraction—"Sergio's girlfriend"—which turned me into another abstraction—"the other woman"—but now here she was in the flesh, and here I was as well. And she was obviously a nice person, and what was I supposed to do with that information? Nothing, for the moment. The only thing I could do was temporarily forget I was having an affair with her fiancé.

Olivia asked me questions about where I grew up and

what had led me to Italy. Once we'd trotted over the basics, silence fell as we savored the greasy saltiness of the meat and mopped up the gravy with chunks of bread. In the background, a television game-show hostess in a sparkly red dress squawked at giggling contestants. Sergio ate very fast, hunched over his soup and meat with focused attention. Halfway through the meal, Bobo began squirming and whining, and Teresa stood up, hoisting the child with her.

"I'm going back to change him," she said.

She left. A moment later a man swung through the front door. He had many of Sergio's features, but more pronounced: the same slim face, but flattened like a run-over nickel; the same olive skin, darkened with five-o'clock shadow; and similar eyebrows, but thicker and uncombed. He held a few envelopes in his hand, which he threw on the table next to Sergio.

"Here you go," he said.

"Anna, this is what you call a thoughtful cousin—he gets the mail for us when he's in town. Nazzaro, this is Anna, from school," Sergio said, as his left hand crawled through the correspondence his cousin had brought.

Nazzaro nodded in my direction and looked me over, then turned back to Sergio. "We bought the part. The hot water heater is waiting for us."

"Off to help Donato," Sergio said, barely glancing at either Olivia or me. He stuck his hands in his jean pockets as he followed his cousin out.

Olivia and I were left alone. She rose and started clearing the table.

"Let me help you clean up," I said.

"Thanks. I'll wash, you can dry."

We stood side by side at the kitchen counter. Olivia wore big black glasses of the kind that were in style in the late '70s, her shoulder-length black hair was pulled back with a rubber band and the stray strands kept down with black bobby pins. She tied an apron around her waist with the smooth coordination of someone doing a familiar task. She had probably started off doing dishes for Sergio and his family with the sense of playing house, and now she did it because it was expected of her. Her patience in the kitchen struck me because my mother had passed on to me a virulent distaste for household chores.

Olivia pointed to the cabinet where the dried dishes went, and I opened it and began stacking them.

"You have such an orderly household," I said.

"It's taken us a while to afford it."

"How long have you and Sergio been together?"

"Five years," she said. "We moved in together three years ago."

"You must have been very young."

"Yes, I was twenty when we met."

"You grew up in Brooklyn?" I asked.

"Yeah, but my mother's Italian, she grew up down the coast, not far from here. She met my father at the end of the war—he was an American GI—and they moved to New York. When my dad died, she decided to bring me and my sister Nina back to Terracina—her hometown just south of here—where her sisters live. Then I spent some time in Rome so I could go to secretarial school. So I never got to go to college." She sighed. "Anyway, when Mauro and Sergio were setting up Multi Lingua, they needed extra help at the beginning. I was working for a temp agency that sent me there. That's how I met Sergio."

"I see."

"My mother disapproved of Sergio from the start. She thought he was too wild for me because he used to come pick me up on a motorcycle—"

Mesmerized by the details of their courtship, I visualized Sergio at twenty-seven on a Vespa, Olivia seated behind him.

"And?" I prompted.

"When we rode the motorcycle at night," she took her hands out of the sink and dried them on a dish towel tucked into her apron pocket, "the mosquitoes would go flying right into my eyeglasses," stepping back from the counter, she gestured in the air to indicate bugs flying toward her, "splat, splat, so I'd come home with these bugs stuck to my glasses and my hair all frizzed out from riding a motorcycle and—my mother was so shocked!" She giggled uncontrollably. Her laughter was infectious. "It was so funny—and the expression on my mother's face! That was pretty funny, too." She opened her mouth wide to demonstrate, then turned back to the sink and stuck her hands back into the soapy water. "Sergio was a wild guy in those days."

"But not so much anymore?"

"We want to have a family, so he's working hard—we're both working hard—to set up a proper household."

"And what happened with your mother?"

"She refuses to talk to either of us because she doesn't approve of our living together before marriage." Olivia looked sad. "I want my children to have a relationship with their grandmother, but if things continue this way, that might not be possible."

"But surely, once you get married—"

"I don't know."

She needed to talk about it, and I listened, riveted by this account of my lover's relationship with his future mother-in-law.

"When are you having the wedding?" I asked.

"I'm not sure," she said. "He hasn't wanted to talk about it recently."

She hadn't mentioned Sergio's annoyance about her family withholding a dowry. Perhaps she attached less importance to it than he did. Of course, his affair with me might also might be causing ripples. I didn't want to think about that.

"I hope everything works out for you." I liked her enough that, bizarrely, my words felt sincere.

"Thanks, Anna." She undid the bow at the small of her back and hung the apron up on a hook. "Let's make up your bed for the night, and then we can go out and do the shopping for dinner."

She led me to the linen closet, a tall, narrow recess in

the long hallway off the kitchen, and placed her fingers on the small brass knob to open it. Inside, on the shelves, were neat stacks of perfectly folded white sheets and pillowcases. There was just what was needed, neither more nor less.

"Gosh, even the inside of your closets and cabinets are orderly and neat," I said, stifling the impulse to relate the argument of *The Feminine Mystique*. But maybe Betty Friedan was wrong and being a housewife was fulfilling for some women.

"Sergio likes it that way." Taking out a stack of clean linens, she smoothed the top with one hand. "And it's satisfying."

As she led me into the formal, spare living room at the back of the building, the quiet of the midday siesta was broken by the sound of a cock crowing. The dark wood tables and bookcases reminded me of the furniture at Multi Lingua. The sun, just past its midday high, slanted in through the window and landed on the carpet with the platinum brightness of spring.

There was a folded cot standing in the middle of the room. Olivia went over and opened it.

"We can make it up now," she said, "because we hardly ever use this room. We pretty much live in the kitchen. Did you bring some pajamas?"

"No, but I can sleep in my T-shirt."

"I have an extra pair I can lend you."

She opened the fitted sheet and together we put it on the cot.

"So what's going on with your living situation?" Olivia asked. "Sergio told me your housemate is driving you crazy."

"Yeah, I live with this guy—" I began. Seeing the question in her eyes, I quickly added, "—he has one bedroom, I have the other. It's completely platonic—and he's lots of fun, but the parties on work nights are tiring. I mean, if I have to be at school first thing in the morning, it's hard."

She unfolded the top sheet, and we tucked it in.

"Well, you can come here to catch up on your sleep anytime you want," she said, then added, with a shy smile, "It'll be nice having an American friend to visit."

"Thanks for having me," I said.

She showed me a folding screen that I could place at the entrance to the living room when I needed privacy. "And now let me show you the rest of the place."

I followed her down the hall. We stepped into a first little room, on the left, with a desk and some bookcases.

"This is Sergio's study. It could be a child's room eventually," she said.

A couple of bookcases held a mix of business textbooks and paperback editions of fiction and poetry. Several piles of hardcover art books with gold lettering on cloth bindings were stacked horizontally; their purchase would have been considered self-indulgent luxuries in Sergio's working-class milieu.

Olivia led me to a second room on the left. In it, a double bed in a wooden four-poster bedframe boasted an intricately carved headboard, making it the most expensive-looking piece of furniture in the apartment.

"Eventually, we're going to move over to the bedroom on the other side of the hall," she said, then added with a smile, "This could be a second child's room."

"You got it all planned out."

"Well," she said, and gave a bit of a grimace, "what Sergio actually wants to do, in the short run, is put his father in here with us, so he can rent out the apartment downstairs."

"You don't like his father?"

"Why should I when he never talks to me, except to ask what's for dinner? The only people he speaks to are Sergio and his sister Robertina across the street. Sometimes a little to Flavio. He doesn't talk to me and he doesn't seem to like me, so why should I do anything for him? Like sew his pants. He's always bringing me his pants to repair. Of course, he doesn't actually *ask* for me to sew them, he just shoves them at me. I don't want to do it, but Sergio says I have to."

Perplexed, I rubbed my nose. Trouble in paradise.

"They fray at the crotch and at the bottom of the legs," Olivia continued, "and it bugs me to have to fix them."

"But you have to."

"I have to. To keep the peace with my future husband." Olivia grimaced, and, sitting down on the bed, absent-mindedly smoothed the white coverlet. Remembering occasions when Sergio had conned me into working longer hours than was humanly possible, I could imagine Sergio having a tyrannical side. "But maybe he's right," she continued with a sigh. "I might as well face it, when Luca—my father-in-law—gets old, I'll have to take care of him. I just wish he could say more to me than *Buon gio'*," she said, truncating *buon giorno* in the Roman style, then projecting her head forward, she gave a funny grunt that made me laugh. "That's exactly what he does—*'Buon gio'*"—she made a grunting sound— "or sometimes *'Buon gio'*"—and she made a double grunt.

As she bent forward with hysterical laughter, I joined her in the high giggle of young women mocking the patriarchs behind their backs. Her words—*we're as good as married, my husband's father, sew his pants*—released a cleansing whirlwind in my head, for whatever it was that I wanted, it wasn't this life in the Italian provinces, with its 1950s definition of a woman's place.

"Really, I shouldn't. If Sergio overheard me, he'd be furious." She stifled her laughter and, wiping the tears from her eyes, stood up. "And rightfully so, because his father has had a really hard time—" She stopped herself.

"How so?"

She shook her head. "I'm not supposed to talk about it. Let me show you the rest of the house."

She led me out of the room to the one across the hall. The largest and brightest of the three hallway rooms, clearly meant to be the master bedroom, it had a raised platform across from a fireplace and two tall windows looking out toward the old town and the sea. There was no furniture yet, only a roll of wall-to-wall carpeting, waiting to be installed.

"The bed will go up there," she said. "I'd like the platform torn out, but Sergio disagreed. However, I got to choose the color of the carpet." She walked over to the roll and turned down a corner to show me. "What do you think?" she asked, back in the role of a young bride setting up house.

"It's lovely," I said. Wall-to-wall carpeting wasn't my thing, but the color—a mix of deep navies and celadon greens—was subtle and appealing. "It could go with anything."

"Yes, you can imagine our antique bed in here, can't you? And Sergio's going to replace the mantelpiece with something nicer." She walked over to the wooden slab and put a hand on it. "He's looking for a piece of marble, reasonably priced. He likes hunting for things."

Naturally, Sergio hadn't shared with me this aspect of his character, scavenger for ideal home with bride. I imagined him on horseback, like a Canadian Mountie, patrolling the entire province of Lazio on the lookout for the right antiques and flooring. If Sergio wanted me to get to know him, the whole of him, quickly, he couldn't have done better than leave me with his fiancée for the afternoon.

Olivia glanced at her watch. "Siesta time is almost over. Let's drive to town to do the shopping."

The back road where Sergio lived led to the old section of Sperlonga, which rose picturesquely ahead of us on a small promontory overlooking the sea. Occasionally a curve in the road opened up a view of a wide arc of sandy beach tucked beneath the southern edge of the headland.

"Oh look, there's Sergio and his pals," Olivia said, pointing, as we passed a café.

Sergio was standing next to an outdoor table with cousins Flavio and Nazzaro, and a fourth man I didn't recognize.

"Who's the other guy?"

"Donato."

"Of the water heater?"

"Yes." She honked, and the guys looked at us and waved as we moved on.

"Nazzaro's an odd one," I said. "You think he'll really go to South America?"

"Who knows?"

The old town came into sight, and Olivia pulled over.

"Easier to find a parking space on the edge of town," she said. "A lot of it is closed to car traffic."

We got out and began walking down narrow streets paved with heavy gray stones and twisting between ragged houses with whitewashed facades and tile roofs. Here and there, a small arch overhead spanned a narrow alley, as though to keep the ancient buildings from leaning into one another. I'd moved south into a Greek-style range of whites, and the warm ochers of Rome felt far away. The Mediterranean flashed in the interstices, between pale plaster walls, from the top of a stone staircase, or in the clearing offered by a piazza.

Olivia hooked her arm through mine. "Let's go for ice cream, then down to the beach. We can go shopping afterward."

I hadn't had a woman friend since leaving Paris, and Sergio had been right—it was what I needed. "Ice cream sounds good," I said, and we walked forward arm in arm.

That evening, back at the apartment, Olivia poked a simmering ox-tail stew with a wooden spoon. It was past eight and Sergio hadn't returned yet. What did he do all afternoon with his male friends? Did Olivia mind his long absences? The two of us—*his little harem,* I thought—had been to the *frutteria,* the butcher's, and the baker's, gathering ingredients for the evening meal. As we chopped celery and parsley in the kitchen and she added vegetables to stew with the browned meat and canned tomatoes, I felt myself filling her loneliness and wondered what her life would be like—an Italian-American girl from Brooklyn dropped into a small town where her husband-to-be had a life already filled with relatives and friends. Who would be her confidante, who would help her when she had her babies? There was Teresa, of course, who would be her cousin-in-law. But one person doesn't make a community for a young bride.

"Why don't you sit down and relax?" Olivia said, still at the stove. "I've got everything under control."

I didn't sit, but went to the window and looked out, glimpsing the sea to the left of the old town. The sight of the falling light landing at a slant on the surface of the water triggered a déjà vu, as though the sea were a familiar dream fragment pursuing me, and for a moment everything, even my affair with Sergio and my duplicitous relationship with Olivia, felt foreordained. But there was an anguish woven around it that cut my breath, as though someone were pulling tight the strings of a corset I was wearing.

"The sunset's beautiful," I said.

Olivia put the spoon down and came over to the window.

"Oh, there's Ser!" she said, lighting up.

Glancing down, I saw Sergio in the street. "Ser"—I didn't know that was his nickname. Just lop a syllable off the end of any Italian word and it sounds better. She clapped her hands with delight, like a little girl. Goddamn, she sure was in love with him. Well, in a few weeks I'd learn whether I'd received that fellowship to teach in Asia. I might be in Hong Kong come next fall.

"Eh," he said, nodding to us both when he swung in a moment later. "Smells good." He went into the bathroom, and I heard the water run as he leaned over the sink and washed his face. His father swung in, wearing an old pair of jeans and a denim work shirt, then sat down at the dining table in the kitchen and picked up the newspaper. Luca would never once make eye contact with me during my many visits.

"*Cosa mangia*?" ("What are we eating?") Luca asked Olivia, not looking up from the paper.

"*Stufato di bue coda.*" ("Ox-tail stew.")

He grunted, and Olivia shot me a conspiratorial glance.

It was a quiet dinner that night, just the four of us. Olivia was a sensible, traditional cook. Pasta, of course, and then the stew and a side of a slightly bitter, cooked greens.

"This is good, Olivia," Sergio said, pointing to a succulent piece of the meat with his knife. "Anna, this is real food. The peasant food of Italy. It's not fancy, but it nourishes."

"It's delicious," I said.

The television was off, and the fatigue of a long day hung silently in the air. Luca was in his own world, Olivia looked tired, and Sergio did, too. After almost a year of living in Rome, I was still puzzled by the whole rhythm of Italian life, which left the work of cooking, cleaning up, and digesting heavy food to the hour right before bedtime. It was understandable in summer when daytime heat cut one's appetite, but felt odd in early spring.

"Tomorrow we have to go to Gaeta," Sergio said. "Someone we barely know is getting married in the cathedral there."

"It's our neighbor downstairs," Olivia explained. "You can come with us. It's a pretty town. You'll enjoy it."

"If you tolerate church weddings," Sergio said.

"You'll come to our wedding, won't you?" Olivia asked me.

Sergio shot me a glance.

"Depends on when it is," I said. "Whether I'm still here or not. I might be in Asia or back in the States."

"Asia?" Olivia asked. "You're going to Asia?"

"I applied for a teaching fellowship in Hong Kong."

"What are you going to do in Hong Kong? I don't get it," Sergio said. "You have a good job here, and Mauro and I are getting you working papers. A job has value—"

"I might also go up to Paris or travel a bit over the summer—if I can get time off from my employer." I tried for a jocular tone.

"Ah. Your ruthless employer," Sergio said, irritably. "In any case, you can do what you want in August. The whole country comes to a stop."

"We were thinking of July," Olivia said. "For the wedding."

"Nothing is settled," Sergio said. "The necessity of marriage I don't understand."

"But you want children," Olivia said.

"Anna will think you are completely unaware of 1968—the upheaval, the protests, the revolution in consciousness—as though none of it ever happened," he said.

"He wants to get married," Olivia said to me, seemingly unbothered. "The socialist talk is just mental exercise."

"But one thing I refuse—a religious wedding. I will not—I cannot—get married by a priest."

"We'll see," Olivia said.

Clearly, they'd had this conversation many times.

"The idea of God sanctifying a union is so much crap," Sergio said. "A union between two people, in the end, serves certain social and economic purposes. It's an arrangement that creates stability for the family, that protects the woman when she is having children, and the children while they are growing up—all that is good and right. But to bring the whole Church into the matter, the priest, saints, angels, the holy water and incense—"

"Now you're going into blasphemy—" Olivia's voice rose as she flushed bright red.

"Since I'm not a Catholic, how can anything I say be blasphemy?"

"You were christened, so you're a Catholic. Your soul—"

"My soul! Show me where my soul is. X-ray me and point to it."

There followed an incomprehensible exchange in which Luca leaned toward his son and asked him a question in dialect, and Sergio responded in the same.

The front door opened, and cousin Flavio came in.

"Grandma has made a tiramisu," he said. "You're all invited next door."

"Flavio's mother, Robertina. My aunt," Sergio said. He wiped his mouth, put his napkin down, and stood up. "Let's go." He had that sharpness to his movements that he got when agitated.

"Go ahead," Olivia said to me, "while I clean up."

It felt wrong to leave her at the sink doing dishes, but

Sergio and Flavio motioned me to follow them, so I grabbed my sweater off the back of my chair and followed the men down the stairs, across the dimly lit street, and past the pumps and garage to a small house with two levels, one a half-flight up, the other a half-flight down underground.

"This way," Flavio said, leading us to the basement, where the lights were on.

In a dank room with a dirt floor, where basic kitchen appliances were positioned haphazardly between improvised counters, Sergio's extended family sat around an enormous farm-style table. Teresa and baby Bobo and the skinny Nazzaro were there, and two elders.

Nazzaro pointed to an empty chair next to him, and I sat down.

"Robertina and Roberto," Sergio said, introducing me to his aunt and uncle. Perhaps one of them had been nicknamed after the other as a result of decades of marriage.

Robertina gave me a smile spotted with the dark spaces of missing teeth then addressed me in an incomprehensible dialect.

"She says," Sergio translated, "that she made the tiramisu especially for you, to welcome you into our family."

"*Grazie,*" I responded.

Nazzaro said something about going dancing.

"That's an idea," Flavio said. "The young people should go dancing."

"What do you think?" Sergio said, turning to look at me with an inscrutable expression. "The discothèque is in the next town—Gaeta. Wouldn't you like a taste of the exciting night life of the provinces?"

"Sure," I said.

"Eh, you see, she wants a good time, and you don't have to be so sarcastic all the time," Nazzaro said, giving Sergio an affectionate slap on the back of the head.

"Is it okay if I go dressed like this?" I was wearing blue jeans and a cotton cardigan over an old tie-dyed T-shirt.

"You look terrific," Nazzaro said. "Very authentic US of A."

Sergio drove, while Flavio sat next to him. In the back seat, Nazzaro appraised me with a steady stare. After a twenty-minute drive down the coast, Sergio stopped before a door that said *Discoteca* in pink neon and nothing more.

"This may be the provinces," Flavio said, "but we know how to show our American friends a good time."

I got out of the car and went over to Sergio's window, which was open.

"Aren't you going to park and come in?" I asked.

"No. We're going to play cards with some friends. We'll come get you in an hour or so."

"But Sergio—"

"Flavio and I are family men. We don't go to discothèques anymore."

"You're safe with Nazzaro," Flavio said, leaning in.

Nazzaro, who'd come to stand by me, repeated, "You're safe with me."

The Mercedes pulled away, and Nazzaro and I looked at each other. He gave me an engaging smile, revealing a gold-capped tooth. A chunky gold ring flashed on a finger as he reached for my hand.

"*Andiam' balla',*" he said. ("Let's go dance.") We headed down some stairs to a stone cellar refurbished as a disco. "I know the DJ here," he added. "Let me introduce you."

I followed Nazzaro up a half-flight of stone stairs to a booth where a cute guy, not more than eighteen, was juggling LPs. Before I knew it, the DJ was making an announcement about the visit of an American, there was a round of applause, and I was sitting in his chair, introducing Marvin Gaye and feeling as giddy as US troops must have felt when they landed in Anzio and were showered with good will. I saw Nazzaro approach a young woman he seemed to know, and they started to dance. He had a stiffness in his upper body suitable for the tango, and I imagined him, after a long day herding cattle on the pampas, stepping into a smoky Buenos Aires club and sweeping some Argentinean beauty in black lace across the dance floor.

The DJ disappeared for a moment, only to reappear with a glass of the potent grappa. This quickly doubled my enjoyment of my new job.

As soon as I introduced a slow number, Nazzaro came up to the booth, grabbed my hand, and dragged me down the stairs and into the dancing mob, where he placed his arms around me and pressed his body against mine. He exuded a smoky smell of rubber tires and hot oil, but I didn't mind because, as Sergio's double, he offered the comfort of a substitute contact.

There followed a series of faster dances, then we were back to body-to-body writhing when Flavio appeared at the entrance and waved to us across the room.

Nazzaro took my hand and led me back outside. There was Sergio, sitting at the wheel. The size of the Mercedes made him look smaller than he really was.

"Have a good time?" he asked.

We all got in and as the car pulled away from the curb, Nazzaro pulled on my arm and drew me toward him for a kiss. His lips came dangerously close, but I resisted.

"*Vieni, vieni,*" he whispered, inviting me closer.

"*No,*" I said pushing back against him.

"Why not?" He passed an arm around my shoulders and, stroking my neck, leaned in to kiss it.

"Because."

"*Che cazzo*—leave her alone, Nazzaro," Sergio said, looking into the rear view mirror.

"*Porca miseria!*" Flavio said, using an expression that literally means, "pig misery" to express "damn it." "She's our guest!"

"Eh!" Nazzaro said, shrugging.

Back at the house, Sergio parked and we all got out.

"Thank you for the lovely evening," Nazzaro said to me.

"Sure."

Nazzaro and Flavio crossed the dimly lit street toward the little house behind the garage, but Sergio didn't move. He just stood leaning against the car. The evening air had a bit of a bite to it, and I pulled my cotton cardigan closed, across my T-shirt, waiting for him.

"It's time to go to sleep," Sergio finally said.

"Yeah," I agreed, but he didn't move. He just stared at me, until Flavio and Nazzaro had disappeared, and we were the only ones on the street in the middle of the night.

"Was there any preparation for that?" Sergio asked, with a nod in the direction of his cousins' house.

"What do you mean?"

"Nazzaro grabbing you in the back of my car? I mean, I don't care what you do, you're free obviously—"

"What? You think I encouraged him? On the contrary, I defended myself!"

"But would you have if I hadn't been there? Obviously, you must have gotten along well enough in the nightclub for him to get the idea to attempt—" He gave an irritated shrug and headed toward the front door, which he opened with a sharp gesture.

"*You* sent me off to the club with him!"

"Why not? Our American guest should have a good time!"

He stomped into his building. Incensed that he presumed me guilty of initiating a flirtation with his cousin, I stomped up the staircase after him.

Entering the apartment, we went into the kitchen.

"You don't really believe I started it, do you?" I said in a low voice. "I can't believe you're being jealous!"

"Yes, I can be an idiot. In fact, I *am* an idiot." He gave me a dark look. "I'm thirsty. You want a Coke?" he asked.

"Uh—sure."

The apartment was quiet. As though to answer my unspoken question, he said, "Olivia is sleeping. She likes to go to bed early."

He put a glass of Coke in front of me and poured himself some, too.

"I hardly saw you all day," I said softly. I couldn't stand the sudden tense divide between us.

"So that's why you carried on with Nazzaro?"

"I did *not* carry on with him!"

"This is a situation that requires delicacy," he sputtered. "What were you expecting?"

"I don't know. But it was like you were running all day, I hardly saw you—"

"But you had a nice time with Olivia?"

"Yes, of course. I like her a lot—"

"Good!"

"Sergio!"

"This is my life, Anna. Many obligations to family and friends going back to the day I was born, and even before. I don't know how you do things in America, but here, if someone needs help, you help out. A friend's water heater breaks and what am I supposed to say to him? 'Sorry, I have to hang out at home today because'—" he dropped his voice "—'my lover is here for the weekend'?"

"*You* invited me."

"Because—because having you near—it's like when we're at work, just having you nearby in the school—it helps me. It helps me—existentially. Even if we can't be alone together, I'm happy knowing you're in the next room teaching, I'm happy hearing your voice on the other side of the wall. Same thing here, now: we can't be alone together, but today, while I was working on the water heater, it made me happy knowing I'd see you at dinner."

His tone was all things at once—clipped and impatient, needy and loving. I couldn't sort it all out.

"I looked forward to seeing you, too."

"Well, then," he said. "So we understand each other, even if we don't know what the hell we're doing." He took a last chug of Coke and set the glass down with a click. "It's three in the morning. Let's get some sleep." He gave me a miserable look and set off down the hallway to the bedroom where Olivia was sleeping.

I went into the living room and, as I leaned over to get my toothbrush out of my Greek bag, I saw a pair of clean white pajamas that Olivia had left for me, neatly folded at the head of the cot.

6. A Female Friend

A cock crowed, making a small tear in the quiet last hour before dawn. I dozed, curled up under a blanket on the cot in Sergio and Olivia's living room. A little later, the first rays of light were slanting in between the wide-slatted shutters when there was a touch on my shoulder, and I floated up from sleep, heard the cock crow again, and opened my eyes to Sergio in his light blue pajamas, kneeling next by my side. It gave me a flash of joy to see him with his morning beard and his chin tucked slightly into his chest as he looked down at me affectionately.

"Are we okay?" I whispered.

"More than okay. I'm sorry I was a jealous ass last night."

"You really were."

"And I apologize for Nazzaro. You know how Italian men are—all hands, very little brain."

We laughed.

With one warm hand he gently stroked my face, with the other he drew my hand toward the gap in his pajama pants. I held him for a moment, then let go as he bent over and kissed my lips.

He stood up and disappeared out the living room and down the corridor.

I fell back asleep. When I woke up again a couple of hours later, I heard Sergio and Olivia heading into the bathroom together for a shower. How sweet—five years together and they were still taking a morning shower together as a matter of course.

"You better get moving," Olivia said to me, stopping at the living room threshold. "We've got that wedding to go to, remember? Help yourself to breakfast."

Sergio didn't look at me, just kept on walking straight ahead and into the bathroom. I heard the door close, some talking, the water running. Damn. Damn him, her, the both of them. I went into the kitchen, poured myself some coffee and rummaged for something to eat. I put some jam on a slice of bread and bit viciously into it as I listened to the sounds coming from the bathroom. When they emerged, Sergio made a beeline for their bedroom, while Olivia stopped in the kitchen and stood before me in her white terry bathrobe. "I bet you didn't bring anything to wear to a wedding, did you? I have something that might work for you."

"Sure."

She went down the hall and returned a moment later holding a navy shift on a hanger and a belt. "Why don't you try this? I'm a couple sizes larger than you, but I bet this would work with a belt and a sweater." After readjusting the screen and turning her back to me out of respect for my modesty (*very Catholic of her,* I thought), she waited while I changed into the dress. It was a well-constructed piece, with a solid satin lining, probably a major purchase. Like many European women, Olivia chose to buy fewer, better-quality garments instead of quantities of cheap products.

"Okay," I said. "Ready for your approval."

"That looks good on you. Maybe cinch it a bit more." Olivia approached, and I could smell her shampoo as she leaned in toward me and tightened the belt around my waist. "Sergio's in a bit of a mood this morning," she said, "because he can't stand church weddings, but I love them." And she looked up at me wistfully.

The wedding was a dull business in a small church in Gaeta, and I fell asleep a couple of times during Mass. Sergio clearly didn't want to be there, and as soon as the ceremony was concluded, he ushered Olivia and me out and to the car. When we got back to his building, we stopped in at the reception in the bridegroom's apartment on the first floor. I was startled to overhear Sergio introduce Olivia to people as *mia moglie*—my wife. Did he call her that in order to deceive those who would have been shocked by their living together before marriage? Maybe there was a small-town acceptance of common law marriage, whereby the very fact of their living together made them man and wife. If, in Rome, I often felt confused by social codes, in Sperlonga I was completely lost.

Olivia hovered over the dining table, loading a paper plate with strawberries, little pastries, and slices of melon wrapped in prosciutto.

"Grab a couple of glasses of wine," she whispered to me, nodding toward the Prosecco. "And let's escape upstairs." She crossed her eyes comically.

"Sounds good to me," I said.

Sergio, who was talking to Flavio, looked at his watch, then joined Olivia and me as we pushed our way out of the room. As the three of us climbed the stairs together, he said he was going back to Donato's to finish working on the hot water heater.

"What about eating something?" Olivia asked.

"I had some melon," he said. "I'm fine."

He disappeared into the back bedroom as soon as we reached the apartment, and Olivia and I went into the kitchen to have lunch. A moment later, Sergio was in jeans and a white T-shirt, waving good-bye.

Olivia opened the fridge door. "How about some cheese to round things out?" She sounded tired.

"Sure." Standing by the window, I looked out and saw Sergio exit the building and head across the street to Flavio's. "And then I guess after lunch I should catch a train back."

"Are you in a rush? Sergio could drive you back," she suggested. "I won't be going with you. I don't have to work tomorrow, so I'm going to stay here and try to finish the curtains."

"All right," I said, my spirits rising, even as, looking at her, I felt mortified. She was so unsuspecting. Yet that wouldn't stop me from grabbing any chance to be alone with Sergio. "By the way, would you mind if I borrowed your sewing machine? I brought with me a dress I need to alter."

"Sure, I'll help you pin it. You want to try it on?"

"That would be great."

I went into the living room where I was camped out, slipped off the dress I'd borrowed from Olivia and put on Doris's long black one, then returned to the kitchen, where Olivia was setting up the sewing machine on the dining table.

"What do you think?" I asked.

"Must be for a pretty fancy party."

"It is, sort of. My aunt runs this club for expats—mostly people who work at the embassies and FAO," I said, referring to the Food and Agriculture Organization, headquartered in Rome. "She calls it the Rome Embassy Club. It feeds into her business as a travel agent. She's always trying to get something out of somebody. So once or twice a year she gets one of the embassies to rent her a hall, where she puts on a formal dinner for a couple hundred people."

"It sounds like a big deal."

"There'll be a banquet and dancing."

"Maybe you'll meet someone," Olivia said, giving me a sly look, then stopped herself. "Or do you have someone already?"

"No. I mean, I've got a sort of ex-boyfriend, far away, but here, there's no one. No one at all."

Sergio returned in the late afternoon, his jeans and T-shirt looking soiled.

"Can you drive Anna back to Rome?" Olivia asked him.

"Sure," he said. "You must have things to do to get ready for the school week?" he asked, turning toward me. "Laundry and so forth? Maybe even a lesson to prepare? I can't remember who your first student is tomorrow morning."

"Renzo," I said, referring to a favorite of the women teachers because, hopelessly in love with his wife, he kept his hands to himself.

"I remember Renzo. He's nice," Olivia said.

"Hey, why don't you all marry Renzo?" Sergio said, throwing his hands up in the air.

"He's already married," I reminded him.

"We'll un-marry him. Multi Lingua will issue the divorce papers."

"I wish you wouldn't joke about divorce," Olivia said.

Sergio looked at me. "Did you know that the Catholic Church not only forbids divorce, but also forbids joking about it?" He shrugged. "I'm going to shower and change."

"Uh, I'm going to get my stuff together," I said, feeling relieved that I had my own life, or semblance thereof, back in the apartment I shared with Nathan on Via Pascoli.

A little later, Sergio and I were alone in his navy Fiat, speeding toward Rome.

"Did you, uh, finish the work on the water heater?" I asked.

"Oh yes. And you had some relaxing time with Olivia, I hope?" He glanced at me as he stepped on the gas and changed lanes.

I looked at the cars whizzing by, interweaving and cutting each other off. I was used to the manic driving of Italy and figured my life was in God's hands anyway.

"It was nice. Olivia is very sweet."

We were repeating the exchange of the previous evening, more kindly, to make it all better.

He cleared his throat. "Well then, everything went okay. I'm glad you like her." An awkward silence fell between us as we drove through an agricultural stretch sectioned into small, flat fields. "Well then," he repeated.

"So your crazy idea worked out fine."

"My crazy idea . . . My first crazy idea was you."

"Thanks." I didn't know how to interpret his tone.

"I didn't mean—Anna, I have no regrets about what we're doing."

He reached for my hand as with the other, he turned the steering wheel and changed lanes again, cutting in front of another speeding Fiat.

"I'm sorry that we didn't have more time together," he continued. "As I tried to explain last night, life in a small town in Italy is very complicated. When an old friend asks for a favor, well, you have to drop everything and go. A tenant in the building is getting married—you go. And I don't mind, on a certain level, because in the end Sperlonga gives me security—Sperlonga and my friends and family, of course."

The idea that family might provide security was alien to me. Family was my mother poking me in the shoulder with two fingers before opening her hand and delivering a slap. Family was my father overworking in his lab to avoid coming home to her drinking. It was my older sister who stayed as far away as possible as my mother sank into alcoholism.

"And you should understand about Olivia," he continued. "Maybe to you she seems—well, I don't know how she seems—but I see her as suitable for a certain role. Wife, mother, and so on. I'm not the kind of man to base my choice of a wife on falling madly in love, because falling madly in love—what kind of guarantee is it for success in making a life with someone? Olivia will be a good *compagna di strada*," he said—literally, a companion for the road—"and it's like any other choice: it only works if you stick to it."

What an odd speech. Was Sergio justifying his choice of partner, as though my opinion mattered? I had a woman's impulse to come to the defense of another of my sex, and his implied belittling of Olivia annoyed me because she had qualities—of authenticity, trust, and commitment—that he didn't have. Besides, why bother discussing Olivia with me? So I wouldn't meddle? So I'd stay in my place?

"I think things are clear," I said, "if that's where you're going with this." I'd learned to speak the way he did—the way Europeans did—never spelling things out completely.

"I'd like them to be clear, but they're not, of course."

I looked at him as he drove. In spite of my irritation, I was touched by his entrapment. I wanted to help him, rescue him. He was a man wanting to leave his provincial origins behind, yet pathetically destined by family ties to fall back into the confining world of his youth. Olivia satisfied his need for the security of a life congruent with his background, whereas with me he could imagine himself as part of a larger world that included travel, art, and intellect.

"I think I understand," I said, softening my tone.

He spoke to my train of thought as though reading my mind: "I felt so important during the agitation of 1968. We demonstrated for so many things—the rights of workers, equality for women, educational reform—we had dreams of a different kind of society, where there would be no social stratification . . ." He sighed. "And now here I am, trying to climb the economic ladder, as though none of that happened."

I gave his arm a squeeze.

"So where are you going to sleep?" I asked. Olivia was back in Sperlonga, and he was probably free.

"Ah."

"I want to make love."

"You're an extraordinary girl," he said, laughing and shaking his head.

"Why not? Why shouldn't we?"

"Truly extraordinary. You're ready at any moment—and any place? Maybe a tree? Let's make love in a tree! What about one of those trees, over there?" He pointed out the window to a dozen Roman pines in a straight line, their dark green headdresses floating high, their long trunks slanting to the right in parallel strokes of sepia against a cornflower blue sky.

"If that's the only place available, then sure!"

"Okay, let's see . . . Back to the Odeon in the Ghetto?"

We rode through peripheral neighborhoods with wide streets and modern buildings then passed under the towering, brick arcades of the city wall, humbling remnants of empire. I lost my sense of direction and didn't get my bearings until we reached the Tiber and I saw the *Isola Tiberina*—the island in the middle of the river—on the left. It was dusk, which Italians, with their sensitivity to color, call the *imbrunire* or "browning" of the day, and the streetlights along the river were reflected in the copper-colored surface of the water below. On the right, we passed the ancient, massive synagogue that faced the island, then headed into the narrow streets.

"Here we are," Sergio said. "Where to park? Oh, look—lovers' luck!" He pulled into a space, and we got out, not far from a patch of ruins with a three-column fragment, part of the Portico d'Ottavia, which marks the edge of the Ghetto.

"Eat or make love first?" He asked me. "Or a visit to the river?"

Sergio took my hand, and his skin, warm and dry, spoke to mine in the language of palms and fingers. Winding into the ancient neighborhood, I lost my sense of direction again, but he seemed to know where we were going as he led me down the cobble-stoned streets, past a couple of restaurants that were opening for the late evening meal. Whenever we encountered an obstacle forcing us to let go of each other— a narrow sidewalk, a couple standing in our way— he stepped ahead to lead the way, keeping an arm turned in and raised a bit backwards, the hand open and inviting mine to slip back into his again, so that we were still holding hands as we crossed the riverside boulevard called the Lungotevere, in order to stand at the parapet, facing the *Isola Tiburtina*. Big clumps of green bushes grew at either end of the island and here and there along the sides. By the water's edge a woman with long straight hair sat with her legs draped over the river, playing the violin. The notes of a Bach partita competed with the traffic behind us.

"That's a hospital there," he said, pointing with his free hand to a massive square building at the center of the island. It had the usual mottled ochre stucco walls, red tiled roof, and big windows. "I had a friend in there, once." He didn't offer details, as though being respectful of that person's privacy. "Looks like it's been freshly painted. What color would you call it?" he asked.

"Well, it's somewhere between beige and peach, so I'd call it—'beige-peach.'"

He laughed. "*Un bello* beige-peach." He nodded toward the violinist. "Have you ever been down there?"

"Yes, last fall. With Nathan. We came along here one night and walked around the island."

In a bush, we'd seen a man with an open pair of pants. A flash of flesh, an arm moving in quick rhythm. The mysterious perversions of solitude.

"There was a man in the shadows, pleasuring himself," I continued. "I wanted to turn back but Nathan of course kept going, and we walked right by him." I shivered remembering that November night, how the sense of human twistedness had mixed with the cold dankness of the river.

"Maybe we should go down now and see if he's still there?" Sergio teased. "The masturbating gentleman, I mean."

"I don't think so," I laughed.

"If he's not there, someone else probably is in his place. There's probably always been some guy there doing his thing— like a sentry post—going all the way back to Julius Caesar."

"No," I said, "tonight the violinist is keeping masturbators at bay."

I wondered where Nathan was that night. We didn't spend as much time together as we used to. In life, love affairs and friendships come one after the other, offering the heart a random sequence of nourishment, like courses taken on the fly in an international food court. This adventure with Sergio, as intense as it felt, might very well be superseded in a year's time by a tumultuous affair with a Hong Kong banker who would teach me Cantonese while making love to me in a pontoon on a velvet-covered banquette. With a sigh, I rested my cheek on Sergio's shoulder. The transience of our story struck me as unbearably sad.

"Anna, Anna," he said, passing his arm around my waist. "You should come back here some time and paint this. Because you would make of it something special—not just one of those silly paintings done for tourists and sold in the shops—" he nodded contemptuously back toward the winding streets we'd come from. "Yes," he continued, "come here and paint it—for us. For you and me. We won't be in the picture, but the picture will be in us."

"Okay. I'll do it," I said.

"Not just a water color, but with real paints, oil or acrylic, whatever you prefer. And I know you'll do something new and interesting with it. Maybe you'll move the violinist to the left or right or, like Chagall, turn her into a dove or a horse."

He stopped talking and, placing his hands on my shoulders, drew me in toward him, stroking my short hair. "It's getting longer. You should get it trimmed. I like it short like a boy's—it's so French that way. What a beautiful woman you are. My wonderful artist."

His tender smile made me feel complete, and for a moment there was nothing but pure presence as we stood there, each the witness of the other's joy.

Then I grabbed him and whispered, "Let's go to the hotel now."

7. In My Aunt's Footsteps

Sergio liked to stay inside me as long as possible after he came, looking softly into my eyes as I looked into his. A ray of light seemed to shine out through the gold fleck in the iris of his left eye. He rolled onto his side, pulling me with him. We talked for a long time with him on his back, my head on his shoulder, my arm across his belly. We'd left the shutters cracked, and the glow from the street lamps filtered in, casting bars of light and shadow on the blanket. Every time we started drifting off to sleep, he'd pull my arm tighter across his belly and whisper, "Tell me another story." I liked feeling his ribs under my fingers as I held his slim frame tight.

Around two in the morning, Sergio was disturbed by a thought or a dream and he woke me up. Yes, he whispered, Olivia was spending the night in Sperlonga, with the plan of driving directly to her job in the morning. But supposing she decided to stop by their Rome apartment on the way to work? For a change of clothes or to pick something up?

"I think I should go back to the apartment," he concluded. "Also, if our neighbor downstairs notices that I didn't come home last night and if Olivia runs into her, then I'm in trouble. That old lady is a real busybody."

He made a motion to get up, and I lifted my head off his shoulder so he could slide out of bed.

"And you?" he asked. "Will you be able to go back to sleep after I leave?"

I propped myself up on a pillow. I didn't want to stay at the Odeon without him, but I also didn't want to go home to Via Pascoli and face Nathan's questioning in the morning.

"How about you drop me at my aunt's?"

"I can do that."

What with getting dressed and driving across town and a dozen delicious kisses before separating, it was three in the morning when I reached my aunt's building and stepped into the old European-style elevator with its oval cage of glass and ornately wrought iron. Reaching her apartment on the fourth floor, I let myself in.

The hallway to the left, where Doris slept with her three terriers, was dark and quiet except for the rhythmic snoring of the oldest one, Tsarina, who was louder than her daughters, Alexandra and Caterina. Doris's life revolved around her dogs, and she made other people's lives revolve around them, too. Across the dark, wide living room, a light glowed from the kitchen, where Halim, Doris's lodger, would be having a snack. A young, handsome refugee from Eritrea—a region in a war with Ethiopia that garnered little media attention in 1979—Halim received free lodging in exchange for helping with the dogs and miscellaneous errands. He was often out late at night, and his one condition was that Doris shouldn't disturb him before eleven a.m. I went to greet him and found him leaning against the counter, eating a chicken leg.

"*Ciao*, Anna," Halim said. "Nathan having another party?"

"Uh, yeah," I lied. I reached into the fridge for a *limonata*, an Italian lemonade.

"Just got back from the café and am going to study a bit," he said. He was hoping to get into medical school so that when he eventually returned to his country he could serve his people.

There was an aristocratic beauty to Halim's profile, with its Eritrean combination of Greek features and milk chocolate coloring, and I wondered if he'd ever let me draw him.

"Were you at Rosy's?" I asked.

Rosy's was a café near the train station where Eritreans

congregated, mostly young men waiting for people who had escaped their country's war of independence and arrived with a single instruction—*meet Halim, or Ahmed, or Karim, at the café called Rosy's, he will take care of you.* When it was Halim's turn to wait, he might be there for eight or ten hours at a time. When it wasn't his turn, he would pop in and visit whoever was on duty.

"Yes, it was my turn."

"Anyone arrive?"

"No, but I'm expecting someone soon," he responded.

"I guess you have to be patient."

"It's okay. I did some studying."

"You're amazing," I said as I pressed the bottle cap back onto the top of the lemonade, but it was a little bent and didn't seal properly. If someone knocked it over, there would be a mess, but I wouldn't be there when it happened. "Well, I'm off to bed," I concluded and stuck my drink back in the fridge.

In the morning, Alexandra and Caterina jumped on my bed and woke me up, nuzzling my face and yapping, while their mother, Tsarina, poor aged thing, trailed in behind them. I'd learned to love Doris's troika of Bedlington terriers the previous summer when I'd first come to Rome and lived in her apartment. I sat up to greet the younger two with a pet and a scratch.

"Anna? Where are you?" Doris shouted. "Get yourself breakfast and come here."

"Be there in a minute."

After sleeping at Doris's, I always took my breakfast into her bedroom and kept her company while she ate in bed. Halim was still sleeping in the little "maid's room" next to the kitchen, so I tried to be quiet as I put a tray together with bread and jam on a plate and an empty cup for coffee. Going into my aunt's room, I found her propped up against several pillows. At bedtime she always placed on her night table a tray with a thermos of hot coffee, a couple of fresh eggs, some tomatoes, and a roll, so that all she had to do in the morning was sit up and move the food to her lap. She was sucking on a raw egg in the Italian fashion, while Tsarina sniffed at the swinging glass doors that led to the little balcony outside the bedroom.

"Let her out, would you?" Doris asked.

After twenty-five years in Rome, my aunt spoke English with an Italian lilt, giving each sentence a musical phrasing. Obediently, I opened the tall widows outward to the balcony, letting in the sounds of women greeting each other across the courtyard: *Come va, Lucia?* (How are you?) Then the answer: *Va be'*—shortened from *va bene*, the Italian "okay." I loved the way colloquial Italian dropped the last syllables of words, though, with my intermediate language skills, I was often confused by the disappearance of verb endings, adjectival gender markers, and random syllables. A faint scent of urine wafted in from outside. Tsarina, unable to wait for her morning walk with Halim, went out on the balcony to do her business. Meanwhile her daughters, both in heat, pathetically offered their reddened rears to each other until Caterina, the more generous soul of the two, gave in and mounted her sister.

"There they go again." Doris chuckled, as she gently poked a second egg with a pointed knife, making a tiny hole at one end and a larger one at the other, which she began sucking on with an expression of bliss. She was a large woman, and the satisfaction of her appetite was her principal joy in life.

"You ought to do something about it," I said. "I mean, get them fixed."

"Why?" Doris asked.

"Don't you think they suffer? From sexual frustration, I mean." I pulled a chair up next to her and sat down, while the "girls," who had completed their mock mating, jumped back on the bed.

"Nah. Look at them. They're fine now," she said, and so they were. "Here, have a raw egg."

"No, thanks."

"So what happened last night?" Doris asked. "What are you up to?"

"This and that. I didn't feel like sleeping at home."

"Another party? Moving in with Nathan—what did you think you were doing?" She always looked amused when taking stock of my youthful follies.

"He's my best friend," I said, forgetting how angry I was with him.

"Can you take the dogs out for a walk?"

"No, I have to be at school by nine-thirty."

My aunt frowned. "Certainly you can spare ten minutes to do something for me. Think of everything I've done for you."

In exchange for granting me the keys to her place, Doris felt entitled to ask me for endless favors, like counting the number of times each of her three terriers pooped when I walked them or cleaning up after Tsarina, the eldest, when she had an accident in the house. Doris got annoyed when I hinted there was something unreasonable about the nature of the tasks she asked me to do. The way she saw it, I was permanently in her debt because she had, with her hospitality, parties, and expeditions, seduced me into the Roman *dolce vita*. But I didn't like being manipulated.

"Really," I said. I wanted desperately to have coffee with Sergio before the day began.

"Hmm. So what are you going to do about your living situation?"

"I don't know. I'd love to get my own apartment when our lease is up."

"Good luck."

It was hard to find an apartment in Rome if you didn't know "somebody who knows somebody," who might (once the proper gratuities had been paid) offer a lead that might (after another gratuity) result in a key.

I sighed. "I know it won't be easy."

"You never know what might come up. You should talk to people at the gala."

There was a pause then I gave in to a confessional impulse. "Okay, this is the story: I'm involved with my boss, and I went down to Sperlonga to spend the weekend with them."

"Oh? And he's married, probably?"

"As good as. How did you know?"

"You said *them*—in the plural. Besides, bosses are always married. Why Sperlonga?"

"They have a second apartment there. That's where he grew up."

She raised her eyebrows and chuckled. "This is really interesting. So how was the weekend?"

"Fine. I know this sounds crazy, but his girlfriend's really nice. And nothing happened with Sergio—I mean, while I was there over the weekend—"

"But there was some hanky-panky right before or after?" Her big breasts and belly bounced with waves of lascivious laughter.

"You're making me feel like an idiot."

"No, I'm happy for you if you're having fun—and being careful."

I wondered whether she was alluding to the usual possibilities of pregnancy and disease or something more dramatic, like a Sicilian drama culminating in gunshot wounds and the discovery of a corpse on the edge of town, while shady, card-playing officials sipped serial espressos in a hot, unlit café, looking the other way.

"Yeah, sure—"

"Good. Hmm . . . And the girlfriend isn't suspicious?"

"She doesn't seem to be."

"A good Catholic girl?"

"Yeah, and half-American," I said.

"A good, half-American, Catholic girl, and probably young? A natural-born sucker, then."

"Maybe she's naïve, but I wouldn't call her a sucker." I bristled at applying the word to Olivia.

"You really liked her?"

"Yeah, I liked her a lot, actually. Which is very confusing."

"Listen, I'm not going to play mommy here, because I don't know how to do that. You know I can't even stand the sight of a pregnant woman. The whole motherhood thing—it's beyond me."

"I'm not expecting you to play mommy."

"I think it's time for you to meet my friend Tito. Why don't you come back tonight and we'll drive to his house for dinner?"

"Remind me again who he is."

"My dearest friend in Rome. You already know his sister, Signora Gianina. She'll be there tonight, if you want to ask for advice."

Although single, Gianina was, because of her age and learning, addressed as *Signora*, a title usually reserved for married women. An art historian in her seventies, she acted as a tour guide for Doris's group expeditions, and I'd followed her tiny, stout form through the Etruscan tombs of Tarquinia, the Renaissance Gardens of Bomarzo, and the hillside towns southeast of Rome. When asked for advice about personal matters, Gianina read palms and used Tarot cards.

"You mean, about Sergio?"

"Yes. She's a fount of wisdom. You'd better brush your hair before you go to school. Use my brush in the bathroom."

I went to brush my hair. *My dearest friend* could only mean one thing: Doris and Tito had been, maybe still were, lovers.

I decided to investigate that evening as she drove us to Tito's in her tiny Fiat. "Tell me more about Tito. Is he married?"

"His wife died a couple of years ago. He lives in the Gianicolo," she said, referring to a luxurious neighborhood on one of Rome's seven hills. "Retired now. He used to be a lawyer so you must address him as *Avvocato*." Pause. "The house has a lovely view of the city."

She didn't seem willing to say more. After years of secrecy, it probably felt unnatural to talk about him with any direct-ness. Glancing sideways at my aunt as we began the winding ascent up the hill, I imagined the struggles of her life abroad. After the War there hadn't been enough men to go around, and many single women had embarked upon long-term rela-tionships with married men. In Italy, such arrangements could go on indefinitely, fostered by the impossibility of divorce and the Italian male's curious mixture of romanticism and loyalty to his mistress. I was younger than Doris had been when she met Tito, but the parallel between her relationship with him and mine with Sergio was obvious, as was the aim of this din-ner: She wanted to give me a lesson of some kind—to show me what might be.

"Now it's your turn," Doris said. "Tell me more about the *fidanzata*. And is she a girlfriend *fidanzata* or a soon-to-be married *fidanzata*?"

After my weekend in Sperlonga, I understood that the word *fidanzata*—literally "fiancée"—had a wide range of meanings. When used repeatedly, it suggested a bond sealed by families and friends, who looked on with the enthusiasm of spectators betting at a horse race.

"She's down-to-earth and very sweet. We had a nice time hanging out together. She helped me take in the dress you gave me for the embassy dinner."

"So she's your new buddy?"

"You're making fun of me. But the fact is, I enjoy her because—because I haven't really made any women friends here, I don't know why—"

"Because you've been too busy chasing your boss, that's why," Doris said, chuckling again.

I shrugged and decided to stop talking. As we drove up streets bordered by straight looming ilex, past villas tucked behind high walls draped with ivy and bougainvillea, a view occasionally opened up over the Roman maze below. Lit up, the larger monuments, such as the Castel San Angelo, the Col-iseum, and the Forum, looked like illuminated toys set down in a mosaic of glowing buildings. The evening light had transformed the warm, daytime reds and ochers of roofs, cupolas, and plastered walls into a range of gleaming ivories and tans. The Tiber, with its course marked by the street lamps it reflected, cut through the city on the left side of the panorama. My eye went to the bridge where Sergio and I had stood, holding hands, before going to the Odeon to make love. I remembered how he'd encouraged me to paint the scene, how he'd run his fingers through my hair, how his tender attention had made the moment magical.

I squeezed my Greek bag, with the letter from Doug inside. I still hadn't answered it, as the idea of him visiting in the middle of my affair with Sergio felt awkward. Yes, I wanted to have lots of lovers, but not simultaneously—that was too complicated—one after another was more my style. Then there was the ugly fact that I was stringing Doug along. I had no intention of returning to him but, cruelly, I kept deferring a total break, so that he continued to hope. I'd told him I couldn't commit *yet*, the *yet* implying that the commitment might come in time. But the fact was that I didn't yearn for him, maybe because the sex hadn't been particularly satisfying. Not in our teenage years together, when we did it in the popcorn-anointed back seat of his car or in the grasses of the beach dunes with a sandy towel under my ass. And not later on, in his single bed in college, when I was distracted by his noisy suite mates on the other side of a flimsy wall. He was an inexperienced lover, and it took me years to say what I needed. Still, there was an attachment and the connection was hard to sever. Doug remained in the background, like a statue recessed in a nook that suddenly appears in the headlight of an approaching car, while I, like a dove on that statue, prepared to take off.

"Signora Gianina is staying with him because he's recovering from a prostate operation," Doris said, parking the car next to a villa gate.

I didn't know what or where the prostate was exactly, only that it was a troublesome part of male sexual anatomy.

"So how did you meet him?"

"Through Gianina. When I bought my apartment, I needed a lawyer and she suggested her brother."

"And one thing led to another—?"

"And one thing led to another."

"Wasn't that awkward for Gianina?"

"No. Why should it have been? Tito has always treated me with respect. You'll like him. He loves art and he's very cultivated."

We passed through the villa gate, my aunt rang the bell, and Signora Gianina opened the door.

"*Allora, Signora,* how is Tito doing?" Doris asked as they embraced.

"Oh, he's fine." Signora Gianina kissed me. "Anna, come meet my brother."

I followed the Signora as she crossed the marble-floored foyer. Her long gray hair was pinned up at the nape of her neck and her clear stockings sagged around her ankles above her flat oxfords. Thick at the waist, she still had a sure-footed step, but her finely striated face revealed age and hardship. As a consequence of wartime poverty, which had entailed periods of near-starvation, seventy in Italian terms looked, for her generation, about five to ten years older than the American equivalent.

The Signora led us into a living room decorated in the old Roman style, with heavy furniture upholstered in sumptuous fabrics and deep red walls hung with paintings and drawings in ornate, gilded frames. Doris approached Tito, who was reading on the couch, and as she sat down next to him and kissed him on the lips, the stardust of their old story shimmered around them. But an impulse to pass judgment dispelled my sentimentalism. Something in me disapproved of their liaison, not because Tito had been married, but because my aunt had agreed to an unequal situation, which I saw as demeaning for her. What I was doing with Sergio was different—transitory. That Doris assumed a parallel between our situations made me feel misunderstood and irritable. But as

Tito stood up to shake my hand, my mood shifted. He looked at me straight on, with a smile that promised good conversation, maybe friendship. In spite of his elderly stoop, he was still tall and distinguished-looking, with a neatly trimmed gray moustache and beard that concealed his years. He looked a few years older than his sister Gianina and so had to be quite a bit older than Doris.

"Good evening, *Avvocato*," I said.

"Doris's lovely niece. She has told me so much about you, and now at long last we meet. Come sit next to me," he said, as Doris stood up and followed Gianina into the kitchen. "I'm rereading *La Princesse de Clèves*," he continued in Italian, showing me a copy in the original French. "Do you know it?"

"Yes, I've read it more than once."

I'd discovered this story of betrayal in a college French class then reread it while living in Paris. *La Princesse de Clèves* tells the story of a woman married to a Prince who adores her, but whom she loves with a feeling that is merely dutiful. Inevitably, she falls passionately in love with someone else, the dashing Duke de Nemours, who woos her assiduously. Although she never sleeps with the Duke, the Prince comes to believe his wife has been unfaithful; he falls ill and dies of a jealous, broken heart. The widowed Princess is now free to be with the Duke, yet she chooses to retreat to a convent instead, not only because she feels responsible for her husband's death, but also because the Duke has a reputation for gallantry, and she imagines that he'll eventually stray. If she marries him, will he be faithful to her? She begins to doubt she can withstand the ups and downs of love. In the end, she withdraws from society and chooses peace of mind—what the French call *repos* or "rest"—over passion. It was a sad story, but in the Princess's proud choice I saw a kind of Plan B for the heart if ever one's love life got too messy. Better to be single than in a relationship that caused continual torment.

"Me, too," Tito said. "In fact, I reread it every year."

His favoring such a morally complex book was puzzling,

given that his affair with my aunt had led him to betray his wife for decades. Compared to what they'd done, my dalliance with Sergio seemed a minor infraction.

Intuiting my thoughts, he continued, "That princess, she lived up to a moral standard few of us could equal."

When I pictured the Princess, it was always the final scene, when she dismissed the Duke. I saw her on a balcony—though why a convent should have a balcony, I don't know—looking down at her suitor, who beseeched her while she said *no* in a noble rewrite of *Romeo and Juliet*. I admired her ability to detach, her determination to hold onto her dignity and independence. I thought of her whenever I began to feel humiliated in relationships.

"Do you think she did the right thing by giving up the Duke?" I asked. We talked about her as though she'd been real and the book a biography instead of a novel.

"She couldn't do otherwise. She felt guilty about her husband's death and haunted by his ghost," he said. "Now, tell me what you're reading."

"Right now, Moravia's *Roman Tales*. They're wonderful."

"An excellent choice. And what do you like about them?"

"The descriptions of common people. The hard side," I said.

He smiled. "Yes, yes. And with this *realistic* sensibility of yours, how do you feel about this city, with its abundance of Baroque art and architecture?"

"Well, I prefer Renaissance art, but I'm learning to appreciate the Baroque." I didn't know how to say "appreciate" in Italian and so invented the word *estimare*, tracing it on the French *estimer*. Whenever I got stuck expressing myself, I fearlessly made up new words modeled on French equivalents.

"The word is *stimare*, not *estimare*," he said, surprising me, for Italians don't correct foreigners' linguistic mistakes the way the French do. "Your French is better than your Italian? *Alors, parlons français.*" He spoke French with a melodious, rolling Italian accent. "So, we were speaking of *le baroque*. Love the Baroque or leave Rome," he went on, smiling. "Doris told me you're a painter. I'm afraid Rome will disappoint you. We have much to offer the sculptor and the architect, but for the painter—alas!—if you don't like the baroque paintings in the churches, you'll end up panting after substance. As for our contemporary artists, they're mediocre and lazy. Too much *dolce vita*, not enough muscle up here," he said pointing to his head. "If you want culture, you should move north—to Milan or Genoa, for example."

"But I love Rome," I said. "I love the colors and the layers of history crumbling all around."

He nodded as I spoke. "I see you've already been seduced. We must make you a reading list, so that the seduction may be complete. Come, follow me to my library," he continued and, standing up uncertainly, reached for my arm. "Let's cross through the garden."

The villa made a U around a planted courtyard, which was dimly lit by light emanating from the living areas. In the air hung the scent of lemon trees; a fountain splashed in a corner of the garden. Tito proceeded slowly, occasionally knocking the toe of his shoe against a paving stone set higher than its neighbors, at which point he would tighten his hold on my arm, then turn his grasp into a caress of my bare skin, so that I had the sense of embarking on a bizarre, if minuscule, erotic adventure with this charming and probably impotent old man.

Tito pushed open the glass door to his study and turned on the light, revealing a heavy wooden desk, walls of books climbing to a high ceiling decorated with ornate moldings, and a dark velvet couch with pillows and a couple of blankets. "Sit here," he said, tucking a blanket around my knees—now I was the one to be coddled and taken care of—and he went over to a phonograph.

"Listen. Pablo Neruda."

He rummaged through his bookcases, chanting along with an old, scratchy recording of the great poet reciting his own poems. I listened, captivated by the cadences, the fragrant air wafting in from the garden, and the weight of the old books, which he placed, each one like a precious gift, on my lap: *I promessi sposi*—a book too long and difficult for me ever to read in the original—and then some more recent works by Natalia Ginzburgh, Svevo, Pirandello. "And some poetry," he said, adding a volume of Montale and another of Ungaretti.

"Thank you," I said, thinking, *I want a home like this, a man like this.* But I knew that Tito was exceptional for Rome and correct when he'd said that, if I wanted to move among cultivated Italians, I'd have to head north. For a split second, I imagined getting Sergio to go with me.

"So young," Tito said, giving me a tender look.

Doris's voice announcing dinner saved me from further reading assignments. Using both hands to carry the books, I didn't have a free arm for Tito, so he put his arm around my waist for balance. As we headed outside, I took in his scent of delicately calibrated musk and camellia, an aftershave I imagined made by a centuries-old apothecary and bottled in a sculptural, masculine flask.

"How beautiful you are," he whispered as he gently pressed my waist. "Ah, if only I were a young man!"

The absurdity of my aunt's aged lover flirting with me behind her back receded as I took in the pathos of this old man's desire, set against the darkness of the night and the beauty of Neruda's voice, which in the background sang of the wide, deep waters that unmoor the human heart: *Soy el desesperado, la palabra sin ecos, / el que lo perdió todo, y el que todo lo ruvo*: *I am the one without hope, the word without echoes, / he who lost everything and he who had everything.*

"You're quite magnificent as you are," I whispered, imagining that, as a younger man, he must have been irresistible.

"*Bella, bella,*" Tito repeated, like an incantation, as we walked by the fountain murmuring in the shadows.

When the four of us sat down to dinner and he reached for my aunt's hand under the table, I thought of Sergio with a pang. I imagined us continuing our affair indefinitely. It was exactly what I wanted. It was exactly what I didn't want. A flash of the surreal came over me as I considered that Doris and Tito had, for decades, carried on their relationship behind the back of his wife—his nameless, trusting wife, now in her grave. And now here was Doris sitting at Tito's dinner table, *in her place*, having won out through longevity. The endurance of their love was romantic; the secrecy and betrayal were awful, creepy even. By the time Gianina brought out coffee and cake, I felt deeply disturbed as I looked at them holding hands, on the tablecloth now.

The conversation turned to the upcoming gala my aunt was organizing for her social club. On this occasion, it would take place at the South African Embassy, a choice that struck me as wildly inappropriate although apartheid wasn't much discussed in Rome at the time.

"Would you say a few words at the dinner?" she asked Signora Gianina.

"About?"

"Something to show our appreciation of their letting us use their space, like about Italy's relationship with South Africa." Doris paused. "What *is* our relationship with them, anyway?" Her use of "our" suggested that she was Italian and Brooklyn a distant nightmare.

"Actually," Gianina said, "there's a very interesting chapter of the last World War, in which a hundred thousand Italian soldiers were taken prisoner in East Africa and sent to South Africa, and some ended up staying on and creating an Italian sub-population—"

"You see?" Doris said to me, delighted. "The woman knows something about everything. Yes, Signora, something like that would be perfect. Italians in South Africa—what a wonderfully interesting topic."

When we'd finished dessert, Doris accompanied Tito to his bedroom to help him get ready for bed. Signora Gianina invited me to sit next to her on the couch.

"You need advice?" she asked.

"I guess."

"A young American girl living in Rome needs advice. I don't have my cards with me, but let's look at your palm." Her ancient hands took one of mine and held it in her lap. "Ah, I see you're an explorer."

Well that had to be obvious.

"By which I mean," she continued, "sometimes you do things just to see what will happen, what the result will be. There are passions involved but also a kind of, how can I put it, scientific spirit at work, as though you were a child in a laboratory, running experiments, with your own life being the stuff in the test tube."

Not so obvious.

She looked up at me. "And as everyone knows, a little girl running wild in a laboratory runs the risk of setting everything, including herself, on fire."

I pulled my hand away, saying nothing. I thought of how Sergio liked to caress my short hair.

"Sometime soon," she said, "you must come to my place, and I'll read the cards for you."

As Doris drove me home through the nightscape of the city with its sculptures, fountains and columns gleaming white against the shadowed ochers, I tried to imagine what my life might be like if I stayed on in Rome, moved out of the apartment I shared with Nathan and into my own place so that Sergio could pay me discreet visits for months, maybe years. My undeveloped moral sense played little part in my thinking; it was my pride that rose up again, rebellious. It was one thing to settle for a fraction of a man temporarily, the way I was

doing with Sergio, quite another to accept such an arrangement indefinitely.

Doris broke the silence. "I'm so glad Gianina will talk at
the embassy dinner." She glanced sideways. "Maybe you'll meet
someone there—someone more appropriate for you—*single*."

"I doubt it."

"You never know. So, what did you think of Tito?" Doris
asked.

"I liked him a lot. He must have been very handsome
when he was young."

"He *was* handsome, in a modest way. Never flashy, like
some Italian men."

"And your story with him was—continuous?" I found
myself using the English translation of *storia* instead of "affair"
or "relationship."

"Yes, it was. Well, there were a couple of intermissions,
but on the whole it's been a long and wonderful story. Sometimes difficult, too, I'll admit."

It was hard to imagine my aunt as a young woman carried away by a passion strong enough to keep her in a lengthy
situation with a married man.

"Which still continues?"

"Yes."

"So, if his wife is gone, why don't you—why can't you—
really be together?"

"Well, we are together when I visit. But if you mean, why
can't I—what?—move in, well, the habits of a lifetime—and
besides, then everyone would know—his wife's family, too."
She smiled. "Really, haven't you lived in Europe long enough
not to be asking such questions?"

I said nothing. Inside me, whispered dreams collided
and crashed.

"I guess it was a stupid question. So then, it was Tito who
kept you from marrying?"

She shrugged. "Maybe." She glanced sideways at me as
she sped through the empty streets. "The fact was that I never

wanted kids, and in Italy it's hard to find a man who doesn't want kids. Our arrangement is common enough here, but not a path I'd recommend. For me—well, it was 1958 and I was in my late twenties when I met Tito. My life had already taken a direction of independence, and he never interfered with what I wanted to do. But for you . . ." She fell silent.

Again I tried to imagine it—a long-term affair with a married man. Guilt, conflict, and bits of intense excitement alternating with long periods of longing. As the years went on, you'd start wondering whether you or your lover's wife would die first. You'd start praying for her death. You might even wonder whether, when all the bodies were dead and buried, you'd have to pay for your behavior with time in hell. And, however passionate Doris's relationship with Tito had been, however deep it still was, he couldn't "be there" for her, and she was alone, except for Halim. There was something pathetic about Doris's arrangement with her Eritrean lodger.

"Don't worry about me," I said. "I'll probably be going to Hong Kong in the fall."

"You've already heard about the teaching fellowship?"

"No, but I think I'll go whether or not I get it. I've been saving up for the airfare and I'm sure I could get a job teaching once I got there. I'm a good teacher."

"I'm glad you've got it all planned out," she said. "A plan will save you when the going gets rough."

"I have some other ideas, too."

"Good for you," she said. "Good for you."

Even as I spoke about Asia, I squeezed my Greek bag, feeling again for Doug's letter. Suddenly I had an urgent need to see him. After all, Sergio had Olivia, why shouldn't I have another partner, too? Maybe I should tell Doug to visit after all. He gave me a sense that some part of me might eventually, after I'd wandered around the globe breaking every possible taboo, land in the country of Normal. For Doug was very normal. He'd been studying for a degree in architecture at MIT and his job prospects were excellent. He'd have a brilliant career, live in a designer house in Cambridge, and send his kids to the best schools. With him in the wings, I'd have two possible escape plans if I got beaten up in this story with Sergio: I could either move on to Asia or—less likely, an emergency solution as I saw it—take up again with my old boyfriend. As Doris and I drove on through the Roman night, I congratulated myself on my foresight. It was shameless of me to use Doug in this way, but the time had come for me to erect a safety net for my heart. I would write him—no, it would be faster if I called him—and tell him I couldn't wait to see him.

8. What the Cards Said

I called Doug and gave him the green light to visit, then promptly went back to my crazy life, including regular weekend visits to Sperlonga. That I was sleeping with Sergio was bad enough, that I had gone down to visit him and his fiancée was bizarre. But that I accepted Olivia's invitation to return several more times in a row was willfully perverse.

The more time I spent with Olivia, the more I liked her, the more I began to think of her as a friend. For when I was in Sperlonga, I spent most of my time with her and hardly saw Sergio, who continued to be busy with his extended family and the refurbishing of his apartment. Nazzaro continued to assess me, and I continued to tolerate him in the way a woman does when flattered by a man's attention. In short, I was no longer carousing with Nathan in Rome, visiting the Falcon Club with our pornographer friend, Peep, or going on outings with my aunt and Signora Gianina. Instead, I was doing something morally indefensible—having an affair during the workweek and spending weekends with my lover's fiancée.

I'd been putting off telling Sergio about Doug's upcoming visit. Certainly I didn't owe it to Sergio to be faithful, but he'd find out one way or another.

It was almost eight p.m. one evening when I found Sergio in his office talking to Melitta, the Greek secretary and teacher.

"The private students need more structure if they are to feel progress," Melitta said. "Don't you think so, Anna?"

In a tight pencil skirt and pressed white blouse, she stood with her arms folded in front of the bookcase with glass doors, looking as fresh as though it were morning. She had a manicure, heavy mascara, and high heels—all the accouterments of conventional femininity. In addition, she could speak and teach five languages. No wonder Nathan was infatuated with her.

"Well, we do, don't we? We follow the usual grammatical curriculum—" Sergio began.

"I'm talking about the advanced students, like Giorgio—" Melitta was referring to a tall, handsome student in his thirties, who was married and a notorious philanderer.

"Giorgio!" Sergio said, throwing his hand up into the air. "Why you always talk to me about Giorgio? His English is better than mine. He's here—you know why—to chase a few skirts—"

"I have no problems with Giorgio. I treat him seriously, and he treats me seriously," Melitta went on. "The point is, I'm drawing up some suggestions I want you to look at, Sergio."

"You know you have to run everything by Mauro, not me." As he paused and sniffed, I realized that working for his childhood best friend didn't always suit him. "I am just a— what am I?—a personnel manager trying to keep everyone happy. Isn't that right, Anna? Am I making you happy?"

"Not enough, actually," I said.

"Ah, there you have it! The truth! What is it you want? More money? Working papers? The working papers, they are coming."

"A shorter day," I said. I'd been at school since nine that morning—eleven hours.

"A shorter day? It's Italy! I can't do that for you! Listen, once upon a time Multi Lingua had a real siesta system. Every day we closed from one to four so that everybody could go home for a nap and get refreshed. But now it's 1979, we have business clients, so no going home for lunch, no nap, and we still have to stay open in the evening for people who want classes on their way home from work. That's the way it is. I'm sorry."

He was destined for a life of overwork. I felt sorry for him.

Melitta persisted. "If you want me to be happy, you'll look at these suggestions before I pass them on to Mauro."

"Okay, I'll look at the suggestions. But in the morning, please. I have no room in my brain for suggestions at the end of the day. And we have to run them by Anna, who has as many private students now as you do."

"All right, Sergio," Melitta said. She looked at me. I'd settled in one of the chairs across from Sergio and she saw I wasn't about to get up. "You have something you want to discuss with Sergio, obviously," she said. "So I'm off for the day." She picked up her bag. "*Buona sera.*"

Sergio and I looked at each other quietly as she left, shutting the door behind her. There was the sound of her footsteps on the staircase, then silence.

"Is everyone gone?" I asked.

"Yes. Your house-mate, too," he said, referring to Nathan.

"Should I have left with her?"

"You mean, does she suspect? You know, people have to be curious before they start to suspect. Melitta, she's not curious about us. She only thinks about the school's curriculum, about how we can get more students—"

"She wants your job."

He shrugged. "And one day, when I leave, she can have it. She would be a great manager. I'm lucky to have a few people who take their jobs seriously. Besides, I'm not going to stay here forever."

A chasm opened up as he referred to a possible life change that would end our seeing each other every day.

"It's late," I said. "Time for me to go home." And I didn't move.

"It's time for me to go home, too," he said and also didn't move. There was a silence. "You're coming down to Sperlonga this weekend as usual, I hope?" He'd switched to Italian, which was the preferred language for talking about our arrangements. "Olivia asked me to invite you again." He cleared his throat nervously.

"I—my aunt is having this fancy dinner for her social club at the South African Embassy on Saturday night—"

"Ah. Olivia will be disappointed. She's become attached to you."

"I like her a lot, too."

"And Nazzaro will be sad, too. He called me this morning and asked after you."

"Great."

"I reconsidered the Nazzaro situation and think the two of you might have a future together—"

"Not funny, Sergio."

"I know. Bad joke. But it provides a kind of smoke screen, don't you think? What about the weekend after—"

"I can't—"

"You don't enjoy Sperlonga?"

"I enjoy it very much, but I have a friend who'll be visiting me from the United States." I suddenly felt irritable. *You want to have your cake and eat it, too.*

"So, after the visit from this friend, you'll come down?"

"Let me think . . . Yes, soon. And did I tell you my cousin Robin is also going to visit—"

"The psychologist?"

"Yes, that's her goal, she's still in graduate school."

"Well, bring her down for the weekend if you like—there's always room for one more—and sounds like this one might be able to give us an analysis of the situation."

"I don't understand you sometimes."

"I've told you: You make me happy, so I don't like being separated." He gave me a loving look.

"Why then, why don't you—you could—make another 'dinner' this week—"

"To make a dinner"—*fare una cena*—was our code expression for the excuse he gave Olivia on the nights we ate together then went to the Odeon Hotel. He would pretend he had to entertain some clients.

"It's always on my mind, when can I 'make another dinner' so as to have a little time with Anna? But the other night Olivia said to me, 'Sergio, why do you have so many dinners recently?' I had to make up a story about how I was trying to get a certain teaching account from an Italian bank and, contrary to what you may think, I hate lies and secrecy. This is not second-nature to me, the way it is to—to lady-chasers like Giorgio, for instance."

I hadn't thought much about what he told Olivia in order to be absent on the occasional evening.

"So do you think *she's* suspicious?" I finally said.

"No, she's not suspicious. But she's curious about the frequent dinners. It's normal. She wants to know."

"So we have to wait a bit?"

"Well, you have the carnival of your life outside of school—Nathan's parties, your aunt's outings and galas, and now your visiting 'friend' to distract you—who is this friend, anyway?"

"Doug."

"Ah, Doug—the ex-boyfriend who is not completely ex?"

I grimaced.

"You could bring him down to Sperlonga, too, if you wanted," he said with a shrug. "I'm warning you, I'm not going to be jealous. Because if either of us starts getting jealous of the other, the game is over."

"I'm not asking you to be jealous and I didn't know this was a 'game.' But I can't see myself bringing Doug down to Sperlonga. Can you?"

"No, I can't. I know that's not reasonable of me, but there it is. So then," he continued, looking dejected, "you'll stay in Rome and be distracted—and satisfied."

"No, I won't be satisfied. Not at all. I don't *want* him the way I—" I stopped. One thing felt taboo and that was any statement of how much we felt for each other. I stood up. "It's time for me to go home."

"Yes, you look tired. Me too. You're right, of course, about the day being much too long." He stood up, pushed his chair neatly under the table. "Let's walk out together. Do you want to ride with me a bit tonight?"

This was one of the absurd ways we extended our time together: in order to have an extra half-hour to gab with him, I would ride in his car part of the way to his Rome apartment, which lay in a different direction from my own home. He'd drop me on the southeast fringe of the city at an open crossroads with ruins on one side and towering stone walls on the others. Waiting to catch a bus back to the center, I always felt vulnerable and exposed, knowing that a woman standing alone on an empty street in the outskirts of a city might, to an Italian male, look like a prostitute hoping for business.

"Sure," I said.

"Let's lock up."

We had our ritual for closing the suite: I turned out the lights in the classrooms in the main area, while he finished tidying up his desk, then went to the annex classroom and closed up there. Usually we'd meet back on the landing, but this time when I closed the front door, he was still inside the extra classroom.

"Sergio, what are you doing?" I stepped into the annex.

"I'm erasing the blackboard. See, this is what I mean. You and Melitta always erase the blackboard at the end of the day. The other teachers don't. The students, they should come in and see a clean blackboard in the morning."

Now that I'd seen his humble origins in Sperlonga and understood his struggle for upward mobility, his seriousness about work touched me. He put the eraser down, looking grumpy. "Your aunt's dinner this weekend," he continued, "means two whole days without seeing you—this doesn't make me happy."

"Me neither, but I promised. I'm supposed to handle the tickets."

"*Va be'*," he said, two little words that mean "it's okay," but can convey, in a tone of despaired resignation, that there's nothing we can do about anything in life, that we're powerless, so let the Roman Empire collapse, the Goths and the

Visigoths descend and pillage the whole peninsula. He sat down on one of the student chairs and sighed. "I don't know what to do about any of it—the school, you, Olivia."

I went over to the door, closed it, came back, and sat on his lap, straddling his legs. He put his arms around me and hugged me and I nestled against his chest, taking in his smell of citrus and sweat.

"Anna, Anna," he murmured. "What a mess we're making."

I started loosening his belt.

"No, Anna. We can't do it at school," he said, "because I'm the boss and you're the employee. I'm trying to run a respectable operation here, not a bordello." He put his hands on my hips, as though to push me away, but didn't.

"Oh, bordello. That could be a fun game."

"All right. I give in." He got up. "Stand over here," he said, leading me to one of the school desks. "You can lean back against it, like that." He unbuttoned the top of my shirt. "Here—let me. You should understand that this is an absolute exception to our rule of not doing it at school, an exception to keep us going until our next 'dinner'." He traced my face with one hand. "I love your eyes. I love your mouth. You're so beautiful, so extraordinary." He kissed me slowly, attentively. Then, in a change of rhythm, his eyes and hands wandered inside my shirt. "Lean back on the desk a little—"

"Like this?"

"Yes, dear. Okay, pull up your skirt a little more, help me out. Let's see what's going on here. Give me your leg. Soon you'll feel much better."

"Sergio—"

"Does this feel good? My fingers on your 'raspberry'?"

"Oh, Sergio—"

"*Amore,* you feel better now, right?"

"*Sì, sì.*"

"Good. Because that's what I want—to make you feel better."

"Sergio—"

"What is it, sweet honey? Tell me."

"You make me happy, Sergio." I looked into his eyes; I bathed in the light emanating from them.

"Anna, dearest."

It was past nine when I got home and found Nathan on the couch, sipping wine and strumming the guitar. A smell of something smoky came from the kitchen.

"What's burning?"

"It was the sauce, but I turned it off. Don't worry, Foxy." He strummed and improvised a tune: "*Oh Foxy, who works late into the night, whose love—*" he made a funny expression as he groped for a rhyme "*— fears the light.*" He frowned, tried again. "*Who works late into the night, her love hidden from sight.*" He strummed a few chords and raised a finger to his lips. "Shh."

"Cut it out." I acted annoyed but was grateful for the company after leaving Sergio.

"I just want you to remember I'm here for you, Foxy, whatever happens." He reached for his wine, took a big swallow.

I went into the kitchen, tasted the sauce.

"Not too burned." I served myself some spaghetti from a bowl on the counter, dolloped on the marinara, and went back to sit across from Nathan. "Hey, do you want to come with me to my aunt's gala tomorrow night?"

"This is kind of last minute, isn't it?"

"I've been debating whether you can be trusted to behave. Anyway, there are still some available seats—"

"And you'd like a ride on my new Vespa, right? That's why you're asking."

I laughed. "Okay, yeah. And I don't want to go alone. Come on, it'll be fun. The food's going to be great, and Doris has invited a princess. Her name's Claudia."

Doris always managed to dig up a bit of royalty for her

events, offering them free tickets in exchange for the right to print their names on the program. How she found these folks was a mystery to me. I imagined her sticking a hand deep into the waste paper basket of Italian nobility, as though it were a lottery jar, and pulling up the names of the lucky winners. With her tall, lithe frame and fifties-style dresses with bouffant chiffon skirts, Princess Claudia was a repeat champion.

"*Oh me, oh my, a gala with Foxy,*" Nathan sang out, improvising on the guitar. He went into a flamenco tune, tapping the body of the guitar for effect. "*Olé!*"

"Oh God. Can I trust you to behave? And do you have a suit?"

"I'll find a suit. A banquet and a princess! I can't wait."

The phone rang. I picked it up.

"Anna," Sergio said in a whisper. "I wanted to hear your voice. I hate separating after we make love."

"Where are you?" I looked at Nathan, then, catching his raised eyebrows, turned my back to him.

"I'm home. Olivia's in the shower."

"What if she overhears—"

"I just wanted to say, I'm sorry I can only give you the minimum, I wish I could give you so much more."

"I appreciate that," I responded dryly.

"Because with this minimum, I can't really express everything I want to, and I really want to give you more—I would if I could—" he stopped. "Sorry, I have to get off the phone now."

I hung up and met Nathan's gaze, sympathetic now instead of mocking. He looked away and went back to humming and strumming the guitar.

I'd promised Doris I'd go to her dinner at the South African Embassy before Sergio and I had become lovers. Now that we were involved, I would have preferred to spend the weekend in Sperlonga with him and Olivia, and so felt a certain despondency as I dressed for the event the following night. But my spirits rose when Nathan and I got on his motorcycle and he cried out, "Hold on, Foxy!" We took off, with me in a treacherous sidesaddle position to accommodate Doris's party dress, which I'd taken in as narrowly as possible and lengthened with a black silk flounce. Nathan, in a black suit and bow-tie, with his face shaven and his light brown moustache trimmed, looked positively respectable and, with my excessive mascara and short hair shined up with pomade, I felt like the incarnation of Parisian chic on a Roman holiday.

"Be careful with the corners!" I cried out after he took a sharp right and the pull of gravity threatened my seating.

"Hold on tighter!"

I pressed my cheek harder into his back as we sped up the Via Merulana, past the train station and through the softly lit, tree-lined residential area east of Villa Borghese, until we reached our destination and Nathan parked the cycle. To ward off the social shyness that came up at my aunt's functions, I hooked my arm through his as we walked toward the entrance of the building.

Stepping in through huge wooden doors fixed open with heavy chains, we ascended a long flight of stone stairs to a landing where Doris was taking tickets. Behind her, in a ballroom hung with enormous tapestries, there were twenty round, white-clothed dinner tables and a couple of buffets with appetizers and bottles of wine. Doris wore a clinging green dress and apricot lipstick, a combination of colors that might work in a Cézanne painting but definitely didn't work on her. Her chubby cheeks glowed with excitement, for these events provided not only social pleasure: Her guests would become potential customers when she advertised her travel agency's services later in the evening.

"Anna, I'm so glad you're here. Would you and Nathan take tickets for a moment? I have to go check up on the kitchen."

As Doris disappeared, Nathan raised his eyebrows and shot me an amused look.

"Who let her out of the house in that dress?" he asked.

"She's a free woman."

"Not for long if the *carabinieri* see her. They'll throw her in the clink for a fashion violation."

We sat down on the folding chairs and took tickets from some tall blonde secretaries who worked at the Finnish consulate, then another group from the Danish embassy.

"This is the best seat in the house," Nathan said, leaning toward me conspiratorially.

"You promised—" I began.

"Oh, Holy Madonna, who's *that?*" he asked, as in walked a tall, thin woman wearing a celadon dress with a skin-tight bodice and a skirt of layered silk chiffon. She had her arm passed through that of an older man.

"That's the Princess Claudia and her father," I whispered.

"*Ciao, Anna,*" said the princess.

"*Buona Sera,* Prince, Princess," I said. "This is my friend, Nathan."

"Is it open or assigned seating?" Claudia asked me.

"It's assigned."

"I'll go shift things around so we can sit together." Claudia had a subversive streak that led her to mess with Doris's seating arrangements. She assessed Nathan. "All of us."

"Make sure Signora Gianina sits with us, too," I said.

"*That* went well," Nathan said, as Claudia floated on into the room with her father. "I think she likes me."

"Do I have to remind you again to behave yourself?"

He tried to look serious. "I *will* behave myself—but is trying to get an invitation to a royal function off-limits? Like a ball? A Mediterranean cruise would be ideal. I long to go to Capri in style." He stroked his moustache. "Though a decadent weekend in the country would suffice, with lots of wine and attractive women."

"And evening strolls in Renaissance gardens?"

"And kisses stolen behind a hedge in a labyrinthine—*la dolce vita*, here I come!"

Suddenly I saw Peep, our photographer and pornographer

friend, coming down the staircase. "Shit, what's he doing here? Did you invite him?"

"He called this morning and I mentioned it in passing and he invited himself—you said there were extra seats."

Peep approached and I scanned his suit, which was fortunately clean and dry. No doggie bag pockets with shellfish hanging out tonight.

"You look good," I said.

"I'm hoping to make a good impression on you, Anna, so you'll agree to go out with me again," he chuckled. "You two look cozy." He couldn't open his mouth without making a reference to my sordid episode with Nathan.

"It's because of comments like that that I won't go out with you—" I started.

"Sense of humor, Anna. More of a sense of humor, that's what you need." He stroked his grizzled Amish-style beard. These men and their facial hair—they couldn't stop touching themselves, as though it were a masturbatory substitute. Of all the men with moustaches that I knew, Sergio was the only one who didn't fondle himself all the time. "How about you let me in free?" Peep asked.

"I'm not going to let you in free."

"You wanna see my empty wallet—"

"I'll pay for him," Nathan said, opening up his.

"All right, go on in," I said. "I'm not sitting with you, though."

"We're not sitting with you," Nathan repeated, straightening his posture and taking a prim look to mock me.

Peep snorted and moved on.

"How could you invite him?" I asked.

"He's desperate for new clients for his portrait business—"

"Terrific. That's really terrific. I hope my aunt doesn't notice him—or find out about his X-rated sideline—"

"So what if she did? What do you care?" He stroked his moustache again.

"Stop that," I said, pulling his arm away from his face.

"I want to look good for the princess."

"Oh, here's someone I really like that you haven't met—Signora Gianina." I waved. She was in her usual black dress, her nude stockings puckered around the ankles above her laced oxfords. "Signora, *come sta?*" I always used the formal address with her, which in Italian was, much to my grammatical misery, the same as the third-person singular, so that I was in this case literally asking, "Signora, how is she?" as though I were a nurse in a mental institution conversing with a multiple personality.

"Good. And you?" She came around the table and kissed me on the cheek.

"This is my friend, Nathan." As I introduced them, my two very different social circles collided with a clink.

"So nice to meet you. So nice," Nathan said, and by God, in his pressed suit, with his recently trimmed moustache, he really did look respectable.

"I asked the princess to seat us together," I said to Gianina.

"I'll go find her," Gianina said and set off, slow and solid, like a good-natured iguana, into the dining hall.

The women outnumbered the men at the princess's table. Claudia sat between her father on the right and Nathan on her left. Gianina sat next to the prince. The space to my left was still empty.

"We need one more man," Princess Claudia said, looking around.

"I'll find someone," Nathan said, and before I could warn him against recruiting Peep, he was gone.

At the podium, my aunt welcomed everyone then invited Gianina up to join her and say a few words. As the Signora gave a thumbnail history of Italian massacres, conquests, and defeats in Africa, Nathan headed straight for Peep, as I'd feared.

I glanced sideways at the loaded buffet tables then at Claudia.

"Yes," she said. "Time to eat."

My aunt's banquets challenged even the most ample stomachs. The selection of dishes was completely changed at each course, so that the display of twenty antipasti would be cleared and replaced by a dozen pasta dishes for the second course, then a collection of meat and fish dishes for the third, and so forth. Each round came with a fresh selection of wines. I stayed close to Claudia, figuring that I should, at the very least, match the portions that my rail-thin acquaintance served herself.

Back at our table, I found Nathan to my right and Peep to my left, and sitting down, I was caught between two strands of conversation. To my left, Peep and Gianina were discussing the gypsies in Rome, a subject I found darkly fascinating as I had twice been assaulted by gypsy children who tried to pick-pocket me. I'd extricated myself by screaming bloody murder and fleeing at a gallop with my Greek bag held high above my head. There followed Peep's stories about beggars in Singapore, where he'd met children mutilated on purpose by their parents to arouse pity. This opened the way to Gianina exploring the difference between the neutering and castration of male animals, which in turn led to both of them discussing the history of eunuchs in Syria.

To my right, Nathan was engaging Claudia and her father in the exploration of the odd lacunae of the Italian language—how there are, for example, no words for privacy or stage fright, two concepts foreign to this extroverted culture. Next came a discussion of words that are the same in English and Italian, which brought Nathan to the word "yacht" and the prince to dropping that he had one—at which point Nathan, coming to attention like a hound sniffing a fox in the distance, mentioned he had an uncle in the Royal Navy, perhaps to signal his readiness for the next princely maritime expedition.

Lost between these two conversations, I stuffed myself to mute my misery. Everything that had once absorbed me in Rome—the parties, the drinking, the expeditions—no longer did. I only wanted to be with Sergio. My eyes were wet with tears when, with perfect timing, Peep turned his attention toward me.

"It's been a while since I last saw you. Have you gone to the dogs yet?" He paused, looked at me. "Yup. I can see you're on your way."

"Don't start in with me—"

He shook his head. "You tolerate me because you know I care. I really do." He put a paw on my bare forearm. "Come to the movies with me, Anna."

"There's really no point in our going out together."

"Not even to the Falcon for a drink?"

"No!"

I stood up and headed for the ladies' room, weaving my way between the tables from which rose a wine-lubricated medley of languages.

The empty restroom provided welcome privacy. I was in front of the mirror trying to repair my make-up when Gianina's tiny, squat form appeared behind me. Facing the mirror next to me, she rearranged the bobby pins in her gray hair bun.

"You're not enjoying yourself," she said.

"Not really."

"Problems of the heart?"

"Yes."

"Why don't you take me home in a taxi after dessert and we'll explore it a bit with my cards? Or did you want to stay and dance?"

"No, not tonight."

"*Va bene.* It's arranged."

Back at the buffet table, the Signora and I loaded up on desserts. A sense of my belly expanding forward through Doris's dress, which I'd taken in too aggressively, didn't stop me from my pursuit of pleasure. I was sinking a large serving spoon deep into a liqueur-drenched trifle when Nathan edged up on my left and whispered, "Don't hold back, Foxy. More, more."

"Looks like you'll be on the high seas with the princess soon."

"I'm working on it."

"Uh-oh, my aunt is starting her announcements. By the

way, I'm about to leave with the Signora. I'll see you at the flat later."

As I sat back down, Doris stepped up to the podium and adjusted the microphone. At the end of her functions, she always delivered a preview of upcoming events with a list of personal announcements appended.

"I want to thank the staff at the South African Embassy for letting us use this marvelous space. Our next dinner, the summer banquet, will be on . . . Our next expedition, to Taormina . . . In September, I'm hoping . . . "

My attention wandered as I focused on my plate of sweets. Glancing around, I had the impression that no one else was listening either.

"The other day I found a dog, a beautiful and well-behaved German Shepherd I've named Antonio, who needs a home . . ."

Okay, we were off to the races now. Doris would request various favors. Bored, people leaned toward each other to resume interrupted conversations in whispers.

"I also have a fourteen-year-old boy from Eritrea who's staying with me and could use a room of his own . . ."

This last request, on Halim's behalf, reminded me of her essential generosity, but it was drowned in a crescendo of voices.

"Please, be quiet!" Doris pleaded. "After all the work I've done organizing this banquet, the least you can do is listen to my announcements." Her face expressed hurt and annoyance.

A chorus of laughter rose from the next table, where some-one was imitating Marcello Mastroianni imitating Groucho Marx.

"You over there, laughing at that table—"

Watching her seek attention, I felt mortified. This was why my family had rejected her. I glanced at Gianina, who stood up and came over to me. "Let's head back toward the ladies' room," she whispered, "that way she won't think we're leaving. Then we'll slip out."

I nodded and, a moment after she headed out, I got up from the table and did the same.

In the taxi on the way to her apartment in Trastevere, the Signora had a good laugh about it.

"Your aunt's quite a character. More Italian than the Italians—she just can't shut up. And what an operator—always trying to get something out of someone! A real survivor."

"I can't tell whether you're praising or criticizing her. It's so embarrassing for me sometimes."

"Oh, my dear, you've had many good times with her."

"But she's not easy."

"If easy is what you want, go to—Canada!" She laughed again.

The taxi let us out at Piazza San Cosimato, where Gianina lived, and a few minutes later I was settling into a rickety chair at a small table in her living room. As she poured me a glass of *amaro*, the bitter herbal liqueur drunk after over-indulging, I looked around the tiny room. With its shelves of books, it had an aura of poverty and studiousness appropriate for a woman who'd avoided marriage and devoted her life to informal scholarship. I guessed that some of the volumes had been borrowed from libraries and never returned. Prints and photographs of ruins and ancient archaeological sites crowded the walls. The centerpiece of the collection was a large antique engraving of gentlemen in formal wear and ladies in long dresses strolling in the Forum.

Gianina rummaged around in the drawer of a little secretary and returned with a deck of cards.

"The Neapolitan deck. It never lies." She smiled and sat down across from me. "Let's lift the lid of the pot and see what's cooking inside."

I sighed; she sighed back. "Yes," she continued, "being young is a miserable business. You're in the process of becoming, but what, who? And who's going to help you? Or obstruct you? And it all happens at the speed of light, determined by forces you have no control over. Yet the ego craves control, so the mind creates an illusion of power, when there's really very little. Thankfully, the cards can help us grab at the straws of self-knowledge, so we can turn all that pathos into something a little more malleable, even dignified."

"You think so?" I gazed at her wrinkled face hopefully.

She nodded, shuffling the cards, then dealt them out, placing them in a pattern. Pages and princes in brightly colored tunics and tights held swords, batons, chalices, or coins. "So, man trouble?"

"Actually there are two," I said, thinking of Doug's upcoming visit.

"But it's the married one who is the problem? What's his name?"

"Sergio. He's not married yet, but might as well be."

"Not legally, but in the eyes of his community?" She looked at the cards. "Yes, I see. He wants her to make babies for him. Two or three. He has a fantasy of maybe even four, good old Catholic-style, serial reproduction. But he's not a practicing Catholic, is he? He's a dangerous mix of instinct and intellect. *Un intelletto-istintivo*, we call it: the instinct-driven intellectual, a sub-type of the Italian male. They're smart, but so busy rebelling against their culture that they lose connection with their hearts. The command alternates between up here and down there—" she pointed to her head then her lap "—with no center here." She placed two fingers on her heart.

I drooped. "Okay."

"And what's going to happen to you, my dear, when they marry?"

"I don't know. I mean, I'm thinking of leaving for Asia."

"Then all this suffering will end soon? Or you haven't decided about Asia?"

"No, I'm not sure." There, inside me, was the thing I hadn't yet confessed to myself—a desire to stick it out, no matter what, to the bitter end. I would only leave if someone punched me in the stomach, knifed and dismembered me.

Wanting Sergio had revealed to me my own secret, shameful taste for melodrama.

"Perhaps Asia is a good plan. Listen, after they marry and they have their first baby, that's the end of it. Every time the baby sniffles, he'll go running home to help *mamma* take care of it. There you'll be, waiting for your lover in your silk negligee, while he's calling the doctor because the baby sneezed. It's an old Italian story, this kind of thing. Do you think I approved of how my brother treated Doris? Of course not! Maybe she figured she couldn't do better. But look at you—you're young, intelligent, beautiful—magnificent! You're magnificent, and this situation you're in is humiliating. Have the courage to face the facts as they are, my dear. And Sergio's type, the *intelletto-istintivo*, is not capable of real love."

"Really?"

"Okay, let's look a little deeper into this man." She gathered up the cards, shuffled, dealt out a new spread, and studied it. "Ah, look here. Maybe I was wrong."

"Wrong about?"

"The way he feels. We say 'love' as though there were only one kind. The Greeks had seven different words for love. Hmm, I see you're in a fix here. He does love you, in his way. Well, you must decide what to do—or not to do. Stay and fight for him, or leave."

"Fight for him? How?"

"I don't know how you do it in America, but here, you write an anonymous letter to the wife telling her what's going on."

"An anonymous letter?"

"Yes. Now, if a man writes the letter, there has to be some kind of threat—a death threat, of course, *a la Siciliana*. You should read *To Each His Own* by Leonardo Sciascia if you want the flavor of the thing. But when the mistress writes a letter to inform the wife, or would-be wife, only the facts are necessary, no violence." She paused, picked up a card, and put it back down. "And when you think about it—if you were her—wouldn't you want to know? Would you want to marry someone who was, right before the wedding, having an affair under your nose? Of course, if you choose to write a letter, you'll face scandal and the judgment of his family and community. But maybe it's worth it." She looked up at me, and our eyes met. "Oh, dear child—you're white as a sheet. I've upset you."

"I'm okay." I sniffed, holding everything in.

"Here," she said, going to the shelf where she kept the liqueurs. "Let me pour you a little grappa. It'll put you back on your feet."

9. The Not-So-Ex Boyfriend

I considered Signora Gianina's suggestion I send Olivia an anonymous letter. I could begin it with, *"An anonymous friend thinks you ought to know . . ."* Or, more ominously, *"Marrying Sergio will bring you unhappiness . . ."* Remembering Gianina's reference to Sciascia's detective novel, *To Each His Own,* which begins with an anonymous letter, I got a copy and started to read it. But the threats of violence and the subsequent murder in that story had little to do with the world I lived in, and I soon lost interest and put it down.

I was obsessed with Sergio, I was in love with him, but did I want him forever and ever?

In any case, I would postpone any action until after Doug's visit.

Doug had a strong jaw. When I'd met him in high school, that jaw had made him seem older than he was. At fourteen, he already towered above me, and the two things together—the jaw and the height—got my attention because a guy with big bone structure seemed like the perfect antidote to an alcoholic mother. Doug made me feel so safe that, even when I outgrew him, I couldn't let go, and he wouldn't either. Once I got to Europe, he even said he was okay with my having other relationships—as long as I didn't tell him the details—because they would make me more confident when the time came to settle down. So I'd written him that I was involved with a married Italian, and he'd told me about a few of his flings, adding that with each other woman he'd known, he'd become more sure I was the right one for him.

It was a warm day in May and I'd asked for the morning off from teaching, when I met Doug at Stazione Termini, at the bus stop for the airport shuttle. We hugged and got on the 16 bus to my apartment. He had one of those huge backpacks that students used before the invention of the Rollaboard. It was an ugly bright orange, and I could see the outline of a few large books pressing against the nylon from the inside: he had his master's exams scheduled for the end of the month and would do some studying while visiting me. We stood holding onto a pole while he steadied the pack on the floor between his knees.

"Your mother wants to know if you're coming home this summer." His expression made it clear he wanted to know, too.

"I haven't decided yet."

"Oh."

"Well, I have a job here—"

He bent a bit to peer out the bus window. "She gave me a care package for you," he said.

"With what kind of stuff?"

"Some candied apricots and iron pills—"

"Candied apricots?"

"Full of potassium or something. She's worried about your nutrition."

"I'm doing fine."

"You look fine."

He smiled, looking at me with desire. I sighed internally, knowing I'd go to bed with him when we reached my apartment. It seemed only fair after he'd come all this way.

"A little overworked at school, maybe," I said.

"But you like teaching?"

"Yeah, it's fun."

"What about the interior design idea?" he asked. We'd talked about one day starting a business that would offer both architectural and decorating services.

"Well, maybe, when I return." His mentioning our old fantasy made me feel the way I felt around my parents—that I was trapped in an old story that wouldn't let me change, or that even if I did change, they wouldn't notice, they would see me as being exactly the same. I looked out the window. "Next stop is ours."

We got off and headed down Via Angelo Poliziano toward my apartment on Via Pascoli.

"So what's this housemate of yours like?"

"Nathan's a great buddy. You'll like him."

"You have privacy?" he asked.

"Yeah, sure. I don't share a room with Nathan, if that's what you're after."

"I'm real tired from the flight but—" he smiled at me.

"Of course." I still liked his smile.

Doug walked looking around and up.

"Gee, I love the cornices on these buildings. What a lovely street," he said.

"Probably built in the mid-nineteenth century, when the new neighborhoods with straight streets were put in."

"Sort of the Roman equivalent of what Haussmann did in Paris?"

"Yes, a little later perhaps. Maybe in the 1870s," I said. We always had things to talk about—urban planning, history, aesthetics.

"So much to see here. I'm excited."

"There'll be a lot for you to do when I'm teaching." Thankfully, I'd continue to see Sergio at school. "Here we are."

As we entered the building complex and crossed the cement courtyard, I watched him take in the charm of the potted plants and hanging laundry against the rust ocher wash of the walls. I wondered whether he would be as moved by the beauty of the city as I had been or whether he would take it all in as an art history lesson, illustrating what he'd learned in class. We went down the steps to my subterranean apartment and I opened the door. Nathan was still teaching, so we were alone.

He set his backpack down in the bedroom and got out

his green toiletry kit and went into the bathroom. I sat on the edge of the bed and listened to him brush his teeth and wash his face. I hadn't seen Doug since the previous summer, when he'd visited me in Paris right before I left for Rome. He came back into the room and bent over his backpack to pull out the box my mother had asked him to bring me.

"She made me promise to give you this straight away," he said.

He sat down on the bed next to me as I tore off the wrapping paper. Inside, under a clear plastic lid, plump apricots glistened with the sugar syrup that had been used to candy them.

"This is such a weird thing to send me," I said.

"Let's face it, your mother can be pretty weird."

"How was she when you saw her?"

"Pretty clear," he said, meaning that it had been early in the day and she hadn't started drinking yet. "She really misses you." He took the box from me and put it down on the bedside table. "Did you want me to shower?"

"No, it's okay."

"You still on the pill?"

"No, I was having migraines so I went off it last summer."

"I thought you might have, so I brought some condoms."

"I'm using a device." In Paris I'd gotten a Dutch cap, a kind of reduced diaphragm fitting just over the cervix. It felt awkward to inform Doug that I'd acquired a new form of birth control since we'd parted, so I didn't bother with explanations. Nor did I mention that I hadn't bothered to put spermicide inside the cap, as I was supposed to. I hated the smell of spermicide and the way it made me itch after having sex. In any case, I hadn't had a period since going off the pill and, though I knew it was theoretically possible to get pregnant, I was convinced my reproductive system had shut down.

"All right," he said, uninterested in the details.

We got undressed.

"I've gotten fatter," I said, feeling self-conscious—something I never felt with Sergio.

"Come here," he said, climbing into bed.

I got in next to him.

"This feels strange," I said. "It's been a long time." He smelled like airplane—a mixture of fuel, plastic, and hot metal—but also like himself—salty like the beach where we first had sex as teenagers, warm like the instant coffee in his dorm room at Columbia, fresh like a crisp fall day on upper Broadway. He smelled like his parents' house, like old wood and his mother's chocolate brownies, and also like my parents' place, French perfume with a dash of turpentine and Scotch whiskey. And just like my parents' house, he was a place that was good to return to, even though I didn't want to stay too long. I would use him, selfishly, as a temporary refuge.

"It's been too long." He stroked my neck. "And you haven't written me enough. I write you these long letters and your answers are so—short."

"I'm sorry. My life here is crazy."

He drew me to him with his large hands. I felt uncomfortable with his heavy body, so unlike my other lover's light frame. Doug's bones were so long and big that it was like having a bulky zoo animal in the bed—a giraffe or a gazelle—but I was, because of Sergio, in a state of perpetual arousal, and my response went off like a rocket.

"Your Italian lover has really opened you up, Annie," Doug said afterwards. "Is that still going on?"

"Sort of." I lay there with the absurd sense of having been unfaithful to Sergio.

Doug stroked my face. "But why? If he's married, it can't possibly lead to anything."

"It doesn't have to lead to anything in order to be good for me."

"Well, obviously, sexually it has been." His tone was neutral. Exhaustion was probably keeping jealousy at bay. "I can't help it," he said, closing his eyes sleepily, "but I have to take a nap now."

"That's okay, I have to work this afternoon. I'll see you when I get back this evening."

"Okay," he said, and a moment later was asleep.

I gazed at him. There was a wooden quality to his body, a kind of stiffness that remained with him even in sleep. His feet stuck off the end of the mattress. He'd grown several inches since that September seven years before, when my father had gotten a research job at the Stony Brook University medical center and we'd moved out to Long Island from the city. That's when my mother sank into constant drink, to the point of having slurred speech and memory lapses. With my father at work all the time and my sister gone, I found myself in a miserable tête-à-tête with a witch. It was to escape her that I threw myself into a teenage relationship. Doug had the stiffness and solidity of a Styrofoam life preserver.

I glanced at the clock. It was a little past noon. I would rummage around for a quick bite in the kitchen, then hop on the trusty 16 to school and still have plenty time for an espresso with Sergio before teaching.

"I don't want to go for coffee." With one elbow on the office chair armrest, the other arm tapping a pencil on the table, Sergio sat behind his desk looking glum. The collar of his black suit jacket hiked up a little above his shirt as he sunk back and away from me. "So the boyfriend, he has arrived on schedule?" He spoke in Italian.

"Yes." It was awkward, no way around it. "The last time I saw him was ten months ago, so of course it's—strange."

"He must be very attached to you. He wants to get married probably, start a family?" His eyes were veiled, like a reptile with two sets of eyelids.

"Americans aren't all in a rush to start a family the way you are here—"

"He sounds, from what you've told me about him, like a good sort of guy"—*un tipo bravo* was the expression he used—"destined for professional success. Reliable, stable—a good comrade for the journey of life, no?"

"I appreciate your stamp of approval."

"Okay, you have a right to be sarcastic. Listen, I have something for you." He cleared his throat, opened a drawer, and took out an envelope. "The notice for your working papers."

I looked at the envelope. "Really?"

He put it back in the drawer. "There's more paperwork to be done—as always in Italy. But we are at the last step here. I have to make up a contract for you with the school, you sign it, we make a photocopy and submit it, and you're done."

"Thank you so much." This meant that, like my aunt Doris, I could have a real life in Rome with a permanent job and health insurance. Maybe one day I could even buy an apartment. It might be worth foregoing my round-the-world plan for a while. I could always pick it up later.

Sergio looked at me. "How long is the boyfriend staying?"

"Not sure. He has a couple of weeks off from school, but he might use some of the time to travel a bit, maybe to Florence."

"You want to go with him?"

"I don't think so."

"I can find someone to substitute for you if you change your mind," Sergio said, switching to English.

"Thanks, but I really don't want to."

"Why doesn't he come and live in Italy for a year?"

"He's in a rush to make a career. He's very driven—that's one thing the two of you have in common, actually."

"One can always find something that two people have in common. For example, you and Olivia, you're both American and from New York."

"Gee, I wonder why that is." I didn't really wonder. I had this whole theory—which I would never articulate to him—that he was attracted to New York girls because we gave him a connection to a broader, more exciting world that he couldn't attain on his own.

"I wish you wouldn't be sarcastic with me. You know,

with our different languages and cultures, sometimes it's hard for me to 'get' it."

"Sorry."

Sergio made his nervous gesture, moving his shoulders up and down in his too-big jacket, then stood up and went to the open window. Spring in Rome is as wonderful as it gets because it goes on and on, making flowers bloom in the crags of ruins and all the colors split with light, and the next words out of his mouth expressed what I was thinking: "Can you feel the air changing? In a couple of months we'll be closing the windows and the shutters against the heat at lunchtime, instead of opening them. Summer is around the corner." He stood looking out with his back to me. "Olivia wants to get married this summer."

"I know."

"Once we get married, I think I will quit Multi Lingua and look for a job near Sperlonga. I can't continue this life with two apartments. And doing business in Rome is too complicated for me."

"How could you possibly want to leave Rome for Sperlonga?"

"I told you, my family is there." He turned back around and looked at me. "My father, especially—I owe him so much, and he's been so lonely since my mother died. Yes, once I had a dream of escaping—in my university years in Rome, I dared to imagine a life in a big city, maybe even in our more civilized north, a life with intelligent, educated people, but it won't happen. The fact is, I wouldn't have had that education if it hadn't been for my father. A truck driver, can you imagine, who had the brains—" he tapped his head— "to imagine that his son might have a better life than he'd had. A normal sort of thing for an American parent, perhaps, but here—very rare. I owe him everything." He paused. "Anna, you and I are in an absurd situation. Impossible and absurd."

"I know." My eyes filled with tears. His ability to stay connected and committed—to Olivia, to his father and family—was one of the things I loved about him, even as I hated it because it stood in the way of our being together. In any case, my own agenda of seeing the world created another set of obstacles. I wanted desperately to go over and hold him but didn't dare. Nathan and the other teachers would be returning from lunch break at any moment.

"Whatever you do," he said, "please don't cry. Then, really, you will put me in crisis." He switched to Italian when emotional: *Mi metterai in crisi.*

"I won't cry then. But, goddammit, I'm not staying on at the school—or in Rome—if you leave!"

"Be reasonable! You almost have your working papers— you should stay in Italy another year or two before continuing your way around the world, no? Master the language, enrich yourself as an artist—and we can still see each other if I'm in Sperlonga—not so often, obviously—and you can come visit us."

I sniffed noisily.

"We must try to enjoy life," he went on, "and enjoy each other in the time that remains. That's the only thing to do." He looked at his watch. "Let's take a walk up to Villa Borghese," he said, referring to a park not from school. "We have time." As Melitta wasn't there to answer the phone, he took it off the hook and grabbed his keys.

We went down the stairs, out through the heavy door, and headed up toward the park through the calm and swanky area just east of Via Veneto. Soon we reached the ancient crumbling city wall and passed under the tall archways that soared over the main roads connecting the center of the metropolis to its outskirts. On the other side was the huge expanse of Villa Borghese. Now that we were a safe distance from school, Sergio took my hand. The feeling of his warm fingers calmed me. At the entrance to the park stood a small movie theater and some stands selling gelato and pretzels. In a field with tiny spring daisies and dandelions, couples interlaced in the sun and mothers watched small children play. The scent of the grass in the midday sun rose up around us.

"This is the way things go," he said. "You meet the right

people at the wrong moments, and the wrong people at the right moments. The right timing—we call it *il tempismo*—only a lucky few have it. But you have to keep going forward, doing what you can with your life even when things aren't exactly how you want them to be. Things are imperfect, disappointing even, but the main thing is to keep your goals in mind."

"I wish I knew what my goals were."

"You Americans—you have too much freedom, that's your problem." He stopped walking. "Let's lie down here."

We lay down in the grass together, and he put his arms around me and drew me to him until my head was on his shoulder. I looked up at the sculptural branches of a Roman pine looming above us against the sky. The greens and browns of the tree vibrated against the blue, and my body vibrated in response, every cell dancing with life. Could this kind of crazy feeling last? Wasn't it just a product of circumstance—of the constraints of a secret affair? Yet again I thought of Signora Gianina's suggestion I write Olivia an anonymous letter. It wouldn't be hard to do. I could make it seem like it came from one of the schoolteachers or students, and Sergio wouldn't blame me for the ensuing maelstrom. *Dear Olivia, a well-intentioned friend wishes to spare you the miseries of a life married to a philandering Italian . . .* Of course, I imagined Sergio wouldn't philander if he were married to me.

"Doug," Sergio said, interrupting my plotting. "What kind of name is that? It must be short for something."

"It's short for Douglas."

"Oh. Like in Kirk Douglas? There's no equivalent in Italian, I don't think." He pondered it.

"No, there isn't." I thought of Doug back at my apartment, sleeping in my bed.

He took my arm and, with a gentle pull, wrapped it even tighter around his waist. He rolled toward me, and I felt his erection through his pants.

"I wish we could go to a hotel," I said.

"We don't have time, dear—you have to teach in forty-five minutes. Besides, sometimes it's better to be like this. Twenty, thirty years from now, you'll remember this moment better than if we went to a hotel. You go to a room and screw, and it's one act of copulation among many. But lying in the grass like this on a beautiful spring day in Rome, having this conversation—well, in a way it's much sweeter, don't you think?"

"I don't know."

"Of course it is. Anyway, it's all we have—here and now."

"So then, under that Marxist, son-of-a-truck-driver exterior, you're a romantic." I stroked his face.

"Perhaps. At least, I know how things work here—" He touched my chest gently, then his own, as though connecting our hearts with a thread. "I know how and what the heart remembers. Because the thing is—I wouldn't want you to forget me," he said. "Ever."

"I won't forget you. I couldn't possibly forget you." A little shiver went through me in spite of the warm sun. "So then, no hotel today."

"No hotel. However," he added, with a dreamy smile, "I do like the feeling of your hand on my pants."

I had classes back-to-back all afternoon. In the interstices of the day, between the group from IBM and private lessons with students like Giorgio the wolf, I thought of Doug waiting for me back at the apartment. What would he think of Nathan when he arrived? Not that it mattered, really. The important thing was for me to clarify things with Doug soon, because my opinion of myself was going to sink dangerously low if I didn't. It was one thing to sleep with him now and again, but I couldn't let him go on believing that settling down with him was in my life plan.

After the last class, I followed the smell of pipe smoke into the office where Mauro was in conference with Sergio.

"Are you still being brilliant with the students, Anna?" Mauro asked me.

"Trying to," I said.

"*Brava*," he said, and gravely puffed his pipe.

Mauro came by only once or twice a week, disturbing the routine Sergio and I had of locking up and leaving together. I quickly placed my books back behind the glass doors. Then, catching Sergio's eye for a brilliant sliver of a second, I gave the two of them a wave and headed out into the spring evening.

I hated leaving without a kiss or a hug, but there was nothing to be done about it.

The apartment was quiet when I got home. A note on the dining table in Nathan's hand read, "Foxy—took Doug to pool hall. Start water for pasta, would you?" The pool hall was just around the corner and I smiled imagining Nathan dragging Doug there.

I sat down to look at the mail. There was an envelope in letterhead stationery from the foundation I'd applied to for a fellowship. It would be the notification about Asia. I took a deep breath, reached for the envelope, and opened it.

"We are happy to inform you—"

I reread the letter several times, jubilant, sad, excited. This meant I could move on—if I still wanted to, if I could withstand the pain of severing my connection with Sergio. I thought of walking along the waterfronts of Hong Kong, of riding the funiculars, of smelling—and eating!—the roasted ducks hung in restaurant windows. Yes, I would be brave, light, and casual about Sergio, and I would leave. And where would I live in Hong Kong? Who would I hang out with? What would the students be like? I hadn't read or spoken Mandarin since college and suddenly China seemed like a crazy idea. One thing made me unequivocally happy, however. Accepting the fellowship would provide me with an excuse not to go home in the coming summer. I would do almost anything to avoid dealing with my mother.

A tight feeling came into my throat. I put a big pot of water up to boil and went to fetch Nathan and Doug for dinner.

The pool hall was around the corner and, like our apartment, a half-flight down from street level. There was no piped-in music, no bar, and not a single painting or poster on the wall. Six pool tables illuminated by overhanging bulbs stood on the black and white tiled floor. The splashes of green against the neutral walls and floor gave the scene the flavor of a sepia photograph with colorized diamonds. It was a place for men and men only—men with cigars, cigarettes, or pipes; short middle-aged men with protruding bellies; and lean, young men, taller than their fathers. The atmosphere was quiet and focused. I felt awkward entering the room but was in fact barely noticed. A *donna qualunque*—some woman or other—coming in to retrieve a man for dinner was accepted, like an Irish woman fishing her hubby out of a pub after work or a French wife getting her man out of the local *bar* or *café*, a reminder that women not only provided pleasure to men but also got in the way of it.

Doug was bent over the table, focusing on his shot, while Nathan leaned in toward him, giving him counsel. The two of them were already buddies. I loved that Nathan's lack of boundaries and inhibitions enabled him to befriend just about anybody in a flash. I imagined the scene earlier in the day: Doug sleeping in my bed, Nathan coming home and realizing someone was in the apartment, then his waking Doug up and Doug sitting up naked as Nathan introduced himself. Nathan would have dragged Doug out to a bar for an aperitif, or a series of, and from there to the pool hall. The two of them had already bonded through drink and pool.

Nathan saw me.

"Hey, Foxy!" he said.

Doug took his shot then turned to look at me, a big grin on his face. He was having a good time. I went up to him.

"What did you do today?"

"I slept hours, then Nathan took me to the Coliseum and a bar next to it."

He looked less wooden, so much the better for a few drinks. I liked him more in this state than when he was sober.

"You getting hungry?"

"Yeah, sort of. I mean, my body clock is confused—but sure, let's eat."

The two of them talked loudly as we walked out into the May evening, which had turned close and damp. It would rain soon. My brain was working overtime: I'd never told Doug that I had applied for a fellowship to go to Asia, but I'd have to tell him now. The delicacy of the May evening belied the cruelty to come.

Back in the apartment, I stared at the sparse contents of the refrigerator. If I'd anticipated Doug's visit with any joy, I would have stocked the kitchen beforehand.

"There's some pancetta and a little cream," Nathan said, peering over my shoulder. "We could improvise something carbonara-like with that." He said "we" but he meant "you," for soon he was at his usual post on the couch in the living room, strumming his guitar.

As I chopped the bacon, I heard Nathan say to Doug, "Pour me another glass of wine, old chap, would you?" I was glad to have him take Doug off my hands for a little bit while I mustered courage for the confrontation that would follow.

After dinner, Doug and I went into the bedroom and closed the door. We could hear Nathan playing softly again in the background. Doug changed into fresh underwear and got into bed. I put my pajamas on.

"You think you'll be able to sleep?" I asked.

"Sooner or later. I shouldn't have slept so long after you left. But what about you? You had a long day."

"I'm a little wired."

"Well then, maybe—" He pulled me closer, and at first I resisted, then gave in. I really didn't need to do it with Doug a second time, but it assuaged my guilt.

Afterward I lay with my head on his shoulder agitated by a crazy voice inside that screamed *get out*. Rain had started hitting the window above my bed.

"Annie," he said, "I think about you all the time. I want you to come home."

"It's been almost two years since I left for Europe. I'm surprised you haven't found another girlfriend."

"I haven't been a saint, you know that. And obviously you haven't been one, either. But you know I don't care about that. We've both had a chance to sow our wild oats, and now it's time for you to come and live with me in Cambridge. I want us to get married."

"I'm living here now."

"It's easy: buy a plane ticket, pack your bags, and come home. I mean, what are you doing here, anyway?"

I disengaged myself and sat up next to him, hugging my knees.

"It's beautiful here. It's so beautiful it's intoxicating. I mean, you went out today, you looked around. Or are you wearing blinders?"

"Come back to me, Annie. Come home." He took my arm and tugged on it a bit, in an attempt to draw me toward him. But I sat still and firm, hugging my knees tighter.

"I like traveling," I said. "I like living in other countries—"

"Eventually, I'll be a self-employed architect. We can go into business together, the way we planned. And then we can travel every year, if that's what you want."

"Doug—"

"Unless you're holding out for this Italian guy—who sounds like a real jerk." He sat up and faced me.

"I'm not 'holding out' for him. I applied for a teaching fellowship in Hong Kong, and I got it."

"You applied for a fellowship? You never told me!"

"I should have but I didn't want you—I didn't want you meddling with—with what I want or don't want! I want to do what I want, and I want to figure out what I want, without your input—"

"Jesus, Annie, I can't keep waiting for you forever. A year in Paris, okay. Another year in Rome—well, it's already too much time apart. But if you're going to start wandering around Asia—"

"I didn't ask you to wait for me—"

"But we left open the possibility—" He looked off into space. "God, what an idiot I am. You're breaking up with me, that's what you're doing. You don't have the fucking guts to say, 'I'm breaking up with you,' so you're going to China."

"How can I be breaking up with you when we haven't been together for two years? And I'm going to Hong Kong because I want to go, that's all. And if that means you need to stop thinking about me, well then—stop thinking about me! Okay, there it is." We'd been through variations of this scene in the US before I left for Paris, then in Paris before I left for Rome, but this time I knew we were at the end.

He threw the bed covers back, got up, pulled his pants on, and started packing.

"Doug, what are you doing? Don't be ridiculous. Stay. It's almost midnight and it's raining."

"I'm sure I can find a room near the train station." He shoved his toiletry kit into his backpack. "You could have had the decency to do this by mail, so I wouldn't have wasted my money on a plane ticket. I'm a graduate student, remember? I'm not rich, you know."

"I only heard about the fellowship today."

"And if you hadn't gotten it? You never had any plans of coming back to me, did you? You've just had me parked in the garage as a kind of—back-up plan."

Doug was right and I felt ashamed. Then I remembered Signora Gianina's words, *Look at you. You're gorgeous. You're splendid.* It was time for me to believe them. "For your information, I don't need a back-up plan."

He buckled his belt with a sharp, angry gesture. "Well, good luck to you, then." Swinging his backpack up and onto his shoulders, he opened the bedroom door, marched out into the living area, saluted Nathan, and stormed out the door.

"It looks like your man is gone," Nathan said.

I sat down on the couch next to him.

"He's gone all right." A pathetic, solitary tear rolled down my cheek.

"That's what you wanted, wasn't it?" Nathan said.

"Yeah, but it's a miserable business anyway."

"Come on over here for a cuddle."

Nathan put his guitar down and extended an arm. Scooting closer to him, I rested my head on his shoulder.

"Poor not-so-little Foxy," he cooed.

"I wish it could have ended on a friendlier note."

"You want me to sleep with you tonight?" Nathan asked. "I mean—keep you company?"

"No," I said. "But thanks for offering."

In my dreams that night, interrupted by the sound of rain, I revisited the little attic apartment Doug had rented in Cambridge, where I'd stayed with him for a month after graduating from college. I was back in time yet knowing the future, knowing how things would inevitably come to an end for us. And this foreknowledge made me cling to him, even as I had the taste of loss in my mouth.

I woke up the next morning yearning for another meeting. My reasons weren't admirable: I wanted Doug to forgive me for having led him on so that I might be relieved of guilt. But I had no way of getting in touch with him. We didn't have cell phones, of course, so my only option was to prowl the neighborhood near the train station, past the pizza joints and cafés with Eritrean refugees, in the hopes of running into him, but chances were I wouldn't find him. He would probably take off for Florence earlier than originally planned; maybe he'd already left. So I didn't go look for him.

I went into the bathroom and sat on the toilet to pee. Looking down I saw, in a puddle of water on the floor near

my feet, a dozen tiny scorpions, all dead, that had washed in
with the rain through the cracked window. There were few
creatures that revolted me as much as the scorpion, and the
sight of their tan, articulated bodies and tails, all curled and
still, sent a series of shudders down my spine.

I stood up from the toilet and leapt over their little bodies.
Hopefully, Nathan would dispose of them when he woke up.

The next morning, a Thursday, Sergio sat at his desk in the
school office and I was in my usual spot in the chair across
from him. He was sympathetic.

"A relationship is like a car—the older it gets, the harder
it becomes to trade it in for another. But at a certain point, you
can't keep on taking it to the garage to be fixed. If it doesn't
run, you have to abandon it by the side of the road and keep
going on your own, even if it means by foot."

I grimaced. Though I wasn't "together" with Sergio, I
wasn't exactly "on my own," either.

"And," he went on, "that leaves you free, either to go
to Asia or to stay here." He rubbed his nose. "What are you
going to do?"

"I'm going to accept the fellowship, I guess."

"And then, afterward, you'll come back to Italy and settle down?"

"I don't know what 'settle down' would mean—"

"I mean, like your aunt—face the fact that you belong
here—"

"How could you possibly know where I belong?"

"You're right. I don't," he said. "But the main thing is
. . ." He paused, visibly perked up. "All this means you're free
this weekend, right?"

I was too astonished to stay angry. Sergio lived so entirely
in the moment that he couldn't project forward in time to my
leaving Italy. And some of that attitude must have rubbed off

on me, because I also couldn't wrap my mind around the idea of leaving. Like some split personality, I had two scenarios going on in my head simultaneously: in one I was headed to Asia, and in the other I stayed put, found myself another apartment, and continued my life in Rome.

"After all," Sergio continued, "you don't want to be alone after a break-up. I'll check with Olivia. I'm sure she'd like you to come. I'm going down to Sperlonga early tomorrow to pick up some supplies for the house, but she could pick you up after school and drive you down tomorrow night or Saturday morning."

There was something on my mind. "You know that every time I come down, Nazzaro asks me to go back to the discothèque with him? And every time I say no."

"But you had fun that time you went with him? Being DJ at the discothèque, you liked it, right?"

"I did—but I'm not interested in him, so why does he keep asking?"

"Because—you have to understand Italian small-town mentality here—you are American, that means you are rich—"

* "What?"

"Yes, American means rich, means landers-at-Anzio, saviors-of-Italy-from-fascist-nightmare, means creators-of-Marshall-Plan, means all kinds of things! And for Nazzaro to be seen at the local disco with an American woman is a kind of—how do you say?—plume in his hat. Besides, I told him, hands off, so you can go out with him and he won't bother you."

"And you won't be jealous?"

"I won't be jealous. Promise. No more silly tantrums."

That evening, Olivia called me at home.

"Sergio told me about the break-up. You must be down in the dumps."

"It wasn't fun, but I'll be okay."

"You want to visit us again this weekend? I'll pick you up tomorrow night at school."

"Sure," I said.

"I had an exhausting week. Do you mind if we stay in Rome tomorrow night and go down early on Saturday? Would that be okay?"

I thought about spending the night alone with Olivia in their Roman apartment. My lover's fiancée was one of the kindest, most hospitable people I'd ever met. How could I continue sleeping with her guy?

"That makes sense," I said. "Let's spend the night in Rome and then drive down the next morning."

10. The Fact of Olivia

Friday after class, Olivia came by to get me and we headed southeast toward the periphery of the city.

"We'll have something simple to eat and try to get to bed early," she said as we entered an outlying neighborhood of fascist-era apartment blocks. "I'd like to set out for Sperlonga by eight or nine tomorrow."

Their Rome apartment lay in the direction of the highway that led to the coast. It would be like stopping in Brooklyn overnight on the way from Manhattan out to the north shore of Long Island.

"Okay," I said. "I'm surprised Sergio went down early. I've never known him to take a day off from work."

"There are some suppliers that aren't open on weekends, in this case the place where we're getting the stone pavers for the bathroom. Sergio's very choosy, so it's not like his cousins can do it for him. He says they have no taste or judgment." She smiled. "He wants everything to be perfect. One should begin things well, he says. Meaning our life together. I like his seriousness about it."

I gazed out the window as we moved into a zone with lower, grit-streaked construction.

"Not that everything is rosy," she went on, her eyes on the traffic. "But I'm not going to go into that while I'm driving. What should I make you for dinner? Maybe some *pappardelle* with meat sauce? Italian comfort food."

Olivia turned off the main road onto a side street and into a parking lot next to a drab apartment complex. As we climbed the cement steps up to the building's second floor and walked down a hallway to a small unit with sad, plastic blinds, I thought of using this time alone with her to spit out the unpleasant truth. No, that might backfire, she might blame me instead of Sergio, it would be better to plant in her mind suspicions of a more general nature about Sergio's fidelity, in which case I—false friend that I was, about to spend the night in her company—should keep my mouth shut and write an anonymous letter, as Signora Gianina had suggested. But did I have the courage—or the heartlessness—necessary to destroy Olivia's plans? Did I want Sergio enough to steal her place? My longing for him crashed against the reef of my compassion for her as she opened the front door, threw her keys into a bowl in the kitchen, and tied an apron around her waist.

"What can I do to help?" I asked.

"There's some stuff for salad in the fridge that you can wash in that colander over there."

As Olivia took a packet of homemade meat sauce out of the freezer, I glanced around. The kitchen was a tiny appendage to the living room and the apartment, also miniature, was poorly furnished compared to their Sperlonga home. The cost of living in Rome was high by Italian standards and this was all they could afford. When they moved back to Sergio's hometown, they would enjoy a higher standard of living.

"So you think it's really over with your boyfriend?" Turning her heart-shaped face away from the pan where she was stirring sauce, Olivia looked at me with sympathy.

"Yes," I said, "we've drifted too far apart." I trotted out the usual platitudes about relationships running their course even as, in the back of my mind, I returned to the idea of the anonymous letter. If Olivia learned that it was *me* who was the Other Woman, our friendship would end and her face would express anger and hatred instead of concern. "Of course, it's very painful, and I feel terribly guilty," I added.

"Guilty about hurting him?"

"Yes."

"But it's the right thing to do if you don't want to marry him," Olivia said. "I mean, you're sure you want to break up with him, right? Because there is no such thing as a perfect relationship."

She spoke with the authority of a woman who'd been married many years or had had many relationships, neither of which was the case.

"Yeah, I know."

The water came to a boil, and we fell silent as she shook some wide noodles into the pot and finished putting together our meal. There was a smooth grace to the way she moved from task to task, a Zen-like attention to detail in the way she chopped garlic and rinsed a bundle of greens in a big pot of water. Sergio had spoken the truth when he'd said she was right for the role of wife and mother. I thought of the pathetic meals I made for Nathan and myself—how I never had the necessary ingredients in the fridge and impatiently skipped steps in recipes. Lacking the discipline needed to be a good homemaker, I felt like both a voyeur and a spy as I studied my rival and collected the information I might need to step into her shoes, if it came to that.

"We have a fold-up cot here," she said, "but you might sleep better in the big bed with me."

After dinner, we went into the bedroom and changed into our nightclothes. She turned her back to me when she undressed, and I noticed she kept her panties and bra on under her pajamas. Was that Catholic modesty? She put on a light bathrobe and, sitting cross-legged on the bed, asked me about the fellowship, and I told her about it.

"Are you going home this summer?" she asked.

"I don't think so. I'd rather go straight from here or Paris to Hong Kong."

"I'm hoping you'll be here for our wedding."

"I might be," I said, hoping not to be.

"You have to come," she said. "It would mean a lot to me." She reached across the bed and gently touched my wrist.

"Well—" I hesitated. Why was she so eager to have me at her wedding? I wanted a way out. "I was thinking of doing some traveling in Europe, maybe with my cousin Robin. Then I'm going to Hong Kong."

"I'll move the wedding up to before you leave. You can bring your cousin— what's her name again?"

"Robin—"

"You can bring Robin to the wedding. I'm fine with that. I want you there. Please."

Great. Because of me, Sergio would get married even earlier. "Okay, I'll be there." I was trapped.

She took a deep breath. "I need the moral support. Because the truth is that things aren't going that well with us right now," she said. "I don't think my family is going to attend."

"What's going on?"

"My mother can't forgive Sergio for taking me to live with him before marriage." Tears welled up in her eyes. "I think I told you that she lives and works in Terracina, which is just twenty minutes down the coast from Sperlonga, but I never see her because she won't have anything to do with me."

She paused as she reached for a tissue. Terracina, a beachside resort, was a favorite destination for working class Italian families. I imagined Olivia's mother in a black dress, with a gold cross on her ample bosom, down on her knees scrubbing a linoleum floor in a restaurant or a hotel there.

Olivia blew her nose then continued. "Yes, what we did was against Catholic law, but it's the 1970s, and I knew from the beginning that Sergio would marry me. But my mother believes I've sinned and will burn in hell for it." She fell silent.

"But you don't think you will—burn in hell—do you?"

"No, of course not. I mean, there's the spirit of the law and the letter of the law. Though, it's caused so much trouble with my mother that I've come to regret living together before marriage. And my aunts agree with her, of course. Only Nina, my younger sister, has been on my side and said she'd come to the wedding no matter what, but I think she's changing her mind now because my mom is putting so much pressure on her. So maybe no one from my family will be there! That's why I want you to come."

My heart went out to her. "I'll be there. Of course I will."

"And Sergio has been more distant recently."

"He's moody by nature, isn't it? That's the way he is at school, anyway."

"Right now it's worse than usual. I know he's angry with my family because they'd promised us money that now they're not going to give us, and he can't forgive their going back on their word. I don't think he'd change his mind about marrying me because I know he wants children more than anything else in the world—but I can't bear it sometimes—he's been so distant with me."

I started perspiring. I was a traitor and an interloper, a creator of discord and trouble.

"Maybe he's worried about the future," I offered. "I mean, if you guys are going to settle down in Sperlonga, he'll have to find a job there, right? Maybe that won't be so easy to do."

"He'll find something. He's smart and hard working. I'm sure he can find a job, if not in Sperlonga, then in Gaeta. There are a lot of businesses there because of the port."

"But maybe *he's* not so confident."

"Maybe you're right," she said. "Maybe I have more confidence in him than he has in himself."

"That's probably it."

"I'm probably underestimating Sergio's concerns about supporting a family. Maybe it's all coming to a head for him as we get closer to the wedding."

"So you just need to be patient and supportive."

"You're right," she said.

Olivia turned off the light and got under the covers, and I did the same, my mind spinning. We lay silently in the dark for a couple of minutes.

"Anna," she whispered, "you still awake?"

"Yeah," I said.

"There's something else that could be bothering him, I don't know." Her voice became even softer. "I like sex, but I'm not able to—to fully enjoy it the way some women are."

"Oh."

"Do you think a man might be bothered by that?"

"I don't know. Have you asked him?"

"No, I haven't." She paused. "Anna, you don't have to answer this if you don't want to, but are you able—were you able with your boyfriend—to—to fully enjoy— intimacy?"

"You mean, was I able to have an orgasm? Is that the question?" I couldn't bear her tiptoeing around the word.

"Yes. Were you?"

It was dark, I couldn't see her face, but I imagined her blushing.

"Yes," I said. So, her sexual inhibitions were feeding Sergio's discontent, along with her lack of interest in books and politics and the wider world. I felt sorry for her, wanted to help, give her hope. "But not at the very beginning. We started young—I was fifteen—"

"Fifteen!"

She fell silent.

"You need to read some books, Olivia, and learn to ask for the stimulation you need—"

"It's not that I'm ignorant, Anna—it's—it's the way I feel about certain things—the things that aren't directly related to procreation . . ."

That word—"procreation"—brought me to a stop. I wasn't about to battle with centuries of Church indoctrination.

"You'll work it out, one way or another," I said.

"I shouldn't let myself get so worked up about everything. Thanks, Anna, thanks for listening to me talk about this."

"I'm happy to listen."

"And Anna," she added, "I'm really hoping you'll come back to Italy when you finish your fellowship year in Hong Kong."

"It's possible. This feels like home now."

"You could be a special auntie for our kids."

"Sure," I said and for an instant, vaguely, I meant it.

As we lay in the dark, a sense of horror at the situation and my part in it exploded within me. Olivia's regular breathing soon suggested she was asleep and, propping myself up on a pillow, I gazed at her still profile in the light filtering in through the curtains. I looked at her enviously, affectionately, guiltily. I wanted to wake her up and confess my sin, not in order to get Sergio for myself but to prevent *her* from entering into a marriage with a man who wouldn't be faithful to her. In terms of intellect, he was her superior, having gone to college and acquired the habit of reading, and he would soon tire of small conversations about food and babies. But in terms of heart, she was truer and deeper than he'd ever be, she was *good* and *honest*—qualities I couldn't claim for myself or anyone else I knew. And when Sergio tired of her in bed, he would find pleasure elsewhere, as he had done with me. If I hurt her now with the truth, I might spare her much suffering down the line. Yes, she should know the truth about Sergio—and about me—she should know that I'd done this ghastly thing of sleeping with her man while befriending her. For hours I stared at her profile, wanting to confess and ask forgiveness, to bludgeon her with the facts and spare her inevitable misery the way you'd shoot a horse with a broken leg or take a rock to the head of a half-chewed rabbit the cat brought home. I swore to myself that I'd do it in the morning.

But when we woke up lying on our sides, facing each other, my nerve failed me. Even with one cheek pressed into the pillow, her face still had a heart shape. If I told Olivia the truth and she broke up with Sergio, she would be a woman stranded without husband or family, an outcast sinner—damaged goods. Wait a minute—what year was it? This was the reality, though, of how she'd see herself and how her family would see her. She'd lived with a man before marriage and no number of confessions, Ave Marias, or holy water could repair the holy hymen.

She opened her eyes and met mine with a sweet smile.

"Thanks again for listening last night," she said. "And I'm sorry. I meant to give you an opportunity to talk about your break-up and instead all I did was talk about Sergio."

"It's okay. After all, things are over with Doug—but just beginning for you and Sergio."

We got up, had toast and weak coffee for breakfast—"We can have the coffee Brooklyn-style since Sergio isn't here," she said—and soon were dressed and off for the coast.

We arrived at the Sperlonga apartment to find Sergio and his cousins, Flavio and Nazzaro, in the kitchen engaged in *scopa*, a popular Italian card game played with the same Neapolitan deck Gianina used for fortune-telling. The brightly colored cards with medieval knights and pages reminded me of my conversation with the Signora. "You must decide what to do—or not to do," she'd said.

"The American girls, they have arrived," Nazzaro said, with an inscrutable glance in my direction.

Sergio stood up. "Come see what we have brought you. A little gift. Eh!" he threw his hands merrily up in the air. "You see, we spent the morning intending to please you."

"Yes, come look at the beauties," Nazzaro said, motioning Olivia and me toward the sink.

I went over and glanced down into a red plastic bucket at a haul of snails, all tightly pulled back into shells glistening with water.

"Might there be something else on the menu, perhaps?" I inquired.

Nazzaro picked one up and holding it in his palm, lifted it to my face.

"The *signorina* doesn't like?" he asked me.

"Not particularly."

"Then we'll have to find something else to please you, won't we?"

He was standing so close to me that I could smell his tobacco-saturated person.

"How long will it take you to think like an Italian?" Sergio said, waving both arms at me in mock impatience. "This"— with a dramatic gesture at the bucket—"is free and delicious, it's all we need."

"I don't think so," I said.

Olivia laughed. "Don't worry, I'll make something else, too."

"Okay," Sergio said. "Do what you like. The three of us are off to get the tiles—"

"I thought you were getting the tiles yesterday," Olivia said, looking unhappy. They didn't have much time alone together.

"I got half of them—they're in the basement—and the other half is waiting for us to pick them up. Because that's the way things are here. Why make one trip when you can make two? You know that, my dear, and you must give Anna some lessons about these things, so that when she comes back to Italy from Asia, she'll be prepared for the way everything practical is impossible here. Everything!"

He spoke in a staccato that was half-humorous, half-wired with exaggerated manic energy. Yes, he had moments of terrible suffering when he thought of my leaving.

The three men were heading toward the door when Nazzaro turned back and pointed a finger toward me.

"Tonight, I am taking you back to the disco, okay? No arguments this time. I told everyone I was bringing back the special, the authentic American DJ."

"Uh, okay—"

"Until later then," he said and gave me a complicitous wink on the way out.

"You going with him?" Olivia asked as the door shut. "It might cheer you up, or at least distract you."

"I suppose. He's kind of strange."

"Oh, not really. Let's go to the butcher's and get you something for lunch —instead of snails."

"I can just have pasta—"

She was already reaching for her net shopping bag. "Don't be ridiculous. You need a proper lunch."

"Fine," I said. The tasks of the day were a welcome distraction after the upheaval with Doug and my night's moral debate. To be in the reality of things as they were—errands, meals, Sergio's family—felt good, and the way Olivia fussed over me was touching. There was no way I'd ever try to take her place.

When we came back from the butcher's, the *frutteria*, and a quick stop for cappuccino and pastry, we found that the snails had woken up, escaped the red bucket, and were now making their way up the edges of the sink, across the counter, and down the cabinet toward the floor, their tiny horns wobbling as they pulled along the shells above them.

The day went by as days did in Sperlonga, with family members and friends coming and going. The snails, gathered and cooked in olive oil, garlic, and white wine, were considered a treat and served up to various visitors over the course of a couple of hours, along with red wine from what Aunt Robertina called her "select" collection. Of course, Sergio whispered to me, there was no such thing as a select collection, only a big wooden barrel storing wine gotten from a friend in the country. Sergio's father appeared just long enough to eat a plateful, grunt at everyone, and go back down to his apartment. Flavio appeared and Teresa with Bobo in her arms, and I shuddered as Bobo ingested a few snails and his parents applauded him. Nazzaro left, saying he'd be back to pick me up between nine and ten. By four o'clock everyone had dispersed for a siesta, except for Sergio and Flavio, who busied themselves with unloading the tiles.

After a nap, it was time to start thinking about the next meal, and the whole routine started all over again. Olivia and I were back in the kitchen when Sergio appeared with an announcement.

"I'm going out for dinner."

"Where?" Olivia asked.

"Flavio and I are going to eat with a guy who has a piece of property we have our eye on."

I must have looked puzzled.

"That's how it's done here," Sergio explained. "You have a good meal together, you talk about the possibility of property changing hands, how much, have some more wine, a little less expensive please, a little more wine, okay, let's compromise, etcetera! No agents, no mortgages. I have the money, he has the land, and we just have to agree to do it. Then, once it's done, starts the Italian nightmare of the contract and the lawyers." He spoke rapidly.

"And what will you do with the land?" I asked.

"Keep it, build on it, trade it—who knows! You see, in Italy if you have money saved up, what to do with it is a problem. If you put it in the bank, some *ufficiale* could declare a surprise tax, no reason needed, happy birthday, whatever! But a piece of land —is a piece of land."

"Well, good luck," Olivia said, "and have a good time."

She turned toward me after he left. "Sergio has this restless side—that's what this property thing is about, more than investing. He likes the excitement. And if he's got to be restless, better the wheeling and dealing than—what a lot of Italian husbands do, if you know what I mean."

"I see your point," I said, temptress that I was. "Though all this activity must be hard on you at times."

"Well, yes, but tonight it makes things easier in a way. No guys. We can make exactly what we want for dinner." She attempted to hide her disappointment.

We were chopping vegetables for minestrone when the phone rang and Olivia picked up.

"Nina!" she said. "Where are you?"

It was the younger sister she'd told me about, the only one in her family who remained in touch. To give her privacy, I stepped out of the room and into Sergio's study.

"Yeah, sure, sure," she was saying from the other room. "But I have someone here—uh-huh, uh-huh. Okay, okay. In an hour or so."

I heard her hang up. She came and found me in the study.

"Listen," she said, "my sister's in Terracina, and she wants me to go stay with her tonight. She's been talking to my mother and thinks that this might be the moment for a reconciliation. This is terribly rude of me, but would you mind if I left you after dinner? You're going to the disco with Nazzaro tonight anyway, right? And I'll be back tomorrow by lunchtime. Terracina is just twenty minutes from here."

"Sure, sure," I said. "That would be great if you and your mom made up. I wouldn't want to get in the way of that."

"Thanks so much, Anna. Nina's really taking my side. I'm so happy."

After dinner, she gathered her sleep things, scribbled Sergio a note, and picked up her car keys.

"He won't mind," she said. "He'll probably be out really late with Flavio anyway." She went to a kitchen drawer for an extra key to the apartment. "Here. Make yourself at home." And she left.

Thus it was that I found myself in the curious position of being alone in Sergio and Olivia's apartment. I walked down the hall and stood on the threshold of their bedroom and looked at their four-poster bed. I headed back into the living room and looked at my little cot with its fluffed up pillow and blanket neatly folded at the foot. Nazzaro would be by to pick me up soon. I went into the study and looked at Sergio's library again. What did the future hold for him, a man of education and culture stuck in a small town where no one, not even his wife-to-be, ever read a newspaper or a book? I wondered what time he'd be back, whether I'd see him before bedtime. I yearned for him with every cell in my stupid body.

The thought that he deserved a more nourishing life led me to wondering what kind of life we might have together. I imagined persuading him to move to a more sophisticated Italian metropolis like Turin or Milan. Although he might be at first reluctant to move north, once we had children, he'd see that Sperlonga would be a stultifying place for them to grow up in, that they deserved a wider opening to the world. Milan, capital of fashion and design, might be our best bet. Living with Sergio, my Italian would soon be good enough for me to continue my studies at a local arts university. In Milan, Sergio would find a managerial job in one of the big companies and I could get in on the creative end—clothes, furniture, automobiles, whatever, I didn't care. We'd have a big apartment with tall windows and ornate moldings running around the ceilings and a fireplace with a marble frontispiece and mantel. When we hosted dinner parties for groups of cosmopolitan guests, the oval table would be set with floral-patterned terracotta dinnerware. I imagined our adorable Italian-American children coming in to say good night, I saw myself planting a kiss upon my daughter's forehead, then on the rosy cheek of a little boy on my lap. Suddenly I wanted all the things that I'd never wanted before—children and a sense of place and community. Because yes, I did love him. This wasn't just a casual affair or another passing relationship; it was the real deal. And I could accept ties that bound me if they were to Sergio and a place like Milan. I would have a man like Tito and a home like his, but unlike Doris, I'd be in a legitimate relationship.

And a life in a capital of culture was something Sergio had once wanted, too, and would want again when I made it possible for him. Certainly it was the life he deserved. If Olivia had to be "sacrificed" in the process, in the long run she'd be better off for it. A break now might free her from her old-fashioned Catholic attitudes and initiate her into the twentieth-century. Certainly it would save her from a marriage with a philandering husband. And Sergio was happy with me sexually so, married to me, he wouldn't philander. Ultimately Olivia would find someone who could be faithful to her, maybe a Catholic believer her mother would accept, so that they could be one big, happy family.

My reverie was interrupted by Nazzaro knocking at the door. He led me down to the so-called family Mercedes.

"You see, I've come for you—*in style,*" he added, switching to English. "For our night out."

"*Bene,*" I said. "Let's go."

As we headed down the shoreline highway to Gaeta, I asked him about his plans to go to South America.

"I'm getting the money together. I'm not sure which country yet. I like the idea of Argentina, of course. We Italians have a special relationship with Argentina."

"You think you'll be happy there?"

He shrugged. "I will go, make a bundle of money, then return."

"How's your Spanish?"

"*Muy bien, muy bien.*" He smiled.

"Sounds like you're all set to go then."

"I'd hoped to have a companion, maybe a lively American, but it looks like the one I was interested in isn't going to work out."

"You'll meet someone there, an exotic Argentinian beauty."

"Who knows? Life is a game of roulette." He turned his thin, flat face toward me and gave me a cryptic look.

It was past ten when we reached the club. A couple of drinks ended my moral debate, leaving me oddly light and cheerful. With Olivia gone for the night, I might have some time alone with Sergio later on, depending on when he came home. Manically energized, I climbed the steps up to the DJ booth, where the guy in charge gave me his seat in front of the turntables as he'd done during my first visit months before. I thought he was good-looking—everyone was that night. A few songs later, I was on the dance floor with Nazzaro, then with a couple of his friends, one after the other. Special status went along with being the only American in the dance joint of a small town, and I was enjoying it. When I got danced out, I went back up to the booth to relieve the cute DJ again.

Around midnight, thinking that Sergio might soon return home, I asked Nazzaro to take me back, screaming over the loud music to be heard. He nodded in agreement. As we headed out, the dancing crowd gave a round of applause for my work in the booth, and I bowed a merry acknowledgment in return.

The air outside felt refreshing after the smoke inside the club. High from drink and dancing, grateful that Nazzaro hadn't tried to put the moves on me again, I felt almost happy. We got into the front seat of the Mercedes. Instead of starting the car, Nazzaro reached into the back seat for a paper bag.

"An apple," he said. "I'm hungry. Want a slice?"

"Uh, sure."

He took a knife out of his pocket, flattened the paper bag across his lap, and began to quarter the apple. Light coming in from a street lamp reflected off the blade of his knife and the chunky gold ring on his left middle finger.

"I sharpened this recently," he said, "so look how easily it slices."

I shifted uneasily in my seat. I was alone at night in a car, in a town most Americans would never have heard of, with a man holding a very sharp knife.

"It's almost like the apple was meant to fall apart," he continued.

He picked up a piece and handed it to me. I ate it slowly, keeping an eye on him.

"So you approve of Olivia?" he asked.

"Yes, of course," I said, surprised. "She's a dear friend."

"We're all very pleased with Olivia. Very, very pleased. She *fits in*, if you know what I mean." There was a long pause as he popped a whole slice of apple into his mouth. The piece made a lump in his cheek then disappeared as he chewed and swallowed it. "And her family owns property in Brooklyn. Perhaps you didn't know that?"

"No, I didn't."

"The problems with her mother will be resolved eventually. The property in Brooklyn, it's a nice thing to have. It's rental property." He looked at me again. "Does your family own land?"

I cleared my throat. "My family has property in New York—the house they live in."

"Not quite the same. Rental property is a particularly beautiful thing."

"Is that what Sergio and Flavio are looking to buy from the guy they're meeting with tonight?" I wanted to change the direction of the conversation.

He nodded. "Yes." He shifted in his seat, turning his upper body to look at me. "And the thing you have to understand about Sergio—" for emphasis, he waved the open knife a little too close—"is how smart he is. I mean, he has a plan to better not only himself but our whole family. And should anyone try to get in the way of that plan—" he stopped waving the knife and held it still in the air, slowly bringing its point up to my chin, "well, we—his family—wouldn't tolerate it. Do you want another slice?" He drew the knife away from me and back to the apple. "Here, let me cut out the core. One must—" he paused, gave me a sharp look—"cut out the bad part first." He extended another piece of apple.

I shook my head. "I've had enough." I felt cold; my heart was racing. "Take me back to the house, Nazzaro."

"Sure." He popped the second slice of apple into his mouth and chewed it. He snapped the knife shut and slid it into his pocket. "As long as you understand what I'm saying."

"I understand."

"And that I'm not leaving for Argentina until I see him safely married to Olivia."

"All right, Nazzaro." The blood was pounding in my ears and I had to pee.

We drove back in silence. At one point, the knife slipped out of his pocket and onto the car seat. With his left hand still on the wheel as he continued to drive, he opened the knife again with the right, casually wiped the blade on his pant leg, then closed it and stuck it deeper into his pocket.

II. The Night of the Rooster

Back in Sergio and Olivia's apartment, I locked the door behind me and shivered, remembering the glint of Nazzaro's gold-capped teeth and the silver gleam of his knife. If he understood that there was something between Sergio and me, how long would it take the rest of his family to figure it out? And Olivia? I'd heard terrible stories about the back country in Italy, about how people "disappeared." Matters of "honor," which, to an American mind, might merit at most a few punches between men or the slaps of a catfight between women, could lead to gruesomeness here. The air was close and humid as I took off my clothes and stretched out, perspiring in my underwear, on the cot in Sergio and Olivia's living room. I'd stay awake until Sergio came home so I could tell him what happened.

Approaching thunder rumbled like the purr of a slumbering cat god when I heard the key in the lock and Sergio's step in the foyer. He turned the lights on and stepped into the kitchen. He would be leaning over the counter, reading Olivia's note explaining she'd gone to her sister's. "*Va bene*," he said to himself. For some reason I said nothing, just listened. There was the sound of the fridge opening and closing, of a glass clinking on the table and being filled, then of his walking back into the foyer and from there into the living room, until he stood over me.

"Anna," he whispered. "Are you awake?"

"Yes."

He sat down next to me on the little cot and unbuttoned his shirt. "Flavio's car broke down, and we had to push it." He took off his T-shirt and handed it to me. "Feel. I'm drenched in sweat."

"You sure are."

The T-shirt, warm and damp, felt nice in my hand—that's how viscerally connected we were. He lay down next to me and drew me close. I moved my head onto his shoulder. There was another low rumble of thunder and a splash of rain on the living room window.

"It should have rained ten minutes ago," he said. "That would have been refreshing."

"What's wrong with the car?"

"I don't know. We'll worry about it tomorrow."

I liked how calm he could be about such an annoyance.

"How did the dinner go?" I asked.

"Fine, fine. The deal is in the bag. And you? Nazzaro behaved?"

"Sergio, he threatened me! I think he knows about us. Or suspects. He wants me gone."

"You mustn't take him seriously—"

"We were in his car and he took out his knife—to peel an apple supposedly, but he actually brought the blade up to my face—while telling me how badly he wants to see you and Olivia married—"

"Jesus! That's the way the mind of the petty Italian works. And the mind of the *contadino*—peasant—gets smaller as you move south. You have to understand, Nazzaro's father, Roberto, is from Sicily. There's a reason my father hardly speaks to either of them. They have no manners and are very primitive in their thinking."

"But Sergio! This was more than bad manners—he seemed serious."

"No, I don't think so. He was bluffing."

"You don't *think* so? I don't find that reassuring. He seems like a Mafioso to me."

"I tell you, it's a southern type. It's as though there were some kind of Italian hoodlum gene—"

"Then how could you send me out with him?"

"This hoodlum gene—if Nazzaro has it—it's recessive! He's rough around the edges, but not dangerous. He likes melodrama, that's all. Really, I don't think he was serious."

"You'll say something to him, won't you? Tell him to leave me alone. Or would that confirm his suspicions?"

"Don't worry about it. I'll make it clear that he's not permitted to make you uncomfortable."

We fell silent. Another roll of thunder then, absurdly, in the middle of the night, the sound of the neighbor's rooster punctuating the darkness.

"Sergio, I want to take you away from here." There it was, the fantasy that had been simmering inside me, now bursting out. "Let's go away, some place north like Milan. We could have a good life there."

"What about work? You think I can get off the train in Milan and say, 'Here I am, look how wonderful I am, hire me'—eh? I have no connections in Milan. You can't just land some place in Italy and get a job if you don't know anybody. Life here is about exchanging favors. I do something for so-and-so, then his cousin, father, whoever, does something for me. Besides, I don't understand the people up north, they're different."

Here was the ancient Italian mentality formed by the history of a peninsula divided into city-states, each with its own ruling class, dialect, and customs. His speech brought home just how provincial he was, but I persisted.

"You're smart, you could find a job."

"And your dreams of going around the world? Of a year in Hong Kong?"

"You've changed my dreams. We can go to Hong Kong together some day."

"And what about my father?"

"We'll take him to Milan with us," I said, though I couldn't quite see Luca at that oval dining table with the tall windows looking out over an elegant boulevard. Our guests would be talking about international politics, Verdi, Pirandello—and Sergio's father would sit there and grunt. Then grunt again.

Sergio fell silent, as though considering my idea seriously. "I don't think my father would be happy there." He shook his head in the shadows. "Besides, my father and I, we're kept in Sperlonga by a ghost, the ghost of my mother. We can't leave."

"What happened to your mother?"

"She died when I was nine, she . . . Anna, I'll tell you some other time. It's too terrible."

"You can tell me now—"

"No, not now. Anyway, not only is there my father, but the rest of my family—they're all counting on me. Roberto and Nazzaro I don't care so much about, but Robertina is my father's sister, and Flavio is a good man, but not so smart. He needs me to help him make his way through life so he can raise little Bobo properly. I'm the only one in my family who will ever make any real money." Pause. Gravitas. "And to bring dishonor on someone else is to bring it on oneself."

"Olivia won't be happy with you. You won't be happy together."

"Probably not. But she's happy enough now, and now is all anybody's got. And I don't know that life is about happiness, my dear."

"You don't think it's important to be happy?"

"That's an American idea. 'Life, liberty, and the pursuit of happiness'! But here, everything is about survival. If I told you the awful things I had to eat as a child when there was nothing in the pantry, your stomach would turn over. A man's duty is, first of all, to put food on the table and to do it *day after day* for self and family; secondly, to do meaningful things for other people. If I could convince Robertina to let me pay to have her teeth fixed, that would be an accomplishment. In short, eat, do a few good deeds for your tribe, and then, *basta*, you can die in peace."

"You could pay for her dental work if you were living somewhere else. People go away to get better jobs, then send money home—"

"But I have to be here to convince her. She thinks it's a waste of money. Eh—here you are in my arms, but what do you understand of the world I come from, of the poverty? I try to explain it to you, but if you haven't lived through it, you can't understand. The fact is, it makes one insecure and cautious. And when I think that one day you'll forget everything I've explained to you and remember me as a louse and a coward—it breaks my heart."

"Sergio—" I moved my hand up to his face. It felt wet, with sweat or tears, I didn't know. "Listen—"

He put a hand between my legs. "*Cara*—sweet, sweet honey—if only, *if only* I could go away with you and start over somewhere else. What a dream! But you must try to see the situation as clearly as I do—how I'm in a trap—then you'd understand that the only moment we have is this one, right here and now." He sat up, pulled off his underwear, then my pajama bottoms. "And with Olivia out, we have all night." He got on top and gently entered me. I was ready; I didn't need foreplay. His body felt light and comfortable above me, my body ecstatic to have him back after Doug. "We'll pay for this, of course," he went on. "With longing and missing and grief. We'll pay for it." He caressed my face, kissed me.

"For how long?"

"Months, years. I don't know."

We started on the cot then continued on the sofa and the floor, and later on, we moved down the hall, into the master bedroom and onto the four-poster bed he shared with Olivia, where we made love, thrashing like wild horses that won't be contained, as we created something in time that would prove inescapable. For that night would come back to me, years and decades later, in all its split, wounded beauty, beating at the door of memory, like a tropical storm hitting a beach and whipping palm branches straight up as the surf, too, goes vertical and boundaries between air and water dissolve. And it would keep coming back for years and decades, in the rumbling of thunder and the freshness of spring rain, in views of the sea and photos of Mediterranean whitewashed towns that would remind me, again and again, of Sperlonga. It would come back, during other travels, in the smell of cold stone and the fragrance of fish soup. It would come back in the first night with every subsequent lover, in the disappointment of not finding again the connection that I'd had with Sergio. It would follow me wherever I went—the rhythm of him moving inside me and the bliss of my giving myself over to him, completely and easily because he was a part of who I was.

When we could couple no more, I fought sleep in order to continue savoring our togetherness, yet when I did give in, there was the grace of the night extending itself through the alleys and byways of dreams that led me away from the realities waiting for us. When a rooster in the neighbor's backyard crowed in the darkness, I knew our night together was running out, and I fought sleep even harder, drinking in the sweetness of being held, as Sergio, also unwilling to drift off, kept pulling me closer. Tell me a story, he said a couple of times, and I'd say, I have no more stories, and we would start drifting off again, when the cock in the neighbor's backyard started in a second time, then for a third, disturbing our sleep, until finally Sergio sat up and, throwing his arms up into the air with comic drama, cried out, "Curse that crazy rooster! I'll eat him for dinner tonight!" I laughed, and he lay back down and curled around me, and I melted into him as I drifted back into a dream of the Italian countryside.

The sun was coming in through the cracks of the heavy shutters, making the dust dance in the rays of morning light, when the rooster went at it again, and Sergio said, "You should probably get up. Olivia will be back soon." He gave me a last kiss, and I sat up on the edge of the bed. He reached for my hand and held it for a moment.

"You have to be brave," he said. "When it's over, try not to look back too much. You have things to do, your path to discover. My life path is already locked in, but for you—anything is possible. And you—you deserve so much more than I can offer."

I looked at him, delirious from too much sex and too little sleep.

"Do you think that's possible—not to look back?"

"No," he said. "I don't. I don't think it's possible."

"My idea of us going to Milan is a good one."

"It's a wonderful idea! Maybe you're right and I'm just a coward. Listen, I'll think about it."

"You will?"

"Yes, I will."

I got up and walked back down the hall to my little cot in the living room, where I fell fast asleep.

Opening my eyes, I'd forgotten the mess I was in. I only felt myself rocking in the physical elation that comes after a passionate night, when I heard Olivia's voice coming from the kitchen and Sergio's responding in low serious tones.

I sat up and put panties and a T-shirt on with a sense of things ending and dying inside me, of little hopes being squelched, like wet grass squeaking under foot after rain.

I reached for my watch, which said noon, and thought of the crazy rooster, but the *gallo pazzo* had gone mute.

I slipped into my skirt and tied the laces of my sneakers.

There was a grumble in Sergio's voice and an insistence in Olivia's that made me grab my fedora with the sense of armoring myself for a blow to come.

As I stood up and went into the kitchen, I remembered pleading with Sergio to come away to Milan with me, how his words, "wonderful idea," had left me with a ray of hope.

Olivia was sitting across the table from Sergio, who had his back to me. She looked up at me and said, "My mother said she'd forgive me if we marry as soon as possible. So we're setting the date."

Sergio gave me a look of mute misery as I sat down across from him and Olivia stood up and headed to the stove, where she picked up the coffee pot and the pan of warm milk to make me a *caffè latte*.

"Soon then?" I asked.

Olivia returned and set the coffee down before me. "Yes. We've already done the *pubblicazione*, so it's just a matter of sending out invitations and reserving a restaurant—"

"What's a *'pubblicazione'*?" I asked.

"The marriage bans," she explained.

"I didn't know that was still done." I gave Sergio a hard look. He shrugged.

"Yes, of course," she said. "Can you come, if it's mid July? My mother is—ashamed of me," she blushed over her sin, "so she might not agree to see Sergio until after the wedding." She gently touched my shoulder. "It would help me so much if you were there. You'll come, won't you?"

"Your mother has caused you enough misery already," Sergio said, hunched over the table. "Why should it matter if she's there or not, as long as she gives us a check?"

"I thought we agreed—" Olivia began.

Sergio stood up. "I could use a shave," he said and left the room.

"He hates her," Olivia said, frowning. "I don't blame him for being angry, but I wish he'd speak about her respectfully." She sat down in his chair. "Things will work out, eventually. I'm sure they'll stop their war when our first child is born."

"Is that to be soon, do you think?" I asked.

She shrugged, lowered her voice. "To be truthful, he hasn't been much interested in that of late. But once we're married, I'm confident things will get back to normal." She gave me a subdued smile.

Her words confirmed my suspicion: Although Sergio wanted to honor his commitment to her, he had disconnected from her sexually because of me. But I didn't feel victorious. I looked at her. She was sweet and pretty and steady, and he'd go back to her as soon as I was gone, and they'd start making babies. I felt sick with jealousy.

"And what kind of wedding are you having?" I asked.

"You know how I want a church wedding and he doesn't. Well, we've compromised. The 'official' wedding will be in court, very short and simple. I'm not even going to wear a white dress, just my blue suit. Afterwards we'll have the traditional big reception and dinner, *in ristorante*, for family and friends and all the Multi Lingua teachers will be invited, too. We'll do the church wedding later in the fall, privately. The nice thing," she said with a mischievous grin, "is that Sergio's father is a die-hard Marxist, so he won't come to that."

"Sergio agreed to a Catholic ceremony?" I asked. He obviously loved her more than he knew.

"Yes, and to our children being baptized."

Stunned, I fell silent, stared off into space.

"What are you thinking?" she asked.

"Oh, uh, sorry—" I groped for something to say. "I was thinking about these scorpions I'm going to have to deal with tonight—they've been coming through the window into the bathroom."

Olivia looked startled.

"We'll drive you home later today," she said, "and Sergio can look at it, maybe come up with a solution to keep them out."

"Thanks."

There was the sound of the bathroom door opening and Sergio walking down the hall.

"I think I'll take my shower now," I said.

A little later, showered and dressed, I was sitting on the cot in the living room stuffing my toiletries into my Greek bag, when Sergio appeared.

"Olivia said you have a problem with scorpions in your bathroom." He looked at me gravely. "That's nasty."

"Oh, they were dead, so there's no need for you to worry—"

He came and stood a little closer to me with his hands in his blue jean pockets.

"They're confused because of the rain," he said. "Usually this is the dry season. You need some kind of barrier along the bottom edge of the window." He cleared his throat in that nervous reflex of his. "About how wide is the window?"

"I don't know. Maybe like this?" I placed my hands two feet apart.

"Or like this, more likely?" He placed his hands three feet apart.

It felt surreal to be discussing my scorpion problem when I'd just learned that his marriage to Olivia was around the corner. I shrugged and, pressing my lips together, gave him a hard stare.

"Why don't you come downstairs with me to the yard and we'll pick out a piece of wood?" he asked, motioning for me to follow him.

I grabbed my fedora and followed him downstairs to the ground floor, where I expected him to lead me outside through a door at the back of the foyer, but instead he continued down another flight down to the cellar. Was he taking me there because he wanted privacy to say something of significance or maybe hold me? No. Turning on the light, he gestured toward a big pile of sand-colored stone tiles and picked one up.

"What do you think?" he asked. "For the master bath?"

"Nice color—subdued and warm."

"Yes." He ran his fingers over the stone, cleared his throat, set it down. "I had some wood planks around here somewhere . . . No, these are too small." He showed me what looked like sawed-off ends of floor planks. "Maybe there's something in the backyard."

"You didn't tell me the marriage bans had already been published," I said, angry.

"It's a medieval tradition of ours. It gives people time to object."

Our eyes met.

"So I could object?"

He nodded. "You could object—and disgrace Olivia and me—and yourself, too."

"Thanks for laying it all out for me."

We went back up the stairs and out through the foyer into the backyard, a mere square of grass with a single lemon tree. On the other side of a wooden fence, a larger backyard held a small vegetable garden and a chicken coop.

"Look—for your hat." Sergio bent to pick up a chicken feather that had made its way to the base of the lemon tree.

He approached and as he reached up to stick it in the ribbon around my fedora, one of the roosters crowed. In spite of our misery, we looked at each other and laughed.

"Crazy rooster!" he said.

"Who lives there?"

"Mauro's family."

"Mauro, owner of Multi Lingua?"

"Yes. Remember, I told you we grew up together."

"Yes, I remember now."

"I have a complicated relationship with his parents right now. You see that fence? It used to be about half a meter to the east," he said, indicating how his yard had once extended further in that direction. "Then they decided they wanted some of my land. So Mauro I talk to, but his parents—no."

"I don't understand. What did they do? Move the fence in the middle of the night?"

"More or less."

"Can't you sue them or something?"

"If you knew how hopeless it is to take anything to court in this country—forget about it! Ah, here is the wood." There were some 1-by-6's leaning against the back wall of the building. "I'll take one of these to your apartment with a handsaw and we'll rig up a barrier." He picked one up and brushed it off with the back of his hand.

"Mauro lives in Rome now, doesn't he?" I asked.

"Insofar as he lives anywhere. Did you know he wants to open a whole string of schools between Rome and Florence, then eventually up to Milan? He wants to beat Berlitz, that's what it's about."

"So he's an example of someone who left Sperlonga—really left—and has been successful! Why shouldn't you do the same?" I kept my voice soft and quiet because, standing in the backyard, we would be visible to Olivia if she looked out of the window.

"Mauro has money from his papa, who has been a successful capitalist with a hotel on the beach here, which he turned into Sperlonga's one and only luxury resort. And using this same business brilliance, Papa provided Mauro the capital necessary to start a chain of schools. You see how it works: there must be a parent, somewhere, who makes enough of a 'cushion' to set the child free. Isn't that how it goes in America, too? The reason you feel free—and brave enough—to wander around the world for a few years is that you have a father to catch you, financially, if you fall flat on your face. Isn't that the case?"

"I've been doing a pretty good job supporting myself," I said. "I don't ask my parents for handouts."

"But in the case of an emergency, you could go home if you needed a roof over your head and a meal."

"I wouldn't go home no matter what. Not just because my mother's a drunk. She's also abusive. She used to hit me. I can't stand being around her. It's like—a physical revulsion." Ashamed of my mother, I'd never before depicted the full gravity of the situation.

"The situation with your mother is terribly sad." He paused to look at me. "I knew when I met you that you'd had a difficult childhood. But, my dear, the fact remains that, if you were stranded someplace, in Shanghai or Tokyo without a penny, your father would wire money to you at the local American Express. But there's no one in my family to catch me if I don't make a go of it." He dropped his voice to a whisper. "If things didn't work out in Milan, I couldn't ask my father or Flavio to send me money. They don't have any."

"Obviously there's nothing I can say that will change the way you see things."

"I'm more of a realist than you are, I guess."

"Let's go," I said.

He went to put the wood in the Fiat, and I climbed the stairs to the third floor. I felt angry, humiliated by having pleaded with him.

When I got back upstairs, I found Olivia, as I'd seen her so many times before, standing over the sink cleaning up. She was wearing her big black-frame glasses and had her black hair up in a bun at the nape of her neck. She unscrewed the top of the espresso maker and dumped the grounds and rinsed it out. Then she set to scrubbing out the little pot used for warming milk. She was destined to do this thousands of times in the course of her marriage. Sergio liked to describe himself as a man who'd had his consciousness raised in the sixties and believed in gender equality, but I'd never once seen him do the dishes. I wasn't cut out for a traditional marriage and never would be, so it was just as well things were ending.

Hearing me enter, Olivia turned her head to smile at me, and I noticed—in spite of her clunky glasses and heavy-set face—how very beautiful she was.

When we drove back to Rome a couple of hours later, I was silent, cramped up in the back seat, while Olivia talked to Sergio about arrangements for the wedding.

"We'll have to give the restaurant a menu," she said. "I was thinking about veal—everyone likes veal, don't they? What do you want to do about the wine, Sergio?"

"We'll use Robertina's, of course."

Sitting behind Sergio, I saw him occasionally glance up into the rear view mirror to look at me. Traffic was heavy. It was Sunday, late afternoon, and people were heading back to Rome after a rest at the beach. We had a long crawl through the periphery then finally reached my apartment on Via Pascoli.

"So this is where you live?" Sergio asked, parking.

"Yes," I said.

He got the plank of wood and his tools out of the back of the car, and the three of us passed through the heavy door and across the courtyard to the stairs down to my apartment. I opened the door to find, much to my relief, that Nathan wasn't there.

"Let me see what's going on in the bathroom," Sergio said.

"You want to show me your room?" Olivia asked me.

As Sergio checked out the scorpion situation, Olivia and I went into my bedroom. I flipped the bright overhead light on inside.

"It's not bad," Olivia said, sitting on the edge of the bed.

I sat down next to her. "Yeah, it's okay, if you don't mind being half-underground."

"So you're really going to Hong Kong?"

"Yes. It's ridiculous, in a way, now that I have working papers. Maybe there's a way to keep them valid until I come back to Rome . . . "

Sergio could be heard hammering in the background.

"I'm sure Mauro would give you your job back when you return. Of course, Sergio probably won't be at Multi Lingua anymore. Hopefully, he'll have found a job in Sperlonga by then."

"A lot of things will be different."

"I might even have a baby. Or a baby on the way." She leaned forward and dropped her voice. "I went off the pill this morning."

"Oh, well. You can go off the pill and your system can be frozen for months," I said. "I haven't had a period since I went off the pill last summer."

"That's weird."

I looked at her. "I doubt that will happen to you," I said. *Little Catholic baby-maker. May you give your life over to serial pregnancies.*

"I hope not."

She smiled sweetly, radiating love, and suddenly I was awe-struck, as though she were some fertility goddess. I couldn't relate to her happy anticipation of motherhood. The memory of my mother, drunk and angry, slapping and pushing me into a closet and locking the door, flitted through a back corridor of my mind again. Motherhood was, as I saw it, a drama destined to end in tragedy. But for Olivia, things would be different.

"I thought Catholics weren't supposed to take the pill," I said.

"The doctor prescribed it because my periods were heavy and painful," she said.

"Oh. That makes it okay, I guess."

"That's right."

Sergio appeared in the bedroom doorway.

"Everything's all cleaned up," he said. "And they won't come in anymore."

Olivia and I stood up and went to the bathroom to look at his work. Sergio had set up a plank along the outside of the bottom windowsill, then sealed the window on the inside with caulk.

"You can take it down in a couple of weeks," he said. "Summer is usually dry, and they won't come in anymore."

"I might be gone. I think I want to do some traveling."

"Yes, of course," he said. "That's what Americans do, I suppose—drop a good job to go on the road."

We had stepped out into the living area when the front door opened and Nathan stepped in with a rucksack over his shoulder and a smile on his face, back from a weekend with his royal connections. He did a double take upon seeing Sergio in our flat.

"Greetings," Nathan said, turning a questioning glance toward me. I gave him a stern look.

"*Ciao*, Nathan," Sergio said. "This is my *fidanzata*, Olivia. I can't remember whether you've met at school."

"I don't think so. Hi there." He extended an arm and they shook hands.

Olivia took him in, wondering, I'm sure, about my odd living arrangement. Then Sergio turned to her. "We should go," he said. He gave me a quick nod. "I'll see you at school in the morning."

They left, and I went into my room and got into bed with my clothes on.

Nathan followed me, and I opened up the covers so he could get in. He slid in next to me, also fully dressed, and we sat propped up on pillows, shoulder to shoulder.

"How was your weekend with Claudia?" I asked.

"Terrific," he said. "She's great, the whole family's great."

I nodded. Although Nathan was a womanizer, he could keep up a civilized front for a couple of days at a time and charm anyone he wanted. By now he probably had the princess's father eating out of his hand.

"The conquest of all conquests for your list?"

"You don't understand," he said. "I'm done with the list. I'm actually thinking of—well—I'm ready to have a steady girlfriend. Claudia's different. And being with her, *I'm* different. She's changed me."

"Or the yachts and champagne have."

He laughed. "What about you? From the bags under your eyes and the roses in your cheeks, I'd say you—"

"Shut up. Just shut up." If he joked once more about *another merge with Serge*, I'd kill him. "It's just about over, anyway."

Nathan gave me a concerned look.

"Come over here." He extended an arm, and I cuddled up to him. "I've been watching you these past weeks, and you've been getting more and more miserable. You're in way too deep with Sergio."

"Uh—duh! And guess what? They're getting married and *soon*. Before I go to Hong Kong, so I'll have to attend—"

"You going to be okay, Foxy?"

"Of course I'll be okay."

The truth was I didn't know whether I'd be okay. It seemed like I'd been living in twenty-four hour increments for weeks, and the only question I ever asked myself was when Sergio and I would next meet at the Odeon or whether I'd get to school early enough to have a cappuccino with him before teaching. But all that was over now.

"You don't seem okay."

"I feel awful," I said and, turning toward him, put my arm across his belly.

Nathan rested his cheek against my head. "You really can't live this way. You're too serious or something."

"Am I?"

"You really are."

"Make me feel better, won't you?" I slid my hand down under the sheet and hooked a couple of fingers into the waist of his pants.

"Oh, Foxy—"

"I did you a favor once, now it's your turn to do me one. Just don't put me on your list—" Sliding my hand down, I found him capable.

"No, of course not—" he said.

"Promise?"

"Promise."

It was the first time we made love, but we were so familiar with each other and I was so used to the way he looked and smelled, that it felt like an encounter between lovers who know each other well, both quiet and exciting. And sleeping with someone, anyone, who wasn't Sergio, made me feel a little better.

When we were done, I made Nathan promise again that he wouldn't put me on his list, and he said, "Okay, wait a minute," and he slid out of bed to go to his diary from his room.

"Watch this," he said when he came back, and he took the list out of his journal, tore it several times, whether for my benefit or the princess's I didn't know, and ceremoniously stuck the pieces into a trash can before getting back in bed. We fell silent, considering things.

"I think I should go away," I finally said. "I could go up to Paris and visit my cousin."

"That sounds like a great idea. Paris is the cure for almost anything. And Sergio will have to give you the time off."

"Yeah, I'm leaving my job soon, anyway. What's he going to do, fire me?"

"Don't worry about it. I'll take your classes or someone else will. You don't owe him a thing."

As we cuddled a little closer, I thought about our eventual separation. I wouldn't sleep with Nathan again, not just because of the princess but because we knew too much about each other. But I was thankful to him for helping me erase Sergio, and there was someone in Paris who could help me with that, too—my Slavic lover, Dimitri. He would be more than willing to help me remember who I'd been before Sergio. Before Italy.

"Yup, Paris is the cure for almost anything," I said.

12. Parisian Remedies

It was the end of the day at school. When I walked into the main office, Sergio stood up behind his desk, sticking his hands into the pockets of his pinstripe suit. I put my Greek bag down on the chair opposite him then slid my course books back onto their shelf in the glass case. We were alone.

"Any more problems with the scorpions?" he asked.

"No. Thanks for taking care of that." I fiddled with the books in order not to look at him.

"Don't be angry with me."

"I'm not angry. I'm—" I faced him squarely, needing to defend my pride. "I'm being realistic."

"'Realistic'?"

"That's the word you used. You said you were more realistic than me. You encouraged me to see that things are impossible, right?"

He cleared his throat. "You're right. In fact, Olivia quit her job. She wants a few weeks in Sperlonga to finish setting up the apartment and prepare for the wedding."

There was a pause. He didn't suggest we should meet for a bittersweet good-bye between the sheets.

"You know, Sergio, the best thing for me right now would be to go up to Paris for a while. Maybe leave tomorrow or the day after tomorrow."

He opened his eyes wider. "We have a full schedule this week—"

"Nathan offered to take my classes. If the schedules overlap, you can find someone else to take my place. Melitta can do it. Olivia could even come back to Rome for a day and substitute in an emergency, right?"

"You have the money for this kind of adventure?"

"I have savings. Besides, it won't cost me much. I'm going to stay in the apartment of an old friend."

He dropped his head, looked at the floor. "Okay. I understand." Then, looking back up at me, "You'll come back for the wedding, won't you? Olivia's counting on you. And, believe it or not, it would help me, too. Your friendship means a lot to me."

"I'll be at the wedding—for Olivia."

He sat down in his chair, inviting me with a gesture to take the seat across from him, but I shook my head and, leaning against the wall, remained standing.

"I know you're upset," he said, "but I want you to know our episode has been very important to me. Intellectually as well as everything else. To have someone to talk to, I mean, to talk to in a real way, about real things—that doesn't happen so often in a lifetime."

He was, in his clumsy way, trying to console me, but all I heard was the past tense, the burial. And his reduction of our affair to an intellectual connection was the final blow. Gianina was right about him being an *intelletto-istintivo*.

"So, I won't be in tomorrow," I said, not responding to his attempt to make sense of things. "I'm going to Paris."

"How long will you be gone?"

"A week or two. I don't know."

"Would you call me when you get there?" he asked.

"Why?" I gave him a hard stare.

"So I know you've arrived safely."

"I'll be fine," I said. "My cousin is meeting me at the train station."

"I know," he said. "But I'll be worrying about you—a young woman, traveling alone."

"How gallant of you. But okay, if you insist," I said.

"I insist. Say, 'I'll call you when I get there.'"

"I'll call you when I get there," I repeated.

"Good." Sergio nodded. "I'll ask the others to take your classes."

I went straight to the train station to buy my ticket. That done, I headed home, where I called Robin, then Dimitri, to tell them I'd be in Paris soon. Dimitri sounded delighted to hear my voice, and we planned on spending my first night there together.

Twenty-four hours later, I was sitting by the window in a second-class compartment on the *Palatino*, the night train from Rome to Paris, which I'd taken several times before. The pleasant anticipation of an erotic interlude with Dimitri was already eclipsing thoughts of Sergio, when five exuberant Polish nuns, some young and others old, entered the cabin and took their seats, their habits swishing around them. With their hair hidden and their bare, ruddy faces, they had a boisterousness incongruous with their chosen path. How lucky! Thanks to these ladies, I wouldn't have in my compartment any shady-looking characters who might search my pockets during the night. I felt even more fortunate a couple of hours later when, as the train passed through Florence, the sisters unpacked their picnic basket and shared with me sausages, savory tortes, and fruit pastries, along with a bottle of wine. The drinking continued past midnight and through several rounds of cards, as they tried to teach me games with rules too complicated to convey in sign language. After much hilarity, I took a top couchette and settled in.

The train chugged up the Ligurian coast, gently rocking me until, in the middle of the night the conductor announced Ventimiglia, the last stop before leaving Italy, and I roused myself to look out the window. It was a moment that always thrilled me, for here, at the border crossing, space underwent an alchemical process that affected the language, culture, and gestures of the people who lived on either side. We'd come to a halt, and I, propped up on my elbows, was taking in the station sign promising change and escape, when the nun in the couchette below me cried out, *"Ave, Ventimiglia!"* A handful of bonbons in colorful wrappers flew up from below, landing by my side like a gift from the Sugar Plum Fairy. I gathered them up greedily as the train groaned and lurched us out of the station and into France.

When we pulled into the Gare d'Austerlitz the next morning, the Polish nuns embraced me and filled my pockets with more candy. I was soon on the platform outside, hugging Robin. She was wearing a tie-dyed T-shirt under a little khaki jacket and, in a nod to Parisian chic, had a floral silk scarf tied around her neck and her short curly hair pinned back with a big tortoise-shell clip. Her summer tan made her look relaxed and healthy.

"Hey," she said, "you look like you didn't sleep much."

Robin was only two years older than me, but I'd always looked up to her, as though she were an aunt with plentiful wisdom. Being with her would make everything better.

"See those Polish nuns over there? They were in my compartment, and we drank wine and played cards until three in the morning, when they started trying to convert me—" I exaggerated a bit for effect.

"Oh, come on, you don't expect me to believe—" Robin laughed.

"Really, I'm not lying. I even got to try on a nun's habit."

"Yeah, right. And how did you know they were Polish? You don't know Polish—"

"I know what it sounds like—"

"All right. Whatever you say."

JESSICA LEVINE

We headed toward the metro to catch a train to the apartment I'd lived in the previous year, when I'd rented a room from Leila, an art history professor I'd become friendly with at Yale. The year after I finished college, Leila took a five-year position running a center for exchange students in Paris, where she was soon happily ensconced in an apartment with Joni, her nervously affectionate Persian cat. Desperate after graduation to escape Doug and my mother, I followed Leila to Paris to work as her research assistant. In that capacity, I helped her catalog and study French engravings of women, many of them erotic, that were held in the Bibliothèque Nationale. After a couple of months, I ended up in the guest room in her apartment. I soon discovered that the conventional lifestyle she led back home was a cover for a gay identity that came out into the open in Paris. By the mid-seventies there was an active and open lesbian community at Yale, but Leila, who wasn't yet tenured, was reluctant to come out of the closet.

Leila took me to le Chat Noir, the Left-Bank lesbian nightclub where Dominique, an artsy free spirit, picked me up and soon had me in her bed. There followed a wild couple of months in which Dominique initiated me not only into the mysteries of my own body, but also into a series of night happenings, including parties, dances, and miscellaneous *réunions* held in private homes, bookstores, and art galleries. I met Dimitri at the opening of an exhibit of his prints of antique dolls, whose heads and bodies he smashed before drawing. Rumor had it that the faces he drew bore a disturbing resemblance to those of his serial lovers. But underneath this suggestion of twisted violence, which I found both dangerous and attractive, I discovered only refinement and tenderness. I should add that Dominique passed me on to Dimitri freely, the way you might circulate a library book that you've finished but are too lazy to return to its rightful home. As the whole business with Dominique felt like a transitory experiment, I willingly let myself be handed over.

If my French adventures had led me to consider Paris the

207

capital of titrated *amours* and cultivated detachment, I would always, after my affair with Sergio, think of Rome as a place of disorderly, outsized passions. But for a moment, as Robin and I exited the metro to the intoxicating scents of green spaces and freshly baked baguettes, as we wandered through the little streets of Leila's tranquil neighborhood between the Luxembourg Garden and Montparnasse, I hoped one day to remember Sergio as a mere parenthetical clause in the picaresque novel of my life.

We climbed the familiar five flights to Leila's refuge filled with antiques and facing the rooftops of other quiet buildings—a view I'd drawn many times in order to practice gradating whites and grays. I set my bag down in the little, bright guest room, used the bathroom, and then returned to the living area, where I joined Robin on the couch. Leila's red phone stared at me from the coffee table.

"I have to call Sergio and tell him I'm here," I said.

"I thought the whole point of coming to Paris was to escape this guy," Robin countered.

"Yes, but—" I remembered the pleading look in Sergio's eyes when he asked me to call. "I have to. Then I'll be done."

She shrugged. "I'll go make some coffee."

I picked up the phone and dialed the code for Italy, then the school number.

"*Pronto.* Multi Lingua." Fortunately, Sergio had answered, not Melitta.

"Hi, Sergio. It's me, calling to say I got here safely."

"Ah, good. And how was the train ride?" There was warmth in his voice, as though he were still my lover.

"Fine. There were nuns in my compartment, so you see, nothing to worry about."

"Nuns?" he laughed. "Oh, you do have a guardian angel! Listen, Anna, can I have your phone number there? You never gave it to me."

"Why do you need my number?" I asked as Robin reappeared at the threshold to the kitchen, mouthing "no" and shaking her head. "Sergio," I said, "I'm not going back to Rome early, even if you're short of teachers."

"I know, but—"

"No," I said, then added, more forcefully, "No, Sergio. You don't need my number."

Robin nodded approvingly and mouthed the words, *Good girl.*

"All right, then. Have a good time," Sergio said.

We said good-bye, and I hung up.

Robin looked at me in disbelief. "Why did he want your number? And if I hadn't been here, would you have given it to him?"

Withholding my phone number from Sergio had cost me all my strength. Tears began running down my face. "I knew—I knew they were going to get married," I stammered, "but somehow when Olivia announced it, I was surprised. Shocked actually, because that came right after—right after—this crazy night we had sex four times, and I suggested we run away to Milan together—"

"And you meant it? I mean, about going to Milan?" Robin asked, sitting down next to me on the couch. "Like an *elopement?*"

"Yes. No. Sort of. I mean, I love him terribly, but I'm only twenty-two. I don't feel old enough, or mature enough, to do what Olivia is doing. I could never—at this point—'settle down' with the plan of popping out babies as soon as possible."

"And you'd be miserable living in his little town," Robin said.

"I know. That's why I suggested Milan—"

"Which he didn't go for?"

"I think living with him in Sperlonga, I might have been happier being miserable with him than being happy with anyone else anyplace else—" I sobbed hysterically.

"What?"

"—and I'd been planning on going to Hong Kong, anyway—"

"It's 'unmaking' you, that's what this affair's doing," Robin mused. "Your usual ways of thinking about things are being dismantled so that you can have an experience of something larger. It's an invitation to transcend—"

"That's crap," I said. "Just shut up."

Robin wanted to comfort me by turning my pain into something meaningful, but it was nothing more than a horrible loss to wade through, and I didn't know whether I had the strength to make it to the other side. As I sat there weeping, dark thoughts spun through my head, about slitting my wrists in a bathtub full of water, or jumping off a building, or throwing myself in front of a moving vehicle, Anna Karenina-style.

"Honey," Robin said, "I'm sorry." She reached for a box of tissues and put it within reach.

"I feel like there's no point in going on. I'm never going to be happy with anyone."

"No, no," she whispered, "not true."

For two hours, Robin whispered soothing words as waves of hysteria washed over me. I cried because I'd lost my lover, because I was alone, because I'd learned how dangerous it is to open yourself completely to love and I would never open myself that much again. I cried because you only get one shot to go that deep into feeling and I'd squandered my heart's innocence on someone unavailable. An old sense of scarcity came up in me, a feeling of always hungering after something that was always receding. In Sergio I'd found what I craved, but for such a short time, just a few months, because my destiny was to live deprived of what I most needed. Drained from weeping, I slumped forward and almost slid off the couch.

"Careful there," Robin said, grabbing my arm. "Why don't you lie down and put your head on my lap?"

I stretched out on the couch, my head on her legs she gently stroked my hair. It was sweet and soothing and I drifted off into something like a nap.

When I opened my eyes and sat up, Robin's head was

back on the couch, her chin tilted up and her mouth open, for she, too, had been sleeping. I gave her a nudge.

"Okay," she said. "Now what?"

My head hurt from crying. "I'm supposed to see Dimitri tonight," I said.

She laughed. "Really? Well, maybe that's what you need."

I nodded. "Dimitri will be good for me."

I went into the bathroom to shower and change. My eyes were puffy and disfigured from crying. Well, I'd had my melodramatic meltdown and could move on now. I leaned over the sink and splashed cold water on my face.

In the May evening, dusted with flowers, Robin walked me to Dimitri's. We stopped for a beer at a café on the Boulevard du Montparnasse.

"So who is this Dimitri guy, anyway? What's he like?" Robin asked.

"He's an artist who has a very active love life with a complicated categorization of lovers—major mistresses, minor ones, and passers-by. He calls himself a libertine."

"How's that different from just being promiscuous?"

"He says his lifestyle is based on a philosophical rejection of conventional morality that goes back centuries to people like Machiavelli and Casanova and Sade."

Robin gave me a skeptical look. "It's handy to have historical precedent, I suppose."

"He catalogs his lovers in his art. Preferably faces, but if you refuse to lend your face, then some other body part, like a breast or a hand. Whatever. He likes men, too." Then I added, uncomfortably, "It's rumored he occasionally picks up young boys."

"That's disgusting," Robin said.

"I don't believe it, myself."

"And where are you in his schema of things?"

"I used to be one of his major mistresses, but I guess I demoted myself to intermittent when I left Paris." I gave her a wry smile.

"Okay," Robin said. "And does he know about Sergio?"

"Yeah, sure. When I called him from Rome, I told him I needed help getting over someone, and he said he'd be happy to help."

"I see you're bouncing back quickly." She paused, then turned serious. "Listen, Anna, I need to tell you something. I'm in an irregular relationship myself."

"Oh?"

"I met someone in Amsterdam." Pause. "He's German and—" She groped for the right words.

In our family, in 1979, the Holocaust was yesterday. We wouldn't visit Germany or buy anything made there. The idea of having sex with a German was grotesque, unthinkable.

"—very sensitive, very aware," Robin continued. "Someone totally working through his country's past—"

"It's okay," I said. "You don't have to justify it."

"I do have to justify it because forgiveness isn't easy. Listen, instead of going straight back to Rome, why don't you come to Germany with me and meet him? We could get a Eurail Pass and bop around a bit, go to Frankfurt and Vienna then into Northern Italy."

"I don't know. I was going to go back and teach for a few more weeks—"

"You short of cash?"

"No, I have some savings."

"We should go traveling, then. And I want you to meet Manfred."

"But you'll come down to Rome with me for the wedding? I have to go for Olivia."

"I think you're crazy, but sure, I'll go with you. Don't worry about it."

There was no elevator in Dimitri's building, and I was a little out of breath by the time I reached the sixth floor. I knocked and heard his footsteps approach the door.

"*Alors, la romaine.*" He kissed me, and I followed him past the workspace crammed with easels and art supplies to his sleeping area. Out the window was a view of the white dome of the Pantheon. Years before, Dimitri had bought and connected three *chambres de bonne*, the attic rooms that nineteenth-century architects constructed for maids. One room was now his bedroom, the other two he'd turned into a studio. He had no kitchen, just a counter with a single electric burner for a coffee pot, which sufficed because he lunched in cafés and dined in the homes of friends and acquaintances. The invitations came in an unceasing stream, for the twisted eroticism of his drawings provoked enough of a *frisson* that he ended up on everyone's guest list.

"Let me take a good look at you, see how you've changed," he said. We spoke in French.

We sat on the edge of the bed—the room was so small that there was no other place to sit—and he took my hands and looked at me.

"You've been crying," he said.

"I couldn't help it."

"You got too serious about this Italian guy and wanted him all to yourself?"

"I guess so."

"I thought I'd taught you to be careful about that," he said, shaking his head. "All that romantic head-garbage, it's seductive but poisonous. The wrong ideals get in the way of enjoying life."

"I'm okay now."

He touched my chest. "A bit of a callus, perhaps?"

I imagined my heart with a dead membrane over part of it. "Yes, a numb zone."

"But not completely, I hope?" His hand moved to my breast, which he caressed.

"Not completely." I was happy to see him. "What about you? How's *your* love life? Your *complicated* love life."

"A little slow at the moment. One young lady went back to her home country—" He didn't specify which, for, in the French fashion, he respected his lovers' privacy. "The other one decided she couldn't see me anymore because she wants to be faithful to her husband. *Bof!* What can you do with such little minds?"

"That's good news for me," I said, unbuttoning his shirt.

"Yes, I have a lot of free time this week." He smiled. "I'm very happy to see you, Anna." He continued to study me, as his hand fondled my other breast. "I worried when you left for Rome that you would fall into the banal and become like all the others."

"Yes, I remember," I said. He'd warned me, *tu vas te banaliser à Rome*—an expression that means something like, you'll lose your originality.

He cocked his head as he studied me. "But I don't think you have."

"Thanks."

Dimitri looked attractive in his white Indian kurta and drawstring silk pants, unconventional garb for a Frenchman. He was tall and slim, of blonde Russian stock, with brilliant blue eyes sunk deep in their eye sockets, as though retreating from the icy air of the steppes. The bed was in the left corner of his room, and along the walls ran a shelf holding votive candles that flickered under other shelves crowded with books. An antique icon of Mother and Child hung over the head of the bed.

"Get undressed," he said. "But leave the hat on. I like that fedora. "

I stood up, unbuttoned my shirt, slid off my pants, and removed my underwear.

"Lie down," he said, reaching for a pencil and a sketchbook. "Tell me more about Rome—move your right leg a little bit toward me—yes, like that—and the other in the opposite direction—that's better. How's your Italian? Improved?"

"Somewhat," I said. It was exciting to watch him draw me.

"Oh, I forgot to offer you a drink—don't move—keep your leg there." He bent over me as he moved it to his liking. "Your thighs are beautiful—and what's between, too. *L'origine du monde.*" He sighed happily as he went over to a bottle of wine on the windowsill. "You'll like this rosé," he said, handing me a glass. He crouched on the floor next to the bed and started sketching. "I'm so glad you're here."

"You mean, since the others have abandoned you? Poor thing!" I laughed.

He threw his sketchbook down with a devilish expression, drew himself up to the edge of the bed. "How dare you mock me?" He reached for my hat, removed it. "I like the feather," he said, "but we can do away with this now, don't you think?"

He threw my fedora toward his desk. As it sailed through the air, the chicken feather that Sergio had stuck in the ribbon around the brim flew off. I made a motion to go after it, but Dimitri took my wrists to detain me.

"You're not going anywhere," he said.

As the feather glided to the floor, he got back on the bed and climbed on top of me. I knew what to expect with Dimitri. Attentive to my needs and wants, he would slowly and deliberately arouse me and, a true gentleman, make sure I came before he did. Dimitri was a spicy cocktail made of two parts Baudelaire, one part André Gide, and a dash of Sade. What he lacked in depth of feeling he made up for with technical expertise, so that one way or the other, I'd be superbly screwed and satisfied and, goddamn Sergio, by morning I'd be back a little closer to the real me—whoever the hell that was.

13. The Nature of Reality

I extended my stay in Paris for a couple of days, then several more, without calling Sergio. During the day, Robin and I wandered through gardens, museums, and little shops, stopping in cafés as needed for refreshments. At night, I returned to my Franco-Slavic lover, who worked on erasing Sergio with his lovemaking and philosophy of open relationships. It was such a relief to be with someone I could see when I wanted to, instead of having to wait and pine for my lover to sneak away to a hotel with me, that I took advantage of Dimitri's availability and gorged on sex for over a week. What helped most was that Dimitri came from a world that was completely different from Sergio's. Whereas Sergio was provincial and family-minded, Dimitri was a cosmopolitan libertine. Whereas Sergio enjoyed shocking his Catholic countrymen with his passionate atheism, Dimitri liked to discuss the fine points of Russian Orthodox doctrine with his priest. As I made a mental list of their opposite characteristics, both men began to seem as though they came from parallel universes so alien that I could never fully inhabit either one. By the time my cousin and I bought our Eurail passes and got on the train for Frankfurt, I felt internally free. I belonged to myself and no other.

Robin and I went to Germany, where I met Manfred and had all my prejudices and preconceptions shaken up. Then we spent another three weeks wandering around Europe. It was cold and damp in Frankfurt, so we headed to the south of France, hitting Avignon and Aix before moving on to Marseilles and across to Nice, Turin, and Milan. We zigzagged down the Italian peninsula, passing through Verona, Padua, Venice, and Bologna, staying in hostels and cheap hotels. Manfred got off from work and joined us in Florence. Having gorged myself on sex in Paris, I now gorged myself on Italian art. All the train travel and the sights and the people we met on the way helped me finish the job of taking emotional distance from Sergio—or so I thought.

When Robin and I arrived in Rome one bright July morning and stepped into my apartment, we found empty bottles of wine and clusters of cigarette butts in the living room, dishes piled high in the kitchen sink, and my bed unmade, having undoubtedly been used by some guests too drunk to get home. Nathan was out.

"You didn't tell me he was a slob," Robin said, looking around.

"Make yourself at home. I'd better call Sergio and tell him I'm back."

"Why go back at all?" Robin asked. She put her backpack down in the bedroom then went to the refrigerator to check it out. "Why not quit now? Just disappear."

"Believe it or not, I'm reasonably paid, and the more money I save up before leaving for Hong Kong, the better. And I have to go to the wedding—because I told Olivia I would. And everyone at school and in Sperlonga would be surprised if I didn't."

"Okay. If that's the way you want to see it."

I dialed Sergio.

"I thought you were coming back weeks ago!" He sounded annoyed. "I had no way of getting in touch with you. Were you in Paris the whole time?"

"No, we went traveling."

"You know we can't hire any new teachers until after the August break—you really left me in the lurch. Can you come in at six this evening? There's a new group starting, and none of the other teachers are free."

"Sure."

Irritated by his businesslike manner, I went into my bedroom, threw myself on the crumpled sheets, and hugged one of the pillows. Robin came in and sat on the edge of the bed, munching a biscuit from a box we'd taken on the train.

"Things a little tense with the boss?" she asked.

"I can't wait till this is over." I sniffed, remembering my meltdown in Paris. I wouldn't allow myself to go there again.

"What do you want to do today?"

"I don't know. Go to Piazza Navona and wander around. Eat gelato. Meet you after you finish teaching and have dinner on some piazza with a bottle of wine."

"Sounds good. Especially the wine."

We went out and started walking and bussing our way toward Piazza Navona. It felt awful being back. The things I'd once loved in Rome—the crenellated cornices and rooftop gardens, the fountains with stone statues, the vistas into cobblestone courtyards—were now devoid of color, spirit, sparkle. When we reached Piazza Navona, the most majestic of all Italian piazzas, which Napoleon had called the drawing room of Europe, I might as well have been looking at an old postcard in which the colors had gone slightly off. Not only was my relationship with Sergio over, but my love affair with the city as well.

I was, however, resolved to discharge my duties as a tourguide and we forged ahead. Unconsciously, I led Robin south toward the Ghetto. As we wandered there—in those days the Ghetto was quiet, with few shops, no tourists, only cobblestone streets and gardens tucked under crumbling arches—my old enchantment broke through the numbing grief, and I lapsed into a sweet daydream of moss and stone, of flowers and sunshine.

We arrived at the Via del Tempio, where the Odeon Hotel was, and I gestured up toward the third floor. "This is where we used to meet," I said.

"So that's why you led me in this direction."

"Just another dumb Italian love story."

"I doubt it," Robin said, passing her arm through mine.

"I have to believe it has changed me for the better," I said. "I got to experience things—feelings—that I'd never had before."

"Sure. You'll be more—what? Sensitive? Interesting? Or just passionate and fun in bed?"

"Something like that. And maybe more careful about getting into messy situations." I sighed and we moved on.

Robin and I parted late in the afternoon, when I caught a bus to Multi Lingua. For the two-hundredth time, I got off in front of the Ministry of Finance and made my way to our building—I thought of it as "our" building and "our" school, just as I thought of the Odeon as "our" hotel.

I pushed open the heavy front doors with their lion-head knockers, climbed the white stone staircase with the gray carpeting, and swung open the door to the school, resolved to be cool and brave. In the office, I saw Sergio sitting in his chair, looking tired as he leaned on his left elbow and gazed down at a ledger, a pen in his right hand.

He got a sweet light in his face when he saw me. "You're back," he said softly.

I sat down in the chair opposite him. "I'm back."

He looked at his watch. "Ten minutes until your class. Things have been very busy while you were gone." He looked back up at me. "Do you feel better after your trip?"

"A little." I examined him with a feeling of detachment. "How are you?"

"I went to Florence to buy a piece of property." He sighed. "You've put me in a state of misery, Anna."

I shrugged. "How's Olivia? Getting ready for the wedding?"

"Yes, she's in Sperlonga, making arrangements."

There was a pause. Since she was down there and he

was in Rome, I wondered—purely out of habit—whether he would suggest a meeting at the Odeon.

"I appreciate your being such a good sport . . ." he continued.

He wasn't going to ask me to dinner or to the Odeon. I felt a little sick to my stomach, as though looking at a squirrel hit by a car and dying by the side of the road. Then, remembering Dimitri's image of a callus on the heart, I shrugged again and asked, "Is there a lot to do?"

"Not that much, really. The menu at the restaurant, that's always the main thing. We are having the banquet at Mauro's father's hotel—to bury the ax about the argument about the fence. Let him have his extra foot of land. Anyway, everyone's invited. You'll bring your cousin, I hope."

"Yes."

"So, tell me about your trip."

"Paris was lovely, then we traveled around. I had a good time." I felt pleased with myself for being cold.

Classes were ending, and students and teachers could be heard moving into the hallway.

"I'll tell you more about it some other time," I said, standing up. "The student list, please?"

In the following week, the scene was repeated many times: we'd have a moment to talk, then it would be cut short by someone looking in and asking something. Several mornings, on arriving, I smelled Mauro's pipe and found the office door closed. Maybe Sergio had given notice and Mauro was trying to convince him to stay on.

The day after Robin arrived, we went to see Doris, who had invited us out to dinner. She was on the phone when we arrived, which meant a long wait, so I found the Campari and poured Robin and me a couple of drinks, and we went to sit on the west-facing balcony. I gradually got a buzz on, and my old awe of the city returned, dispelling my depression, as we took in the view of rooftop gardens and church cupolas flashing rose and gold against a sunset sky.

Robin waved a hand at the view. "You sure you want to leave this? It's so gorgeous."

"I have to," I said. "It's time." I filled my Campari back up to the brim.

Around nine p.m., Doris emerged from her home office. She hugged Robin energetically, for she hadn't seen her in years.

"And how is Sarah?" Doris asked, inquiring about Robin's mother, who lived in San Francisco. "What do I have to do to get my sisters to visit me?" She seemed unaware that they wanted nothing to do with her. Then she reached for me, so she could hug Robin and me at the same time. "Both of my nieces! At once! *Che piacere!* Okay now, shall we go eat?"

"You know," I said to Doris on our way out, "it's time for you to buy me that ticket to Hong Kong."

"Sure," she said. "I'll find you some cheap last-minute deal. So, Robin, you sure you don't want to stay here, where you can have your own room?"

I'd warned Robin that if she accepted Doris's invitation, she'd become her errand-runner and dog poop counter, so she had a ready answer.

"Thanks for being so generous, but we have cousin stuff in the works." And she leaned toward me and squeezed my arm.

Robin stayed with me for ten days. Nathan was assiduous in his attentions to her, although still professing loyalty to the princess. He'd bring out the brandy after dinner to get her talking and make her laugh with his stories. But she remained steady and resisted his charms.

I no longer rushed in for the morning coffee with Sergio. Sometimes I showed up late on purpose, to irritate him. A couple of days before the wedding, I arrived for a lesson with a private student, but learned that the student had called saying he would be late. Sergio was free and wanting to talk to me. The other teachers had already started their classes, and we were alone.

"I'm going straight down to Sperlonga after work tonight," he said. "But I have to go home and get some clean socks at lunchtime. You want to come with me?"

"What about eating lunch?" I asked. The trip to his Roman apartment would take a good thirty to forty-five minutes each way and consume most of the midday break. Besides, I no longer organized my life around attempts to snatch extra time with him.

"We'll pick something up on the way back."

"I don't know," I said. "I'll want a real meal." The emotions of recent weeks had made my stomach sensitive to stress, and it was uncomfortable when empty.

"Come on," he said. "We have to find our way through this and be friends."

"All right."

My pupil finally arrived and we had our lesson. An hour later, I followed Sergio down to his Fiat, telling myself that it was important for us to transition back to an amicable relationship so that I might leave Rome on a civil note. The way an affair ends conditions one's memory of it.

"Are you enjoying your cousin's visit?" he asked.

"Yes, it's been very nice. Very therapeutic," I said.

"I'm glad. I mean, I'm happy you have something to distract you right now."

We got into his car and set off toward the drab periphery. As Sergio dodged the darting cars with his quick reflexes, desire chugged away inside me, a reaction to being alone with him that operated independently of my muted emotions.

He cleared his throat to interrupt the silence. "I found a job in Sperlonga."

"You did?"

"Yes, a managerial position in a local company. I've already told Mauro I'm quitting in a few weeks. It'll be after you've left. I know this sounds crazy, but it's just hitting me now that you're going away."

"Really?"

He glanced sideways at me then back at the road. "Probably you don't think very highly of me at the moment. But maybe you'll agree, all these changes, they're distractions, so a good thing. You'll have a new life in Hong Kong; I'll have my new life in Sperlonga—" He laughed bitterly. "We're each accomplishing our 'destiny,' no?"

I thought about it. "You're right. We're each doing what we've always wanted to do."

We made some small talk about whether Mauro would ask Melitta to take Sergio's place, whether I would fly directly to Hong Kong, and so forth. Soon we arrived at the dreary apartment block where I'd once spent the night with Olivia and almost confessed my misdeeds to her. He parked, and I followed him up the cement staircase and down the grungy hallway to their front door. He opened it and we went in.

It was as orderly and spotless as it had been when I'd visited before.

"So you won't be needing this place anymore," I said.

"We handed in our notice. We'll move out end of the month."

I followed him into the bedroom and sat on the bed, while he went over to the tall dresser, opened the top drawer, and grabbed two pairs of socks, which he stuck in the pockets of his jacket. Then he stopped as though remembering something, removed his jacket, threw it on a chair, approached me and pushed me back on the bed. Consciously or unconsciously, I don't know, he had asked me to accompany him back to his apartment so that he might fuck me one last time. And fucking it was—not making love. He went at it quickly and unceremoniously, without a moment of perfunctory foreplay. *He really is a peasant,* I thought. I was annoyed but, because I never stopped wanting him no matter how wounded and angry I got, my sex was wet and I didn't object, I just lay there and went along with it. And because I attributed his absence of bedroom manners to his doomed passion for me, I forgave him and it felt unutterably pleasurable, the way it always did.

It was only when he was done that he became affectionate, stroking my face and telling me how beautiful I was, how he'd miss me. We'd been so distant since the night of the rooster—since the morning of Olivia's wedding announcement—that I felt detached as I listened and stared at the light speck in his left eye. I felt emotion-deaf the way one might be hard of hearing after a long airplane ride.

"Promise me," he said, stroking my face, "that if ever I want to see you again, you'll say yes."

"I can't promise that, but I probably would."

He put his nose against my neck.

"I'm memorizing you," he said. "How you feel and smell." He kissed me. "How you taste."

He was expressing his love for me, but I remembered how in Paris I had wanted to kill myself and resolved never to feel that way again. He hadn't gone through that paroxysm of loss yet, but he would, in his own time and way. I sat up, feeling a little sick to my stomach.

"I need to eat before classes start again," I said. "I have a long afternoon ahead."

He looked at his watch. "Yes, we have to get going. But wait a minute, I got you something."

He went to the closet and brought back a large object wrapped in tissue paper.

"For you. I haven't had time to wrap it properly."

Removing the tissue paper, I found an old-fashioned briefcase tailored for a woman, made of soft brown leather and adorned with brass buckles.

"It's beautiful," I said.

"This is the real reason I wanted to come back to the apartment," he said. "I forgot to bring it with me to the office this morning."

"Thank you." The gift touched me through the layers of numbness.

"I got it for you when I was in Florence. You can use it in Hong Kong, instead of that ridiculous Greek bag. You're a professional, you should look like one."

I wondered whether he'd put it in the closet to hide it from Olivia, or maybe she knew about it, maybe he'd told her it was a going-away present for me, and she hadn't thought twice about it. I'd never know. It didn't matter anymore.

"It's lovely."

He put his dark suit jacket back on, double-checking the pockets for the goddamn socks, and I followed him back downstairs to the car, with the satchel under my arm. We were still in the ugly outer periphery of the city when we saw a dilapidated café with a parking space in front of it, and Sergio pulled up and ran in. A moment later he ran back out, bringing me a tired-looking sandwich of mortadella and mozzarella with wilted lettuce, which I ate in silence as he drove in silence, both of us twice as miserable as we'd been an hour before.

On the morning of Sergio and Olivia's wedding, I opened my eyes, was hit by nausea, and went to the bathroom to vomit. Then I woke Robin up.

"We've got to get going. And my stomach is really upset. I just threw up."

"Why are you doing this to yourself? It's positively masochistic," Robin said.

"It's a point of honor. To show I don't care."

"You're an idiot."

I meant what I said because I was determined to have lots of lovers and, in order to do that, I needed to learn how to withstand sentimental suffering. So I got Nathan up and grilled some toast for the three of us, and we took the 16 to Stazione Termini where we met Melitta. The plan was for the four of us to take the train down to Formia, where Flavio would pick us up.

As soon as we met Melitta, I flipped the social switch to "on" and began putting on a happy act. For the rest of the day, I'd laugh and joke with my friends.

An hour later, Flavio picked us up at the station and explained the plan in the car: "Anna, we have to stop at the apartment before going to the courthouse, because Olivia needs your help."

"What's up?" I asked.

"She'd like you to do her hair because her mother—her mother isn't available."

"She's not coming to the wedding?"

"She's coming but—she's not available to do Olivia's hair."

"All right," I said. A knot tightened in my stomach as I anticipated my last moment alone with Olivia before the wedding.

After taking the usual route a couple of miles up the coast, we stopped at Sergio's Sperlonga apartment. Flavio, Robin, and Nathan joined a crowd that had gathered in the front yard near a table with glasses of wine, while I went upstairs and entered the kitchen. Sergio's father and Nazzaro, with his nephew Bobo on his lap, were sitting at the kitchen dining table, while Teresa was arranging snacks on a ceramic platter. A restaurant meal was to follow the ceremony, but eating and imbibing would take place both before and after.

"Where's Olivia?" I asked.

"In the bedroom," Teresa said. "I'm hopeless with hair. *Grazie, grazie* for helping."

Sergio was nowhere to be seen as I went down the hall to the master bedroom, where I found Olivia wearing a light blue suit over a lace blouse and looking at herself in the mirror.

"Hi." She hugged me. "You were gone a long time. Sergio told me you traveled around."

"That's right," I said.

"You'll have to tell me all about it . . . Look, I've been trying to put my hair up and I'm hopeless at it." She gestured toward a bun in disarray.

"Sit down and let me fix it."

Her hair, cool and soft between my fingers, smelled pleasantly of the shampoo she'd used that morning. Here was my last opportunity to say or do something to change the course of events, but I was paralyzed. All I could mutter was, "That's a pretty blouse."

"It's my substitute for a wedding dress," she said.

"Did you want one?"

"Not really. I agree with Sergio that it's a waste of money."

"I thought your mom and sister would be with you."

"My mother won't set foot in the apartment until after we're married. Because this is where we've lived in sin, blah-blah-blah. And she won't let Nina come up either." Olivia grimaced.

"Well, she's of a different generation," I said. *Don't you see, Olivia, the omens aren't good for this marriage, listen, I have to tell you something—*

Olivia shook her head. "It's impossible to escape being a Catholic. I went to confession last Sunday and I felt so much better afterward that it made me realize I'd been feeling guilty all along. I wanted to be modern about living together before marriage, but deep down, I've been feeling that my mother— and the Church—were right about it. And that I was wrong."

I could barely breathe as my fantasy of objecting fell into the abyss. Instead, I had to bow before her developed moral sense and her desire to respect the holy precepts.

"I know you can't understand, just the way Sergio can't," she continued. "But I was raised that way, so it's real for me."

"You've chosen to live within a certain set of rules and you feel uncomfortable about having broken them. Is that it?"

"It's not just rules, Anna. It's God's law."

"God's law." I nodded, wanting to be respectful. Her faith was the cornerstone of her existence. "Okay, I see. Well, the priest gave you absolution, right? And you're getting married in an hour, so everything's okay now, right?" Then I added, a little maliciously perhaps, "And you'll live happily ever after."

A shadow fell across her face. "I'm not an idiot. I know that marrying an Italian is risky business."

"Is it?"

"You know what I mean—the reputation Italian husbands have for—"

She gave me a hard look, and for a dreadful second I wondered whether she had suspicions about Sergio and me.

"You think they're worse than others?"

"I don't know." She shrugged. "That's what life is, I guess. One leap of faith after another."

"Sergio loves you very much," I said. My hands felt a little shaky as I put the last pins in her hair. "There."

She stood up and looked at herself in the mirror. "Thank you," she said then hugged me, glowing again. "I hope that one day you'll be as happy as I am today."

"I'm happy right now, Olivia. Happy everything is resolved for you."

"Thank you."

"I'm happy—and relieved for you, really relieved." I cared for her, so my words weren't completely insincere.

"And now you'd better go find yourself a ride to the courthouse."

I went downstairs and found Nathan and Robin standing outside, whispering in deep conversation. Was he still trying to seduce her? Had he forgotten about the princess? Or were they gossiping about me? Melitta must have already gotten a ride as she was nowhere to be seen. I was looking around for Flavio when Nazzaro pulled up in the Mercedes. It was the first time I'd seen him shaved and in a suit. He almost looked respectable.

"Over here, Anglos, ride with me." He leaned sideways to open the passenger door and beckoned to me. "Best teacher in front, everyone else in the back."

I got in next to him and our eyes met.

"The wedding is finally happening," he said. "A good thing, no?"

"I'm very happy for them."

"You should be."

I took in his gold-capped teeth as he grinned. Now that Sergio was getting married, Nazzaro wouldn't threaten me anymore.

We drove down the coast to Gaeta, parked, and went into the courthouse. There, in the ceremony room, I finally met Olivia's mother, a stout woman in middle age who spoke English with a heavy Italian accent. She sat with Olivia's sister, Nina, in the row in front of me and every now and then I heard her whisper *chiesa* this and *chiesa* that. She was obviously unhappy about the proceedings, but a church ceremony would happen later. The old lady had made her case until Sergio gave in.

As Sergio and Olivia stood before the judge, he in his business three-piece and she in her light blue suit, I went into a self-anesthetizing trance that lasted through the ceremony and the dinner at the hotel Mauro's dad owned. The huge crowd at the restaurant included everyone I knew in Sperlonga—Sergio's dad, Flavio with Teresa and Bobo, Nazzaro, Roberto and Robertina, neighbors and friends of relatives—as well as the teachers at Multi Lingua. My memory would eventually condense the long evening to a series of short clips, only one of which I recall clearly: In the hotel dining room, which had a view of the Mediterranean, three long tables were set up in a U-shape, with Sergio and Olivia in the middle. The food and drink kept coming as family and friends made toasts. I sat between Robin and Nathan, talking and laughing. At one point I was leaning toward Robin with some brilliant witticism, when my peripheral vision caught Sergio as he shot a glance in my direction, then looked down at a fork he was playing with, smiling to himself. A sad, affectionate smile as, newly married, he remembered sweet times with his ex-mistress.

Well, fuck him. And thank God this ridiculous story was over. I averted my eyes and gulped down some more wine. Then I felt Nathan take my free hand under the table and give it a squeeze.

I turned to look at him. "Thanks," I said.

"You're much too good for him," Nathan said. "Don't forget that."

I looked out at the sea—the thirst-making and thirst-quenching sea—and nodded.

The next morning, back in Rome, I woke up with nausea and a dull headache. Robin was sound asleep next to me. Getting up, I dragged myself into Nathan's bedroom.

"Hey, Foxy," Nathan said, opening his eyes.

"Move over," I said, climbing in.

"Sure." He scooted over, and I got in next to him.

We both fell back asleep. The silence of Sunday morning was broken occasionally by distant church bells calling the faithful to Mass. I was reawakened by nausea and wanting to put a little something in my stomach.

"Nathan," I said. "I have to sit up. Come keep me company on the couch."

"All right, Foxy."

I went to the kitchen cabinet and grabbed a box of the crackers I'd started keeping in the house and sat down on the living room couch next to Nathan. I was trying to get a cracker down when Robin got up and came out of the bedroom.

"It's those feelings you've got bottled up inside that are making you sick," she said, sitting in the rattan armchair across from us. "You have to stop acting okay and just give in to the misery of it. Scream, cry, throw things. Do whatever you need to do to get it out of your system."

"I did that already in Paris. I'm not doing it again," I said.

"I knew from the moment I met Sergio that he was a bad egg," Nathan said. "I should have put a stop to it."

"It wasn't your job to 'put as stop to it.' And Sergio isn't a bad egg," I said.

"Oh, fuck it. Stop defending him," Robin said.

I looked at them miserably then the nausea came over me again. "Oh no," I said, and ran to the bathroom.

When I was through, I returned to the living room couch and resumed my position propped up against Nathan. I hated throwing up more than anything in the world. Robin came over and put her hand on my forehead.

"No fever."

"I don't have a fever. I'm just upset and hung-over. I'm never going to drink again."

Robin sat down next to me.

"That might not be a bad idea, given your mother's history, but . . . you threw up yesterday *before* the wedding and all the eating and drinking. So yeah, maybe you're giving yourself an ulcer from bottling things up inside, but can I ask you—I don't want to freak you out but—when did you last have your period?"

"I haven't had a period since I went off the pill almost a year ago. So what you're thinking of is unlikely."

Robin looked at me, aghast. "Are you an idiot or what? If your system started up again and you ovulated, how would you know? Didn't you ever bother to get the basics from *Our Bodies, Our Selves?*"

Out of the corner of my eye, I saw Nathan turn pale.

"Foxy—" he began.

"Don't worry," I said to him, "I've been feeling nauseous since before we did it." I was lying: the nausea had started more recently. Suddenly I felt light-headed. "Jesus."

"Goddammit, Anna," Robin said. "I think you'd better go get yourself a fucking pregnancy test."

14. The Letter

When the American doctor I'd visited for the pregnancy test called me with the results, I was home alone for the siesta hour, which I no longer spent at school. "I don't know how many weeks pregnant you are," he said.

"Oh," I said.

"Do you know what you'll do?" he asked, kindness in his voice.

"No, I don't," I said.

"Can the father help?" he suggested.

"No, he can't," I said. Of course, I didn't know who the father was, but I didn't tell him that.

My body was full of knots and nausea. What to do? What to do? I hung up, pulled out my diary, and went over it:

May 17th, sex with Doug. If he were the father, I'd be sucked back into the dark life back home that I'd escaped.

May 19th, the night of the rooster.

May 20th, sex with Nathan. Had I really had sex with Nathan right after my night with Sergio? If Nathan were the father, it would be one big cosmic joke.

Trip to Paris: May 24th, sex with Dimitri. Also the 25th, 26th, 27th, 28th. We'd skipped the 29th, and then I'd seen him again on the 30th. I shuddered at the possibility that this twisted libertine might have impregnated me.

What were the odds in each case?

I tried to remember when I'd used my mini diaphragm,

when I hadn't. Even when I'd inserted it, I'd sometimes been careless, not bothering to fill it with spermicide. How I wanted Sergio to be the father! I wanted it so much that at moments I believed he was, but I kept coming back to the fact that I couldn't be sure. I'd spent more nights with Dimitri than with the others, so the odds were that he was the one who'd gotten me pregnant. A sense of horror, almost revulsion, came over me again at that possibility. How could I have slept with four men in such a short period of time? And how could I have been so sloppy about birth control? I was too smart for something like this to happen to me, but I'd deluded myself into thinking I was infertile because I hadn't had a period since going off the pill. My shame had less to do with having been "promiscuous" —after all, if Nathan could have serial lovers, why shouldn't I?—than with the sense of being caught, like a small child, doing something beyond her age, like driving a car. I'd been more than careless. I'd proven myself *incompetent*. At life. At adulthood.

There was something about having relationships in other languages and countries that made them feel unreal, as though Sergio and Dimitri didn't "count" because I'd spoken Italian and French in bed with them. Doug didn't count because he was an ex. Nathan didn't count because our relationship was basically platonic. Living abroad had induced a mental state of make-believe, but now, as I sat on the wicker couch in my half-subterranean apartment, I fell back into reality as fast as a satellite falling to Earth. My grasp of that dimension —"reality"—had been tenuous since I'd left the United States two years before and adopted the persona of a carefree globe-trotter, careening along in one continuous, mind-altering party. I'd been pretending to be someone else for so long that the role had finally stuck. Now there was this cluster of cells in my abdomen making it all real. And what was "reality"? It was a path toward a future that would be very problematic within a finite period of time. I couldn't just drift now, I'd have to take some kind of action, and whatever I did—or didn't do—would by definition be drastic.

My breath grew shallow, my spine vibrated. Nathan and

Robin were out and I was alone in the apartment. I needed to talk to someone immediately. Doris couldn't stand the sight of a pregnant woman, so no point going to her for advice. I couldn't call home because my mother would say that she wasn't interested in helping me take care of a baby at this point in her life and she wouldn't hold my hand through an abortion, either. She'd given me a similar kind of speech once when I was a junior in high school, sleeping with Doug, and she discovered rubbers in my room. "I was happy to see condoms in your dresser because if you get in trouble, you can't count on me." Those were her exact words.

I thought of Signora Gianina, who might use her Tarot cards again to divine what Fate wanted of me, and I called her.

"*Aspetto un bambino,*" I said, using the Italian euphemism: I'm waiting for a child.

"Come over straight away."

I went out and started the trip to Trastevere, one bus then another. The whole time, my heart was beating hard, and the city outside, with its shops shuttered for the siesta hour and its quiet courtyards, had a frozen look, as though from a science fiction movie in which time had stopped.

Finally, I arrived at Piazza San Cosimato and rang Signora Gianina's doorbell.

She opened the door and I stooped down to hug her ancient form.

"You really are a lost child," she said and, taking my hand, led me into her tiny living room.

I sat on the couch and she went to get me a glass of mineral water. The nineteenth-century engraving of the Forum caught my eye again. Had things really changed much since then, when it came to a single woman getting pregnant? Theoretically, I could do whatever I wanted with my life, but my mother, if no one else, would work hard to make me feel ashamed every day of my pregnancy and for the rest of my life. There was no way I could have a child without a partner, support, or country that felt like home.

"What am I going to do?" I asked.

"Tell the father."

"Signora, I'm not sure—I don't know who the father is."

She shook her head. "I thought you were a modern woman, but I was mistaken. Well, you know the options. You can spend your pregnancy in some Catholic 'women's retreat' here, then give the child up for adoption."

I imagined living in a convent dormitory with a herd of young women at different stages of pregnancy, all of them waiting to deliver, like cows in a stable, while a crucifix loomed above them. I shook my head energetically in the negative.

"Or if you want to keep it," Gianina continued, "you go home to America and have the baby. I don't know if your parents would help or support you—"

"No, they wouldn't."

"Are you sure?"

"I'd rather die than ask. I loathe my mother."

"That's not a reasonable attitude."

"It's the way things are." If only I'd had one person who could help me—a lover, relative, or friend—but I had no one.

"Well, you know the other option. Abortion is legal in Italy now, but I don't recommend it. I've heard the best places are Paris and Amsterdam."

I thought of Leila, the art history professor with the apartment Robin and I had stayed in when we met in Paris. Leila was back now and had lots of feminist friends who would know where to go for the procedure. The thought of telling her about my predicament triggered more feelings of shame, and I wept.

"Okay, back to square one," Gianina said. "You need a father—"

"Oh, Gianina, if only I knew it was Sergio! If only I hadn't slept with anyone else." I sobbed.

"If Sergio's the one you care about, let him be the father—"

"But what—what if the child has blue eyes?" I said, thinking of Dimitri.

"The child will be so adorable that people won't gossip."

"His whole family will hate me. Olivia and her family will hate me. Everyone in Sperlonga will hate me."

"Yes, there would be a huge scandal, with uncertain results. They might ostracize the both of you, and he might no longer be able to appear in his hometown, which he might hold against you for life. Not a great way to start a marriage."

"So then?"

"The classic solution: You write the wife an anonymous letter, then she may ask him—not for a divorce, of course, but for an annulment. So soon after the wedding, I think they could get an annulment." She smiled. "Yes, they could get one even though they've been having sex for years—sorry, dear— that's how hypocritical we are in our culture."

"How does that avoid scandal?"

"It doesn't avoid scandal, but it helps everyone save face. The wife asks for an annulment, he asks why, she tells him about the letter. It's all done privately. This enables him to take a stand on his own, so you don't feel like you're twisting his arm. Down the line, you and your lover marry, before or after you have the baby, I don't know—" She stopped and reflected. "I'm not sure how it would all go. It's true they'll gossip in the town, it could be unpleasant."

"We could go to Milan," I said as I wondered what would happen if, as he feared, Sergio couldn't find a job there. Well, he would find one. And even if he were miserable about dishonoring Olivia and leaving his family, he would be happy to be with me and our child.

"You could have a good life in Milan," she said. "That would be a fine solution."

"Would you help me write the letter?"

"Let me get some paper."

She went over to a diminutive secretary and rummaged for a sheet of paper and a pen, which she placed before me on the little coffee table.

"It must be anonymous. Sergio may suspect you wrote it, but if he can't prove it, that's better for you."

I leaned over and wrote in Italian:

Olivia, you should know that your husband recently had a relationship with another woman, who is now expecting his child.

I chose to think of "expecting his child" not as a lie, but as an uncertainty. I showed it to Gianina. "Is the Italian correct?"

"Yes. But now I'm thinking—one of them might recognize your handwriting, no?"

"Would you write it for me, then?"

She looked uncomfortable, then nodded. "Yes, it's the only way." She took a fresh piece of paper and transcribed what I'd written, tweaking the language, then handed it back to me.

"I need to put this in the mail before I lose my nerve," I said.

"I have stamps."

She returned to her desk for an envelope, and I dictated Olivia's name and address in Sperlonga. She sealed it, put a stamp on it.

"Okay," I said. "I'm taking this to a mailbox now."

She smiled at me. "You're so young. If the marriage doesn't work out, you can always leave him—and Italy. When your child is eighteen and you'll only be, what?"

"Forty," I said.

"Still young enough to start over." Her wrinkled face broke into a gentle smile.

After posting the letter in a box on the piazza, I took the bus home. Stepping into my apartment, I didn't say hello to Robin and Nathan, who were hanging out in the living room, but went straight to my room, where I got into bed and pulled the bedspread over my head.

I heard Nathan come in.

"You okay?" he asked, standing over me.

"The doctor called earlier. I'm pregnant."

He sat down on the edge of my bed. "Listen, Foxy, we could get married," he said.

"Who? You and me?" Astonished by this gentlemanly reflex, I pulled the cover down to look at him. Robin was standing in the doorframe.

"Why not? We're all set up for it. We could renew the lease on the apartment—" he said.

"Don't be ridiculous. I told you I don't think it's yours. And you know there wasn't only Sergio, there was Doug and Dimitri, so the chances—"

"So what! I can be the father. I like living with you and—"

"But what about the princess? " I asked.

"Well, yes, there's that, but the fact is—you're more important to me than Claudia."

"That's sweet, but you don't mean it."

"Oh, sweetie," he said.

"Please don't feel sorry for me," I said.

My cousin approached and sat down cross-legged at the foot of the bed. With her curls and big silver earrings, she was the original free spirit of which I was a poor imitation. In my shoes, Robin would have had the baby, slung it on her back, and gotten on with things.

"Where have you been all afternoon?" she asked.

"I went to see an old friend," I said, "and she advised me to write an anonymous letter to Sergio . . ."

Their eyes grew wide as I delivered my tale, and I braced myself, wondering if they would challenge the logic of what I'd done. But they were only silent, astonished perhaps, until Nathan said, "I see." Perhaps he was hurt that I'd turned down his "proposal."

"You've got chutzpah," Robin finally said. "You're testing him."

"In a way, yes, I guess I am."

"Supposing Olivia reads the letter and doesn't say anything?" she asked. "Supposing she decides just to swallow it, or ignore it, because she wants to stay married? Why don't you just tell him?"

"I can't," I said. "Don't ask me why." I couldn't explain how much I cared for Olivia—it was absurd and unbelievable under the circumstances—and I couldn't explain that I wanted Sergio to have a choice in the matter. "I just know that this is the right way to go about it."

In the days that followed, there were moments when I wondered whether I was really pregnant. But my breasts were already changing and the nausea kept on and not just in the morning. Every time I stuck a toothbrush in my mouth, I thought I was going to throw up. In the meantime, I continued teaching at school, where I watched Sergio with a hyped up sixth sense, wondering when Olivia would get the letter and the situation would explode. I'd seen Gianina and posted the letter on a Wednesday. Italian mail was slow and unreliable, but when Friday and then the following Monday rolled around and he still hadn't said anything, I thought I'd go crazy. If we'd had a moment alone together, I might have grabbed him and blurted out my news. But the summer session was hectic, with students constantly swarming in and out, so there was no opportunity, and I was too upset to create one.

Monday night, I was about to leave when Sergio snagged me.

"Your aunt called," he said. "She wants you to call her. She has your ticket to Hong Kong."

"Oh," I said.

"When are you leaving?"

"In a couple of weeks." But was I really going to leave? Weren't we going to move to Milan together and have a baby? The back of my neck went into a spasm.

"All right, then," he said, just as a couple of the other teachers came in, ending our conversation.

I decided to call Doris from the corner café instead of using the phone in the office. Rushing down the stairs, I almost tripped on the last step. I took a left out the front door and then it was a few steps into the café, past the cashier, and to the phone in the back corner.

"Anna?" Doris answered. "When do you want to come over and get your ticket?"

"Can I come now? Doris—I'm pregnant," I said, glancing sideways at the cashier in her miniskirt.

"I thought you were smarter than that."

"What am I going to do?"

"I'm not your mother."

"But can I come over?"

"Of course you can come over. I've got your ticket. You fly out from Luxembourg."

I walked over to Doris's and let myself in. On hearing me, she came to the foyer.

"What a mess you've got yourself in—" she said.

"Is Halim here?" I said, dropping my voice. "I don't want to discuss this in front of him."

"No, he's walking the dogs. Don't you use contraception?"

"I haven't had a period in a year. I didn't think I could get pregnant, and sometimes I didn't have my device with me, and it was so spontaneous, like, like—"

"Like—at school—on the floor? Okay, I got it. So, what are you going to do? You know I can't help you. I'm not good around pregnant women."

"I'm not asking you to help me," I said, annoyed.

"But I want to know how you're going to dig yourself out of this."

"Gianina suggested I write an anonymous letter—"

"A traditional Italian move," she said, nodding.

"And we wrote it and I sent it. So maybe Sergio and I will move to Milan, then you won't have to see me as I expand—"

"Honey, I can't help it, but I just couldn't—"

"And if it doesn't work out, I'll need that plane ticket. So where is it?" Angry now at Doris for not being more helpful, I was impatient to leave.

"Follow me."

We went into her home office, where she switched on a lamp and picked up a thick envelope.

"I got the fare heavily discounted. I hope you appreciate that."

"I'll bring the cash next time I come over. Is it refundable?"

"Until forty-eight hours before."

"Thanks. I'd better be going."

"You don't want to stay for dinner? Call Robin and have her come over, too."

"No, I want to go home."

I was disappointed in Doris, who ought to have been willing to stand by me in this crisis. An existential vertigo came over me as I stuck the ticket deep in the leather satchel Sergio had given me. I didn't know whether I was heading for a life in Milan with a husband who might not be happy about the path forced upon him, or for an abortion and more global wanderings. I still very much wanted to go to Hong Kong. Ever since leaving the States, I'd enjoyed a Dionysian drunkenness of spirit that had remedied the miseries of a childhood parented by an alcoholic, narcissistic mother, and part of me wanted more of this remedy, even as another part whispered that life with Sergio and his child might provide a deeper cure.

"You know, I'm not sure I agree with Gianina's tactics," Doris said as I stood on the threshold about to leave. "Such an old-fashioned, Machiavellian approach. You're an American girl, that's why Sergio is attracted to you. Be direct. Just tell him you're pregnant."

"I don't want to force his hand."

"But you are, with the letter."

"No, not really. I mean, he could pretend he never got it. I want him to *choose* me. And it's not just about him. It's about Olivia. I want her to be able to save face." I didn't mention that I wasn't sure Sergio was the father.

Doris shrugged. "Sometimes I think you love her more than him. All right then. Call me when there's a development."

It was dusk as I made my way home. Getting off the number 16 bus at Via Angelo Poliziano, I heaved a sigh and slowed my pace. It was comforting to be back in my neighborhood with its modest little shops and dimly lit storefront windows. I stopped at a *frutteria* for some strawberry jam, thinking it might be appetizing on crackers for breakfast. Then, as I turned the corner onto Via Pascoli, I saw leaning against my building, next to the heavy wooden door, the flat lean figure of a man smoking a cigarette. For a split second I thought it was Sergio, who would have had the time, while I'd made the detour to my aunt's, to make his way from school to my place. My heart leapt up hopefully, imagining that Olivia had received the letter and called him from Sperlonga and that now he was here to tell me that things were over with her and he was ready to do what was needed in order to be with me, because it was meant to be, because the baby I was carrying—actually I didn't think of it as a baby, I thought of it as a cluster of cells that would turn into a baby, the way a sack of flour might, with care and attention, be turned into a loaf of bread—the "it" I was carrying was a sign from Fate that we were meant to be together.

But when I got closer, I saw it wasn't Sergio. It was his dark double, Nazzaro.

He stood in the classic pose of the waiting loafer—his back against the stone building, his feet a couple of feet forward so that his legs, straight and thin, went at a forty-five degree angle from wall to sidewalk. His left hand was deep in his pocket, his right hand held a cigarette. He wore jeans and a white T-shirt and looked absolutely average, except that he knew too much about me. And the closer I got, the more dread came over me. Was he degenerate enough to murder or rape? Whatever happened, I wouldn't invite him into my apartment. Of course, if he intended aggression, he could find a quiet moment to assault me in the waning light of dusk. I glanced at the street for some sign of a familiar vehicle and saw none. *So, no car nearby for him to cart my body away in.* Wait a moment, this was absurd. This was

Nazzaro, Sergio's cousin, we'd gone dancing together. He was just a hick who liked to throw his weight around. But how had he found out where I lived?

"*Ciao,* Nazzaro. What are you doing here?"

"*Ciao,*" he said on seeing me. "I was hoping you'd have a drink with me."

"All right. There's a place at the entrance to the park."

In dead silence, we walked a few short blocks to the Esquilino. Next to a heap of brick ruins stood a green, hexagonal booth with a drink stand, still open for business, and a dozen little tables, painted a matching green faded by weather. Thankfully, we were not alone, but in the company of a number of people unwinding at the end of the day with a soda, juice, or espresso.

"An apricot juice, please," I said to Nazzaro. Sitting at one of the metal tables, I might have been a young woman out on a date, waiting for her escort to bring her a refreshing drink as the warm June air touched her face. But no, alas, that wasn't me.

He came back to the table and set two glasses and two little bottles down. His silence unsettled me, which was exactly what he wanted.

"You didn't come up from Sperlonga to drink fruit juice with me," I said. "How did you find out where I live?"

"It wasn't difficult. Sergio has an address book he takes everywhere with him. It has all the teachers' addresses and phone numbers in it."

"So?"

"I have something for you," he said.

He reached into his pocket and took out the anonymous letter that I'd posted on Piazza Cosimato after meeting with Signora Gianina. The stamp was canceled, so my missive had reached its destination—or had it? Noticing that the envelope had been opened, I reached for it, but he quickly extended two fingers and pulled it back toward him.

"What's that?" I asked.

"I did a little intercepting. I'm no idiot, Anna. An anonymous letter to Olivia! In Italy, a letter with no return address—we know what that is. Let me repeat: I'm not stupid."

"I don't know what you're talking about."

"Of course you do."

"I don't."

"Then you won't mind if I tear it up."

He picked up the envelope, folded it carefully crosswise, then reached into his pocket and took out his knife, which he opened and used to cut the letter in two. The two resulting pieces were carefully folded in two, one at a time, and each ripped with the knife once again, until there were four quarters.

"Okay," I said.

"You want the pieces?"

"No."

He put them in his pocket, leaving the knife open on the table in front of him.

"You think—because you want it to be so—that the baby you're carrying is Sergio's, but do you think anyone else, in Sperlonga or elsewhere, will be so sure? A woman like you, American, who lives with a man friend, who has old boyfriends visiting her in her apartment, who hops off to Paris, where certainly she has a lover or two in reserve—such a woman, how can she possibly know who the father of her baby is? Even Sergio will have his doubts."

I said nothing, stunned. I'd been in such denial about my behavior that it had never occurred to me that Sergio would question his paternity.

"Sergio might believe you at first," Nazzaro continued, "but his thinking will eventually be contaminated by those around him—his *family*, who have loved and known him since birth—who will whisper in his ear, *are you sure? Are you sure?* And he'll start to wonder whether he wants to give up Olivia and his family for a whore"—*puttana* was the word he used—"who visited his bed in between one lover and the next."

"None of this is your business, Nazzaro—"

"Of course, you could write the letter again or simply see Olivia and tell her. And she would be shocked and angry with both you and Sergio—but she, too, would doubt the baby is his, and eventually she'd forgive him. That's what Italian wives do."

"Damn you."

He leaned in, grabbed my wrist, and pressed it into the little table with painful pressure while his other hand went for the pocketknife, still open between us, which he pointed in my direction. "You underestimate me. I would do *anything* to protect Sergio and my family. So I advise you to be very, very careful." He let go of me and stood up. "I think we're done now. Good night." He snapped the knife shut, stuck it in his pocket, and walked away.

I sat there perspiring as he exited the park. I'd wait a few more minutes before going home. No need to run into him a second time.

Finally, legs shaking, I stood up and made my way toward Via Pascoli—the lovely street where, nine months earlier, a young American woman in full bloom had landed for a marvelous adventure. It was now a narrowing tunnel, and I felt trapped, as though I were in a slow-motion version of that classic scene in thriller movies, in which a heroic spy is imprisoned in a room and about to be crushed by walls moving closer together. Nazzaro was right: Sergio treasured his family and his hometown. Could he be persuaded to give them up for—*me?* For a *slut?* Most likely not. Faint and drenched in sweat, I reached my building. The front door felt almost too heavy to open. I crossed the courtyard, made my way down the half-flight of stairs and into my apartment, where I found Robin cooking and Nathan on the couch with his guitar, as usual.

I sat down on the couch next to Nathan, who stopped playing the guitar and looked at me, concerned.

"You okay, Foxy?" he asked.

Robin came in from the kitchen and looked at me.

"Anna, what happened?" she asked.

I looked up at her. "We have to go back to Paris. And we have to do it straight away."

On my last morning in Rome, a bright June day, Nathan accompanied Robin and me on the 16 bus to the train station. There, we threaded our way through the tourist sharks and gypsies to the platform, where a crowd was waiting to board the *Palatino*. Nathan and I had a moment alone together when Robin went to the restroom.

"You sure you don't want to get married, Foxy?" he asked.

"Not that again! You can't possible be serious."

"But I am. Why not? It would be great to have a kid together."

"Even if it's not yours?"

"I said before that I didn't care, and I thought about it some more, and I really don't."

"You're years from settling down, and so am I, for that matter. And I don't want to hurt the princess."

"It's okay. I can break up with her." He suddenly grabbed and hugged me. "We've made a mess of things—you and me, I mean."

"It couldn't have been otherwise," I said, recalling the inventory of conquests that, yes, he'd torn up, but he'd soon start another. I could never be serious about someone who made lists, Don Giovanni style, of the women he'd slept with.

"I'm not sure about that," he said.

Robin reappeared and picked up her bag. The three of us walked down the platform until we reached our wagon.

"Time to say good-bye," Robin said.

Nathan kissed me gently on the lips. "You'll call me and tell me how it went, right?"

"Yes," I said. But I never would.

Robin and I climbed up the metal stairs into the train then shuffled down the corridor until we found our compartment.

After we'd hoisted our bags onto the rack, I sat down and saw Nathan still standing on the platform, looking at me mournfully. I opened the window and he came closer.

"It was a lot of fun living together," I said. "Some of it, anyway."

"You're terrific, Foxy." He had tears in his eyes.

"You too, Nathan."

He extended an arm, and I reached my hand out through the window and squeezed his fingers until the train groaned and, lurching forward, pulled our hands apart. He waved, while I, hit by the sadness in his expression, sank back into my seat and watched him recede.

15. Paris, Again

I'd called Leila Behrens before leaving Rome and told her I wanted to visit, but I didn't tell her why until Robin and I reached her place. I'd barely put my bags down when my whole story came out in a rush, while my cousin sat next to me in silence.

"So I've come to Paris for an abortion," I concluded.

Leila sat me down and gave me a hard look.

"You sure about this?" she asked. Solidly built, with a stare that went right through her tortoise shell glasses and cut to the matter at hand, Leila inspired trust. Even her bangs, perfectly trimmed, suggested an orderly lifestyle, and the wrinkles at the corners of her mouth gave her a responsible air.

"Pretty sure."

"Honey, abortion became legal in France four years ago, but it's not available to foreigners."

"It's not available?" I laughed bitterly as I remembered that scene in *Casablanca* when Captain Renault asks Rick why he's come to Casablanca. "My health. I came to Casablanca for the waters," Rick answers. "Waters? What waters? We're in the desert," Renault says. "I was misinformed," Rick says.

"What's so funny?" Leila asked.

"I was misinformed," I said, thinking of Gianina. "And I feel like an idiot."

"Maybe you could do it in Amsterdam," Leila said. "Or go home. If you're sure you want an abortion, that is."

"I don't see any other choice. I mean, where would I spend my pregnancy? How would I support myself and a child?"

"What about the father?"

"I'm not sure who the father is."

"Oh," she said.

"You don't need to know the details."

"The details could be important, if you want to have the child."

"I thought you believed in a woman's right to decide—"

"Yes, I do. I just want to make sure . . ." Leila stared at an undefined spot on the rug. "One day you might have regrets. Maybe you don't want a child now, but you might want one later on and—and not be able to have one." She looked at me again. "I had an abortion once."

"I thought you were gay," I said, rather stupidly.

"Before I was gay, I had a boyfriend." She looked back at that spot on the rug. "Anyway, sometimes I think I should have kept it, then I'd have a child now."

Robin and I absorbed her revelation in silence.

"It was 1955," Leila went on, "and pretty awful."

"I'm sorry," I said.

"Yeah," Robin said.

"Thankfully, things are different now, your fertility probably wouldn't be compromised, but still, you never know what can happen. And sometimes there is no right choice. If I'd had the child, I probably wouldn't have been able to have a teaching career, I'd be working in a supermarket." She sighed, looked back at me. "I'll take you to a doctor, we'll find out how far along you are and how much time you have to think it through."

If I hadn't expected my own last-minute uncertainty, I'd expected practical obstacles even less. I'd thought I could just sail into a clinic and have the "procedure" done and sail out, but now I was faced with the nitty-gritty of where and how. The only thing I was sure of was that I didn't want to go back to the States. So the next day Leila accompanied me to an obstetrical office in a hospital called La Pitié, which was near the Jardin des Plantes. I didn't have health insurance in France and had to pay out of pocket, but it wasn't very much. After a long wait, I was ushered into a tiny examination room. I'd come in through one door and was sitting on a chair waiting, when a doctor came in through another door and sat across from me. He had delicate facial features, the way small-boned French men do.

"*Alors*, when was your last menstrual period?"

When I said I didn't know, he invited me to undress and get on the examination table. It struck me as very French that you were supposed to take your clothes off right in front of the doctor, that they did without the hypocrisy of a screened changing area and a paper gown. As the doctor examined my cervix, I confessed that I didn't know who the father was. Going over my story in French, I was once again overcome with the sense of altered reality that I'd often had since moving abroad, but that quickly passed when I got off the table and he suggested I go to another hospital for an *échographie*, an ultrasound to help determine how many weeks pregnant I was.

"We don't have the equipment here," he explained.

I dressed while he wrote the information I needed on a piece of paper.

"I'm thinking of having an abortion," I said.

"You're at around six weeks, so it's early enough," he said. "But as a foreigner, you can't do it in France."

"I know," I said.

After the exam, I went out and met Leila in the waiting area. "So?" she asked, and I gave her the report as we walked out. We fell silent as we walked through a park with trees planted in careful rows and over to the Boulevard de l'Hôpital, where, following the elevated metro with its engineered metal tracks supported by Ionic columns, we continued in the direction of the Seine. The streets grew jammed with buses, and the sidewalks with café tables and pedestrians, after the tracks veered away from the avenue. We were approaching the Gare d'Austerlitz, the train station where I'd first caught the train to Rome a little over a year before. If I'd known what lay ahead, would I have accepted Doris's invitation to visit her there? Maybe not. The heat and the crowds, the pregnancy hormones and depression all intensified my fatigue, and I followed Leila with heavy feet. When Paris wasn't invigorating, it was huge and shapeless and exhausting. The river was near when we made a left toward the Jardin des Plantes, where we found a bench in a quiet spot and sat down. A woman walked by holding the hand of a cranky toddler. I thought about going for the sonogram and seeing a picture of the fetus. The idea that Dimitri might be the father still made me shudder and want to abort, but the possibility that the child growing inside me might be Sergio's had new meaning. And suddenly I wanted to hold onto it for as long as I could. Even if I would eventually give it up.

I reached into my pocket, fished out the piece of paper the doctor had given me, and handed it to Leila.

"This is where I'm supposed to go for the sonogram."

She pushed her big glasses up on her nose and looked at it for a long moment.

"If you don't want an abortion, you could stay with me," she said.

"Stay with you?" I turned to look at her. Even though this was the rescue I needed, I shook my head in the negative. "I can't impose in that way," I said.

"I want to help you. I can't explain why, but I want to."

"I don't know."

"You can have your old job back as my assistant to cover your expenses. We'll get your *carte de séjour* renewed and you can live with me, as you did before."

"Okay," I said. "I'll think about it."

Years later, I would ask Leila why she'd been so willing to have her life disrupted by a miserable young person, and she would confess that, as soon as I said I couldn't take care of a baby, she started thinking about adopting it herself. She told me that this fantasy continued for a few months, until she became involved with a woman, Martine, who didn't want the responsibility of a child. It was rare in those days for lesbians to raise children, and Leila's new partner didn't have the courage for it.

A few days later, cousin Robin left for Germany and another tryst with Manfred, and I settled into Leila's guest room. In a comforting return to an old routine, I went back to work as her research assistant, writing descriptions for her project cataloging French prints, as I'd done during my time in Paris two years before. I also wrote the foundation that had awarded me the Hong Kong scholarship and asked if I could put it off for a year. They said yes. And so my life plan was modified: I would have the baby, give it up, and return to my identity as a globetrotter. I'd gotten into trouble, but— *miracolo!*—I'd come up with a survival plan. Briefly, I congratulated myself on my resourcefulness and ingenuity.

But as I moved further into pregnancy and the baby began to move, serious depression set in. Memory has condensed those months because all the days were the same, and all were difficult. Leila found in a used clothing store a men's gray tweed coat big enough for my expanding belly, and I trudged through the winter rains wrapped in its wet wool smell. Mentally, I'd moved into a bit of a dissociated state: I was deep in my body and its processes, but also outside it. Foolishly, when I decided to keep the baby, I imagined I could grow and birth him without getting attached. What happened instead was a journey into love. I truly loved this unknown child, but felt unworthy of him. What stood in the way of my keeping him was, in the end, not my lack of home, partner, income, or family support, nor was it my desire for adventure, it was simply the deep belief that I couldn't be a good mother. Might I rage against this baby the way my mother had raged against me? Might I, in a moment of wretchedness, even harm him? I assumed that, if I had a child, I would have the same disastrous relationship with him that my mother had had with me. Someone else could parent him better. Anyone else.

Leila kept me afloat during that dark time. I had a knack in those years for finding mother substitutes, who provided the road maps I needed on my journey. And Leila's routines gave me security. Her habit of trimming her bangs on Sunday night, the orderliness of her research, and the punctuality with which she served dinner at eight o'clock sharp, French-style—all this held and contained me like an emotional swaddling, without which I would have fallen apart.

It was a night in March 1980 when I went into labor. I'd taken a couple of Lamaze classes but dropped out because I hated being the only unwed mother there. Now, as the pain increased, I regretted it. When the contractions started coming closer together, Leila took me to a hospital in a taxi. *I'll survive this the way billions of other women have,* I thought, but as the waves grew more intense and the hours went on, my courage left me. I would give my baby up, so there was no purpose to my suffering, nothing for me to gain from it, no reason to survive it. For hours they told me not to push, then someone commanded the opposite, but my body wouldn't listen. Part of me wanted to birth the child, but another part wanted to keep it, because pushing it out would mean separation. And so, in a room of metal and ceramic tile, the pain increased until I had in my mouth the taste of death, acrid like the dark blood of an evil god flying through the skies of my despair. Perhaps there were women equipped for such suffering, but I wasn't one of them. Finally, they gave me anesthesia and there was a hole in time, spacious and forgiving. A baby's cry was heard, and in a hallucination I saw a chunk of my heart, pink and bleeding, fall out of my chest and onto the tile floor.

I'd told the nurses I didn't want to see the baby, but they asked again, do you want to hold him, and I said, no. And I really didn't want to, because I didn't want to contaminate him with the self-loathing that was inside me. That too—the self-loathing—was a kind of dead-tasting bad blood that might sicken a child and make him die. Turned inside out, drained and drugged, I could barely hear my own *no* over the sounds in the room. And though I didn't want to see him, I did, alas, glimpse something—was it baby's feet?—as he was carried out of the room. Tiny and pink and fragile-looking. Or perhaps that, too, was hallucination. I heard someone say *trop de sang*, and in my altered state I thought that meant I had too much blood in my body, I didn't understand I was hemorrhaging until I was floating above and saw them starting the transfusion. A woman's voice said, *God is merciful*, and I saw a face set against a gold halo, as in a painting of a saint or a Buddha, and I said, *I'm not sure I understand what merciful means. Does it mean I'll be forgiven, or that God feels my pain and is sorry for me? I don't get it.* And the woman spoke again, more insistently, *truly, truly merciful*. Crying felt good, and I was still alive, so maybe God was merciful, after all. In the morning, if it ever came, I would consider whether life was worth continuing. For now, there was only sinking deeper into a turbid, oceanic sleep.

A bell from a church near the hospital kept ringing as time passed in a series of frozen, contrary stills: day, night, day, night, and day again. Nurses came by to monitor my bleeding: the placenta, exiting my body, had torn off a bit of the lining of my uterus. Finally the flow subsided and a doctor said I could be released. Leila came to get me and, as we walked out of the maternity ward, we passed the glass-walled room where the babies were kept in their bassinets. My baby wasn't there, having already gone to his new mother. I stopped and stared at the infants, leaning my forehead against the window. Well, not now, but maybe later. Maybe one day I'd be deserving and equal to the task. Of course, I didn't want my baby until he was taken away. But I bowed before my decision as the only possible one. I was a person of fortunate birth, well-fed and educated in a country that exported its wars—a person of privilege, in short—but in spite of all that, also a woman without roots or support, caught in a siege laid by the convergence of biology with my own stupidity.

Leila took me back to her apartment. There followed weeks of exhaustion and depression spent in bed. She offered to find me a doctor, a therapist, a support group. I refused. The cat rubbed its head against my face when I wept.

Finally, the weeping stopped. In May, my energy returned and I became so irritable that I couldn't bear to be in the apartment and so spent days walking, hoping that physical exhaustion would help me sleep. The most beautiful neighborhoods, the most splendid parks, had no effect on me as I passed through them. The gorgeous bridges of the Seine—so what? The quaint little streets of Saint-Germain—who cared? I was not *in* my own life, which was too grim a place to be. My life was something external, at a distance, and my connection with it felt remote.

Every day I walked in a different direction until nearing the point of collapse, then I'd drag myself to a metro station or a bus stop and ride back. Sometimes I stopped in one café, then another, for a glass of wine or a cocktail. One day I wandered all the way up into the 19th arrondissement. After several glasses of wine, I had a couple of coffees with brandy that left me feeling unwell. With my legs not quite obeying, I made my way into the hilly Buttes-Chaumont Park, where I wandered up and down paths, the picturesqueness of the site being so much noise as I grew more and more out of breath. Taking my own life would rid me of feeling the pain of my loss, but how might it be done? I went through my options—putting rocks in my pocket and jumping into the Seine, slashing my wrists, etc.— but quickly saw I wasn't desperate enough to follow through. The nature of living things was so goddamn persistent.

The wanting very much to *get off*, to *end things*, was a familiar feeling that came from my early years, something a small child, trapped, neglected, and abused, might feel, but that was now being felt by the adult me who had, full of love for her child and loathing for her self, given up her baby a couple of months before. The misery felt dark and *permanent*. I might eventually be able to put layers of other experience over it, but it would always be there. For I'd given away more than a healthy seven-pound baby boy. I'd given away that boy's first words and steps. I'd given away his smiles and laughter, his blossoming and development into a teenager, then a man. I'd relinquished years, decades of connection to another human being. It was an amputation of one of my heart's tentacles.

Drunk and heaving, I made my way to a bench, sat down, and promptly threw up. Wiping my mouth, I became dimly aware of a pair of eyes on me, then another, but no one asked *are you okay, do you need help?* Did I look like a woman with morning sickness or a drunkard? I didn't know. The vomiting continued, again and again. What came up and out of me was not only drink, but also bilious hatred—of myself for not being worthy of my child, of my mother for not having been worthy of me. Heaving, I expelled all the bad mothering that had brewed in me and my mother and my grandmothers and great-grandmothers all the way back to Eve. At last I was done and, emotionally as well as physically purged, stood up and headed back to the metro station and Leila's apartment.

How strange, almost unbelievable, that I managed, for years afterward, to put it all behind me, to resist wanting my little boy back or another child to replace him. When, after Sergio and Hong Kong, I returned to the States and had a series of relationships that didn't work out, in each case my partner's lack of desire to have kids confirmed me in my belief that I wasn't meant to be a mother. It was only when Robin had her child, Serena, a decade later, and I, dumbstruck by joy, held her in my arms for the first time that my armor of self-loathing fell away and I understood I would never be whole until I had another baby.

When I got back to Leila's place, I found her working at one end of the long dining table where we kept the documents and note cards for her cataloging project.

"What happened to you?" she asked, looking up at me through her big tortoise-shell glasses. "You look terrible."

"I was sick."

She put her pen down and went to get me a glass of water. When she joined me in the living room, I realized that it had been weeks since I'd cooked a meal or done any cataloging for her. I'd given up trying to earn my keep.

"I'm sorry I haven't done anything around the house in a while," I said.

"Don't worry about it," she said, sitting down next to me on the little couch. "You know, you're always going to be sad about this, but you have to move forward. You have to."

"I know."

"And you have to stop drinking."

"I know that, too," I said. She could smell alcohol on my breath. How humiliating. I swore to myself I'd never get drunk again. It was a promise I'd keep.

"You should leave Paris," she said. "I'm fine with your living here as long as you need to, but I think you're staying now for the wrong reasons. You need to leave France and move on."

For a moment I felt like I didn't have the energy or desire to go to anywhere. Then I saw she was right, I needed to move on. Leila didn't spell it out, but she knew I was staying in Paris because somewhere, in the maze of apartments and little houses, of courtyards and gardens, was the family who had adopted my baby. More than once, I'd had the crazy fantasy of finding and kidnapping the child and taking him back to Italy with me, presenting him to Sergio and saying, *look, look at what I got here. Yours. Maybe. Maybe, but let's pretend he's yours.* I said nothing, while Leila stroked my hair.

"Wasn't your original plan to go to Hong Kong early?" she continued. "You have some money saved up, right? Or you could go home for the summer."

"I can't go home. You know that."

"Then go to Hong Kong and enroll in a language class."

I met her eyes, big and brown through her glasses. In spite of her visits to lesbian nightclubs and her dream of a feminist revolution, Leila was a conventional academic: She believed that acquiring more knowledge was the solution to almost any ill. Though I didn't always agree with that, in this case her words were magic. Language study had always organized and regenerated my brain. Drawing, learning French, and Doug had gotten me through my dreadful adolescence. In the end, art, languages, and sex were the unholy trinity that had saved me repeatedly and would again. I laughed, remembering my fantasy of having sex on a pontoon with a Hong Kong banker who would teach me Cantonese between one caress and the next. It would be a while before I felt like having sex again.

"What's so funny?" Leila asked.

"Nothing. You think I can go to Hong Kong and not get in trouble?"

"I think so."

Yes, if I got to Hong Kong early, I could do some drawing and study language before I had to start teaching. There it was, underneath the devastation—the shreds of life desire and curiosity that I needed. For I still did want to travel in Asia and study Mandarin and Cantonese. Maybe if I kept moving, I'd somehow find a way to make peace with myself, I'd learn something or find something that would help me survive and bear my loss. Maybe one day I'd find my way back to joy, or something like joy.

"You're right," I agreed. "That's what I have to do. I'll go to Hong Kong early."

By the time I left Paris, I'd convinced myself that whoever had taken in my boy was the right family, and I would stay with that belief over the years. I was unfit to be a mother, and this child, removed from me and my dark heritage, would have a better upbringing than I could possibly ever give him. Destiny had brought me huge suffering, but it had also arranged things in the best possible way for my son. I could only hope he wouldn't suffer too much from being adopted.

As for Sergio, when I thought of him, there remained a big mix of feelings and impressions. The way he tapped a pencil on the desk blotter during our quiet conversations in the school office, our passionate nights at the Odeon making love as the smell of pasta sauce and curry drifted down the hall, our magical afternoon lying on the grass in Villa Borghese, and the fleeting fantasy of another life in Milan that we entertained on the night of the rooster—these were beautiful things etched in my heart. That I didn't know whether he was the father of my child, that I would never know just how much he'd loved me, that I'd enjoyed Olivia's friendship while sleeping with her man, and that, because of me, Sergio's marriage had begun with betrayal—these were terrible things I wanted to forget.

The worst was that I'd left without saying a proper goodbye. In the end, our love story was like a tattered book with the last chapters and back cover ripped off—begging resolution.

PART III

16. Flash Forward: 2004

Twenty-five years later, I was at my mother's place on Long Island, feeling both touched and remorseful as I mulled over my last phone call with Sergio, in which he'd revealed that he and Olivia had named their daughter Anna. Then, thinking about how I'd had a child who might have borne Sergio's last name, I reached for the letter from the French adoption agency informing me that the son I'd relinquished wanted to get in touch with me and, if possible, his birth father as well. The time had come to do whatever was necessary in order to find out who my son's dad was, and I wanted to—I owed him that. I had reconnected with one of the possible fathers, and the others might be findable for DNA testing. Jean-Paul would be twenty-four now, a young man wanting to know his origins as he made his place in the world. I wondered what he looked like and what kind of a person he was, whether he was married and working or still in school.

I was alone that morning because Chantal, the aide, had driven my mother to a group support meeting at the detox center and Cousin Julia had taken Esther into New York for the night. A few days had passed since I'd last spoken to Michael, who was back in our Berkeley home after his last trip. The divide between us felt so enormous that I didn't ask myself whether the time had come to tell him the truth about Italy and my first child. Eventually I'd tell him, but not yet. For now, my problems were mine alone, and I lay on the bed in my sister's room, transfixed by the messes of the past that had caught up with me.

I sat up. Outside the window, the oak trees and a single willow danced in the spring wind blowing in from Long Island Sound. Wanting to take advantage of my solitude to call Sergio, I went to my handbag to get the phone card I'd bought at the drugstore the day before, the kind that got you reduced rates for calling abroad. The numeric activation code was so long and I was so agitated that I kept on making mistakes plugging it in, but finally I got it right and heard Sergio's line ring.

"I'm so happy to hear your voice again," he said.

The connection was sharp and clear.

"Sergio, I have to tell you why I left Rome."

"Tell me, dear."

My story came out piece by piece—how I learned I was pregnant, how I went to Paris intending to get an abortion but ended up having the baby and giving it up.

"Why didn't you tell me you were pregnant?" His voice broke.

"I almost did." I stopped, remembering how Nazzaro had threatened me that evening in the park. "I wanted to—I really did—but, Sergio . . . I wasn't sure who the father was. I thought it was you, but I wasn't absolutely sure." Incredibly, twenty-five years later, a blush of shame warmed my face.

"So there were others—"

"Yeah, around the time of your wedding, because I was so upset—"

"And that's why you left without saying good-bye? Oh, Anna, why didn't you tell me?"

"Would it have changed anything if I'd told you right after you and Olivia had signed the marriage license? When I didn't know if you were the father? When I felt like a—*puttana*?" I said, using the Italian for whore.

"Don't blame yourself. It was all my fault. You wouldn't have slept with the others if I'd acted sooner. Anna, I was a very stupid young man, obstinate and confused."

"I'm still angry you didn't choose me, Sergio. Twenty-five years later, I'm still jealous of Olivia and wish you'd chosen me instead."

"That I made a mistake, okay, but how can you be jealous when you have your own family now? When you know things didn't work out with Olivia—"

"I guess I'm feeling now the jealousy I wouldn't let myself feel then."

"If only you weren't so far away now and we could meet face to face and talk about what happened—if only I could hold you and comfort you—"

"Sergio, I wanted to tell you, I tried—"

"What do you mean?"

"I wrote an anonymous letter to Olivia, but Nazzaro intercepted it. He said that everyone would call me a slut. And he threatened me with a knife."

"Damn that cousin of mine! Did he hurt you?" he asked.

"No, thank God. What ever happened to him?"

"He went to Argentina and never came back." There was a long silence, a bit of static. "Anna, why are you telling me this now?"

"I got a letter from the agency in Paris that placed my baby. My son wants to know who his birth parents are." Silence again. "Sergio, you still there?"

"Yes, dear, I am. What's his name?"

"Jean-Paul Macon."

"How strange," he said. "Your son—maybe our son—a Frenchman."

Another pause.

"What are you thinking, Sergio?"

"We have to go find him. We'll go together."

"You'll have to have a DNA test. He will, too. It'll be awkward," I said.

"Not if he needs to know. And I want to know, too. Anna, are you okay?"

"I don't know. The whole thing was so traumatic that I can't think straight about it."

There was a vibration in my body, a kind of shivering without sensation of cold, as my brain retrieved from long ago that glimpse of baby feet disappearing out the door of the birthing room—an image that, as the years went by, had come to seem more like a morphine-induced hallucination than a memory.

"Okay, here's a plan." Sergio's voice brought me back to reality. "Come to Italy in the middle of August. I'll have a couple of weeks off from work, we'll spend time together and get reacquainted, you'll see the apartment—then we'll go find him."

"Sergio, I'm frightened. I would do anything for him, and whatever he needs of me now, I'm prepared to give. But I'm afraid of what he'll think of me."

"Don't be. I'll be there. Paris, the two of us together, will be wonderful. As for your son, maybe *our* son, we'll mop up as best we can."

"If it makes him happy to find his biological parents, I might be able to . . . forgive myself."

"I hope so. It's time," he said.

"Sergio, we haven't exchanged pictures yet. I don't look twenty-two anymore."

"That doesn't matter to me. Underneath, I'm the same, you're the same. Don't you feel it?"

"I feel *we're* the same—our connection is the same—but I . . . I've turned into my opposite. I'm not the same person I was." The journey of life and the changes I'd undergone felt surreal. "Maybe you won't like the person I turned into."

"Don't worry about it."

"Okay."

"And I'll send you a photo now—to diminish the shock." He chuckled.

"Okay, I'll do that, too."

We said good-bye, and I went to stand at the window and look out toward my mother's studio in the backyard, where the trees were still dancing in the wind. It still drove me crazy to think that, in terms of probability, Dimitri was most likely the father because I'd had sex with him non-stop for a week. Yes, it had been fun at the time, but retrospectively what an idiotic episode! Then there'd been Doug, too . . . Damn, there I was going over the whole thing for the thousandth time. Well, maybe getting the facts would force acceptance. Sigh. At that moment in mid-June, in Rome, the flowers would have finished blooming, the tree canopies on Via Merulana would be dense and the birds chirping madly. I thought about how Sergio and I used to meet at the Odeon, how we'd had sex at school and at his apartment in Sperlonga. Even when I tortured myself about the other men I'd slept with, I continued to fantasize that I'd gotten pregnant the night of the rooster— that crazy night Olivia was at her mother's and Sergio and I made love until dawn. Incredibly, after everything I'd been through, the memory of that night could still get me aroused. I was standing there, flushed with desire, when my cell phone rang. It was Sergio again.

"Hi," he said.

"You okay?" I asked. His voice sounded raw.

"I'm thinking about everything you told me—what you must have gone through . . . those months of your pregnancy—and after you gave away the child, it must have been terrible. Were you alone?"

"I had a friend in Paris who took care of me."

"Do you think—do you think you might have gotten pregnant the night of the rooster? You remember the night of the rooster, don't you? What an incredible night . . ."

"Of course I remember it. I was just asking myself that question again."

"But you can't be sure it was that night?"

"My periods stopped when I went off the birth control pill, so no, I can't be sure."

"That was quite a night," he said, his voice breaking.

"Sergio, you never said you loved me. I wish you had."

"Where I come from, when a man speaks those words, they constitute a pledge with big consequences—almost a proposal—so I couldn't say them, given the particular circumstances, but I did love you. And I love you still."

"I love you, too, Sergio. If only we could get in a time machine and go back! Do you have a time machine?"

"No, *cara*. I wish I did. You were so adorable with that short haircut—"

"I'll cut it again for you."

"Would you really? Crazy girl! Anna, what are you wearing today?"

"Jeans and a blouse. Why?"

"What kind of blouse?" he asked.

"With a red floral print—"

"I loved your printed skirts, your wild outfits—and what kind of jeans?"

"Low on the hips, the kind that's in fashion now."

"So if you take your shirt off, I can imagine your belly, my hand on it, caressing you, your soft skin—"

"Sergio—"

"Unzip your jeans, put your hand where it's supposed to be—where mine should be—"

"Okay . . ."

"Do you have a finger on your berry? Remember how we used to call it that?"

"I'm remembering everything, Sergio, more and more of it."

Phone sex was a betrayal, but how much of a betrayal? This was the question I pondered later that day, and the next, and during the trip back to California. Just as I had led Sergio to betray Olivia twenty-five years before, he had now led me to betray Michael. The symmetry felt equitable, like the completion of a pattern. I felt guilty and not, at the same time. Certainly I felt less remorse when, arriving in California after a twelve-hour trip—the train from my mother's into New York, a bus out to JFK airport, then the flight to San Francisco and shuttle bus home—Esther and I found the house in a shambles. A slob by nature, Michael had, in the first years of our marriage, made an attempt to pick up after himself, but now that he was successful, traveling a lot and overworking, he didn't give a fuck. There were dishes piled up in the kitchen sink, greasy take-out boxes on the dining table, papers covering the couch, and clothes on the floor in the bedroom.

"Kind of messy, isn't it?" Esther said.

"Yeah," I said. "Hey, you have school tomorrow."

"I want a snack."

We wheeled our suitcases into our respective rooms then met in the kitchen a few minutes later. As Esther poured herself some cold cereal, I saw a note in Michael's hand on the breakfast table: "Gig in Sacramento. Home late."

It aggravated me that he still accepted gigs when he had a steady teaching job and his compositions were being performed in major venues. I knew his habit of going after every possible penny, at whatever cost to health and family, came out of a musician's lifetime of poverty, but his overworking meant that I had to pick up after him while he used the house as a hotel.

"What was the best part of the trip for you?" I asked Esther.

"Going into New York with Aunt Julia," she said.

"I'm glad you had a good time."

"Julia said she and Uncle Ben might provide me with a cousin."

"She told you they're thinking of adopting?"

"Yeah. I'm pretty excited. I'd be the older one. I don't like being the younger one all the time, the way I am with Serena," she said, referring to Robin's seventeen-year-old daughter, who lived in San Francisco. "How does it work anyway?"

"How does what work?"

"Adoption."

For a moment I wondered whether she knew my secret. No, it wasn't possible. She couldn't *know* but maybe she *intuited*, in the way that intimates do.

"If a woman can't take care of her child, she finds someone who can. Well, usually it's an agency that does."

"Oh," she said, looking puzzled.

I had a lot to tell her. One day. When I got a handle on things.

After we finished our snack, I went into the bedroom, threw Michael's clothes into the laundry basket, and closed his drawers. I picked up the half-smoked joint next to his side of the bed and, although I hated his habit, put it in a plastic bag instead of throwing it away, because pot was expensive and he'd only buy more. Michael lived so much in his head, in his music and ears, that he was indifferent to his surroundings. I'd known this before I married him, yet I couldn't make peace with it. As I put the joint in his bedside drawer, a voice inside whispered, *This is trivial, stay the course and recommit—for Esther's sake.* But another voice whispered, *Maybe not. Maybe—enough.*

I thought of the rooms at Buddhaland, where I occasionally went on retreat. They were monastically devoid of things, and being there always soothed my ruffled feathers. The next time Michael was home for a weekend, I'd go up there to decompress and figure everything out—Sergio and the son I'd given up and my marriage and where it was all going. Maybe if I went away, I would get some clarity about Michael and remember why I'd chosen him. I had to figure things out because the situation I'd slipped into was feeling increasingly unstable. That I'd been in correspondence with Sergio was bad enough. Worse was that, since having phone sex with him, I'd been in a slightly altered state—living neither in the present nor in the past, but in some place deep in my brain that opened onto a fifth dimension where Sergio and I were connected. And the more I allowed myself to love him, the more I regretted what I'd done and wondered how I was ever going to forgive myself.

Later that week, we exchanged photographs of ourselves. When I clicked on Sergio's to open it, I was shocked by how much he'd changed. His hair had gone completely gray; his face had thickened. But the smile was the same, as was the beauty mark on his right cheek.

One early morning I had a dream in which I was somewhere in Italy, looking out the window at the Mediterranean, which lay beyond a port. I was under a heavy dress and finding it hard to breathe. There was a tremor of excitement in my body. I was aware I was dreaming and said to myself, look, here I've landed in some corny scene from a period piece movie—a young woman waiting for her suitor, all a-flutter. Then the door opened and suddenly everything was as real as anything I'd ever lived. A man walked in, someone who felt familiar and beloved—and I understood it was a previous incarnation of Sergio. When I looked into his eyes, it was as though I were looking into a mirror reflecting another mirror across from it, so that I was peering down a tunnel of reflections set one into the other and growing ever smaller. And when I saw that this tunnel went back, through layers of the past, to a lifetime in which Sergio and I had known enormous happiness together, my heart was flooded with light and my whole body warm with joy.

When I opened my eyes, they were wet with tears.

The dream felt huge, and I longed to share it with someone. There had been too much going on in my life that I'd been keeping to myself, and I needed a confidante to release some of the pressure. Only Robin would understand. I thought about how she had accompanied me to Sergio's wedding, how she'd supported me when I learned I was pregnant that awful day in Rome, how she'd gone back to Paris with me and been there when I decided to carry my baby to term. So I called her and asked if she was free so I could visit. She said she had time in the afternoon, so later that day I drove across the Bay to see her.

Robin lived in the Richmond area of San Francisco, where the avenues leading out toward the ocean are often covered by fog, in a house around the corner from a wide avenue lined with cafés, Asian grocery stores, and little boutiques with last year's fashions in the windows.

I rang the doorbell and she opened the door. She was wearing green corduroy pants and a denim shirt. The silver necklaces around her neck, dotted with turquoise and bearing pendants depicting a deer, a wolf, and a hawk testified to her interest in Native American spirituality and ancient practices of healing soul and body. I followed her into the kitchen, where she put a kettle up for tea.

"So, what's up?" she asked.

"I've been in touch with Sergio again."

"Sergio?" Robin frowned.

"Yes." I told her about my correspondence with Sergio. "He declared his love to me over the phone."

"Past love or—present?"

"Both. I don't think time enters into it."

"Okay. Have you told him?" She was referring to my little boy. We never talked about it, though she knew everything.

"Yes, I did. Not immediately. But finally I had to because I got a letter from the agency in Paris. It seems my son wants to meet me, so Sergio and I are going to go to Paris to find him."

"Okay. But you've never told Michael about it, have you?"

She had an upset, almost cross look. More than once over the years, Robin had suggested I tell Michael my secret, and each time I'd given reasons not to.

"No." As I went over it with her, the extent of my cover-up came home to me. There had only been one other point in my life when I'd been so aware of it: When I was carrying Esther, I'd asked my obstetrician not to share with my husband that it was my second pregnancy, and Michael never asked himself why I delivered her in record time. "Robin, I don't know where all this is going, but I'm afraid. For my marriage."

"You feel . . . uncertain?"

"I feel . . . destabilized."

"Michael isn't easy," Robin said. "And parenting is hard.

It puts a lot of strain on a marriage. Sometimes I think I've had it good being a single parent."

"But you aren't single, exactly. You've had Gloria," I said, referring to the woman she'd lived with for twenty years. In an unusual arrangement, they'd helped each other raise their children.

"True," she said. She poured boiling water into the cups. "Let's go down to the cave."

"Cave" was her name for the downstairs space where she saw therapy clients and ran groups focused on spiritual development. In a square room with a single set of windows looking out onto a backyard, shelves displayed feather fans, decorated gourd rattles from Peru, and stone figurines of animals made by the Zuni tribe of New Mexico. On the walls were hide drums and Native Mexican "paintings" that used brightly colored yarn pressed into wax to depict gods, birds, and deer. Bronze figures of the Buddha and Kwan Yin were scattered here and there.

We sat cross-legged, and she placed the tray with teapot and cups between us. Comforted by the sacred art around me, I took a deep breath and relaxed. For a moment, we sat quietly, mindfully coming into the present moment.

"Sometimes this kind of obsessive, recurring relationship," Robin finally prompted, "comes from another lifetime."

Her words, so on target, startled me, for my dream about meeting Sergio's previous incarnation had been following me all morning and afternoon. Sometimes truth lies in the interstices of thought and perception, in the work of the imagination rather than our daily experience. In that dream, I'd glimpsed something huge and essential to my being—a fragment of another lifetime with particular meaning. Was it possible that the idea of important relationships recurring over lifetimes wasn't a New Age cliché but an element of ancient knowledge lost to modern man?

"I had a dream last night—that kind of dream."

"About?"

I'd wanted to tell her everything, but now the details felt too private. I stayed vague. "We knew each other in another lifetime," I said. "The feeling was so uncanny. There was this sense of familiarity, of an enormous connection between us."

So enormous, I realized, that in other lifetimes we continued to yearn and look for each other. Thus it happened that, in all of our lives, we contrived to meet again and again, even when circumstances were against us.

"You know—"

"It's—an absolute bond, beyond and outside of time."

Remembering my dream as I sat with Robin in her quiet, sacred space, I suddenly had the sense of all points in time and space coexisting simultaneously, as though my previous and subsequent lifetimes, including those with Sergio, still and always floated in another kind of Now, an alternate, temporally unified dimension in which we were always together. The wonder was that I could, in loving him, tap into the sense of my soul's journey.

Love is a mystical experience that takes you on its space ship to a place in the universe where you can be made whole.

"Go on," Robin prompted.

"Whatever happens," I continued, "I'll be okay. I'm seeing that we've been together in other lifetimes, and that those times of our togetherness still exist, are still happening, somewhere out there, or deep in here"—I touched my sternum—"in the dimension where all space and time are One."

With a warning to drive carefully, Robin sent me off into the dusk, and I drove home across the Bay Bridge with a sense of having been touched by a sacred insight. But the inevitable, precipitous fall from the mystical back into the mundane came an hour later at the dinner table, when I found myself jarred by an argument Esther and Michael were having before me.

"I don't want to take piano lessons anymore, and that's final!" Esther screamed.

"I won't let you give it up when you've come so far, that's what's final!" Michael screamed back.

"I hate it, I hate it!" The child had tears of fury in her eyes. Michael put his fork down, looked at me. "Don't glare at me, support me."

"I wasn't glaring at you, but I can't support you, because I don't agree with you," I said. "If she's not musically inclined, why force her? Why not let things be? She's been struggling with it for five years, without enjoyment."

"I thought we decided we wouldn't contradict each other in front of Esther. Especially when one of us has already reached a decision." With his voice booming, Michael seemed twice his usual size, inflated with the determination to turn his unmusical child into his image.

"You reached that decision without me," I said.

"See, Mommy agrees with me," Esther said.

"I thought I was in charge of her musical education!" Michael said, furious.

"Well, her musical education is now over!" I said. "So you're not in charge anymore!"

I got up, threw my napkin on the table, and, leaving the kitchen, headed toward the bedroom, where I sat on the edge of the bed, feeling powerless. Esther, fully in the adolescent phase of worshipping her father, was riding on a hysteria coming out of two conflicting needs—a desperate need to please him and an equally desperate need to assert her own agenda. She wanted his approval more than anything else, but the piano lessons were torture for her, and feeling stupid at the keyboard on a daily basis so threatened her self-esteem that rebellion was her only option.

I was focusing on my breathing when my cell rang. It was Robin.

"You doing okay?" she asked.

"Sort of," I said. "We've been fighting here. All three of us."

"I'm so sorry. You want me to call back later?"

"No, it's all right. I left the room. And thanks for listening to me today."

"I'm calling because you seemed elated and—I want you to be careful—"

"Driving home over the bridge, I decided to go to Rome for the last two weeks of August, before school starts—"

"Are you sure? "

In the background, I heard Michael and Esther snapping at each other. If I intervened, I'd only make things worse, so I ignored them.

"Talking to you made me realize that this thing with Sergio is real."

"Listen," Robin said, "you need to slow down. You think you're in love with Sergio again, but you might not be attracted to him when you see him. Twenty-five years have passed. You might not like the way he looks or the way he smells—"

"He'll smell like all Italian men—of garlic and aftershave," I said, laughing.

"You sound giddy, which isn't necessarily the best way to—"

"Don't worry about me. I'm going on retreat for a few days, so I'll have a chance to think things through. We'll talk about it more when I get back, okay?"

After hanging up, I took refuge in the bathroom, locking the door behind me. Putting the lid down on the toilet, I sat and listened. There was a last round of screaming then the ruckus in the kitchen subsided, and Michael and Esther were talking in softer voices.

I got up, stared at myself in the mirror. When Sergio and I finally met, what would he think of me? The way my face had puffed and fallen with the years made me think of the way skin loosens on a parboiled tomato. My long auburn hair, frizzy and streaked with gray, wasn't flattering. I remembered the short haircut I'd had in Rome, how it had lent me an androgynous mix of masculine power and feminine chic.

Opening the drawer in the sink commode, I grabbed the clips and scissors I used to trim my hair and Esther's. My intention was drastic transformation. I pinned up the top layers of hair, exposing the under layer, and took a deep breath: I was an artist; I could do this. I began to cut, letting the tresses fall into the sink.

Dishes clattered in the kitchen. Father and daughter had resolved their differences and were cleaning up together. I continued my work. Sometimes I grabbed too much hair and the clump resisted the blades, but I exerted force and kept going. I continued until the mane was gone and the sink full of hair. I locked eyes with my reflection. I looked like that wild, passionate young woman who had once lived in Rome. I looked like an aging Buddhist nun. I was both those things. I was neither. I put the scissors down, satisfied with my handiwork.

I planned on sorting things out while on retreat, as I'd told Robin I would, but before I left I purchased my plane ticket.

From: Anna Stark
To: Sergio Buria
Dearest,
Tomorrow I'm going up to the Buddhist center for a while, so if you don't hear from me for a bit, you'll know why. I have to hand over my cell phone when I arrive and won't have access to email.

I'm so glad I told you my secret and that you want to come with me to find my child. Of course I'm hoping that he's yours, too, but, either way, your going with me will make things easier. We'll meet with someone at the agency in Paris who'll set up a time for us to see him. There are papers to sign, and so forth. It's France, so lots of bureaucracy.

I'm flying to Rome on August 14th! I can't wait to see you. Sergio, since we made love on the phone, I can't stop thinking about you—and desiring you.

Kisses,
Anna

17. Retreat

When I got to my room at Buddhaland—so pleasingly stark and quiet it was—I put on my black novitiate's robe. Changing dress helped me shift my consciousness in the direction of meditation and prayer. As I tied the sash around my waist, I thought about how I'd had phone sex with Sergio, then written him confessing my desire. Feelings of shame and foolishness came over me. It was all deeply confusing, but I could use the quiet time on retreat to reflect on the meaning and consequences of my actions.

Breathe in, breathe out. Early morning meditations in my dormitory room. Silent meals, vegetarian of course, in the cafeteria with fellow visitors and the resident monks and nuns. Twice a day, I found refuge in the Great Hall, where hundreds of foot-high Buddha statues behind glass lined the walls. Donated by worshippers over the years, the figurines came from many countries and traditions. Some were of bronze or wood adorned with gold paint, others of ceramic or terracotta. The Buddha was depicted in various postures—extending the bowl of healing, or with hands on his knees, or one hand resting inside the other. A sense of compassion and patience emanated from these representations, offering what I needed to repair my heart.

The days were filled with summer heat and soft gongs and prayer, the nights with mantras, the eerie meow of peacocks, and the music of frogs by the pond and crickets in the grass.

Listening to prayers, some of them in English, others in Mandarin, I recalled my time in Hong Kong, which had marked the beginning of my spiritual quest. Faced with the raw pain of having given up my child and still yearning for Sergio, I'd exiled myself to a continent where I had to start all over again, without friends or family. Prayer was the only remedy for my desolation, and I prayed in whatever temple I chanced upon, to whatever deity presented itself—the Buddha of course, but also the goddess of mercy, the god slayer of demons, the goddess of fishermen, the god of longevity—it didn't matter. If there was a temple, I stepped in, bought a stick of incense, and prayed.

Now here I was, a quarter of century later, praying again with the same fervor. I returned to the meditation exercise in which I saw myself as a Taoist monk sitting in a mountain-side cave, hosting dark feelings that took the shape of visiting dragons. When guilt and loss came up about the child I'd relinquished, the only thing I could do was sit with my feelings and journal them until they moved out of mind and body. Meditating and mourning as the days went by, I released some of my self-hatred and inched forward to self-forgiveness. I saw that the time for secrecy was over, that I had to tell Michael about my emotional re-involvement with Sergio and the baby I'd given up. I wanted to protect Esther, but I also needed to go to Paris to find my son and learn who his father was. If Sergio wasn't the father, I would look for my other partners so that we could do DNA testing. Doug, Dimitri, Nathan—it might not be possible to find them all, but I had to give it a try. My son had lived his life with too much not knowing.

I also had to face the implications and consequences of desiring Sergio again. The Buddhist precepts for right living, including the one against sexual misconduct, had provided me with a road map for some years. I no longer had the emotional stamina for the subterfuge I'd engaged in during my youthful affair with Sergio, so if we became lovers again, I'd have to ask Michael for a separation, although I hated the idea of shaking up Esther's world. I imagined leaving Michael, spending the school year with Esther in Berkeley and the summer with Sergio in Rome. When the time was right, I would take Esther to Italy with me so that she could get to know Sergio. Depending on how things went with Jean-Paul, I would also take her to Paris so she could meet her half-brother.

But wait a minute—I was getting ahead of myself. Sergio in the flesh would be different from Sergio long-distance. It was absurd to be on the crest of raw lust after so many years when, as Robin had said, I didn't know how I'd feel on seeing him. And maybe he loved me, but did he want to be with me? He and Olivia were divorced, but he still visited her, spent time with her and his daughters. Maybe he still thought of me as "lover" —the *amante* a man has a *storia* with but never commits to, the woman purveyor of pleasure and diversion. And I wasn't about to go there again. Then there was the possibility that Sergio and I might not mesh again, that our reunion might be brief or unsatisfactory. But I had to be open to whatever might happen.

There were moments when, fearful of the uncertainties that lay ahead, I questioned my direction, but the clearer I became inside, the more I saw that I also had to make the outside clear. I kept on coming back to the fact that I needed to spend time with Sergio in order to get closure over losing him years before, even if that meant risking my marriage. Dissolution of my marriage would feel like a failure, but failure would be the price of authenticity.

I thought about Michael again. When we'd first been together, I'd found him inspiring and believed he was a kindred spirit. Then, after Esther's birth and his musical success, when free hours became a luxury, I'd found myself getting the short end of the stick. Michael's genius and obsessive composing had made him the dominant partner, and I was tired of it. Could I re-balance things by periodically running away to a Buddhist retreat? Or would Michael continue to do exactly as he pleased, not caring to discuss or compromise? Part of me still wanted to make a go of it, to find the generosity of spirit I needed to continue living in an arrangement that wasn't quite right for me. But another part wondered whether I'd clung to "for better or for worse" for too long. If I released my old habits of self-punishment, what might happen? How might life open itself up to me?

The uncertainty of the moment had little anguish in this sacred place. Rather, it hung in the air, full of magic and possibility, like a hummingbird suspended before a flower.

I was passing the front desk on the way from my room to the meditation hall when Mei Xing stopped me.

"There's a message for you, Bai An," she said, using my Chinese name.

"Thanks."

I approached the desk and bowed as she handed me a note taken by someone in the main office.

Michael called and will be visiting tomorrow with Esther and Julia.

So much for my peaceful mood! I hadn't known Julia was on the West Coast. Was she staying with Michael and Esther in Berkeley or with Robin in San Francisco? The idea of Julia staying in my house with Michael while I was away struck me as a violation of some rule of propriety—absurd, of course, given that their relationship in college had been platonic. And Esther would function as a chaperone.

The next morning, I was meditating when Mei Xing knocked at my door. I opened it and we bowed to each other.

"Your visitors are here," she said.

I nodded and followed her down the corridor.

There they were, the three of them—daughter, husband, cousin. My heart filled with joy on seeing Esther, whom I'd missed terribly without realizing it.

"You're delicious," I said, hugging her.

"Mommy!"

I kissed Julia, then Michael, on the cheek. In some corner of my contradictory heart, I'd hoped I would experience a surge of love on seeing my husband again, if only to avoid the pain and disruption of separation. But instead there was muted anger and a longing for exit.

"When did you get in?" I asked Julia.

"A couple of days ago," she said.

We stepped outside. The heat felt pleasant after the coolness of my little room. The campus was quiet as the hour between eleven and noon, coming after the completion of morning chores and before the midday meal, was a time of meditation, either private or in the communal hall. Michael and Julia sat on a bench while Esther and I wandered in the direction of "peacock pond," where a dozen or more of the large birds congregated, occasionally piercing the silence with their high-pitched cries.

"How was camp last week?" I asked my daughter.

"Boring, I don't like being a CIT."

"I'm so sorry." I stroked her hair. "You said last summer that you wanted to do it, and now I'm afraid you're committed. At least it's only day camp, not sleep-away."

"I know." She shrugged then looked up at me with her child's eyes. "Tell me the Buddha's story again. The part about when he left the palace."

I stopped and leaned against an old oak tree, feeling its bark through the back of my novitiate's robe.

"Siddhartha Gautama was born a prince in India, many centuries ago. He grew up in a palace where he married and stayed for many years without ever stepping outside, because his father wanted to protect him from knowing the evils of life. Well, one day when he was twenty-nine, Gautama decided he wanted to go out to meet his subjects. That's when he had his three meetings with reality—with the realities of human suffering, that is."

"His three meetings with reality," Esther repeated. She

crouched down to the ground and picked up a stick. "One," she prompted, drawing a line in the dirt.

"One, he encountered an old man, which made him realize that people age. And that aging can bring suffering."

"Okay," she said. Clearly she felt *that* would never happen to her.

"After that, he wanted to know the whole truth—not to be shielded anymore—so he went back out and on that second outing he saw a sick man—"

"And he realized people can get sick. I've been sick," she said, drawing a number two.

"Yes, but you've never been very sick, thank God, knock wood, and all that."

"And then what happened?"

"Of course Gautama wanted to know absolutely everything, so he went out a third time, and that's when he saw a corpse."

"I've never seen a corpse. Only in movies. Have you?"

"When my father died," I said. "You were very little at the time."

We both fell silent. She looked back at the ground and drew the number three.

"And it was after he saw the corpse that he decided to leave the palace for good?" she finally said.

"That's right."

"Well, if *he* decided to leave the palace, why did *you* decide to come up here? Daddy said you're 'seluding' yourself."

"The word is 'seclude,'" I said, startled by her misunderstanding of Buddha's story. "This isn't exactly a palace—"

"It's the same idea, isn't it?"

"No, it's different." I paused, trying to sort out her comparison. "This is more like—like sleep-away camp for grownups. I'll be home soon," I said. "I promise."

Michael and Julia were approaching as Esther looked up at me with an expression I'll never forget—the expression of a child's intelligence shining out and shimmying as it collides with an unpleasant thing racing toward her. Then it was gone. She stood up and, throwing her stick to the side, ran toward her father. "Let's go to the pond, Daddy."

"Sure," he said.

Julia hung back as the two of them wandered toward the peacock pond.

"It's good to see you, Julia. I didn't know you were coming out to California this summer."

"It seemed like Michael could use some help with Esther."

Julia's dry tone implied that I was neglecting my duties. She undoubtedly saw me as involved with some weird New Age sect. I'd grown up imbued with that same secular skepticism before my suffering and travels created the conditions for spiritual emergence.

"This isn't one of those crazy California cults that New Yorkers like to denigrate," I said. "Master Lun Yi belongs to a wisdom tradition that goes right back to the Chan Buddhism of ancient China—"

"And they teach that it's okay to abandon your children?"

"I haven't been gone that long. For heaven's sake, when we were kids, we went away to summer camp for two months at a time!"

Julia's readiness to censure me was galling, yet the fact of our relatedness made me want her understanding, her support even. I tried to explain the value of a spiritual retreat, but her expression remained stiff, superior. My cousin had a moral rigidity that kept me from revealing anything about Sergio and my son. I'd never told her about my first pregnancy for a reason: she would have judged me a monster for relinquishing my child. Decades later, she hadn't changed much. In any case, I couldn't tell her before I told Michael.

"How about I take you for a tour?" I suggested. "I want to show you the Great Hall."

We'd come to the main building, where two Chinese frescoes depicting dancing gods rose twenty feet on either side of the double front door.

I opened the door for Julia. "This is where I'm at peace," I said as we stepped inside.

"It's very—impressive," she said, gazing at the statues.

I looked at her sideways, uncomfortable with her and the situation. Of course, that's what she and Michael wanted—to make me uncomfortable. Going on a spiritual retreat if you're a mother is more than a violation of convention and routine, it's a revolutionary act.

Leaving her to look about on her own, I sat down on one of the benches. *May all beings be happy. May all beings be free.* I prayed all the time now, and praying for others often felt more comforting than praying for myself. Some of the prayers, in Chinese, resonated internally like incantations from another dimension, and murmuring them afforded tranquil pleasure.

After a few minutes, Julia joined me and we exited the hall, then wandered about until we found Michael and Esther by the pond where the peacocks gathered. Julia paired off with Esther, and I had a moment alone with Michael.

"It's nice to see Julia," I said.

"She's a good auntie."

We fell silent.

"We're on our way to Mendocino to spend the weekend with Val," he said, referring to a friend who lived in a pictur-esque village on a cliff overlooking the Pacific. Val's daughter and Esther were great friends. "I thought Julia might like to see some of Northern California, and I'm going to help Val with a photography class."

"Do you think Esther really doesn't like being a CIT?" I asked.

"I don't know why she says that. She seems to love it. She's full of stories when I pick her up in the afternoon." He paused. "You've been gone three weeks." Accusing.

"Has it been that long?" I was honestly surprised.

"Anna, we have to talk."

"Yes, we do—"

"You've been so distant for—what—three months? Or has it been three years? Something has to give—"

"You've been distant, too!"

"Do you want a separation?" he asked.

"We should talk about it at some point."

"Okay. What do you have to say?"

"Well—" I turned toward him, wanting to tell him everything then and there, but the gray, angry expression on his face stopped me short. His dry lips were pressed together, as though stamped shut. I wouldn't have an ugly scene with Esther nearby, in a place that felt sacred to me.

"We can't have that kind of conversation now, with Esther here."

"All right."

We fell silent. The campus was coming to life as people emerged from the dormitories and headed toward the Great Hall. I gazed at Esther across the lawn. Julia was on her cell phone, probably talking to her husband in New York. Then she and Esther wandered into a building.

As though to take advantage of Esther's absence, Michael started in on his attack again. "Anyway, I can't have a real conversation with you in those ridiculous robes." He gestured up and down at my novitiate's garment.

"Wearing this helps me shift into retreat mode—"

"And I can't get used to your short hair. Why the hell did you lop it off? You gonna become a nun or something?"

"You know what, this isn't the place—" I started. We had walked back to the Great Hall and I looked inside with longing.

"I thought we were in agreement when we got married. I thought we wanted the same things—a child, a family."

"We did. But sometimes it doesn't work out."

"I'm not going to put up with this forever—the way you keep disappearing."

I welcomed the words because I wanted the decision to separate to be mutual. But I wouldn't take all the blame.

"You're being unreasonable. You go away all the time for per-formances—I'm not taking more time than you ever have."

"I take lots of short trips, yeah, but that's different from just going away and not saying when you're coming back—"

Just as he was building up a head of steam for a fight, monks and novitiates in robes and townspeople in day clothes began filing past us and into the hall in silence. That was where I also wanted to be, inside with the Buddhas and the incense and the dust-speckled light angling in through the clerestory windows. A gong clanged gently, announcing the imminent beginning of the service.

"I'm going in," I said. "Kiss Esther good-bye for me. Then how about you leave her with Julia for a day and come back by yourself?" I said. "We'll go off campus for coffee and a talk." I bowed good-bye and went inside.

The idea of leaving my husband brought up all my fears. I'd already been a bad mother once, and now I'd be one again. I felt cursed, as though I'd inherited the bad mother gene from my own mother. I hated the idea of Esther shut-tling between her parents or, worse, living with one and not having the experience of two. But we couldn't escape what was coming. So I made my plan for my conversation with Michael—which café we'd go to in the town near the retreat center, what I'd say and ask for. I'd suggest that we work with a mediator instead of a lawyer, that we share custody of Esther. I planned to remain calm, no matter how reactive Michael became. My sense was that he was equally ready to separate, so I felt optimistic we could proceed amicably. Maybe we could even continue to cohabitate while I looked for another place to live.

A couple of days later, I felt prepared for his return. But my equanimity disappeared after morning meditation when, stepping out of the Great Hall, I saw him and Julia sitting together, holding hands. Esther was nowhere to be seen. Julia was leaning toward Michael, her head on his shoulder.

Shock. For a moment I didn't move, I just stood staring at them. Then came a surge of fury, chasing heat into my face. This had been years in the making, I'd been correct in suspecting Michael betrayed me long ago with Julia. When, where, exactly? At Yale or ten years later, in New York? I flashed back to a crazy dinner party he and Ben held in their apartment on Orange Street when we were in college. That was the night my cousins and I met him, this genius of a graduate student, tall, handsome, and brilliant, but also self-destructive and messy. Robin quickly sunk her claws into him, but there was something between him and Julia from the start. The way she stood next to the piano that night and sang while he played, the way they were soon drinking tea and chatting on the couch all the time, how they used to hang out in New York over school vacations—their secret alliance had continued right under my nose, but I'd been too dumb to put two and two together. I'd suspected it and stupidly denied it. Well, fuck them, maybe it was for the best, it would make things easier.

Their heads were strangely huge in my field of vision, their faces gleaming like moons in the night sky of an alternate universe as I approached.

"There's been a development, I see." My voice came from outside of me.

"Julia's going to move out to California to live with me," Michael said. His skin looked oddly translucent, varnished by layers of anguish and joy.

"You're leaving Ben?" I asked, turning toward my cousin. "Somehow I'm not completely surprised." I stopped, shut up. I did, and didn't, want to know the details.

"Sorry," Julia said in a low voice. She had a frightened, guilty look on her face.

"You know, you've been coming and going for a while now," Michael said.

"Fuck you, and fuck you, Julia." Idiotically, I felt hurt, as though I'd forgotten that I, too, wanted a separation. I felt betrayed even though I'd brought their betrayal upon myself by loving Sergio again.

"Okay, I'm going to let you two work it out," Julia said. As she stood up and stepped away, my loathing of her was upended by the realization that she was doing to me *exactly* what I'd done to Olivia years before. Well, maybe not exactly. A version of, better or worse I didn't know. In this place, which was to me so sacred, I was being shown the workings of the law of just desserts, the great cosmic boomerang called karma. For I could no longer doubt there was such a thing.

"You said it was over," Michael said, and I realized that when he'd asked me during his previous visit if I wanted a separation, he'd been looking for permission to act on his feelings for Julia. "And it's for the best. We can't be good parents if we're fighting all the time."

That was certainly true. For a moment I said nothing. Looking away, I saw Julia, off at a distance, talking on the phone.

"There was something between the two of you at Yale, wasn't there?" I asked. I couldn't help wanting to know *something*.

"Nothing that led to anything, if that's what you mean."

"You wouldn't tell me the truth, anyway, so I don't know why I'm asking."

"I'm sorry. I'm sorry it hasn't worked out." He reached for my arm.

"It is as it should be, I suppose." I stepped back.

"You can have the house," he said.

"I don't want the house. I don't want to stay in a place where we were together," I snapped, even as I wondered where I'd go. In the short run, I could stay with Robin in San Francisco, but I'd have to start looking for a place in Berkeley immediately in order to find something before Esther went back to school. Now that the reality of separation was before me, my mind raced about the economics of my situation. Michael earned more than I did, and we'd always pooled our resources. I wouldn't be able to support myself with the part-time teaching I did. Maybe I could get some income out of the apartment in Rome.

"We'll talk when we get back to Berkeley. But don't worry about money, I'll take care of you," he said, reading my mind.

"Did you leave Esther in Mendocino today?"

"Yes, she's with Val's family—"

"I'm going to drive over and get her."

"How about I tell her about me and Jul first?"

His calling Julia "Jul" seemed in poor taste to me, a display of their long intimacy. "You haven't told her yet?"

"No," he said. "The plan was to tell her tonight when we get back."

"Okay," I said. "I'll come get her tomorrow."

"I'm hoping for something equitable in terms of custody," he said. "She'll probably have to—go back and forth."

"Like millions of kids of divorced parents do, right?"

Now that our split was real, I hated both of us for putting our daughter in that position. There was no way of assessing what the collateral damage would be down the line, and I feared that Esther, like many children of divorced parents, wouldn't be able to have a healthy relationship or a family. Would she "believe" in marriage? Was marriage something worth believing in? Or was it, like monarchy and slavery, an institution that belonged to the past, that no social movement could reform because it was at odds with the mutability of human nature?

"We'll have to find a way to do this amicably," Michael said. "For Esther's sake."

That willingness to be *amicable* was exactly what I wanted. I calmed down.

"I want to take her with me to Robin's for a few days," I said.

"Fair enough."

I felt jealous, blameful. But later I would mull again over the fact that I'd sowed the seeds for everything that happened.

I sowed the first round when I slept with Sergio, continued the affair in spite of my friendship with Olivia, and didn't keep my baby. I sowed the second round when I didn't tell Michael about that first pregnancy, when I allowed that secret to keep me from fully committing to my marriage, and when I reconnected with Sergio years later. I can't point to any single one of those actions and say, there, that was the signal moment when I erred from a wiser, more ethical path. No, there was a whole series of interlocking steps that I took—steps triggered by the low self-esteem of a child parented by an alcoholic, steps motivated by desire and neediness—while all the time mistakenly believing I was heading in the right direction, toward some form of emotional relief.

After Michael and Julia left, my brain, adrenalized, spun with a thousand thoughts and feelings as I headed back to my dormitory. I stopped at the front desk to talk to Mei Xing.

"Everything okay, Bai An?" she asked.

"Something's come up, I have to leave tomorrow. Can I—uh—break the rules? I really need to make a phone call."

She gave me a severe look but reached into a drawer and pulled out my cell phone.

"Take it. You coming back?"

"I won't be leaving till tomorrow but I—I need to go off campus right now."

I hurried down the hall with the thought of calling Robin. Under my fury with Michael and Julia was a shard of excitement at the prospect of liberation. I'd been wanting an escape for a long time. Then I thought about my economic situation again. Why had I so readily conceded the house to Michael? He'd put up the down payment for it and had made the lion's share of the mortgage payments, yet, under California law, it was community property and I was entitled to half. It occurred to me that I could probably exact some kind of cash payment in exchange for my share—Julia could buy me out. Like a snake anxious to shed its skin, I would eventually have a place that was all mine, that had no trace of him in it. I thought of Kali, the Hindu goddess of creation and destruction, of the joyful rebirth inherent in cataclysm.

As soon as I reached my room, I dialed Robin. She picked up and I told her what happened.

"I'm so, so sorry," she kept saying. "You feel ready for this?"

I wasn't in the mood for a therapist's taking stock. "Did you know anything about them?"

"No, not at all. Never."

"You sure?"

"Really," she said.

"I wonder if they had an affair at Yale. After you." I paused to process the insanity of my husband having slept with both of my cousins at different points in his life.

"I don't know. I don't think so."

"Can I come stay with you for a bit?"

"Of course. You can have Gloria's room," Robin said, referring to her housemate. "She's away on vacation, and I'd love to have company."

"I'm going to drive over to Mendocino tomorrow and get Esther, then we'll swing through Berkeley to get a few things— "

"Do whatever you need to do," she said.

After hanging up, I didn't know what to do with myself. I wouldn't be able to collect Esther until the following day. What could I do in the meantime? Meditation was out of the question at this point. An hour south were the wineries of Sonoma, always open to tourists. No, better to avoid alcohol. I'd go east to the nearby regional park and hike until I was dusty and tired and clear of mind. I took off my robe and sandals, changed into shorts and sneakers, put my wallet and phone in a mini backpack. Did I need my inhaler? I grabbed it even as I noticed that my lungs felt spacious and free. Because that's what I would be now, all of me—spacious and (more or less) free. I went out into the hot parking lot, got into my car, and buckled my seat belt. Julia's intrusion had relieved me of the necessity of telling Michael about Sergio and the baby I'd given up for adoption. Hey, now that Michael was running off with Julia, I could do what I wanted, go where I wanted, sleep with whom I wanted, and not tell him a thing. I could take up with Sergio again without worrying about that bothersome Buddhist precept against sexual misconduct.

Laughing bitterly at the absurdity of life, I turned the keys in the ignition and headed out to the woods.

18. An Imperfect Circle

From: Anna Stark
To: Sergio Buria
Hello dear,
Much has happened since my retreat. I've moved out of my house and into my cousin's because Michael and I are splitting up. It seems that, while I was getting ready to ask him for a divorce, he and Julia were "connecting." Honestly, I don't know how I feel about everything. Of course I'm furious with Michael and Julia for the betrayal, though I have no "right" to be. I'll tell you all the gory details when I see you. The main thing is that this leaves me "free," though what that means for us, with you in Italy and me needing to be in California for Esther, I don't know.

Are you making arrangements for us to travel up to Paris and find Jean-Paul? I'd like to take the night train. I have to sign some forms at the adoption agency before they can put me in touch with him—there's a rule against email communication before meeting. I'm impatient to see him but anxious that he'll judge me.

It'll be a shock to see you after so many years. I hope you won't find me too changed. Recently I cut my hair so it's

*short again, like when I knew you in Rome. I can't wait
to see you.*

Much love and kisses,
Anna

From: Sergio Buria
To: Anna Stark
Dearest Anna,
*I'm sad to learn about you and Michael. But the fact that
you're now free, even with us separated by continents and
oceans, makes me happy. As for the meeting with Jean-
Paul, it'll be huge and surreal at the same time. I can
understand why you're afraid.*

*I'll drive up to Rome from Sperlonga and meet you at the
apartment the day you arrive. If you get there first, you'll find
under the mat the key I've been keeping there for workmen.
I hope you like the remodeling done in the kitchen and
bathroom . . . but mostly I hope you like—me! Yes, it could
be a shock to see each other—or maybe not. What I do know
is that I used to love so much your full mouth, your green
eyes, and short red hair. I expect to love them again.*

Because I belong to you.

Kisses,
Sergio

A couple of weeks later, I was in Rome, going up to my aunt's
apartment in the rickety European-style elevator with its
ornate wrought-iron doors and glass case. I'd taken a night

flight, during which I'd barely slept, and arrived in a city baking in August heat. But the stone building was cool inside. Stepping out of the elevator, I saw my aunt's name, Doris Lipski, by the buzzer. Was she really dead? A surge of nostalgia was soon swept away by another question, the only one that mattered at that moment—had Sergio arrived yet? I rang; there was no answer. I bent down and, lifting the doormat, found the key.

Stepping in, I saw in the foyer the same little beat-up table where Doris used to put her mail. Marcella, the daughter of Doris's lover, Tito, had left a manila envelope addressed to me and containing the deed, a copy of the will, and other documents I'd already seen as email attachments. In the living room, the black and white checked marble floor was the same. I pulled aside the worn gauze curtains in order to step out onto the balcony and take in the view of rooftop gardens and church cupolas, as fascinating as it had ever been. Then the heat hit me, and I retreated inside, moved on toward the kitchen, where Sergio had retiled the floor with terracotta pavers. The wooden counters were gone, replaced with a pale gray marble from one of the quarries he visited. The tiered wire basket no longer had tomatoes in it; that would be easy enough to fix.

I was walking down the hall toward the bedrooms when the bell rang, startling my heart into a rapid beat. A second later, I was at the front door, and there was Sergio, beaming— the same and not the same. He'd gained weight and had a bit of a double chin. The moustache was gone, but the beauty mark on his left cheek and the gold fleck in the brown iris of his left eye were the same.

"Here I am," he said, and he gestured toward himself, the way a magician might toward a rabbit he'd pulled out of a hat. "*Me voilà!*"

"Oh, you speak French now?"

"I've been brushing up, for our trip to Paris."

"You going to come in or not?"

"*Bien sûr!*"

He stepped in and I threw my arms around his neck. "Sergio!"

He grabbed me and kissed me hard.

"I can't believe it!" I laughed.

"Isn't this amazing? Isn't this wonderful?"

"Absolutely!"

"Let's go in." He took my hand, led me to my aunt's couch. "How do you like the apartment? Are you pleased with what you've seen so far? Have my men done a good job?"

"I think so—"

"You're gorgeous," he said. "You've had facelifts, California-style?"

"Of course not—"

"Look, look," he fumbled in his pockets. "I have a gift." He took out a wooden box with a hinged lid. "Open it."

Inside was a beautiful cameo in a beaded gold setting. "It's beautiful!"

"It was my mother's. I wanted to give it to you years ago as a good-bye present, but you left without saying good-bye."

"You gave me a leather briefcase, don't you remember?"

"Not enough."

I took the little box and gazed at the cameo. "I'm surprised you never gave this to Olivia."

"It would have looked ridiculous on Olivia. I don't mean that in a nasty way but—you know what I mean."

"Yes, I know."

"Here, look. You can wear it as a pin, or you can put a gold chain through the loop here and turn it into a pendant." He reached into his pocket.

"And you just so happen to have a chain in your pocket."

He threaded the chain through the loop. "Of course. Here, let me." He moved closer to me, reached around my neck. "So miraculous to find you again, Anna."

He fastened it, sat back down next to me, caressed my neck, and kissed me hard again.

"Calm down," I said, laughing. "Give me a minute to get used to you."

"You think I've changed?"

"Just a little." He had thickened in the face and neck and waist, as Italian men do with age, and I wondered whether, if I had crossed him on some Roman street unexpectedly, I would have recognized him. Perhaps not, unless he'd smiled at me. I would have recognized the smile and the beauty mark on his right cheek, the gold fleck in the brown iris of his left eye. "You look more important now. Like, like a diplomat or a wealthy businessman." I stroked the skin under his jaw, which was lax and soft and clean-shaven.

He laughed, too. "Well, not a diplomat, but an almost wealthy businessman. I can confess to that." He stroked my neck. "You used to me yet? Did you see the bedroom?"

"No, not yet."

"You want to?"

"I can't wait to see the bedroom." I threw my arms around him.

The palm of his hand cradled my face as I touched his hair, which felt cool and fine between my fingers.

"You smell good," I said. He smelled not of lemons and garlic, as I'd expected, but of cinnamon and rosewater, like some exotic dessert.

"You *feel* good," he said, slipping two fingers inside me.

The dive into skin and flesh, kisses and caresses, felt familiar and strange at once. This was the Sergio I'd once known, and I had with him the trust and ease of long ago. At the same time, he was so different—with more padding around the waist, age spots on his hands, and darker, sun-beaten skin—that I might as well have been in bed with a stranger. I had fantasized about this reunion so many times that, even as it happened, I didn't quite know where I was or what I was doing—only that I was throwing myself into it and he was, too, and that the moment was binding us together with solemnity and crazy joy.

Afterward, as I lay in Sergio's arms, he kept taking my arm and wrapping it tighter around his waist and tighter still.

"I remember you used to do that," I said.

"Do what?"

"Pick my arm up and wrap it tighter around your waist."

"That's how it should be. Very tight." He took my arm again and pulled me even closer.

"I thought you'd be angry when I told you that I'd slept with three other men at the end."

"Twenty-five years later? You thought I'd be angry?" He shrugged. "You know, I don't think I'd have been angry back then, if you'd told me."

"You don't? You seemed jealous of Nazzaro's attentions to me."

"Because you deserved better. Anyway, I behaved terribly, so how could I have said anything?"

"And I thought you'd be angry with me for giving up the child."

"You know, the older I get, the more fascinated I am by normal people who do . . . unexpected things. Knowing how your mother abused you, I'm not surprised that at twenty-two you wouldn't have felt ready for a child. Anyway, given my own family history, I wouldn't be one to judge. Do you remember the story about my mother?"

"You never told me what happened."

"I guess I wasn't talking about it much back then. My mother committed suicide shortly after my younger sister was born. I was around nine. And she took my sister with her."

"How horrible."

"It was hardest on my father."

"And you, how did you survive it?"

"Oh," he shrugged. "It was the decade after the war. All of us kids were wild back then, running around all day in a gang, playing, of course, but also—incredible to think about it now—looking for food. Mussels on the beach. Snails, berries, and mushrooms in the countryside. The poverty in Italy was terrible at the time. Anyway, about my mother—post-partum depression was what people said. My father never recovered."

"Is that why he was always so—"

"Difficult? Grumpy? Yes. I know he didn't make a good impression on you, but I owe him everything—my home, my education, my ability to carry on. So you see, there wasn't just the matter of Olivia. I couldn't have left Sperlonga and moved to Milan with you. It would have killed my father."

"It helps to know all that.'"

"And you were so full of adventure and passion, Anna, that to have taken you as my wife would have been like capturing a wild bird and putting it in a cage. It was inconceivable."

"Damn my passions."

"Why damn your passions?" he said. "They were one of the most beautiful things about you. To be passionate is to be fully human."

Suddenly hot, I slipped out of his arms to open the French doors onto the balcony where Doris's aging dog used to pee. A late-afternoon breeze wafted in through the slightly open window.

"It doesn't smell bad anymore," I said.

"My guy retiled it. What a mess."

I turned, got back into bed, and he took my arm and again wrapped it tight around his waist. "So, what do you think of the bed?" he asked.

"It's very comfortable." I thought of how my aunt had met with Tito in this place. Or had they met at hotels, the way Sergio and I once had?

"I replaced the mattress."

"Oh, so there was an ulterior motive to your wanting to fix up the apartment for me," I teased.

"Yes—getting the right mattress." He laughed. "And what about the rest of the apartment? You're happy?"

"It's wonderful."

"You'll keep it," he said.

"Of course I'll keep it."

"So tell me everything, the bad as well as the good."

"I just signed the lease on a place in Berkeley . . . " I began.

I had a lot to report. Since splitting up with Michael, I'd found a two-bedroom apartment on the second floor of an old house in Berkeley. Esther would be with her father and Julia while I was in Italy, then she would move in with me. My soon-to-be ex and I hadn't worked out the details yet, but I felt optimistic I'd get my share of my daughter because Michael and Julia had their hands full. A day after Michael and Julia visited me at Buddhaland, Michael had a little car accident in Northern California caused by a minor stroke that affected his left arm, so he was now in physical therapy, and Julia spent much time driving him to appointments and taking care of him. Sometimes I felt sorry for him and guilty about his accident. If I hadn't been on retreat, Michael wouldn't have been driving in the wilds of California west of Buddhaland and he might have gotten emergency care earlier, or maybe the stroke wouldn't even have happened. A few times right after the accident, I'd woken up in the middle of the night thinking, in an instinctive reflex, that I had to go to my husband and take care of him. Then I'd remember how he'd betrayed me with Julia. Now, lying in bed with Sergio, the facts of Michael's health and love life seemed remote, and I felt neither guilty nor blaming, but simply a cog in a machine of events and forces, precise and inexorable, that acted and reacted against each other.

Sergio listened to my narrative and reflections, nodding thoughtfully every now and then. "So now your life is as complicated and messed up as mine. And you have an apartment there and an apartment here," he said.

"So what about you? I don't understand exactly your situation with Olivia. You're divorced but you still visit her?"

"Yes, I still visit now and then—sleeping in separate rooms, of course—to help her with the house I gave her, one of my properties in Florence, and so that we can spend time together with our daughters, as a family."

"Your daughters—one of whom is named Anna. Which is both lovely and weird."

"Yes." He squeezed my arm.

"And why did you divorce?"

He cleared his throat. "Things didn't go very well in the bedroom and I could not go, year after year, without the physical, so finally I—I was not a good husband, I broke the rules a couple of times. And the second time, she found out about it and couldn't forgive me and, even worse, she blamed herself for not having been sufficient in that arena—and we lacked the skills to—to fix things . . . "

"I see."

"Probably in America you would, I don't know, see a special therapist for that kind of thing. But honestly, for Olivia and me, Italians from working-class backgrounds, it was inconceivable to talk about our sex life with a third party . . ."

We fell silent. I imagined in flitting mental images the affairs he'd had, the fights with Olivia, her casting him out. To stop the thinking, I snuggled down under the sheet, buried my face in his chest, and took in his fragrance. Our togetherness was absolute joy, and anything less than this would be painful. Buddhism teaches that the source of suffering is desire, in particular the ever-renewability of desire that causes us to keep grasping for more, and, sure enough, a huge clinging feeling rose up in me as I pressed myself into Sergio's body.

My meditation teacher used to say that there are two ways to hold a coin: with an open hand or with a closed fist. Although the higher, more peaceful path lies in the open hand, our instinct is to close our fists in order to hold on to what we've got. The impulse to grasp and hoard comes out of what Buddhists call *tanha*—the thirst or craving for more that accompanies desire, creating insatiability.

In spite of all the spiritual instruction I'd received, I felt, lying in Sergio's arms, like one big fist that wanted, anxiously and restlessly, to hold onto him forever. If Sergio and I had been younger, if I hadn't just been on a plane for twelve hours, I would have wanted to make love again. But another round wouldn't have done the trick either. I would still have been left wanting more.

"Darling," Sergio whispered, wrapping my arm tighter around his waist.

"I'm tired," I whispered, and closed my eyes.

"Me too," he said.

It was dusk when we woke up from our siesta.

"We should go out," he said, "some place lively, like Trastevere, and have dinner."

"I'd love that."

Trastevere, the Bohemian neighborhood where Signora Gianina used to live, seemed like an excellent destination. Magic had become more elusive with the passing of years, but it was upon me again when we stepped out into the falling Roman night of late summer. In gardened stone courtyards, small wall fountains splashed and stucco shrines sheltered open-air altars to Madonnas. Oblivious to the waning light, flocks of birds chattered in the trees. My passion for the place made me feel I belonged there, just as my love for Sergio made me feel I belonged with him.

"You know I spend little time in Rome now, so I have no idea which bus to take over there," he said as we walked aimlessly down Via Piave. "Rome—still too big, too complicated for this country boy." He laughed.

"The only bus route I remember is the 16, which used to take me from my apartment to school and back."

"My car then. We'll park this side of the river and walk across the bridge."

We reached his Audi.

"I see you still like fancy cars," I said.

"What do you mean? This belongs to my company."

"What about the 'family Mercedes' you used to have in Sperlonga?"

"We never had a Mercedes."

"Yeah you did. You and Flavio and Nazzaro—"

"Oh that!" He laughed. "Every time you visited, we borrowed it from a rich doctor friend on weekends—to impress you!"

"Really?" Taken aback, I wondered in what other ways I'd been conned.

"Really."

We got into the car and drove across the city, past its stone ruins, fountains, and palazzos, until the river came in sight. Sergio found a parking place between the Circo Massimo and the water, and we headed across the Palatino bridge just south of the Tiber island. There we stopped to take in the view of another, older and crumbling bridge right next to it, which Romans call *Ponte Rotto* or broken bridge, because it extends halfway across the river before stopping midway. The disintegration brought me more sharply into the present. All those people, generations, layers of civilization were gone, and one day I would go with them, but for the moment there I was, alive, the street lights reflecting in the river, the summer night air on my face, Sergio's hand in mine.

Reaching the other side of the Tiber, we walked along its bank.

"Let's sit for a moment," I asked. There was a low wall where I stopped and sat down. Jet lag had caught up with me.

He sat next to me. "We have to find a restaurant, there are dozens. I don't even know how you like to eat anymore. Do you want something traditional or *nouvelle*?" He looked at me. "You're a Buddhist now, does that mean you're a vegetarian?"

"No, I'm not."

"Hmm."

My elation was dampened again by the clinging feeling, triggered by anguish about what lay ahead.

"So basically you . . . you commute up to Florence to see Olivia," I said.

He looked at me. "About once a month which isn't so often, so I think I'm a little bit more free, but you—you're a lot less so, with your daughter in California."

"What is it about you Italians that you specialize in impossible relationships?" I asked.

"It's all totally possible because the situation with Olivia isn't what you may think. Because, well, she met someone else, so the dynamic is changing fast. I'll be staying in a hotel the next time I go to Florence to visit my daughters."

"Olivia met someone?"

He cleared his throat. "Some American guy who's in the import/export business. Olive oil, I think. He's Episcopalian, which turned out to be very convenient."

"Convenient?"

"A couple of years ago, Olivia began to believe again and wanted to go back to the Catholic Church, but our having divorced made it difficult . . . "

"But as an Episcopalian—"

"As an Episcopalian, yes, it's all okay. She's in the process of converting in order to be with her new boyfriend. So you see, I really am free to be with you."

"The only problem then is that we live on different continents."

"Yes. It's not ideal," he said. "There will be a lot of flying back and forth. I can't ask you to move to Italy, at least not until Esther graduates."

"No, and I can't separate her from her father."

There was an anxious silence. I wondered if we could hack it—I knew too many long distance relationships that had failed.

"But you can bring her to Italy in the summer, right? And maybe I can find a reason to spend stretches of time in California," he said. "Maybe I can get my company to look for export markets there." Pause. "I don't know. We'll work it out."

"I want to, I really want to."

I sighed as it came up again inside me, the grasping feeling that goes with being in love. I'd forgotten how plain uncomfortable it could be. When we were apart, there would be a hundred avenues toward suffering. How would I feel when the time came to get back on the airplane, unsure of exactly when we'd meet again? Or maybe having a plan for the next meeting, but not the meeting after the next one? And what impact would separation have on our relationship? A miserable sense of having gotten in way over my head combined with the crazy joy of our reunion, but my willingness to be vulnerable felt like a step forward. I remembered my youthful obsession with *La Princesse de Clèves*, how I'd once admired the heroine of that novel for her dignified rejection of her lover and her decision to be on her own. The princess now seemed like a coward to me. She'd chosen longing and the safety of the convent over the ups and downs, the uncertainties and compromises of love. And in the process she'd missed the flower of life.

"We'll work it out," Sergio repeated. "Maybe I can retire early. The main thing is not to worry. Now let's go find a place to eat. The Roman night is waiting for us."

The days were hot, so Sergio and I went out in the early morning for walks, then spent the afternoon in bed in the cool apartment. When we made love, it felt like he was filling my whole body—not only my sex, but my heart and brain, too. I had a huge sense of being deeply nourished and pacified, like a baby getting the feeding she needs, and I would have made love every day if he'd been capable.

"You're just as insatiable as you were at twenty-two," he said, laughing one time when he couldn't achieve an erection. "I'm almost sixty, I can't do it every day."

"That's okay. I'll just breathe you in instead." My head on his chest, I pressed my nose into his skin in order to take in his intoxicating smell of cinnamon and rosewater.

We also spent time looking at Italian magazines about architecture and design. I needed to do a few more things for the apartment, such as replace the kitchen appliances, upgrade the electrical situation for the computer age, and buy a new couch and curtains. Although most businesses were closed for the August holiday, Sergio got workmen to come give us bids on jobs. I was happy to have a week in Rome with Sergio before heading up to Paris, which I remembered as the place I'd spent my dreadful first pregnancy. Though I longed to meet Jean-Paul, I was like a disaster survivor not wanting to return to the scene of trauma.

Doris's apartment felt like a second home and refuge, the way it had years before. I knew I wouldn't sell it but would rent it out to tourists for part of the year and use it myself at other times, for Sergio and I would probably want my aunt's apartment as a meeting place when I came to Italy. I couldn't handle the awkwardness of visiting him in Sperlonga, where his family and friends would realize we'd been lovers twenty-five years before.

Then there was the matter of Olivia. She, too, would realize Sergio and I had been lovers right before their marriage. That might add to her bitterness and anger. Well, she'd found another partner; she'd moved on, we all had to.

Sergio had bought us first-class tickets for the *Palatino*, the overnight train to Paris that I wanted to take. Having the compartment to ourselves felt luxurious compared to my previous rides in second class. I tried not to think about the last, terrible journey, when, pregnant, I'd fled Rome for Paris, but recalled instead my night playing cards with the Polish nuns, how jolly they were, how they threw candies up into my couchette after I went to bed. So long ago. Sergio and I ate our picnic dinner sitting next to each other, looking out the window at the coast and hills dimming and dipping into the late summer night. When we were done eating, we sat with arms intertwined. The olive skin on the back of his hands was speckled from the Italian sun and the passage of time; the fingers were fleshier than they'd once been.

"I love holding hands with you," I said. "I guess we didn't hold hands much back then, for fear of being seen."

"Sometimes we did. Remember that day at Villa Borghese?" Sergio paused.

"Of course I do."

The lights and housing outside were increasing in density when the train conductor announced the next stop, Florence.

"Another stop," Sergio said, sounding nervous.

This was where Olivia lived. As the train pulled into the station, the thought of her nearness gripped me. She was real—neither a memory nor ghost, but a middle-aged woman who'd made a mistaken marriage, who was now in another relationship, yet still connected by children and property to the man next to me. What if, suddenly, her face appeared in the crowd at the platform? What if she had her own reasons to go to Paris? Maybe she and her Episcopalian beau had decided to take a weekend holiday in France. As I imagined her in middle-age—heavier set, jowly about the mouth, but still pretty—I nervously scanned the crowd on the platform, but she was nowhere to be seen. Glancing sideways, I saw that the same thought was crossing Sergio's mind. There was an almost audible sigh of relief when the train conductor announced our departure over the speaker.

"They'll come by to make the beds soon," Sergio whispered.

I thought about the implications of our being openly together. There were things I needed to say and questions I had to ask.

"If Jean-Paul is your son," I finally said, "then he would be a half-brother to your daughters—"

"Yes, he would be. True."

"I wonder—" I fell silent.

"Yes," he said. "There are many things that will be awkward." Pause. "Have you told Esther about him?"

"Not yet. But eventually I will."

The train picked up speed as we left Florence—and Olivia—behind. I leaned my head on Sergio's shoulder. The rocking movement of the car and the rhythmic noise of its wheels soothed me. But something nagged at me. I felt disturbed at the idea of Olivia having left the Church. I picked my head up.

"Olivia was so Catholic," I said. "I'm surprised she granted you a divorce. I'm guessing she lost her faith because you stepped out. But women can find out about their husbands' adulteries without losing their faith in God."

"She felt angry with God for not . . . having given her more ability to enjoy sex. And for having made me . . . need it so much."

He looked so unhappy talking about it that I resolved to stop asking questions. But he went on.

"I don't know if you can understand all this," he said. "It's such an Italian story. The way she saw it, my being an atheist was a contributing factor. She thought that my not being a practicing Catholic had diminished the effectiveness of our vows, as though the sacrament had failed because I hadn't brought to it the seriousness of a believer."

I put my head back down on his shoulder. "You don't have to talk about if you don't want," I said.

"It's okay," he said. "The time has come for you to ask me anything you want. You should know everything."

I thought about the affairs he'd had. I picked my head up again and looked at him squarely. "So, who were they? The other women?" I couldn't keep the reproach out of my voice, as though it had been me he'd betrayed.

"Anna! Can you not understand why a man whose wife doesn't like sex might seek another partner now and then?"

I fell silent. Of course I did understand, but a wave of painful jealousy hit me: Had he loved any of his lovers more than me?

"When did Olivia find out?"

"Five years ago. I was seeing a woman at the time—a philosophy professor, a very fine person of great intelligence—and I got carried away, I was absent too much, I'd come home late, etcetera. All the usual stupid stuff. One day, Olivia started questioning and accusing me, finally I confessed, and we were in the middle of a terrible scene when Olivia's phone rang. She picked her phone up, saw our daughter's name, *Anna*, on the little screen, and then—suddenly!—twenty years after the fact, she made the connection about you. About you and me, that is. She looked at me and said, 'And you did this before our wedding, didn't you?' She never mentioned your name, but it was obvious she understood what had happened, what we'd done."

So she already knew. "How awful." I shivered, feeling cold.

"I know." He sighed. "When I first read your aunt's obituary, I almost didn't get in touch with you, because I didn't want to have to tell you that Olivia had figured things out. But then, selfishly, I needed to find you." He squeezed my hand.

"I'm glad you found me, and I'm glad you told me. Though it's awful."

I'd wanted to imagine that she'd divorced Sergio because of his subsequent infidelities, not because of me. But I was implicated in the suffering she must have gone through. That time of leaving the Catholic Church, of being without faith, albeit temporary, must have been the darkest night of the soul for her. I felt for her suffering, as one might feel for the suffering any dear friend has experienced. And there was the matter of what she must have thought of me when she put two and two together. I would no longer be remembered as a dear friend from youth, but as some demonic Other Woman.

"After we divorced," Sergio continued, " she refused to have anything to do with me for a couple of years. Then she agreed to see me at family gatherings and let me help her around the house. I thought she might even want us to cohabit again or remarry—when, surprise, surprise, she meets Mr. Import/ Export and decides to become Episcopalian." He looked sad. "You know, even though she seems happy with this guy and it was probably all for the best, I still feel terribly guilty."

"I wonder if I'll have occasion . . . to see her again—"

"I imagine at some point, yes, that might happen."

We looked at each other blankly for a moment as we tried to imagine it.

"I hate to think I hurt her," I said.

"It was my fault," he said, looking out the window. "She loved you, you know."

"I loved her, too."

He took my hand again, and we sat there in silence as the train sped toward France.

19. A Son in Paris

I didn't want to stay any place near Leila's apartment or the hospital where I'd given birth, so I'd chosen a hotel not far from the Place des Vosges. The Right Bank, in the general direction of Jean-Paul's place in the 10th arrondissement, but not too close to it, seemed right. After Sergio and I left our bags in our room, we went to the adoption agency, where I signed a bunch of forms. The administrator then called Jean-Paul to made arrangements for us to meet at his place the following day.

"Thank you for not trying to communicate directly before meeting," the woman said. "Too many misunderstandings can happen that way. Reunions usually go better if they start in person."

What she meant, I imagined, was that an abandoned child was more likely to spill accusations and resentment in an email to his birth mother than face to face. Of course, that might happen anyway. Maybe Jean-Paul wanted to meet in order to spit out hateful things and get them off his chest for once and for all. A protective numbness came over me as I considered what might lie ahead. Sergio and I were quiet when we left her office, and later that night in the bistro where we had dinner, and during an evening walk and back in our hotel room. Suddenly there was nothing to say, and I saw in his still face a reflection of my own apprehension. I felt tight, intense, and empty all at the same time. Every now and then Sergio reached for my hand and gave it a squeeze, and the warmth of his skin brought me back into something like reality. Mostly there was a sudden crazy impatience to meet Jean-Paul, to get it over with, as it were. It felt awful being back in Paris, and I wanted to overwrite the wounds of the past with something new—almost any other experience, good or bad, would do.

The next morning we took the metro to Saint-Lazare and walked toward the address the social worker had given us. Jean-Paul lived in a neighborhood that in my youth had been scruffy but was now being gentrified. I didn't know what to expect. We'd learned my son made documentaries, but I didn't know whether he was employed or self-employed, whether he was artistic or a techno-nerd. I didn't know what he looked like, what language we'd speak when we met, whether there would be a sense of connection or an unbridgeable chasm. Maybe having Sergio with me would increase the awkwardness of our meeting but I wanted him there for support.

Our path took us toward the Canal St. Martin. The sight of the water, running straight and slow between cement embankments, was pleasing in the summer heat.

"Anna," he said, stopping in his tracks. "Dear one."

"Yes?"

"I want you to know that, for me, whether or not he's my son, I'm okay with it."

"Really? You don't have a feeling about it one way or the other?" I turned toward him. "That you'd like it if he was your son, or maybe it would make you so sad that it would be better if he wasn't? Or that if he isn't, you'll have some kind of judgment about my behavior—"

"The main thing here is you—your reconnecting with him. It's you who went through the pain and anguish. The father in these things, he's responsible but not very important. Men are . . . idiots, and the sperm is—what?—a little fertilizer around the lemon tree."

"But that's how I feel. I want you to be the father." I pulled him toward me.

He smiled. "I've always wanted a son, and a reason to visit Paris!" We laughed. "I mean," he added, more seriously, "if he wants to be visited."

"I wonder," I went on, "when we meet him, if we'll shake hands or do the polite French *bises*, one on each cheek. I wonder what his politics are. Maybe he'll be a member of the *Front National*," I said, referring to an extreme-right political party that was a blight on the French scene.

Sergio burst out laughing. "So, maybe you won't love him because he's a fascist? Now you're tormenting yourself needlessly, for sure." He started walking again. "You know," he added, "I'm nervous, too."

My heart was beating hard as I thought of meeting Jean-Paul. *Soon—now—I'll see him, my son.* We walked along the left bank of the canal and up onto the little bridge named after the Rue Bichat that leads into it on one side. A dozen people had gathered to look at the locks being manipulated for an approaching tourist boat. I'd never seen locks in operation before and, as fascinated as a small child, I leaned over the bridge railing and watched as the boat, at a standstill between the two sets of locks, gradually rose with the level of water. It felt good to take a breath and slow things down a bit. Sergio stopped, too, and for a moment we forgot our quest and dissolved into the watching crowd. Then the locks on the up side opened and the boat moved forward. *As the boat goes forward, so will we.* Glancing sideways at Sergio, I asked myself whether he would be faithful to me.

"I wonder if you'll have other lovers besides me," I said.

"Now, where did that come from?" Sergio seemed honestly surprised. "You're wrong. I won't."

"You don't think so? When I'm in California taking care of Esther, and you're here, unable to visit me because you're working?"

"I can't go a decade without having sex, but six months, a

year even—no problem. I don't have the energy, emotional or physical, for that kind of thing anymore. Besides, we won't go that long without seeing each other. Have you ever counted the saints' holidays in our calendar? And if you recall, for each one there's the opportunity to *fare il ponte* in order to get away," he said, referring to the Italian habit of "making a bridge" between the weekend and a vacation day in the middle of the week.

"I guess I want security, I want an idyll, the two of us in some little stone house in Tuscany forever."

He laughed. "That's an American dream. The Italian dream is a little white-washed house in Iberia."

"I could handle that," I said.

"Retirement in Spain, then." He smiled. "It's important to keep dreaming. And now, let's go meet that son of yours."

Holding hands, we crossed the bridge to the other side, walked by the seventeenth-century Hôpital St. Louis with its lovely combination of beige stone and red brick, and threaded our way to the little street where Jean-Paul lived. We reached his building and rang the outside buzzer to his apartment.

The buzzer rang back and the front door clicked open.

We climbed an old wooden staircase to the third floor and rang a doorbell with Jean-Paul's name next to it.

The door opened.

A lanky young man with olive skin, on the tall side, wearing a pressed white shirt and a pair of old blue jeans, stood before us.

"*Ma mère,*" Jean-Paul said.

For a second there was a veil in his gaze, then it vanished and he reached for me. We gave each other a long hug, and I felt the thin form of a young man in my arms. Breathless, I let go and took a good look at him.

He had a beauty mark on his right cheek and a gold fleck in the velvet brown iris of his left eye.

Stepping back, I watched Jean-Paul turn toward Sergio, and Sergio turn toward Jean-Paul.

"You must be my father," Jean-Paul said in French.

"Looks like it," Sergio answered.

As the two men, each a reflection of the other, moved into an embrace, the pieces of my past, scattered for so long, came together. Then Jean-Paul motioned for us to follow him. We moved into a room filled with light, the northern light of Paris that puts a hint of silver on everything it touches. *He has good taste*, I thought, looking around. The decoration was sparse and modern, with huge, blown-up black and white photographs, portraits of friends perhaps, on brilliant white walls. Hung up high, a single abstract oil painting in dark colors; on the burnished wooden floor, a thread-worn oriental rug; and in the corner, a huge computer screen and a heap of cameras. These were the markers of his life, a life unknown to me, but I'd get to know it. As Sergio and I sat down on the couch across from our son, I wondered what he'd experienced, what loves and successes, what losses and disappointments. I didn't know anything about his past, but I saw myself and his father in his future. There would be moments of joy and bouts of sorrow. There were stories to be told, amends to be made. And in the stillness of the morning light, I smiled, took a breath, and looked ahead.

THE END

Acknowledgments

M y deepest gratitude goes to my agent, April Eberhardt, who supported me through the completion of this book. As was the case with *The Geometry of Love*, April provided crucial feedback to early versions of *Nothing Forgotten* and was a partner in its creation. Thanks also go to Brooke Warner, Cait Levin, and the rest of the staff at She Writes Press for their superb work.

Additional thanks go to my terrific developmental editor, Andrea Hurst, and to my friends Kristine Cristobal, Veronica Reilly-Granach, Betsy Marks-Smith, and Richard DeVore for their feedback on the manuscript. And thank you, Lan Samantha Chang, for the valuable suggestions you gave me at the Napa Valley Writers' Conference.

I am grateful to Charlie Trueheart, the American Library in Paris, and the students I met there for their warm welcome during 2014-15 when I was finishing this book in France.

Last but not least, thanks go to Tim, Emily, and Sophia for their love and support.

About the Author

Jessica Levine is the author of *The Geometry of Love* (She Writes Press, 2014), a Top 10 Women's Fiction Title in the American Library Association's *Booklist* in 2015. She is also the author of *Delicate Pursuit: Discretion in Henry James and Edith Wharton* (Routledge, 2002). Her essays, short stories, and poetry have appeared in many publications including *The Southern Review* and *The Huffington Post*. She has translated several books from French and Italian into English.

Jessica holds a Ph.D. in English Literature from the University of California at Berkeley, where she was a Mellon Fellow. She was born in New York City and now lives in Northern California. You can find her at www.jessicalevine.com.

Author photo © Chris Loomis

Selected Titles from She Writes Press

She Writes Press is an independent publishing
company founded to serve women writers everywhere.
Visit us at www.shewritespress.com.

The Geometry of Love by Jessica Levine. $16.95, 978-1-938314-62-9.
Torn between her need for stability and her desire for independence,
an aspiring poet grapples with questions of artistic inspiration, erotic
love, and infidelity.

A Cup of Redemption by Carole Bumpus. $16.95, 978-1-938314-90-2.
Three women, each with their own secrets and shames, seek to make
peace with their pasts and carve out new identities for themselves.

Eden by Jeanne Blasberg. $16.95, 978-1-63152-188-1. As her chil-
dren and grandchildren assemble for Fourth of July weekend at
Eden, the Meister family's grand summer cottage on the Rhode
Island shore, Becca decides it's time to introduce the daughter she
gave up for adoption fifty years ago.

Center Ring by Nicole Waggoner. $17.95, 978-1-63152-034-1. When
a startling confession rattles a group of tightly knit women to its
core, the friends are left analyzing their own roads not taken and
the vastly different choices they've made in life and love.

Play for Me by Céline Keating. $16.95, 978-1-63152-972-6. Middle-
aged Lily impulsively joins a touring folk-rock band, leaving her
job and marriage behind in an attempt to find a second chance at
life, passion, and art.

Shelter Us by Laura Diamond. $16.95, 978-1-63152-970-2. Lawyer-
turned-stay-at-home-mom Sarah Shaw is still struggling to find a
steady happiness after the death of her infant daughter when she
meets a young homeless mother and toddler she can't get out of her
mind—and becomes determined to rescue them.